Just One Day

WINTER

Hope you enjoy the
series

Love
Susan Buchanan
x x x

Also by Susan Buchanan

Sign of the Times
The Dating Game
The Christmas Spirit
Return of the Christmas Spirit

Just One Day

WINTER

SUSAN BUCHANAN

First published in 2021 by Susan Buchanan

A CIP catalogue record of this title is available from the British Library

Paperback – 978-0-9931851-5-1
eBook – 978-0-9931851-6-8

DEDICATION

For Margaret and Robert
The best sister and brother a girl could have
Love you xxx

ABOUT THE AUTHOR

Susan Buchanan lives in Scotland with her husband, their two young children and a crazy Labrador called Benji. She has been reading since the age of four and had to get an adult library card early as she had read the entire children's section by the age of ten. As a freelance book editor, she has books for breakfast, lunch and dinner and in her personal reading always has several books on the go at any one time.

If she's not reading, editing or writing, she's thinking about it. She loves romantic fiction, psychological thrillers, crime fiction and legal thrillers, but her favourite books feature books themselves.

In her past life she worked in International Sales as she speaks five languages. She has travelled to 51 countries and her travel knowledge tends to pop up in her writing. Collecting books on her travels, even in languages she doesn't speak, became a bit of a hobby.

Susan writes contemporary fiction, often partly set in Scotland, usually featuring travel, food or Christmas. When not working, writing, or caring for her two delightful cherubs, Susan loves reading (obviously), the theatre, quiz shows and eating out – not necessarily in that order!

You can connect with Susan via her website www.susanbuchananauthor.com, on Facebook www.facebook.com/susan.buchanan.author, on Twitter @susan_buchanan or on Instagram AuthorSusanBuchanan

ACKNOWLEDGEMENTS

Huge thanks to
Wendy Janes for proofreading
(www.wendyproof.co.uk)

Jaboof Design Studio for my gorgeous cover.
I love it so much!
Claire@jaboofdesignstudio.com

Catherine Ferguson, Katy Ferguson, Karen Furk,
Georgina Wyatt, Kathy Simmonds, Hazel Elkin
and Babs Wilkie for agreeing to be beta readers.

And to my Advance Review team.
And finally to the Word Wranglers for making me
accountable and for chivvying me along.

Chapter One

Happy New Year! I stand in the middle of the living room, Bear, my Labrador, rubbing his head against me, reminding me it's time for his breakfast. I take a deep breath in and vow to myself that this year will be different. This year I will defeat the to-do list, even if it's just for one day.

My husband Ronnie works on a rig in the North Sea and has the usual oil-worker shift pattern of two weeks on, two weeks off. You'd think I'd be used to it by now, but no. Two weeks of the month I am rational and invigorated, the other two weeks I'd aspire to exhaustion. Since he left on the thirtieth and I have our rather large, extended family coming for lunch today, I'm tipping towards exhaustion again.

Ah, there's my phone. Wait. I have twenty-four unread WhatsApps and seventeen text messages. What? I know it's New Year, but I checked my messages before I went to bed at two. Don't these people sleep?

I bash out a couple of texts.

Hi Mum, Happy New Year. Is dessert in hand? Look forward to seeing you and Dad later x

Hi Rhys, Happy New Year. Can't wait to see you guys today. Are you staying over? If you could let me know so I

1

can get the spare room ready.

I don't add that its décor currently includes a box of bathroom tiles, a broken vacuum cleaner, two pairs of hiking boots, an ice-axe, Christmas presents that still have to be given out to those we didn't see before Christmas, and about five days' worth of clean washing hanging up to dry.

My phone pings. Mum.

My maple pecan pie is a triumph if I say so myself. You won't be disappointed x

I tap out a reply to Mum. *Glad to hear it. I'm sure it will go down well x*

A WhatsApp notification pings in. I check on the children. They seem happy enough in the playroom – teddies are everywhere in various stages of undress and with several items of food heaped onto their plates. Hugo is enjoying himself every bit as much as Aria, and I smile fondly at my boy. Clearly being sandwiched in between a younger sister and an elder one has rubbed off on him.

I open my Sisters Like These WhatsApp group – it's my sister Wendy.

Hi, Louisa, I'm really sorry, but Kayla and Hallie have been up vomiting all night. I don't think we can make it today. We're all shattered, and I don't want to pass anything on to you all. We're going back to bed but will call later x

Shit. Hope they're OK. Then a selfish thought crosses my mind. I hope it's a twenty-four-hour thing and we haven't been in close enough contact with them to catch it.

Nightmare! Hope they feel better soon. Give them a hug from me and get some rest x

I round on my two youngest. 'Who's coming for a shower?'

'Me,' shrieks Aria, beating Hugo by a millisecond.

'Hugo, you can watch TV if you want whilst Aria's in the shower.'

He mumbles, 'Nah, I'm OK,' and it makes me smile. Yep, he's going to continue to play teddy bears' picnic even after his little sister leaves the room. I shepherd Aria upstairs.

Drat, Wendy was bringing the starter. What can we have instead? I run through the possibilities, trying to figure out if I can rustle up something suitable from the contents of my fridge.

I'm towelling Aria dry when my phone rings. Jo. My other sister.

'Hey, Jo. Happy New Year.'

'Happy New Year! How are you? All set?'

'Kind of. Did you see Wendy's message?' I run a detangling brush through Aria's curls.

'No. Why?'

I fill her in and she makes the right noises in the right places.

'Do you need me to do anything?'

I look to the heavens and praise God.

'Actually, could you pick up some haggis and mashed potato, and something for the kids? Wendy was bringing the starter.'

'Eh, sure.' Jo responds like someone who didn't expect you to take them up on their offer. Tough. She asked and I accepted, and anyway, she always gets off lightly. 'Don't know how long we will be, though. Travis has to pop into the city centre first.'

'On New Year's Day?'

'You know I don't keep tabs on him, and I have even less interest in the restaurant. Anyway, once he's done what he has to do, it should only take us fifteen minutes or so to get from Glasgow to Ferniehall.'

'Well, there won't be any traffic on New Year's Day, so hopefully you won't be too long.'

A creaky floorboard near the bathroom alerts me that my eldest daughter has arisen. It's five past ten. Not bad going for an almost teenager, particularly since she stayed up past midnight. It was lovely, just her and me ringing in the bells together, some rare Mummy/girl time. Now she's twelve, I am no longer the centre of her world.

'Gotta go, Jo.'

'OK, see you later.'

Whilst I have been on the phone, Aria has unearthed her Pocahontas outfit from her dress-up box and is trying to shimmy into it.

'Aria, you're not dry yet. Come here.' I pat her beautiful blonde curls dry and then her body, but when I reach for her party dress, she pouts. 'Want to wear Pocahontas.' She runs off and her feet patter downstairs.

I follow her. 'Aria, it's a special day today, so we need to wear our best clothes.'

'Pocahontas is best.' Her eyes shine with defiance as she crosses her arms at the foot of the stairs.

I sigh and decide to fight that battle later as I slip the outfit over her head.

'Morning, darling.' I kiss Genevieve's head as she reaches the bottom of the stairs.

She grunts something unintelligible as she passes me and heads for the living room where she wraps herself in a fleece blanket laid out on the couch, only coming out of hibernation to retrieve her phone from the coffee table.

'Would you like some tea?'

'Please,' she croaks.

Oh God, don't let her be coming down with something.

4

I go back to the kitchen, make Genevieve some tea and take it through. She doesn't glance up from her phone. No doubt she has tons of friends texting her Happy New Year and asking what her plans are for the day. I leave her to it and finally go for a shower.

I've no sooner started lathering myself up when a voice comes through the door. 'Mum, can I play on the Xbox?'

Honestly, there is never a minute's peace in this house.

'Hugo, I'm in the shower. Couldn't your question wait until I come out?'

There's a pause as if he's pondering this. Then he says, 'Well, can I?'

If I wasn't in the shower, it would be my turn to roll my eyes at him, but I don't fancy getting soap in them. 'Fine,' I call through the door.

Ten minutes later, and with no further interruptions, I exit the bathroom, refreshed and energised. I sit on my bed to towel dry my hair, and see that I have a few more texts and WhatsApp messages. I'll have to do something about those soon. I demur over whether to put on my default smart casual clothes – black trousers and a red sparkly top – then opt for jeans and a T-shirt for now; I still have a lot of cleaning to do.

I blast my hair with the hairdryer then sling it up into a messy chignon. I don't really know how to do any other kind, plus the idea of a chignon appeals to me. It's sophisticated when I'm feeling anything but. What's the saying? Fake it till you make it. At least I am partly ready for the party now. I smile at the thought then jog downstairs. 'Gen, do you want some breakfast?'

'Yes, please.'

When silence ensues, I realise no further information is going to be forthcoming, so I pop my head round the living room door and say, 'What would you like?'

'Roll and sausage?' Gen asks, the inflexion in her voice indicating she knows she's pushing it. We're having a big lunch in a few hours and I still have a lot to do. But she's my girl, so I don't let her know I wish she'd said cornflakes, and instead say, 'Ten minutes.'

Whilst Genevieve's sausage is sizzling away in the pan, I finally get to those WhatsApp messages.

Hi, Louisa. Happy New Year. Yes, if it's OK, can we stay? We'll head off about 11 tomorrow. Thx, Rhys

That's fine. See you later.

I then turn to the Three Amigas group, comprised of me and my two best friends, Sam and Nicky. They're having lunch together today, with Sam's husband and kids and Nicky's son. Nicky's partner unfortunately is long gone.

Lou, Happy New Year. Wish you were coming to ours today. Can we do a play date this week? Will sort details later, Sam x

Happy New Year to you too, I type. *Have a great time today. Would be great to meet up. Wish Erik and the girls Happy New Year from us too x*

Hey missus, Happy New Year from me and Xander. Hope you have a great day with the family. When are we meeting up? Haven't seen you this year. Nic x

Hi Nic, Happy New Year to you both. Are you looking forward to going to Sam's? She messaged in the group about a play date x

I flip Gen's sausage, butter the bread and fetch a plate for it.

'Here you go, darling. Would you mind helping me move the dining tables around later? Aunt Wendy and the gang can't come as Kayla and Hallie are sick.'

'Oh no! Are they OK?' Genevieve's eyes are wide with

6

concern and she pauses in her texting.

'They've got a bug. Hopefully, it's a twenty-four-hour thing, but they're poorly and Aunt Wendy doesn't want to risk passing it on.'

Gen nods. 'That's a shame. I love the twins, they're so cute.'

She's right, they're gorgeous. In fact, with their blonde curls, sometimes it's hard to tell them and Aria apart.

'They are indeed. So, dining table after you've dressed,' I say meaningfully.

Gen nods again as she takes a huge bite out of her roll.

I check the time and go into the kitchen to take stock. I can't do anything about the starter until Jo brings the ingredients. The pastry is defrosting ready for the meat to go in. The meat has been slow-cooking since seven o'clock.

I make the most of Gen's sunny disposition today to ask for a bit more assistance than I would usually. It's not generally worth the angst. As we move the first dining table, I wonder if it's the advent of a new year that has caused her to be so amenable, as my daughter isn't always sweetness and light. However, she's still quick to escape back upstairs when we're done, no doubt to chat on social media with her friends.

'Can I help, Mummy?' asks a small voice.

I turn to see Aria, still in her Pocahontas outfit. I'll need to do something about that soon. I pray it's not a screaming match to get it off her. It is only family, I suppose. They wouldn't mind. Maybe I will spare myself any aggro and let her keep it on.

'Can you ask Hugo to give you the cloth napkins, the white ones, out of the drawer in the spare room?'

My phone rings. It's Ronnie FaceTiming me.

'Happy New Year, darling. Yes, not bad. Trying to get everything organised for everyone coming.' I look at my husband. I love FaceTime. If I didn't have FaceTime I'd be even more disconnected from Ronnie. Although it's hard keeping on top of everything, that's not the only area where I find his long absences difficult. I miss Ronnie terribly, even when he's being a pain. I even miss us arguing over what to watch on TV, but he redresses the balance on all counts when he's back for his two weeks.

'Are Rhys and Sandra staying then?'

'Yes, he texted me this morning.'

'It makes sense. They're going up to see Sandra's parents tomorrow. No point in them going back down to Kelso tonight.'

'No. So what did you do to ring in the bells?'

'Well, we had the TV on in the background with the usual street party stuff, and we broke out the Monopoly about half twelve.'

My husband regales me with tales of the rig, and I listen, thinking wistfully of how much I would like him to be here. He misses so many of our family parties. When you have an extended family as large as ours, it's always someone's birthday or anniversary, christening, first communion or school play.

When he finishes, I tell him about Wendy's predicament.

'Poor Wendy. That's a terrible start to the year. Wish her well from me.'

'I will.'

'Can I speak to the kids?'

'Of course. You can talk to Gen first then I'll put the other two on.'

'Great. Listen, Lou, I know how hard it is for you when I'm away, particularly when there are these big events, so promise me you'll take some time to chill, and delegate. It should have been Jo's turn to host. Make sure she makes up for it by helping you.'

'I know, I promise.' If Jo brings what I asked her for the starter, that will be enough.

'Come back on once I've spoken to the kids, won't you?' His voice cracks with emotion. Either that or he has the makings of a cold.

'I will, don't worry.' I go up to Gen's room and knock. 'Dad's on FaceTime.'

Instantly, her head appears round the door. 'Dad!'

I nod and she thunders down the stairs and barrels into the living room then starts talking animatedly with Ronnie. My heart aches. I wish for all our sakes that he didn't have to work offshore and we saw him every night. It seems my kids think so too. I leave her to some privacy with her father and go into the playroom to check on her siblings. They really do play well together. They are both jabbering away like budgies.

'Daddy's on the phone.'

'Daddy, Daddy!' Aria shouts, jumping up and down.

'Gen's talking to him in the living room. On you go.'

Hugo has a huge grin across his face as Aria takes his hand and drags him into the living room.

'Hi, Daddy!' Aria shouts. Gen cuts off talking to Ronnie whilst Aria and Hugo say their hellos.

After five minutes, I say, 'Gen, why don't you help me with the spare bed whilst Dad talks to Aria and Hugo? We can come and talk to him again afterwards.'

'Bye, Dad,' she says. 'Speak to you in a bit. Don't hang up without talking to me again.'

'I won't, princess. Don't worry.'

I smile at his term of endearment. Gen is 'princess',

Aria is 'angel', and Hugo is 'little man', although for how much longer Ronnie will get away with that, I'm not sure. At eight, our son is growing fast, but Ronnie is six one, so Hugo is still little in his dad's eyes.

'So, Sam and Nicky want us to do something together on Monday. What do you think?' I say.

Genevieve glances up from where she is folding the sheet under the mattress. Her eyebrows raise as if she can't believe I'm asking her opinion.

'Well, it has to be something we'll all enjoy. How about trampolining? Or the cinema and then something to eat afterwards? Or sledging?'

She's clearly on a roll now. I think it's good to empower the kids. They get so fed up with us parents telling them what to do all the time.

'Those ideas all sound great. Can you find out what's showing at the cinema, and what the minimum age is for sledging? Emily's only three, same as Aria, remember. Same for trampolining. I'm sure they'd love both but I'd hate for us to arrive and then they couldn't get in.'

Gen's face lights up, as if I've entrusted her with a top-secret mission. 'I'm on it,' she announces as she fluffs the final pillows. 'Right, I'm going to talk to Dad again.'

I follow her downstairs. 'Aria, time to get dressed.'

'But I'm not Aria, Mummy, I'm Pocahontas,' she wails.

I let it go as the doorbell rings. I peer out the window, and see, to my horror, that my in-laws are already here. I glance at the clock. They're more than an hour early. I'm not ready yet. I'm in my cleaning clothes, the house isn't completely tidy and we haven't finalised the dining arrangements.

I answer the door, plastering on my biggest smile. It is

New Year after all.

'Annabelle, Phillip, Happy New Year.' I fold them in my embrace and kiss them on both cheeks.

'Louisa, darling, how are you? Oh, I see you haven't had time to change yet,' Annabelle says, her gaze sweeping over my grubby top and faded jeans.

For once she's right. Usually when she makes a comment like this, I'm clad in my best clothes and she has clearly found me lacking.

'I'm good, thanks. And no, I've been cleaning. I was making sure the kids were ready first,' I say, hoping she doesn't miss the 'Aren't I a great mum?' hint I've tried to include, putting my children before myself, as I always do.

'Ronnie's on FaceTime with the kids. Why don't you go through whilst I change?'

Annabelle's face distorts in distaste. 'FaceTime? Children are exposed to too much technology too young.'

I manage to keep myself in check and wave a hand towards the living room, indicating that's where the action is, then I rush upstairs and strip off. Excited shrieks reach my ears. The kids have noticed their grandparents. Good – they can watch them for now. I throw on my black trousers and spangly top then cast around for a hairbrush. I drag it through my hair, trying to make myself look less frantic madwoman and instead channel sophisticated mother-of-three who takes hosting dinner parties in her stride. Unfortunately, I still have time to notice the beginnings of grey hairs creeping into my dark curls. I wave a mascara wand over my lashes. Good. It makes the green of my eyes pop. I look less haggard now.

'Mum, I'm hungry.' I swivel round. Hugo is standing at my bedroom door, his tongue hanging out like a gazelle that has been chased through the savannah by a lion.

'Will a ham sandwich do you until lunch?'

'Two ham sandwiches?' he pleads.

'Fine, but you had better eat your lunch,' I say, slinging my arm around him and pulling him to me as we head back downstairs. God, I've turned into my mother, or worse, Annabelle.

I wave to Ronnie when I return to the living room. He grins and shoots me a knowing look, then turns his attention back to his parents. His mother had fortunately been distracted by Genevieve, whom I now rope in to helping me move the furniture.

'Oh, Phillip will give you a hand with that,' says Annabelle, shooing her husband over in our direction.

To his credit, Phillip does help as I tell him and Gen where to position the chairs and the second table. I note Annabelle didn't offer her own services.

'Thanks, Phillip. Would you like a drink?' I ask, realising that I left them to their own devices whilst I changed.

'Whisky would be good,' he announces then retreats back to the living room, his duty done.

I think it's a bit early in the day for spirits, but maybe I should embrace his philosophy. Hmm, on second thoughts, better not, I still have lunch to cook. Talking of lunch, it's about time I rolled out the pastry. Ready-made, of course. I haven't got time to make it from scratch, especially with guests arriving more than an hour early.

I unearth a bottle of Glenfiddich one of Ronnie's oil-rig friends bought him.

'Here you go, Phillip,' I say, handing him the generous measure I've poured.

He sniffs it. Initially, I'm unsure if he's ascertaining whether it's palatable or not, but then he says, 'Glenfiddich, fifteen-year-old.'

I breathe a sigh of relief. It seems to have met with his approval.

'Annabelle, what would you like to drink?'

'White wine spritzer.'

I notice the absence of a please but simply say, 'Coming right up,' deciding she can wait for it as I turn the oven on and start to roll out the pastry. That's what she gets for having no manners.

I'm turning the oven on when the doorbell goes again, and I dash to answer it.

'Mum, Dad, Happy New Year. Come in.' I hug Dad to me tight. Sometimes even when you're an adult, giving your mum or dad a cuddle makes everything better. Since I can't hug my husband as often as I'd like, being able to hug my parents is a good backup.

'Happy New Year, Louisa.' My dad gives me a smacker on the cheek then offers me a lump of coal as he does every year. He's used to being my 'first foot'. I don't have the heart to tell him that because Annabelle and Phillip turned up early, he isn't. He'll work it out soon enough. Anyway, I can pretend. Annabelle and Phillip aren't up on Scottish traditions. Phillip has an excuse. He's from Stoke-on-Trent, but Annabelle's from Musselburgh, so she knows the tradition of the tall, dark, handsome stranger who bears a gift of coal and that it's a harbinger of good luck.

Mum can't hug me because she is carrying a pie dish, but she kisses me on the cheek as notes of Viktor & Rolf's Flowerbomb waft towards me.

'Where are the cherubs?' she says, her eyes darting all over the place as if I've hidden them.

'In the living room. They're on a FaceTime call with Ronnie.'

'Ooh, I love FaceTime,' Mum says. That's not

surprising; it's how she and Dad communicate with us most of the time, since they are almost always away on one cruise or another.

She hands me the dish and waltzes through to the living room. Dad catches my eye and grins. My mother is a force to be reckoned with, which is just as well, when Annabelle's around.

'Annabelle, Phillip, Happy New Year. I didn't realise you were already here. Hi, Ronnie. Happy New Year to you too.'

Murmured conversation follows.

'Dad, fancy helping me in the kitchen?'

He nods, his eyes widening in gratitude. It's not that my mum and dad don't like Annabelle and Phillip, but two more different couples you couldn't meet.

'Could you make some ham sandwiches for Hugo whilst I deal with this pastry?' I ask Dad as I pull on an apron.

'Of course.' Dad is at home in my house and helps himself to what he needs from the fridge whilst we chat easily about his and Mum's upcoming trip.

'She's already looking to book another, you know,' he confides to me.

'Really? I thought the deal was you always came back from one and booked another.'

'It is, but you know what your mother's like.'

I do.

'So where to next?' I ask as I crimp the edges of the pastry around the pie dish then use the remaining pieces to make leaves.

'The Arctic.'

'The Arctic? I thought Mum was a sun-worshipper.'

'She is, usually, but she watched some documentary

about the unexploited Russian Arctic and how it's renowned for its "abundance" of polar bears–' I roll my eyes at this '–and she's intent on going now.'

My poor dad. I wonder how much, if any, say he had in this. I know he prefers sailing round the Med. And he last spoke to me about wanting to visit Jura, Mull, Luing and Shuna. He would have preferred a tour of the Hebrides on a luxury ship looking for seals, although I imagine they have seals in Russian waters too.

Dad takes Hugo's sandwich through to him, and immediately I hear Aria moan that she wants one too. OK, it has been a while since breakfast. They were up far earlier than Genevieve. I pop the pie in the oven and am about to open the fridge to make some more sandwiches when the doorbell goes again. Honestly, Piccadilly Circus must be quieter than here. The clock shows it's only twelve thirty. No one was meant to be here until one.

I walk into the hall only for Aria to accost me. 'Mummy, I want a ham sandwich too,' she whines.

'In a minute, poppet.' I disentangle her limbs from mine and get to the door as Hugo shouts, 'It's Uncle Rhys. I can see his car. Uncle Rhys, Uncle Rhys!'

I open the door and don't even get 'Happy New Year' out before Hugo jumps up on Rhys and Rhys ruffles his hair and makes a fuss of him, setting his glasses askew as he does so. Hugo feigns indignation whilst Sandra chuckles. I beckon her inside, where Aria emulates her brother and makes a big deal of her aunt's arrival.

'Mummy, Aunt Sandra's earrings have a number one on them.'

'That's because today is the first, sweetheart,' Sandra says. 'And the first is the same as one.'

'Sandra, can I take your coat?' I ask.

She undoes her coat and I see just how huge her stomach is.

'Wow! I can't believe how much more pregnant you look than last time.' I avoid saying 'bigger'. People can be so sensitive, although it never bothered me when I was pregnant.

Sandra grins. 'I know. Although I suppose I am seven and a half months pregnant.'

'Really? Where has the time gone?'

'That's what I was saying. There'll be no peace soon,' my brother-in-law chips in.

'Hi, Rhys.' I grin. Rhys and I have always got on well. He's like a little brother to me.

'Hi, sis.' He leans in to give me a peck and then hugs me. 'Happy New Year.'

'Happy New Year. Drink?'

'Are my folks here yet?' he asks.

'Yes,' I reply.

'In that case, make it a double.'

We all laugh. Rhys has a love/put-up-with relationship with his parents. How two such stuffy individuals raised such relaxed children as Rhys and Ronnie I'll never know.

'But seriously, if you have any Guinness, that would go down well.'

'I'll get you one in a sec. Let me fix Aria a sandwich first,' I say, glancing at my daughter, who is eyeing me mutinously, then staring at her brother's half-eaten sandwich. 'Everyone's in the living room. Sandra, what about you?'

'No-alcohol Prosecco. I brought two bottles. I even chilled them in the cool box in the car.'

'I'm impressed.' I take them from her, putting one on the worktop and the other in the fridge.

'Figured I'd need to get good at planning ahead. Where can I put this bag of chocolates and treats for the kids?'

'On the table for now, thanks.'

'Can I help?' she asks.

'Actually, would you mind getting Rhys a drink, if you're feeling up to it? And I forgot to get Annabelle's white wine spritzer.' I roll my eyes and we giggle.

'That won't do at all. I'm on it.'

'Who's taking care of the dogs whilst you're up here?' I ask her as she pours drinks and I slap some ham on thinly buttered brown bread for Aria.

'Our neighbour Milo has them. He and his boyfriend are spending a quiet New Year together, as it's their anniversary, so they were more than happy to have Max and Benji.'

'Aw, that's nice.' Sounds blissful. For a second I wonder what it would be like planning a New Year's meal for fewer than twenty people.

Excited chatter emanates from the living room. Annabelle has obviously discovered her youngest son has arrived.

I go through with her white wine spritzer and Aria's sandwich. The living room is filling up. It's still fairly festive, even though I took down the Christmas cards.

'Oh, you did remember. I was just telling your mum I thought you'd forgotten all about me.' Annabelle titters.

I plaster on the same smile as earlier and hand her glass to her. Of course, nobody has noticed I don't have one, then Sandra turns from where she was standing talking to Dad.

'Louisa, here you go.' She hands me a glass of Prosecco and finally I can breathe for a second, not because of the chance to gulp down some alcohol but because I have an excuse to stop whizzing around. OK, my brain is still racing, thinking, *Everyone is here but Jo and she has the ingredients for the starter.*

'Mum.' Aria is pulling at the bottom of my blouse. I glance down and see a stain on the front of her Pocahontas dress. I put my finger to my lips then twirl her round. Yep, soaking. She's had another 'accident'.

'C'mon, let's put your pretty dress on,' I say, and the smile she gives me lights up her whole face.

I rest my Prosecco glass on the low bookcase and lead my daughter by the hand upstairs, where I divest her of her clothes, clean her up and slip her party dress over her head. She manages the underwear herself.

With Aria squeaky clean, I usher her downstairs whilst I carry, at arm's length, her saturated bundle of clothes.

The doorbell rings. I'm getting déjà vu. It can only be Jo and her brood, surely. There isn't anyone else left to arrive, is there? I rack my brain. Nope, all here, except the one with the food.

I open the door. 'Happy New Year. In you come. I'm en route to the washing machine, so I won't hug you, yet. Jo, follow me with those bags, will you? Hello, Aurora, what a pretty dress. And how handsome are you, Jackson?' I turn to my brother-in-law. 'Travis, can you take the kids, Aria too, into the living room? Everyone's in there.'

I draw breath and trot off to throw the stuff in the wash. I'm busy pouring fabric conditioner into the washing machine compartment when Jo comes in behind me.

'What's up?'

'Nothing,' I say. 'But Aria wet herself again. I need to wash her costume or it will stink the utility room out.'

'Ah. I thought she was doing so much better too,' Jo says as she sets the shopping on the worktop and starts extracting the items from the bags, placing some things in the fridge and glancing around as if looking for homes for the others.

'She was,' I say as I fiddle with the knobs and turn the machine on. 'But when something exciting's happening, that's when she has lapses.'

'Such as today, with everyone coming round?' Jo asks.

'Exactly.'

Jo comes to hug me.

'You might want to wait until I've washed my hands,' I say, making a beeline for the sink.

'Good point,' says my eldest sister.

'So, did you get everything?'

'I could only get tinned haggis, but they'll never know. They're not that discerning. Anyway, the good thing is it won't take so long to make. Let me say hi to everyone and I'll come back and help you cook it.'

'What, ping stuff?' I look at the five packets of pre-prepared mash and neeps that Jo has bought. Where she bought them on New Year's Day confounds me, but I am thankful she has.

'Ha ha. I can plate up.'

She makes it sound like silver service.

'Fine. All help's welcome. What do you want to drink?'

'I'll get something myself in a sec. Get zapping, I'm starving!'

My sister always makes me laugh. Even though she is the eldest of us three siblings, you'd think it was the other way around. Wendy is more serious and a born organiser, Jo is ditzy, last-minute and not the most reliable, but her heart is in the right place.

'Oh, what did you get for the kids?' I call after her as she vanishes into the living room.

She sticks her head back round the door long enough to say 'Breadsticks,' and then she's gone.

Breadsticks? Breadsticks? How's that going to feed them? They'll have ages to wait before the steak pie is ready. I bend down and check. Yep, rising nicely, but it still has a long way to go, plus the adults are having haggis first. Maybe I will try the kids with haggis. I have eight tins of it.

My phone pings.

Ronnie: *Hey, babe, sorry I didn't get to say goodbye. You know what Mum's like. Don't let her negativity get you down. Have a great day and say hi to everyone I missed on the call. Love you. I'll call in two days. R x P.S. Did you get my text the other day about the kitchen fitters?*

Wendy: *Just realised I was meant to be bringing the starter. So sorry. Was so tired didn't even think about suggesting earlier that Jo could pick it up. Apologies. I'm feeling a bit yucky myself now. Going to get some sleep. Love you x*

The third is from a number I don't recognise. *Hi, Louisa, sorry to bother you on New Year's Day, but I've received word from the supplier that they won't be able to do the foil stamping for the McIvor wedding until the week after next due to a backlog. Thought I should let you know, Sue, Ferguson's Stationery Supplies.*

Crap. Alison Coughlan, soon to be McIvor, has been on the phone three times asking about the invitations, as the supplier for the specific type of foil they wanted has delayed three times now. What on earth am I going to tell her?

When you're self-employed, you initially think everything's going to be within your control, you can make your own decisions. You soon learn that you are still at the mercy of a supply chain. I run my own wedding stationery business, Wedded Bliss. I design it all and I can do small print runs of some types of stationery in-house, but I need to outsource the bigger weddings as well as the more complicated finishes. I still do all the design, and it's frustrating when I deliver for the client and do my piece, only for someone else to let both me and the client down. Aargh! Happy New Year. It's so unprofessional. But, no time to think about that right now, I have more haggis to ping. I'll reply to Wendy and Ronnie after starters.

True to her word, Jo comes back into the kitchen, even bringing me my now lukewarm glass of Prosecco. I open the fridge and pour in another glug to help bring the temperature to a drinkable level.

'Thanks. Can you dish up?' I point to the sizzling mounds of haggis, which she starts to turn over with a fork so it doesn't have quite the consistency of Pedigree Chum. It's fine for Bear, but I have no inclination to eat it myself.

Finally, we are all around the two dining tables, well, three if you count the kids' table. To my surprise most of the kids are attacking the haggis as if they've never seen food. With the cream sauce I added to it, it tastes fine, although I did add whisky for the adults' version. There is a momentary lull in the hullabaloo that is inevitable in the presence of five children and nine adults.

I am just glad to have time to eat my food. I'm starving. I sound like Hugo now, but it's half one and I've had a bowl of granola all day, which my growling stomach has reminded me of on more than one occasion in the past few hours.

As I serve the kids and myself, I hear an 'Oh God' from further down the table. I look up to see a stricken Sandra.

'You OK?'

'Not exactly.' There's a pause before she says, 'I think my waters have just broken.'

Chapter Two

All hell breaks loose at Sandra's announcement. Rhys jumps up, knocking over the water jug I've placed in the centre of the table and sending streams of water down the table.

'Ugh!' shout the kids as the water drips on to them.

Annabelle, surprisingly, remains hands-off with the advice for once. Perhaps she feels she will be called upon to help with the messy side of things.

Rhys puts his hands on Sandra's shoulders and says softly, 'What do you need?'

'Another pair of trousers for a start.'

He looks down at Sandra's lap then up at me. 'Oh! I don't suppose you have a spare pair of trousers, Lou?'

'I have some joggers that might do.'

Sandra's eyes send up a silent plea. I can tell she's uncomfortable, understatement, with this having happened at our dining table and with so many spectators.

'Sandra, why don't we get you to the bathroom? Rhys, can you call the Queen Elizabeth? That's the nearest hospital. Mum, can you help Sandra and I'll grab a change of clothes for her?'

We all swing into action whilst the others remain at the

23

table, the haggis fast going cold. Philip still has his fork in his hand as if unsure if he should continue eating or not. He will be torn between not wanting food to go to waste and being hungry, and displaying poor etiquette. But it's his grandchild we're talking about here.

Suddenly two things occur to me: one, the baby is early, and two, this is a fantastic surprise, although I would have preferred if Sandra could have held on until after lunch. My stomach rumbles for about five seconds as if to remind me I'm starving. I don't need reminding.

'Rhys, I'm scared,' Sandra whispers. 'I'm only thirty-four weeks.'

'Sandra, it will be fine,' I reassure her. Rhys' shoulders relax. He doesn't have any experience to fall back on; this is their first baby. 'Aria was born at thirty-six weeks.'

'I don't even have my notes with me. And I'm going to have to deliver in a different hospital.'

'They'll send your notes over. Don't worry. And believe me, birth plans go out the window. Have you had any contractions yet?'

'I don't think so. I'd know, right? I've had some Braxton Hicks before, but nothing recently.'

'Any chance you have your hospital bag with you?'

Sandra tears up. 'I was waiting until thirty-six weeks before doing that.'

I can see she is on the verge of a meltdown, so I say, 'Good thing you were staying here overnight then. You'll have more stuff than you know from your overnight bag, plus I'm bound to have some of the things you need.'

'But what about the baby clothes and the car seat and the maternity pyjamas?' Sandra's tears spill over.

'We don't know you're going to need those yet. And I still have the kids' baby clothes and car seats. I can put the clothes in the wash so if baby decides to put in an appearance, we're ready.'

Sandra visibly relaxes a little. 'Thank you, Louisa.'

We all spring into action to perform our various tasks.

'Jo, you guys may as well eat. Can you keep an eye on the steak pie, Dad?'

Rhys returns a few minutes later. Mum is still helping Sandra with the clothes I passed her.

'The hospital says we've to come in,' he says, excitement and concern battling for position in his voice.

'Right. Rhys, go upstairs and grab Sandra's overnight bag. Make sure she has toiletries, pyjamas, a book, phone charger, dressing gown and underwear. I'll see what I have that may be of use to her.'

Rhys bounds up the stairs and I go and relay the news to Sandra and Mum.

What a way to start the New Year. I just wish Ronnie were here too to share in his brother's excitement. I wonder if Rhys has had a chance to text him. I am guessing not. One thing's for sure: in a few hours there will be another baby in this family, and I can't wait – especially as I am not the one giving birth.

Chapter Three

Saturday 2 January

To-do list – items carried over – 27
New list items
Try to get gravy stain out of carpet in dining room
Wash dining chair covers
Check prices for leather chairs in sales (will avoid having to wash them every time Phillip is over. He's messier than a toddler)
Eggs
Place online Asda order for Thursday
Reattach playroom curtain (it was used by Aurora as a vine for swinging through the jungle, but didn't quite hold)
Email the McIvors about their wedding stationery
(Remainder of) items from 1st that didn't action

The phone ringing wakes me at five thirty. Rhys.

'I'm a dad! I can't believe it.'

'Oh, Rhys, that's fantastic news. When was the baby born? How's Sandra?'

We'd received various updates last night, and by the time I went to bed at one, Sandra had been in labour for three hours.

'She was amazing. I'm so proud of her. My God, what

you women have to go through. I never appreciated how horrific it is until now.'

'Horrific?'

'And beautiful, of course,' Rhys amends hastily, 'but seriously, I was freaked out sometimes by the amount of screaming, people in other rooms were doing. I thought I was in a secure unit not a maternity hospital.'

I smile. 'Anyway, enough of that. Do you have a baby girl or boy?'

'Girl. A wee baby girl. I can't believe it. You're an auntie again.'

'Aw, I'm so happy for you both. Have you named her yet?'

'Yep, Isabella. And she is, very *bella*.'

'Oh, I can't wait to meet her. Are we going to be able to visit?'

'Not sure yet. She's in the neonatal unit as she was small.'

'What weight was she?'

'Four pounds three ounces.'

I try not to gasp. That is pretty light. But Rhys hasn't mentioned she's having any difficulties breathing or otherwise, so I guess she's OK.

'I take it that means Sandra and Isabella will be in hospital for a little while yet then.'

'Yes. Actually, I have a favour to ask.'

Before he can continue, I say, 'Of course you can stay.'

'Thanks, Lou. I really appreciate it.'

'No problem. I'll let you go then as I need to see if those baby clothes I washed last night are dry. Are you coming back here now?'

'Yes, I'm shattered. I don't want to leave them, but I know I need to, and Sandra has given me a list of things to buy. I'll pick those up when I go back in around one.'

'Sounds like a plan. Right, come home and get some sleep then. I can't believe I have a niece.'

'I can't believe I have a daughter. See you soon.'

A new baby. A new family member. Wow. When something like this happens, you simply have to stop and draw breath to appreciate it. It's humbling.

I almost leap out of bed, throw some clothes on and head downstairs. My house is like a bomb site. Much as I love Wendy and her clan, I am so glad there were only five children here yesterday, instead of the expected nine. I don't want to imagine the level of damage they would have inflicted on my furniture. As it is, there's marker pen on the cream leather couch in the playroom that wasn't there yesterday morning and that clearly the elves did as according to the children, it wasn't any of them. I have my suspicions but won't name names, albeit I think the child in question thinks she's Tarzan.

I hare round doing a quick tidy, then grabbing a Post-it pad, I scribble down the food items for the Asda order then pull my laptop towards me and start sorting through the new emails that have come in. *Quote. Stationery request. Thank you cards. Can you provide a box for guests to put their cards in too? Change of font request. Need another 35 invites – cost please.*

Did these people not have a New Year celebration? Honestly. I'm still trying to catch up after the Christmas period. I turn my attention to the three most pressing enquiries from yesterday, including the McIvors', asking them if they wish at this point to change their choice of foil, or change from foil altogether, given the production issues. I then reply to a few other important messages from yesterday and scan the list of outstanding items from over the Christmas break. Great, I've missed one completely. I must have opened it and become distracted. Fabulous. Apology time. I manage twenty minutes' work, which must be a record, before the sound of a door opening and a small voice calling 'Mummy' interrupts me.

I go into the hall. Aria is standing at the top of the stairs, her unicorn plush under her arm.

'Morning, sweetheart,' I say as I go upstairs to collect her. She always waits on the top step for me.

'I need the toilet.'

'Let's use the one downstairs as everyone else is still sleeping.'

She curls herself into my body as I head back downstairs, then disentangles herself at the bottom as I put on the light of the WC and wait for her.

'I dreamt about unicorns last night, Mummy, in a forest. There were no bad guys this time.'

'It's so much better when there are only good guys.'

She nods sagely then jumps down and washes her hands. 'Mummy, I'm thirsty. Can we do a puzzle? Where are my slippers?'

I process her statement and questions then say, 'I'll get you some milk. Yes, which puzzle do you want to do? Your slippers are under the table in the dining room.'

'Dora the Explorer. No, Thomas. Can we do both, Mummy?'

I smile at my daughter and take her hand as she leads me to the toy cupboard in the playroom. 'Of course we can.'

I retrieve the puzzles for her then shake the pieces out of the Dora box onto her train table. Fortunately, all the train paraphernalia has been stored away and we can use the top for doing her puzzle.

'Why don't you start and I'll get your milk?'

'Mummy, can you help me sort the edges first?'

'You know how to do the edges, Aria.'

'I like it better when we do it together,' she says, her bottom lip jutting out.

'OK.' I quickly separate the pieces into edges and middles, then leave her to it whilst I put the kettle on and sort her some milk. I notice there's not much left. I'm not even sure how that's possible. I bought eight pints the other day.

I walk through to the playroom with Aria's milk and smile when I see she has only two of the sixteen pieces to finish. She's a whizz-kid. I crouch down beside her, placing her milk on the table and watch her finish.

'Mummy, I'm all done.'

'Well done. High-five?'

She slaps her small hand against mine and then pulls the Thomas puzzle towards her. She tries to open the box, but the lid jams so she offers it to me. These are the moments when all is right with the world, when I can sit with my daughter without feeling I have to rush off to do something more pressing. It's hard to sit still when so much else needs done but sometimes you have to make yourself. I open the box for her and we separate the pieces. She completes the puzzle in record time.

'Frozen, Mummy, and the alphabet one, please,' she says, anticipating my next question.

I bring her the requested puzzles, thirty-five pieces this time, and as if she has rote-learned the order of each piece, she completes the Frozen puzzle in about two minutes.

'Back in a sec.' I step into the kitchen, make my coffee, then realise how much dirty laundry is still in the basket and throw on a dark wash.

'Mummy, I'm done,' calls Aria.

I carry my coffee through to the playroom and she has indeed finished. This girl will go far. We sit together for half an hour doing a few more puzzles. Aria had to show me where some of the pieces in the sixty-piece one went. Nothing like your three-year-old making you feel dim. I'm so proud of her abilities.

'Mummy, I'm hungry. Can I have a bagel with jam?'

'Magic word?'

'Please,' she says.

'OK. Guess what? You have a new little cousin.'

Aria's eyes go wide. 'Is that Aunt Sandra's baby?'

I nod. 'It's a baby girl. Isabella.'

Aria tilts her head, thinks for a minute then says, 'I like that name.' I'm glad it meets with her approval. 'Can I give her one of my teddies?'

'That's very kind, sweetie, but I think we will buy her a new teddy. Tell you what, why don't you help me choose it?'

Aria's eyes shine. She loves making decisions and being asked for her opinion. 'Yes, please.'

'Good. We'll have a look later. Do you want to watch something whilst you eat?'

'Shimmer and Shine.'

One thing about my younger daughter, she is very decisive. Maybe she will lead the country one day.

I turn on the TV and go to prepare her bagel. When I bring it through, she sits obediently at the table, taking huge bites as if she has been starved for three days, and not as if there is a surplus of food in the fridge which would easily feed ten people.

Sitting down with my coffee, I glance at my list again. *Check prices for leather chairs in sales.* Yes, if I can get a

31

good deal, I might take the plunge, as leather ones would wipe down and I wouldn't have to wash the covers after we've had the family round. It's such a pain as they are so awkward to get off. The problem is our dining table seats ten. Ten chairs. The best I can find is £140 for a pair. Not as much of a discount as I'd hoped, but better than nothing. When I get time, I'll look at the bank balances and see how feasible that is.

I jot down on my list – *Check banking*.

What's next on the list? Those damned dining chair covers. Well, I suppose I'll have to wrestle with them later, but right now I can't put them in the wash because there's already one on. I smile smugly to myself. One point to me!

I refer to my list from yesterday. Whilst it's only me and Aria, I can do some of the online stuff. She has finished breakfast and is now playing with Duplo.

Pushing out of my mind the fact I should really clear her plate away, I bow my head and try to get through some of the items which involve using a computer. Banking, check. Nursery fees, check. Client emails – two of ten most pressing, check.

'Mum!' Hugo calls.

I walk into the hall. 'Hugo, why are you shouting?' I whisper. 'Come down here and talk to me.'

He makes his way downstairs and says, 'Where's my new Spider-Man T-shirt? The one I got for Christmas.'

'I don't know.' It's possible it's still festering at the bottom of the ironing basket, or worse, the dirty laundry basket. Depends when he wore it. I cast my mind back but draw a blank.

'But I want to wear it today,' he wails.

Hugo is generally very good but sometimes, like now, he has meltdowns over the most trivial things.

'It might be in the ironing basket,' I suggest.

His face falls then his mouth twists as if he's about to argue with me, or suggest I check, but I adopt my stern, no-nonsense face, which must work as he trots off.

A sleepy Genevieve appears two minutes later. 'Why was Hugo shouting?'

'Spider-Man T-shirt,' I mumble as my eyes chase the columns of figures across the page. 'You have a new cousin by the way.'

'Yay!' says Gen, suddenly more awake, a grin splitting her face. 'Boy or girl?'

'Girl. Isabella.' I smile at her. 'Aunt Sandra and the baby are doing well and Uncle Rhys is going to stay here for a few days whilst they're in hospital. He's on his way back now as he's been awake all night.'

The doorbell rings and Gen rushes to answer it. 'Uncle Rhys, congratulations! I'm a big cousin again.'

'That's right. And I know you'll look out for her, won't you?'

Already Rhys has that protective daddy armour on. Nothing and nobody will hurt his little girl.

'Of course. Do you want some toast? You must be hungry.'

I stare at Gen. I have never known her to offer to make anyone food. This is a landmark day indeed.

It's lunchtime before the house is in any kind of order. We're having a chillout day of sorts. Genevieve asked to go round to her friend Tasha's house as they're having a party with some of her school friends. That leaves Aria, Hugo and me in the house. I told them they could have a movie each, with a break for play in the middle. If it stops tipping it down outside, maybe I can get them out to the park. It would give Bear a good run too.

Rhys went to sleep as soon as he'd had a cup of tea and the toast Gen made him and slept for four hours or so, then headed off to the shops to buy the essentials he'd been asked to pick up. I packed a bag with a selection of the cute baby clothes I kept from when the two girls were born.

The afternoon passes pleasantly enough with copious amounts of hot chocolate, mainly for Hugo, and marshmallows, mainly for Aria, the little ones you use in baking. And whilst the kids are ensconced under a blanket on the living room sofa, I iron as much of the contents of the basket as I can stomach before putting it away and raiding the freezer to see what's for dinner.

School shoes. Drat, I knew there was something else. Where's my phone? I find it on the plant stand beside where I had the ironing board propped up. I tap in *Go to Clarks and get Hugo's and Aria's feet measured – new shoes/trainers?*

In theory we could do this today, it's early enough, but the mood is too relaxed, even if I have spent the past two hours ironing. Ironing whilst watching *The Lion King* somehow makes it more palatable. Did I mention I love animated movies? No? I always have.

Genevieve returns around six and I dig out a ratatouille I froze a week ago. Yes, I know, ratatouille. Ooh la la. She's giving her kids ratatouille. I plate up the ratatouille and Genevieve's eyes light up. Not sure what they fed her, if anything, round at Tasha's, but ratatouille it wasn't. I put Hugo's plate before him and he eyes it curiously. If I'd put a dead pigeon in front of him, it would probably have elicited the same response. Aria, bless her, albeit she regards it with suspicion, dips her fork into it and raises it to her mouth, but then declares, 'Mummy, I don't like it. It smells funny.'

And there you have it, home-cooked meals. A one in three chance of anyone eating them.

'It tastes delicious, honey. Try a bit,' I say to Aria, but she has already pushed her plate away. I know the drill. She's not eating it. With Aria, you could make her sit there for three hours, she still wouldn't eat it. I can't even tempt her with pudding as it won't make any difference. Hugo, on the other hand, is another matter.

'Hugo, there's strawberry cheesecake for afters if you eat some ratatouille.'

'Rat-atooey,' he repeats. 'Are there actual rats in it?' His eyes gleam as if he would be delighted if the answer were yes.

'Fortunately, no. It's full of–' just in time I stop myself from saying 'vegetables' and instead say '–goodness.'

Hugo bestows upon me the look Aria gave the ratatouille earlier: suspicion.

Exasperated, but trying not to show it, I say as calmly as I can, 'What's the worst that could happen? Try it.'

Hugo appears to mull this over then puts a tiny amount onto his fork and tentatively places it in his mouth. 'Hmm, it's OK. Mmm, it's really nice. Ugh, no, it's disgusting.' He almost spits it out again onto the plate but my death glare has him reaching for his napkin and being more discreet than he originally intended. So much for my attempts to make the kids eat more healthily.

'Go play for a bit and I'll make you both some pizza.'

'Yay!' Hugo cries, holding his hand out to Aria, who has already jumped down from her chair. Frozen pizzas it is then: margherita for Aria, pepperoni for Hugo. Ten minutes later they are feasting upon those. Meanwhile, Genevieve, to her credit, has eaten all her ratatouille and refused strawberry cheesecake in favour of more ratatouille. Is she definitely my daughter? Even I don't have second helpings of ratatouille, and I made it.

Aria tires easily after dinner and I have to devise a plan to keep her awake as the last thing I want is her napping late and being a nightmare to put to bed later. So, I coax everyone into playing board games, one choice each. Genevieve has always loved Guess Who? Hugo opts for Twister and Aria for KerPlunk. It descends into chaos quickly after. Genevieve with her long legs has a distinct advantage at Twister, Aria's too little to put the sticks in properly in KerPlunk and Hugo thinks Genevieve is cheating at Guess Who?, as the people he has left to choose from bear no relation to the card in Genevieve's hand.

The games take us until bedtime. Aria has flaked out on the couch. It has been a late one for her. She usually goes an hour before Hugo. Even Hugo is yawning now. I settle Aria in bed then pick up Hugo's pyjamas from his room and take them downstairs.

'Hugo, here's your pyjamas. Can you get changed and I will come up and read you your new Anthony Horowitz book?'

I love that my son still enjoys cuddles and Mummy/ boy time. I read a chapter, then turn to see sparkling dark lashes lying on rosy cheeks. My boy is asleep. I cuddle into Hugo until there is the chance of my falling asleep too, then I shift my weight, rise from the bed and go to see how my eldest daughter is faring. Somehow I don't think she'll want a story.

Chapter Four

To-do list – items outstanding – 17
Actioned yesterday – 8
New items
Order more laundry labels
Fix kitchen cupboard door, hinge broken

'Mum, we need to go or we'll miss our trampolining slot,' Genevieve hollers from the bottom of the stairs.

'Give me a minute. I'm looking for another pair of trampoline socks.'

'We can buy them there,' she replies, annoyance underpinning her tone.

'Aha!' I exclaim, holding aloft the socks I knew all along were there. Every time we go trampolining I have to shell out for socks as we can never find them. Then, the very next day, I find them in the unlikeliest of places. Last time it was the fruit bowl.

I race down the stairs and Gen virtually shepherds me out of the house. You'd think she was the mother the way she's going on. I know I gave her this as a pet project, but she has taken it a little too far. We're not trying to escape an alien invasion or an impending hurricane, we're going to Bounce High, the newest trampolining sensation in the area. In addition to the trampolines, there are eight bouncy castles, as well as *It's-a-Knockout*-style games and a *Gladiators*-type duel. Last but not least, a sticky wall, where you put on a Velcro suit, run at a wall and, you've got it, you stick to it. The kids will love it.

Xander, Nicky's son, is fizzing with excitement, Nicky's words not mine. She texted me, telling me not to be late, as she doesn't want to be sitting in the car with him waiting for us in case he explodes.

I drive the five miles to Bounce High. It's next to an out-of-town retail park, and as I see some of the store signs, it reminds me that I need to buy a couple of presents. I mentally add them to my list.

Birthday present for Sam – Cath Kidston? Next voucher? Perfume? Nice stationery?

Present for Gethin – google £10–£15 toys later

Gethin's mother invited Hugo via a Facebook group message to the mums. They're not terribly close and it seems a big party for an eight-year-old, thirty-two children, but Hugo wants to go, so I can hardly deny him.

I zone back in to the chatter in the car. I am so looking forward to catching up with the girls. I haven't seen them since before Christmas. I realise the monkeys are with us, but hopefully they will play by themselves and we can have a latte and a chat whilst keeping an eye on them. I am glad Genevieve is now old enough to watch Aria a little as last time I went trampolining with Aria, she wouldn't go on the trampoline without me and I wasn't wearing a sports bra. It wasn't the most comfortable in every sense of the word. I mean, I'm not chesty, 34C, but things do still jiggle, plus I kept thinking everyone was watching me.

I pull into the car park and see that Sam's and Nicky's

cars are already there, parked side by side. I undo Aria's seat belt and soon the children and adults are all together heading towards the trampoline building, which resembles an aircraft hangar.

Haircut for Genevieve and Aria. I caught a glimpse of Genevieve's split ends when I glanced in the rear-view mirror. I'll call from the trampoline park and see if I can book them in tomorrow. They go back to school in two days.

We pay at the desk, go through to the changing area, everyone changes, then we head for the debriefing room. Honestly, you'd think it was NASA's Mission Control Centre. I don't recall having ten-minute lessons on how to jump on a trampoline responsibly. Aria is pulling at me, keen to get on the trampolines; Hugo and Xander, who get on really well, are whispering throughout; and Genevieve is rolling her eyes as if the majority of the statements the automated presentation is making is a load of codswallop. I tend to agree with her. And of course, they are all going to break the 'one person to a trampoline at a time' rule, as well as the 'no running between trampolines'. They're kids, for goodness' sake. Don't the organisers know that the more you give kids rules, the more they want to break them?

I gather the various jackets, shoes and bags that belong to my offspring and clutch them to me as I follow Nicky to the table she has already plonked herself at.

'And relax,' says Sam, exhaling heavily as we all sit down.

I nod then stifle a yawn. 'So sorry, I'm shattered. Late night.'

'How come?' asks Nicky, taking her purse out and placing it on the table.

'I talked to Rhys for a bit once the kids went to bed, then when he went up, I was replying to emails until one o'clock.'

'You're joking!' Sam says. 'No wonder you're knackered. You could have cancelled if you were too tired.'

I give her a look.

'Yeah, maybe not. We need this. It keeps us sane,' she concedes. 'On that note, lattes all round?'

Nicky and I murmur our approval.

'Cake?'

I hesitate then decide, stuff it, I will. I don't make New Year's resolutions. There seems little point; they all get broken by around the fifth. So, I don't feel obligated to reduce my sugar intake now that we're in the month where many try to abstain from their vices.

Nicky and I catch up for a few minutes whilst Sam orders the coffees. She waves away our offer of cash.

'So, how is baby Isabella?' she asks.

'Doing really well. In fact, we should be able to see her tonight.'

'Aw, that's wonderful. You must be made up.'

'I am. And I'm so pleased for Sandra and Rhys. They'll be fantastic parents.'

'And how are you managing with the added stress of a house guest and all the excitement?'

I take a deep breath. 'Rhys is no problem, and he's hardly been there. As for the rest, I'm running on empty, to be honest. I love having the kids home, but I'm pulled in too many directions all of the time. If the business gets any busier, I might have to consider taking on some part-time help.'

'That's good though, isn't it?' Nicky pulls her cardigan around her more tightly. It's January after all and I wasn't wrong about the aircraft hangar. It has the same insulation properties. It must be about -2 °C in here.

'Yeah, I suppose,' I admit. 'Although I really have to hold off until Aria starts school in case there isn't enough work for both of us.'

'Well, people are always going to get married,' she points out.

'That's true, but I don't want to take someone on and train them up, only to have to let them go six to nine months later.'

'I see where you're coming from,' Nicky says, resting her hand on her chin, 'but you don't need to overthink this. Can't you hire someone on a zero-hours contract to do the more basic things for you? What's the worst that can happen? And you'd have more time with the kids, guilt-free.'

I mull over what she has said. It might work. 'I'll give it some thought.'

'Definitely think you should do that,' she says as Sam sets our coffees in front of us.

'Mummy!'

I turn to see Aria wiggling from side to side. 'OK, let's go,' I say to her, grabbing her Dora the Explorer backpack and bustling her to the toilets.

'Mummy,' she says tearfully, 'when I jumped up and down on the trampoline, a little bit came out.'

'Don't worry. It happens sometimes. The important thing is to tell me. OK, on you go,' I tell her as she sits up on the toilet and I pull fresh pants and leggings out of her bag. I take the spare carrier bag I always carry for emergencies and remove the bottom half of her clothing once she's done and bundle it into the bag before returning it to the backpack.

All cleaned up and changed, we head back out to the trampoline area where my latte is quickly growing cold.

'Can I have a drink, Mummy?'

'Magic word,' I say on autopilot.

'Pleeeeeeeezeeeeeeee.'

The girls eye me sympathetically. It's the bane of a parent's life never to get to drink a hot drink when it's still hot.

'OK.' I exhale and search in my bag for my purse. 'What will your guys take?' I ask Sam and Nicky. We may as well get it over in one go. When I have their order, I go to the café and fork out twelve pounds for six children's drinks. I must be off my head. I remember having to live on fifteen pounds a week when I was at university.

Aria sits on my lap whilst she drinks her blackcurrant juice. I try to cajole her to sit on the seat next to me, by moving the various backpacks, but she is having none of it.

'I want to sit on your knee, Mummy.' Her voice has risen an octave and I debate which is less of a chore, having cold coffee or listening to her whining. Oh well, the coffee was getting cold. Maybe I'll get another when she goes back on the trampoline.

Aria soon decides she's had enough of her drink, although she has gulped down about three-quarters of it. The three of us settle back in relief at having time to speak with each other again and catch up on some of the gossip. Sam has new neighbours, the Sharmas, with two young children, which is good as Emily and Ava will have someone to play with next door. Nicky's ex has been in touch again. A sore point. He hasn't been in contact for months. They split when Xander was only four and he's barely seen him in the intervening years. But we're not prepared for Nicky's news.

'Brittany's pregnant.'

'You're joking!' Sam and I say at the same time.

'Nope, six months apparently, and now he wants to see Xander more, involve Xander in his new little family unit. Says he knows he messed up with Xander and wants to put it right. Even apologised for doing the dirty on me and treating me so shabbily, not that I believe him for a minute.' Nicky swipes at her eyes to displace the tears that have betrayed her.

'When did you find out?' I ask her, trying to put my jaw back in its usual position, or at least raise it from the floor, where it's currently residing.

'New Year's Day. He phoned me to wish me Happy New Year. He has never done that. I don't know why I answered. I don't owe him anything. But I thought maybe he was phoning to wish Xander Happy New Year.' Her voice cracks; it's obvious that wasn't the reason for his call.

Nicky hasn't dated since Sebastian, her ex, left. Even though it has been six years, she hasn't even looked at anyone else. Part of that, Sam and I feel, is because, despite everything, she still loves him, and part of it is because she has dedicated herself wholly to Xander and making sure she's both mum and dad to him.

Sam tries not to stumble over her words. 'I can't believe it. I assumed as they didn't have kids already that they, you know, couldn't, or that Sebastian had decided one was enough.'

'Yeah, well, apparently not. And bear in mind, Brittany–' she emphasises her name '–is only twenty-eight now. They could go on to have a whole football team if they wanted.'

That's right. Sebastian left his four-year-old son and fiancée for a nubile twenty-two-year-old. What a cliché.

Nicky was only thirty-two but it almost destroyed her. And Brittany was everything Nicky wasn't: auburn curls, blue eyes, five two and curves, to Nicky's brunette with poker-straight hair and green eyes, five ten, slim, boyish figure. Plus with Brittany only being twenty-eight, Nicky's right, she could easily have several more kids. My heart goes out to Nicky. I feel her pain as if it's my own. I'd do anything to alleviate it. Nicky would have loved to have more children, but since she doesn't socialise much with unattached males, it's unlikely that situation will change anytime soon.

'Why didn't you tell us before?' I ask her, thinking of how she must have had to deal with all this on her own the past few days. What a way to start the year, and what a git Sebastian is for deciding New Year's was the best time to tell her. As if she wouldn't be feeling lonely enough, he had to rub salt in the wounds. I never liked Sebastian. Too sure of himself. Of course, I didn't tell Nicky that when they were engaged. The only saving grace was that she didn't marry him before he had second thoughts and moved in with Brittany.

I give her a sympathetic smile and squeeze her hand. 'When we stand up, I'm hugging you, OK,' I say. 'I'd do it now, but I don't think it would work with us sitting down. We'd look weird.'

Xander appears, Hugo right behind him. 'We're thirsty,' they chorus.

'Here.' I hand Hugo his lemonade; he likes the old-fashioned English kind. Xander stares at it, then at his Orange Fruit Shoot in disgust.

'Xander, would you like what Hugo has?' I ask. I've put myself in the mood for one too, and since my coffee is the consistency of cold porridge and probably as disgusting,

I'll have something that can't go cold – the bonus is, given the aircraft hangar-esque central heating properties the trampoline park enjoys, it won't get warm.

His head bobs up and down like one of those nodding dogs you used to see on car dashboards.

'Right, give me a minute. You guys want anything else?' I ask the girls, but they shake their heads.

'Mum, can I have a sandwich?' Xander says.

'Wait half an hour, Xan, and then we can all eat together, yeah?' Nicky says to him.

Xander, unusually at ten, flings his arms round his mum and gives her a huge kiss on the cheek. It's as if the boy is making up for the lack of warmth his father showed his mum. He's the only male who lavishes affection on her as Nicky's father died a long time ago. From the smile on Nicky's face, his action has had the required effect.

I fetch the drinks and the boys sit at the table next to us, as there are only four chairs per table. They talk Nintendo and PlayStation and I zone out of their chat and back into ours.

I've missed what was said and Nicky says, 'So, have you started your prep?'

'For what? Sorry, I was listening to the boys.' Mums are always apologising.

'For the wedding fair.'

I sigh. 'No, not a chance. Too much going on.'

'It's a month tomorrow, and from now until then it'll fly in,' Nicky reminds me.

Nicky's a photographer. She doesn't only cover weddings. In fact, until recently she didn't shoot many weddings, but it's lucrative and bizarrely, she loves weddings, despite her own being cancelled due to Sebastian's infidelity.

'Do you want me to send you a list of things I've done so far? I know we don't have exactly the same needs, but you can cherry-pick what you want.'

'I'd really appreciate that, thanks.'

'No problem. Xander has been giving me a hand. It's good having older kids, they can help out.' She grins.

We chat for a bit, one of us checking on the kids every now and then, although Genevieve is doing a great job of looking after the wee ones. She's taking it in turns to bounce with Aria, Ava and Emily on the various trampolines and bouncy castles, and their smiles say it all.

Xander and Hugo are on the *Gladiators*-style battle beam, teeth gritted, each clearly unwilling to let the other be the victor. Despite being great friends, they are both very competitive.

'So, you looking forward to going back to school?' I ask Sam.

Sam's eyes light up. 'Definitely. I can't believe I am dying to get back to primary four, but I keep thinking about the progress I made with one of my pupils before the end of term. His reading is so much better and I'm hoping it hasn't regressed over the holidays.'

Sam loves her job. She has always wanted to be a teacher, so as soon as she left school, she went to college and then straight into teaching. She has been lucky too. Her placements were never too far from home, and now she teaches at the school Hugo goes to, and where Aria will be next year.

'Hey, the queue has gone down. Will I grab some lunch for everyone?' Nicky asks.

'Sounds like a plan,' I say as Sam calls the kids over to take their orders.

Ten minutes later, Genevieve brings the little ones to

have lunch. Their faces are shiny with sweat and rosy from exertion, but a little thrill courses through me at the children in front of me, munching away on their sandwiches and chatting excitedly to each other.

It's one of those days that you don't want to end. I'm about to suggest they all come back to ours and play, but then I remember the state the house is in and the fact I haven't called the hairdresser yet. And although I placed a supermarket order a few days ago, we are running out of food again. I have no idea where the kids put it. Some days I half expect to walk into Hugo's room and find a hamper full of food. And, of course, we still have to visit baby Isabella.

'See you soon. Bye,' I call to the others as my family loads into the car.

'Next stop, hospital,' I say to the kids.

'Yay,' shouts Aria. 'I want to give 'Sabella the teddy I bought for her.' It's a Lamaze octopus. I thought I was going to have problems making Aria part with it, she liked it so much, but she seems resolved to give it to her special little cousin.

When we arrive, Mum is there. 'Hi, Mum.' I kiss her on the cheek and she rubs my arm.

'She's beautiful,' she says, 'all rosebud mouth and a generous shock of dark hair. The photos they sent didn't do her justice. She's perfect.'

'Happy nana.' I smile. 'How many are allowed in at the same time?'

'Three. Dad's the only one in just now.'

'Would you stay with Gen and Hugo and I will take Aria in?' I turn to Gen and Hugo. 'That OK with you?' I tilt my head towards Aria. 'Someone is desperate to give the baby her new present.'

They both smile. 'Fine,' says Gen. 'Cool,' says Hugo.

'Are you ready to meet your new cousin, Aria?'

She is almost jumping up and down with excitement.

'You need to be very quiet and calm, OK? The baby may be sleeping.'

She nods earnestly.

We go in to the room and immediately spot Sandra, who beams at us.

'Hi, Aria. Can I have a cuddle? I've missed you.'

Aria climbs up on the bed. I refrain from telling her not to. Sandra invited her, after all.

'I missed you too. Where's the baby?'

Subtle, as ever, my daughter. Then she spots Isabella lying in the tiny crib, at the same time I do.

'Oh, she's adorable,' I gasp, taking in the dark hair and innocent little pink face, perfect little eyelashes and fingernails. I turn to Sandra. 'Well done, Mummy.'

Sandra's face glows with pleasure. I remember how I felt the first few times someone addressed me as Mummy or Mum. Amazing. Incredible. Awestruck.

'I'm so happy for you both.' I lean over and give her a hug then kiss her on the cheek. 'Where's Rhys?'

'When your mum and dad came in, I sent him to the canteen to get something to eat. He barely leaves here. And of course, with us getting home tomorrow, I want him sharp, especially as we have to drive back to Kelso.'

'Good point. Can I hold her?'

'Of course. Oh, and thanks again for the clothes you sent in. Godsend.'

'You're welcome. Just glad another little Halliday is able to wear them.'

I lift baby Isabella out of her crib and she opens her eyes, then her mouth. For a moment, I think she is about to bawl the place down, but I position her against my shoulder and whisper to her and she soon settles against me. Solid. Warm. Sweet-smelling. Oh, I miss these times. Feels like ages since I had Aria. I'd forgotten just how tiny small babies are, although none of the babies I've ever handled have been this small. I kiss her on the top of her head. It's so soft. Almost fuzzy. Like felt. Her little mouth comes up as if trying to suck something.

'I think she may be hungry,' I say, passing her to Sandra.

Sandra looks at the clock. 'Oops, I think you may be right.'

'We'll give you some privacy, but is it OK if I send Gen and Hugo in shortly? They're dying to see her.'

'I can't wait for them to meet her.'

'I love baby Isabella,' announces Aria on the way home. 'I'm going to keep all my toys for her so that when she grows big, she can play with them.'

'Very admirable, Aria. Great idea,' I say.

'She's so tiny,' says Hugo. He was so thrilled by the whole experience. 'I love her little toes and fingers.'

'I love the way she smells,' Gen adds.

'But not the bottom end!' Hugo can't resist.

'She still smells better than you, smelly boy.' Gen gives him a playful push and they are soon jabbering away whilst I try to gather my thoughts.

We've had a lovely day out with friends, met our new family member and now we have only one more day left before the kids go back to school and nursery, so I need to get organised.

And then there's the to-do list. Always there. Waiting.

Chapter Five

Thursday 7 January

To-do list
PE Kit (outdoor) Hugo
Packed lunch (Hugo)
Transfer funds to Genevieve's school account for dinner money
Spare clothes for Aria (messy play day scheduled at nursery)
Go through list from yesterday
Start wedding fair prep
Check best place to get more business cards made – same place could do flyers for wedding fair?
Ring Mum
Answer 25 texts and WhatsApp messages haven't managed in past 2 days

Should I be putting the flags out? On the one hand, I feel terrible for even thinking that, on the other hand perhaps it's only natural to be glad to have some time to myself, where I can *think* without being interrupted.

It's quarter past five. I've been up for fifteen minutes. My Labrador, Bear, and I have already been out; his bladder wouldn't hold, and I'm hugging my coffee cup as

I pore over my list. I cross out the items from earlier lists, amalgamating them into one list. One thing I can do whilst I am drinking coffee is search for a present for Sam. Her birthday's a week today and if I don't order it online now, I will only panic that it won't arrive in time. It's pointless buying her stationery as she always gets loads of that from pupils as gifts. What about a journal though? Maybe something from Papier. I could get her one of those and something else, but what? I drum my pen against my lips. No, I'll have to come back to it. I order the journal then go to sort out the schoolbags.

I'm walking through the hall when my foot snags on something and I stumble forward, lose my balance and go over on my ankle. Ow, ow, ow! That really hurts. I fight back the urge to cry and drag myself over to the bottom step of the staircase, where I sit and tenderly touch my ankle. I've sprained it, I think. Bloomin' typical. Just what I don't need this morning. It's as well I got up early. I turn to see what I fell over – Aria's nursery bag. It's one of those drawstring ones with the nursery's logo emblazoned across the front. Stupid thing. It was bound to trip someone up at some point.

I stand up and immediately sit back down, grimacing in pain. Oh my…ow! I tentatively try again, placing one foot in front of the other and attempt to weight-bear, but I can't. Oh no, what am I going to do? The kids are due back at school today. Genevieve could get the bus at a push to her school in Hamwell, but I have to take Aria to nursery in Lymeburn, the next village, then Hugo to school here in Ferniehall. My ankle is already ballooning. How ironic that Rhys has been staying here for a week and left only yesterday. The one person who could have helped me easily enough with the kids. That sort of luck is the story of my life. I cast around for answers and then remember Mum and Dad aren't due to go on holiday for a few days. Maybe they can help. It's too early to call them but perhaps if I get everything ready then phone them around seven, they can come and ferry the kids to school. I can't have them missing school and there's no way I can drive.

Once I've taken some ibuprofen and hobbled back to the sofa, I order the laundry labels, send out some invoice reminders, order various types of card, place some orders with my specialist suppliers and make a list of whose stationery orders need processed next.

McMillan, Hope, Jenner, Abercrombie, Ferris, Jameson
Sort expenses

Time to wake the kids. I stand, or rather sway, then limp to the house phone.

Three rings. 'Hello?'

'Mum, it's me.'

'Louisa, is everything OK?' Mum's voice is laced with panic.

'Not really, no. I've twisted my ankle. I can't put any weight on it.'

'Oh, you poor thing. Do you need some help? Ask Genevieve to give you a hand round the house today. Stick a movie on for the little ones, they'll be delighted.'

'Eh, Mum, they go back to school today.'

'Today? Already?'

I don't like to point out that most parents consider two and a half weeks long enough both for their pockets and their sanity, so I keep shtum.

'Yes, Mum. Actually, I need a favour.'

My parents arrive with just enough time to get the kids to school and nursery and I usher them inside.

52

'I don't want to go to nursery. I want to stay with you, Mummy.' Aria's eyes are full of tears. I'm not sure if it's a nursery avoidance tactic or if she feels sorry for me and wants to look after me.

Hugo has been really sweet. He tidied up and dressed himself without complaint. He fetched the various items of his outdoor PE kit, double-checked the contents of his bag for me, and even said he would go without a packed lunch today and have school dinners. He asked me questions to make sure he had everything and then Genevieve made me a cup of tea, just the way I like it. She's been practising, supervised, over the holidays. I'm still apprehensive about her being around a kettle full of boiling water, but I'll get used to it eventually, I'm sure.

Mum and Dad envelop the kids in warm embraces, then in a no-nonsense way – you can tell my mother was head of the PTA – Mum issues instructions to the three children.

'Gen, can you put Aria in her car seat, please? Hugo, can you bring Gen's bag? Aria, backpack on, my love.'

She makes it all seem so effortless, although I suppose she hasn't had to prepare anything for them, or get them out of bed. That's often the hardest part, especially with Genevieve as she's at that difficult age. Teenagers, albeit she's not quite one yet, require a lot of sleep, and she has taken to embracing this need rather earlier than I had hoped. But when I told her this morning I'd fallen and injured myself, she sat up on her bed, yawning, and five minutes later she was downstairs. She can deliver when it's required. And she has been great over the holidays. I pray that doesn't deteriorate once she returns to school.

'We'll pop back once I've dropped the children off,' Mum says.

'Really, you don't have to,' I protest. 'You're doing

enough.' Then it comes to me. 'You will be able to pick them up again this afternoon, won't you?'

My mother pales. 'I can't. I've got a hospital appointment at three.'

'Hospital?' My face mirrors my mother's. 'What for?'

'Nothing serious, don't worry. I have a lump and the doctor thinks it's a hernia. I'm seeing the consultant – preliminary appointment.'

I sag with relief. Nothing life-threatening then. Now I'm worrying about both my children and my parents. Still, it's an operation and might have complications. I try to think of best-case scenarios only.

'Dad can pick them up,' Mum says.

'But I need to collect you from the hospital,' Dad says. Eyeing me, he says, 'Maybe I should be taking you with us, get your ankle looked at.'

'No, Dad, seriously, I'm fine. I just need to rest it. It's a sprain.'

'Martin, you can collect the kids. I'll manage. You can drop me off a little earlier so you're back in time for the school run.'

Then I remember Aria isn't in nursery a full day today, only until twelve. I feel as if my head is about to swivel off. So much for their going back to school making my life easier. Now the logistics are tying me in knots.

'Can we talk about this when you come back? I need to sort something for Aria.'

Mum cottons on. 'Oh, this is the day she's only at nursery in the morning, isn't it? Well, never mind, we can take her for the afternoon, and then she can go collect Hugo with Dad.'

Aria jumps up and down. 'Please, Mummy, can I, can I? I want to go to big school.'

Aria loves going to school. I hope she loves it as much when she starts in the summer.

I sigh, pain shooting through my ankle again. 'OK. Mum, in theory that's OK. Dad, I'll let you know later how my ankle is. I might take you up on that offer to get it checked out.'

'Let me see it,' Mum says, already bending down.

I suppress my exasperation; they are after all going out of their way to help me, but if they don't leave right now, they will hit heavier traffic and Hugo will be late for school.

'Mum, I can wait until you come back. Oh, is that the time?' I feign nonchalance.

'What time is it? Half past. Oh right, yes, we had better go. C'mon, you lot, into Papa's car.'

I kiss them all by the door, even Genevieve, who usually baulks at such a display. Mum shepherds them out, and when they've gone, I lower myself to the sofa in relief. It doesn't last long. Dragging me back to my main priority at the moment, my ankle chooses that moment to hurt like nobody's business. What am I going to do? Ronnie's not home until next week. How will I manage getting the kids to school and dealing with all the day-to-day stuff, never mind work?

I try not to panic and pull my phone towards me, then I work out what we need to rearrange or cancel if I can't find a way to get the kids there or have someone else take them: swimming lessons, Hugo's taekwondo, Genevieve's gymnastics and after-school oboe lesson, her horse-riding lesson. My head starts to hurt as well as my ankle. Painkillers, first and foremost. I haul myself off the sofa, go into the kitchen, switch the kettle on, and whilst I'm waiting for it to boil, I take two paracetamol.

Over coffee, I try to sort my jumbled thoughts. Gone

is my list from this morning. Firstly, I need to sort out the logistical problems that arise from being unable to put weight on my ankle. I prop my foot on a footstool then remember ice helps reduce swelling. Why didn't I think of that earlier? If it had been one of the kids I would have thought of that straight away. I hobble back through to the kitchen and grab some frozen peas and a tea towel then return to my position on the sofa.

My thoughts swirl in my brain. Mum and Dad can pick them up today. Even someone taking them to school and collecting them will cause an issue for the next few days, especially as Mum and Dad go away on Sunday and Ronnie isn't back until next Wednesday.

Apart from my parents, everyone else has their own school and nursery travel commitments. If I can't drive, I'll have to keep them off. And that means keeping them entertained too. Not ideal when I am under par and when I already have a jam-packed schedule. I had planned on being back to work 'full time' today.

Well, if there's the possibility I won't have peace to work later in the week, I had better make the most of it now. I prop my lap desk on my thighs and go through my emails, answering as many as I can, ordering supplies and I even glance at the checklist Nicky sent through about the wedding fair.

Time flies and before I know it, my parents are back.

'Sorry we were so long. Dad thought it might help to pick up a few essentials for you on our way back. Right, let me see that ankle.'

You'd think Mum had worked as a nurse instead of being an office manager, the way she goes on. Or maybe it's the mother in her. Even when you're thirty-eight, your mum still looks after you. It's in the blood.

Dad smiles at me as he trudges into the kitchen laden with bags.

'It is pretty swollen. Did you put ice on it?'

'Eventually. I forgot to begin with.'

Mum gives me a look. She doesn't need to tell me that was dim of me.

She prods gently, but pain shoots up my ankle. She rotates it, or tries to, but a squeal from me and my almost jumping off the chair towards the ceiling mean she doesn't do it twice.

'I think you should get it seen to. Why don't you come with me to the hospital? Dad can deal with the kids.'

Finally, I relent. It makes sense.

'Well, it's not broken.'

I exhale in relief.

'But I think you may have torn your ligaments from how swollen it is and the lack of mobility,' the young, fresh-faced, terribly handsome doctor (clichéd, I know) tells me. 'The nurse will fit you with a boot and get you some painkillers. You should try to stay off it for the next few days at least.'

He clearly doesn't have kids. If I was ten years younger, not married and with no kids… Well, there has to be some upside to feeling this miserable.

'It's not really feasible. How soon do you think it will be better and I can drive?'

'Well, it depends, but generally when you no longer feel a shooting pain when you depress the clutch or brake, you're ready. Basically you need to be able to do an emergency stop.'

The thought of putting my ankle into that position makes my stomach heave.

'I guess I won't be driving for a bit then.'

'No. How are you getting home?'

I am almost too mortified to say my mum brought me. It makes me feel about six.

Crutches would be more of a hazard than a help in my house, so I decline the doctor's offer of them.

I half hop, half hobble round to Outpatients. Mum is sitting reading her Kindle, a latte on the table next to her.

'Mum.'

She glances up from her book. 'How did you get on?'

'Torn ligaments.'

'Poor you. I suppose it could be worse.'

How? I have three children to ferry to nursery, school and after-school activities and a husband who works in the North Sea. I'm not seeing the positives here.

'What about you? How did you get on?'

'Yes, he's pretty sure it is a hernia, but he's sending me for an MRI to be sure.'

'How long will that take?'

'I don't know. Half an hour?'

I sigh. 'No, Mum, I meant, how long will you have to wait to get an appointment?'

'Oh, I didn't ask.'

Briefly, I close my eyes. What is it about my parents' generation that they don't question things? I'd want to know how many weeks or months I'd have to wait.

'So, are you in a lot of pain normally from it?'

'Comes and goes. Anyway, let's go. Hold on to me if you need support,' Mum says in her usual no-nonsense tone.

It would be churlish of me not to lean on her, so although I feel as if our roles are somewhat reversed, I let her help me as we make our way to the car park.

Ten excruciating minutes later we make it to the car. Ah,

so that's why car parks are free at most Scottish hospitals: you have to park in the next county to get a space. I really wish I had requested a wheelchair. Sweat is pouring down my face, despite the cold January air, and my skin is sizzling from the exertion.

I have never been so relieved to get in a car before, and that's saying something with Mum driving. She's the most politely spoken woman ever, but get her behind the wheel of a car and it's a different story.

Back home, Dad's beaming smile greets us at the door. 'How's the invalid?'

'They wanted to give me crutches.'

'Ah, not really practical,' Dad agrees.

'Mum, are you OK?' Hugo asks me, his forehead scrunching up in concern.

'I'll be fine. Just need to rest.'

'I'll kiss it better, Mummy,' Aria says, ready to place her lips on my moon boot.

'No, that's OK, honey, but thanks.'

She twirls round. 'Papa, you said you would play Soggy Doggy.'

'Not again,' Hugo says. 'It's my turn. I want to play Buckaroo.'

At least they're not attached to their tablets all day long. My father's face is pale and he's almost wheezing. Yes, they are hard work, much as I love them, and that's just the children I'm talking about.

'Thanks, Dad.' I lean into his shoulder, well, fall would be more appropriate.

'So, what's the verdict?'

I regale him with the events at the hospital and he tells tales on which child tried to steal Percy Pigs from the jar, who accidentally dropped the Steiff sloth down the toilet and who was responsible for an entire punnet of blueberries adorning the kitchen tiles.

Mum heats me up some macaroni she found in the freezer. How alien for my parents to be taking care of me. It's always me looking after everyone else. It throws me a little off kilter. Even Genevieve is fussing around me, and Aria is bringing books over for me to read to her rather than telling me to go get them. Weird.

I take some painkillers after dinner and try to rotate my ankle – not a chance, and despite my resting it, it's still ridiculously swollen. Maybe a good night's sleep will help, but in this house, there's no guarantee of that.

Chapter Six

Sunday 10 January

To-do list
Order football boots for Hugo
Redo Broadband package
Take elec and gas meter readings
Book Gen's laptop in to get seen to (keeps getting blue screen of doom)
Watch battery
Groom for Bear (can they collect?) – he's shedding everywhere. Doesn't he know it's still winter?
Tennis balls for Bear – others have been chewed to pieces

My parents have been a godsend over the past few days. I try to rest my ankle as much as I can but it's nigh on impossible. Luckily, Mum sent her cleaner round or the house would be a disaster area of nuclear proportions.

Showering is a struggle, although I've been fortunate enough that the kids' friends' parents have offered to take the children to school and nursery this week. I have no idea how I would have coped if they had been here under my feet all day. As it is, I immerse myself in work, which involves minimal movement from the sofa. The only positive in this is, I finally make time to prepare for the wedding fair.

Ronnie thought I was kidding when I told him, until I showed him the moon boot during our FaceTime call. His eyes nearly bulged out of his head. Clearly he was wondering how I would manage to do everything I do. He wasn't the only one. The first few days I woke up in a panic every hour on the hour.

Mum and Dad went off on their cruise today, so I am relying on the kids, my sisters popping by, and Sam and Nicky. Everyone has promised to chip in until Ronnie gets back on Wednesday. The biggest hurdle is the transport. Now that's taken care of, everything else will be a breeze.

'Mum, I can't find my maths book. Do you think Nana took it?' Genevieve is standing in the doorway of my bedroom, rummaging in her backpack.

'What would Nana want with your maths book? She's away on a cruise not swotting up on trig,' I point out.

'Well, it's not on the dining table where I was doing my homework.'

'Did you leave it at school?'

'No, I was using it for my homework.'

I want to tell her to keep her knickers on, or in this case leotard, as she is dressed for her gymnastics class, but instead say, 'Right.' Sometimes you have to choose your battles and I need her onside right now, what with the gammy ankle. Plus, she has been very well behaved of late.

'Kitchen?'

'No.' She sighs.

After some further grilling, I hobble downstairs and help her look for it. Hugo is playing with his tablet. I relaxed the rules, since enforcing them in my current state isn't the easiest; and Aria is colouring in, leaning on what looks to me suspiciously like a maths book – the aquamarine cover is a bit of a giveaway.

Gen adopts the hangdog expression her father does so well.

Crisis averted, I slump back on the sofa, thankful that Gen can take the bus to gymnastics. I try to tick off some of the items on my list. I manage four but then add eight more, including *Beg doctor for stronger painkillers* and *Hire au pair*. I can dream, can't I?

Chapter Seven

Wednesday 13 January

To-do list
Ensure have dinner ready for Ronnie coming in – he'll be starving
Send Gen to Tesco Express for missing ingredients for fish pie
Craft day since can't drive
Text Ronnie and ask him to bring wine in, and bread and milk, cocktail sausages, Pot Noodles, toilet paper (where does it all go?), *handwash* (ditto) – although I did find Aria washing her dollies with it the other day.

Ronnie's late. He's almost never late. He was due four hours ago. I've checked the forecast because sometimes the weather can cause the helicopter to be delayed, as for safety reasons they no longer take off when it's too gusty. According to the Met Office, there shouldn't be any problem. Plus, he usually calls me from Aberdeen to say he's en route. I had thought maybe his phone was just dead, but I'm starting to worry now. I know it's irrational, he'll be absolutely fine, but I can't help but fret. I'm fielding the kids' questions as best I can as they are so excited for his return.

I try to distract myself from pacing the floor by suggesting we play a game of Family Trivial Pursuit.

'Can't we wait until Dad gets here?' asks Hugo. 'I want to be on his team.'

'Traitor,' I say with a smile, in an attempt to deflect attention from mention of Ronnie. 'Of course we can wait.'

It's well past dinner time and I've been holding off until I hear from Ronnie, and I know the kids will want to eat with him, but time is really marching on. Aria should be going to bed soon.

'Right, I'm going to start dinner now.' Hugo opens his mouth to protest, but I silence him with a, 'I know we usually eat with Dad, but he has obviously been delayed, so we'll have our welcome home meal tomorrow night instead.'

The corners of Hugo's mouth turn down, but he mumbles an 'OK'. Gen, gauging her brother's disconsolate mood, puts her arm round him and says, 'C'mon, I'll play on the Xbox with you.'

Hugo's eyes light up. 'Really?'

When Gen nods, he says, 'You're on. Thanks, Gen.'

I smile at Gen to convey my thanks in helping me out with her brother and turn my attention to Aria. A new colouring book I'd been keeping for a rainy day solves that problem. The three of them traipse off to the playroom whilst I start making dinner.

I turn on the TV and tune in to a news channel then begin chopping onions and carrots ready for the spag bol I'm making.

An update on the helicopter forced to make an emergency landing at Sumburgh Airport in Shetland after taking off from the Callan oil rig. It is understood there were some aboard who received injuries and they have been transferred to either Gilbert Bain Hospital in Lerwick or Aberdeen Royal Infirmary. No one was available from Callan or the aviation company to comment.

I feel sick. Ronnie works at Callan. He's late. How many helicopters leave the rig per day? I've never needed to ask. My heart is pounding in my chest. I feel like I'm going to pass out. Am I having a panic attack? I pick up my phone. No messages. I dial Ronnie's number. Voicemail. Please God let him be OK. I try to think back. Did they say there were no casualties? If they didn't, does that mean they don't know or there weren't? Thoughts race through my mind at a hundred miles per hour.

'Mummy, what do you think?' Aria brings me back to earth by showing me the dragon she has coloured in. It has yellow polka dots and green stripes. Bizarre that I am focusing on that right now. Spots dance in front of my eyes, and they have nothing to do with Aria's colouring in.

'It's lovely. Well done. I'll be back in a minute.'

I take the stairs two at a time, desperate to put some space between me and my children. I don't want to scare them. I sit on the bed and dial Wendy's number.

'Hi, Lou, how you?'

'Not great.' I burst into tears.

'Hey, hey, hey, calm down. Deep breaths. Count.'

I do as instructed. I haven't had a proper panic attack in years, but when I used to have them, they were terrifying; that feeling of being unable to breathe haunted my dreams for months after they stopped.

When I've sufficiently collected myself, Wendy says, 'Take your time and tell me what's wrong.'

'Have you seen the news?'

'Not today, no. Why?'

'A helicopter from Callan had to make an emergency

landing at Sumburgh. I haven't heard from Ronnie. He was due home four and a half hours ago.'

'Lou, listen to me. The likelihood of Ronnie being on that helicopter is slim. There's more than one chopper leaves on changeover day, isn't there?'

I nod through my tears, then realise Wendy won't be able to see me. 'There must be.'

Wendy goes on in a soothing tone, 'So, there's no point worrying. Ronnie's probably just been held up. Maybe his helicopter was delayed.'

When I don't manage to respond, Wendy says, 'Tell you what, let me see what I can find out. I'll contact Callan.'

'Would you?' My shoulders drop, the tension easing out of them.

'I'll call them when we get off the phone, but, Lou, I mean it, try to remain calm.'

'I will. Thanks, Wendy.'

I hang up and turn to see Gen standing in the doorway behind me, her eyes wide.

'Has something happened to Dad?' she asks, coming into the room.

'No, no, Dad's fine,' I say, wishing I was a better liar.

'So, what was all that on the phone? Who were you talking to?'

'Just Aunt Wendy.' I try to keep my statements as brief as possible as I hate lying.

'About Dad? Why would you be talking to Aunt Wendy about Dad?'

'Gen, are you coming back to play Xbox?' Hugo asks, ducking his head into the room.

What is it with my children following me upstairs?

I look at Gen, my eyes imploring her not to say anything. She gives me a long, hard look then says, 'Sure.'

Hugo skips happily downstairs again then Gen turns to me and says, 'I know something is going on,' before she follows her brother down.

My phone rings. Wendy.

'I wasn't able to find much out since I'm not what they consider immediate family. I tried telling them I was calling on your behalf, but they were having none of it. They did tell me, however, that there were no fatalities.'

I breathe a sigh of relief. That's one thing to be thankful for. Silent tears run down my face and I gulp in the stale air in the room.

'Sorry I couldn't help more. Do you want me to come round?'

'No, you have enough on your plate. Let me make the kids dinner and if I'm struggling later, I'll let you know.'

The doorbell rings.

'Wendy, that's the door. I better get it.'

'Love you. And stay calm.' She hangs up.

I race down the stairs, but the kids have beaten me to it.

'Daddy!' Aria launches herself into her father's arms as Hugo stands mutely to one side, a huge grin on his face. Gen usually hangs in the background, a little unsure, when Ronnie has been away, but today she catapults into his broad North-Face-clad chest, and he grabs her in a bear hug. She holds on to him just that little bit tighter, as if she knows about the helicopter incident.

Ronnie radiates happiness. He always does when he returns from the rig. I'm sure it's a dream to be away from the drudgery of everyday life, and the responsibility, although the rig has a different set of challenges, but the moment he walks through the door he is in full-on doting-dad mode. With Aria perched on one arm, Hugo hugging him round the waist and Ronnie's other arm encircling

Genevieve, I let them have their moment. My body almost deflates with relief. I am just glad he is OK. He can tell me later why he was so delayed, but right now I only care that he is in one piece and home. Tears prick my eyes as I think of what might have been the outcome, but I steel myself – he's fine. It may take a while for my heart rate to return to normal though.

I look forward to being able to give my husband a proper hug too, but there will be plenty of time for us to catch up later tonight and over the coming two weeks. Two weeks. It's always two weeks, yet this time his absence has felt considerably longer. Over the heads of our children, Ronnie raises his eyebrows and flashes me his signature grin, then stretches a little to see my foot, shaking his head.

'Right, you lot,' Ronnie says, 'let's get into the living room and maybe I might have a surprise for you.'

'Yay!' the children shriek as one. I hope it's not a chocolate-laden surprise. They are bursting with energy as it is, and it only serves to remind me how missing my own is at the minute. They follow their dad and calls of 'Monopoly,' 'Whac-a-Mole,' 'Snakes and Ladders,' soon greet my ear. I guess they're staying up late and we're having a board-game evening.

I quickly text Wendy to let her know all is well, then assemble the fish pie and pop it in the oven. That was actually quite relaxing. It's amazing the difference the presence of another adult in the house makes, knowing you're not solely responsible for the children. And somehow when it's not their other parent, it's different. Although my family have been fabulous and pitched in a great deal over the past week, I didn't quite feel I could pass responsibility entirely to them. Their dad, on the other hand, absolutely I can.

I sit on the sofa observing my idyllic family – OK, perhaps I've gone too far there – playing Junior Monopoly. I take it Gen won then. She hates Whac-a-Mole – thinks it's not humane. Sends out the wrong message. Her siblings love it. I often have to referee to ensure they don't whack each other. Much though they love each other really, they have their disagreements, but Whac-a-Mole sends them into a frenzy, and they would quite possibly bop each other on the head continuously if I didn't intervene.

The junior version of Monopoly is far too easy for Gen now but she happily plays it with her little brother and sister. I'm enjoying being the observer, for once. I must say they are nice and calm. Why aren't they like that for me? Ah, because they are home, and Ronnie isn't trying to take them anywhere. I relax back into the sofa and lean my head against the cushion – bliss.

The beeping of the oven timer tells me dinner is ready.

'I don't like fish pie,' Aria says mutinously.

Oh-oh. The end of harmony is in sight.

'Don't be silly, angel, you love fish pie,' Ronnie says, tickling her under her chin.

She giggles and says, *'OK, Daddy.'*

What? Who? Is that it? These children, my children, our children, never simply capitulate with me. When they are good, they are very good, but when they are in unhelpful, ungrateful little so-and-so mode, it usually remains that way for quite some time. OK, Daddy? I'm practically fizzing at the unfairness of it all.

Aria sits up at the table, places her napkin in her lap and picks up her fork. Hugo looks as if he wants to say something but changes his mind. He too picks up his cutlery and begins eating. Genevieve sits down then says,

'Mum, I'm going to become vegetarian,' and stands up again.

'Gen, sit down, please, and eat your food. Mum has spent a good part of today making this meal. The least we can do is eat it.'

I stare at Ronnie, astounded, then I turn to Gen, even more flabbergasted. She stares at her father then nods and starts eating.

'That was delicious,' says Ronnie when he finishes. 'Any pudding?' He glances towards the fridge.

'No, you can have a Kit Kat,' I say.

'A Kit Kat?' His face falls.

I stop myself from saying, 'Do you think I have an apple crumble I can pull out of my jacksie?' and say, 'I haven't exactly had a lot of time to think about pudding this week,' then glance at my moon boot.

'Sorry, my stomach was getting the better of me there.'

'Indeed.'

'Daddy, I'm full up,' says Hugo, having polished off the lot. 'Can I go play?'

'Sure.' He smiles at our son and musses his hair as he passes.

'Daa-ad!'

Ronnie grins.

'Wait for me,' says Aria, skipping down from her chair.

Once Gen leaves, I turn to Ronnie, trying to keep calm. 'How come you were so late?'

'Yeah, there was some sort of delay with the helicopters. Something about a technical issue at their base. Didn't you get my message?'

'What message? I was going out of my mind, Ronnie. Do you not know why?'

Ronnie scrunches his forehead. 'No?'

I can tell he feels that's the wrong answer but he doesn't want to lie.

'A helicopter from Callan had to make an emergency landing on Sumburgh today.'

'Really? I didn't hear anything about that.'

'No? And you were five hours late getting home? Didn't you think to text me?'

'But I just told you, I did. Look.' He thrusts his phone towards me and shows me the message.

'Ronnie, that's in your drafts.'

'What?' He takes the phone from me, looks at it then raises his eyes to meet mine. 'Lou, I am so, so sorry. What an idiot. Come here.'

He cradles me in his arms and I burst into noisy sobs. 'I thought something had happened to you. I honestly did. When you didn't come home…'

'Shh, it's fine. I'm here. Look at me.' I look up. 'Could I be any more solid?' He smiles.

I hug him to me and after a few minutes Ronnie plants a kiss on my forehead. 'Right, now we've ascertained I'm fine, maybe I can have my *dessert* later.'

Dessert later? Oh, he means me. Normally, I'd be excited at the prospect but the very thought of all the jostling around and panting, with my ankle as it is, doesn't inspire me. He must see the expression on my face as his smile falters and I glance in dismay at my leg again. Blasted thing.

'Oh right. Yes, I hadn't quite considered the logistics of that.' He has the good grace to look sheepish. What was I thinking the other night about how men and women differed? Oh yes, women think of everyone's needs, and men, well, men think of their own. I can tell him right now that when I am bandaged to the hilt and doped up on as many painkillers as I am allowed, bedroom acrobatics isn't my idea of a good night in, even if he was dicing with death earlier this afternoon. The whole episode has drained me. A thriller on Netflix or in book form, a glass of wine and a box of Heroes would make me happier tonight. And I can't help thinking what that says about our marriage.

Chapter Eight

Thursday 21 January

To-do list
Book paintball
Order more Vanish or ask for recommendations as can't get Hugo's taekwondo suit clean
Monthly book order for everyone
Charity shop – kids need to help with what gets donated
All the other things from past week's list I haven't managed to do

'Dad, hurry up. We'll miss the start of the movie.'

'OK, OK, I'm coming.' Ronnie rushes past me, giving me a peck on the cheek as he goes.

'Aria's backpack.' I point to the area under the stairs.

'Backpack?'

'Yes, in case she has any *accidents*.'

'Oh, I see.'

I'm not sure he does, so I say, 'She will need to go to the toilet at some point during the film. Don't let her kid you. If she starts jiggling or moving around too much, it's not because she's dancing to the music as she'll tell you, but because she needs the loo. Take her.'

'Right.'

'And make sure you put toilet paper down on the toilet seat so she doesn't catch any germs.'

'OK.'

'In fact, tell Gen to take her. I don't want her going into the Gents.'

'Are you sure you wouldn't like to come with us?'

I can't tell if Ronnie's question is hopeful or if he's being sarcastic. 'Quite sure, now scram. I have work to do,' I say, smiling sweetly.

His shoulders slump, then a chorus of 'Dad!' from the car jerks him into action. 'We'll miss the trailers, and I want a hot dog,' shouts Hugo.

'Have fun,' I call to his retreating back.

I'm almost beside myself with glee, and the sad thing is I won't be sitting watching a film at home on my own, hot chocolate and marshmallows in hand; instead I'll be frantically pulling together everything I need for the wedding show. I put the kettle on and settle down to my task. My aim is to get at least twenty items off this list before my family gets back. Normally, I would have gone with them, but needs must, and they'll benefit from some time alone with their dad, if only so Dad can see how bloomin' difficult it is sometimes. Not that I wish a hard time on my beloved husband, but wouldn't it be good if he could appreciate how nerve-wracking taking them to the cinema is? Hopefully, the tickets don't fail to print, Aria doesn't spill her popcorn on the way to screen eight and the ketchup from Hugo's hot dog doesn't shoot out all over the head of the lady in front of him. That would be a nightmare, right? No, just my regular existence. Not necessarily all at once, but they've all happened.

I have coffee, I have my list, let's go. But first I need to add an item to my show list:

Hire temp

Last year I did this show by myself, and it was possibly the worst thing I could have done. At times I was so busy I missed out on potential business. I thought I could simply ask the stallholder next to me, to keep an eye on things whilst I nipped to the loo. How green was I?

Advise agency of type of skills temp needs

Pay final amount of invoice for stall

Banners for stall

Pack the merchandise I already have – see separate list

Need more navy pocket-fold wallets

Double-check when new business cards are due to arrive – ditto flyers (ordered on next-day service, not here yet)

I breeze through another few items, but although I am still only halfway through the list, I realise I can't put on hold all of my other commitments. I turn to my work list – yes, I keep separate to-do lists. Work. Extra (such as the show), Home, Appointments. If the phone could colour code them or mark them in order of importance for me that would be great, but unfortunately although advanced, my phone isn't that advanced.

I prioritise, working out what I can lump together. *Organisers* jumps out at me. They're, funnily enough, responsible for quite a few things. I track down everything I want to ask them and once I've checked it, twice, I fire off an email. Yay – one down, two zillion to go.

For once I'm not doing any family stuff. The laundry, the banking, the shopping, the housework will have to wait. I need to get this done. I'm up against it and I have a three-hour window, tops, where I can pour all my energies into my show arrangements without anyone disturbing me.

Ding-dong.

Postman. Wonder what he has for me today. Maybe it's something for the show. I open the door, ready to give my cheery 'Hi, how are you?' but standing in front of me are my parents.

'What the–?'

'Hi, darling.' My mother enfolds me in a hug and my father hangs back his usual two steps whenever my mother is present.

'But…'

'I'll explain once we're inside. It's perishing out here.' Mum clasps the front of her cashmere coat to her and stares at me until I snap out of it.

'Sorry, come in.'

'Ah, the leg's on the mend, I see.' Nothing gets past my mum.

'It's a lot better, thanks, although I won't be running any marathons for a while…' *Or ever*.

My parents sit on the sofa and I go to join them but Dad says, 'I'd love a cup of tea. Anyone else?'

'I'll get it,' I say. They did so much for me when I hurt my ankle and was unable to move around easily, the least I can do is make them tea, but I am dying to know why they aren't on their cruise. As the kettle boils, I calculate they still had six days left.

I hand them their tea and then decide enough is enough. 'So, why aren't you on your cruise?'

'Oh well, there was a nasty bug on the ship and there weren't enough doctors to cope, so the ship had to turn around and head for the UK.'

'But I saw that on the news. That wasn't your ship. You were on the *Excelsior*, not the *Excalibur*.'

'Ah ha, the plot thickens,' Mum says. She seems to be enjoying relating the tale. She can be a little macabre sometimes. 'We were meant to be on the *Excelsior* but when we arrived at the port, the *Excelsior* had experienced some issues with Norovirus, so about fifty passengers, including us, were given the option of changing to *Excalibur*, which is a much more luxurious ship.'

'Right,' I say.

'So, we changed ship, and then all was fine at first. We had a great time. The Pitons in Saint Lucia were absolutely incredible, Saint Vincent was idyllic, although the shopping wasn't as good as in Cayman, but then when we went to Saint Martin, all hell broke loose. Everyone was getting ill. Everyone we had met at dinner, been sitting beside at the pool, been playing bingo with–'

'Don't forget quiz afternoon. Our team was decimated,' Dad said.

'Quite. Pretty much everyone we had spent time with since arriving was ill. The ship was in uproar. All these people had paid all that money to go on a luxury cruise and they were now confined to their cabins.'

'Stateroom, dear,' Dad corrects.

'That's what I said.' Mum shoots Dad a look. He stays quiet after that.

'So, eventually there was a meeting and the cruise director told us that those passengers who were well enough could fly home if they wanted to, and receive a credit towards another cruise later in the year. Most of the common areas: the library, the majority of the restaurants, the swimming pools, virtually everything had to be shut down.'

'That's a nightmare,' I say, appalled. I hope it hasn't put my parents off cruising. They love it. 'So how come you two are so full of beans?'

'Oh, they put us up in the Marriott Harbor Beach hotel

in Fort Lauderdale for two nights whilst we waited for our flight back and then we were upgraded to business class, so it wasn't all bad,' Mum says.

My parents are amazing. They take everything in their stride. Why, then, am I such a stress head?

'And it was a suite,' Dad says.

'Anyway,' Mum says, 'how have you been? How are my grandchildren? And Ronnie?'

Taking care to process the questions and answer them in the right order, I say, 'Better than I was, the same and fine.'

'Good. So why are you on your own? That doesn't happen often.'

Like I said, nothing gets past my mum.

'Ronnie's taken the kids to see some new superhero movie.'

'You going to chill in front of a movie?' Mum asks, in a poor attempt to act 'down with the kids', if those kids were in their late-thirties, early forties. I'm not sure what kids say nowadays, but I'm sure it's not 'down with the kids'. It's just me who hasn't moved on.

'Well, actually–'

Suddenly, Mum's eyes rest on the flyers for the wedding show. 'Oh, the show. You're trying to get organised for the show. And we're interrupting you. We'll go–'

'No, Mum, don't be silly.' Although secretly I'm wondering when else I will have time to do it.

'I've had a eureka moment.' Mum waves her hand in the air in triumph. 'I'll stay here and help you. You have boxes to pack, merchandise to organise, things to tick off a list, am I right?'

'Yes.' I get my obsession with lists from my mother in case you hadn't guessed already.

'Well, we'll do that and Dad can get us a few things from the shops. We weren't expecting to be home obviously, so we have very little in. What do you think, Martin?'

Dad has perked up. 'Excellent idea. I'll leave you girls to it.'

Dad trots off to Sainsbury's, his happy place. He can grab a coffee and a newspaper and sit in their café afterwards.

The door closes and Mum turns to me. 'Right, where do I start?' She is one hundred per cent in her element. She's wasted being retired. An idea comes to me. I wonder…

Chapter Nine

Tuesday 26 January

To-do list
Buy narwhal plush for Aria
Wrap Aria's presents
Change temp agency but hire temp as need one
Toilet Duck
Renew Next yearly pass

'Mum, Dad, you'll never believe it.' Gen comes into the living room, literally jumping up and down. She thrusts a piece of paper at us.

'Genevieve Halliday has been selected to perform in the regional championships to be held at the SEC Glasgow on Saturday 3 April – discipline: balance beam.'

I leap out of my chair and fling my arms around Gen. 'Well done, sweetheart. I'm so proud of you.' I kiss her on the head. 'Just a chip off the old block.'

'Yeah, that'll be right,' scoffs Ronnie. 'Twinkletoes you ain't.' He comes up and envelops us both in a hug. 'Ditto what Mum said. I'm really proud of you.'

'Thanks, Dad. Will you be there to watch me?'

Ronnie looks at me uncertainly. We both know his shift patterns off by heart. The dates are indelibly marked into our minds.

He gives her a rueful smile. 'I'm sorry, princess, I don't get back until the seventh.' Gen's face falls. 'But I'll be rooting for you, and I'll have all of Callan behind you, cheering you on. And Mum will be there, and I'm sure Aunt Wendy and Aunt Jo and Nana and Papa and Grandma and Grandpa will be there, if they can make it.'

I nod.

'I know you can't help it, Dad. I just wish you could be there sometimes. Knowing you are there gives me confidence. I feel like I can do it. I can see myself holding that trophy.' She shrugs. 'I don't know why, but it helps.'

'Princess, believe you me, the very first time I am able to come watch you in a championship, I'm there. I'll have one of those giant hands you see the spectators waving at American basketball games. I'll be shouting so loud, I'll raise the roof, literally.'

Gen grins. 'No thanks. You might put me off. Or I might get rained on. Or you might embarrass me. Don't know which is worse.'

'That's my girl. You can do it. I know you can.'

She skips out of the room and soon the thud of feet on stairs can be heard.

'I can't believe you're going back tomorrow again.' I sigh.

Ronnie rolls towards me and snuggles into me. 'I know. I feel as if I've only been home about four days.'

I smile at this. If he feels like this after having our three kids to contend with, we're doing something right.

'We didn't even manage a night out,' I wail.

'Well, we can make up for it by having a night in.' The wicked gleam in my husband's eye makes my laughter burst forth and I squeal as he launches himself at me.

Maybe there is truth in 'absence makes the heart grow fonder'.

Chapter Ten

Wednesday 3 February

To-do list

Ensure am on top of work emails by today as taking a day off this week for Aria's birthday
Ask nursery if Aria can stay in full time tomorrow
Change dental appointment for Hugo as it now falls same day as Valentine's disco – 10th
Buy new filter for hoover
Ensure have all of Aria's presents – that they've all arrived – have forgotten what I've bought

February is the month of love. Yeah, right. Must be parental love then. Or familial love. I haven't even seen my husband this month – seven more days to go, not that I'm counting. His last trip home whizzed past. We need to make some time for ourselves next time he's home.

And I am inundated with work. I'm really hoping the wedding show will be worth it. I can't prepare any more than I have. Everything has been packed, checked, double-checked, and I've enlisted my secret weapon: Mum. I have to be careful she doesn't try to take over, and instead does as I've asked and fields clients on the day, and lets me go for the occasional loo break and coffee run.

I miss Ronnie. When things become overwhelming, that's when you really appreciate another adult in the house – not that I wouldn't love him to be here all the time, but when out of the ordinary things occur and mess with your day, a helping hand would be welcome.

Gen was late home last night and didn't call me, so I was freaking out. Had she been hit by a bus, abducted, put in detention, what? Two hours. I was frantic. I almost called the police when it started to get dark.

After ascertaining she was OK, I berated her at length for putting the fear into me. She then revealed she had been with a couple of guys and girls at the new coffee shop in town, Brio. I wasn't even aware she had any money and told her so. She blushed and told me one of her friends had paid for her, and she'd return the favour when she had some money.

I sense a boy in this equation. And money? After putting me through hell, I don't think so. She didn't take that too well when I told her, storming off to her room, which was fine. Saved me shouting at her for a bit and allowed my face to go back to its normal colour. Then Aria half-popped her head round the kitchen door, and I knew she'd heard us. I don't shout at the kids often, but nobody's perfect and when they push the boundaries too far, I generally remove myself from the situation, but I can't when they put 'the fear' into me as Genevieve did. She's old enough to know better.

Aria curled into me and I stroked her blonde mop, speaking to her in a low voice, apologising for shouting. Then I went through to the living room and gasped in horror. Aria, I assume, had scrawled over the wooden coffee table in gold pen. I'm not sure how I kept calm, but

I did, kneeling down beside her, as the books tell you to, so I was the same height, and asking her why she did it. She told me it was boring and she wanted it to look pretty. Yet when she came into the kitchen, her eyes held a note of defiance.

Thank heavens for Hugo. The extent of his misdemeanours last night was to have too much time on his Xbox.

It has all left me feeling rather drained this morning. I need a day off. I make a promise to myself that when Ronnie's back next week, and after the wedding fair, I'm having a day out with Sam and Nicky. I need it.

The thump thump of tiny feet sounds on the stairs. Aria. I walk into the hall and turn on the light. She's standing there, clutching her favourite unicorn teddy, Cornie. Her eyes are red and hazy with sleep.

'Hey, honey, good morning,' I say.

Her lip trembles and she starts to cry. 'Mummy, I had a nightmare.' She launches herself at me and I sweep her into a hug, stroking her hair.

'It was just a bad dream. You're OK. I'm here now.'

'An alligator, a big one, bigger than a house, was trying to climb onto my bed.'

She has a thing about alligators and crocodiles. I knew Ronnie shouldn't have let her watch that nature programme. They can be quite graphic. He turned it off when the gazelle met an inauspicious end.

Aria buries her little face into my shoulder, sobbing.

'Ssh, it's OK,' I tell her as I carry her through to the kitchen.

'Mummy, I'm sorry, I peed my bed.'

'Mummy will deal with that, don't you worry.'

Her face is red and blotchy. I hope she isn't coming

down with something. There's nothing worse than when one of your kids is sick, well, apart from more than one of them being sick. She's also hot to the touch.

'I'll be back in a sec, sweetheart.' I retrieve the thermometer from the bathroom upstairs and when I return Aria is staring into space.

'I'm going to check your temperature, OK?'

She gives a slight nod. Definitely not her usual exuberant little self. I hold the thermometer to her forehead: 38.5 °C. Hmm, she appears to have a temperature.

No nursery for her today. I push away the thoughts of work that crowd in on me and set about making my baby comfortable. Irrationally, I think, I hope she's not ill for her birthday. That would be such a shame. I fetch a syringe and some liquid paracetamol and she takes it without any problem. That worries me. Aria hates taking medicine. I sit on the sofa beside her and she clambers up into my lap, curling her little body into mine. It's not like her. I mean, she's snuggly and affectionate, but she's never this quiet. Aria always jabbers away like a budgie. There's nothing, in some ways, worse than a quiet child. They're either poorly or drawing on your walls…

Chapter Eleven

Thursday 4 February

To-do list
Same as yesterday – didn't do any of it as Aria was ill, apart from answer a few client emails
Ask Mum if she can come round and help prepare for the show/watch Aria
Check with agency re possibility of getting a temp last-minute
Decide whether Aria needs to see doc
Call nursery to tell them she won't be in again today
Make list of things to do for Aria's birthday – cake, balloons, candles, banners

Aria's off nursery again. The poor wee thing has barely slept all night and neither have I. In fact, I brought her into my bed as it was easier than listening to her cough and worrying about her. Her temperature came down a little with the paracetamol but not enough. I really didn't want to move her this morning as she was exhausted, so I called Dad and asked if he would take Hugo to school and asked Genevieve if she would mind getting the bus for once. Since Gen adores her little sister, she didn't cause an argument over it, but the not coming home on time issue is still simmering away between us. As soon as I get a second, I need to address that.

Once Dad has gone and I've waved Gen away to the bus stop, I jump in the shower. I may not get another chance today. When your kids are sick, they take priority, even if it means you're in the same pair of jeans for three days and haven't washed your hair. I fully anticipate Aria being clingy again today and who can blame her.

Back downstairs, I scan my to-do list. I can barely make it out. I'm not sure if I'm overtired or, as I refuse to admit to myself, I need glasses. Another one of those things that gets put on the back-burner.

Schedule optician appointment for myself (if get time)

I decide to make some calls before she wakes up, especially now I've sorted her siblings' journeys to school. Her body obviously needs rest, so I'll let her sleep until she wakes up naturally. I call the nursery, who wish Aria a speedy recovery, then ring Mum.

'Hello, 627871.'

Hardly anyone answers their phone these days giving their phone number but old habits die hard for my mother. She should have been a switchboard operator.

'Hi, Mum, it's me. Listen, I need a favour, another one. I'm really behind with my preparation for the show and I still have my regular work to do. Could you come over at some point today and sit with Aria or help me put the packs together?'

'No problem. What time do you need me?'

My mum is at her best when there's a crisis.

'Sometime before the kids get back from school.'

'I'll be there in half an hour.'

As I said, no nonsense with my mum.

Within twenty minutes my mother arrives. During that time, I've managed to book the optician appointment I know I sorely need. Next Wednesday. That should give Aria enough time to recuperate. I'm fed up squinting at food packaging instructions and straining to see anything smaller than the number plate on a car.

I must look terrible as Mum gives me a hug when she comes in.

'How's Aria?' Her tone is full of concern. My mother and my youngest child have a special relationship. Although Aria is very sweet, she is also three going on thirty, so my mother speaks to her almost as if she's an adult, and they get on really well.

'Not great. I'm letting her sleep.'

'Has she been sick?' Mum asks.

'No, but her temperature is high.'

It's half past nine and Aria hasn't stirred, not even when I went to check on her twenty minutes ago. Her cheeks are rosy red but not in a healthy way. Such a worry, and equally a dilemma. I don't want to call for a doctor's appointment as they will only tell me to make sure she gets plenty of liquids, takes paracetamol and gets rest, but at the back of my mind there's the nagging doubt that it could be something more serious.

Mum and I sit down with the tea I've made then I give her the rundown on how she can help me prepare. Samples still need displayed on vision boards and I have to make up packs containing the different types of card, with various fonts and finishes.

'Mum, you know how you're helping me at the show, do you think Dad would manage with Aria if she's still poorly?'

'Of course. Would do them good to have some bonding

time.'

'Yes, well she's Nana's girl, that's for sure.'

'That she is,' Mum agrees.

'But will Dad cope if she's upset?' I ask, worried.

'Louisa, your dad and I have had enough children, and grandchildren, to know how to cope with any illness. Now stop worrying.'

'I know, you're right. I just worry she'll ask for me and I'll be at the show unable to do anything about it.'

'We have it in hand, so let's crack on with this so we can get as much done as possible before Aria wakes up.'

She's right. Once Aria's up, she'll be permanently affixed to one of us like a limpet. I'm so glad my ankle is almost better. One illness in the family at a time is enough.

Aria wakes an hour later, her hair plastered to her head and her eyes heavy. I've never seen her so listless. Even my mother seems taken aback. Aria usually catapults herself towards her nana, but today she barely acknowledges her and instead makes her way to me, tears rolling down her cheeks.

'Mummy, I don't feel well,' she says then vomits all over me, herself and a large section of the carpet before bursting into tears.

'It's OK, honey, that's why you weren't feeling well,' I tell her as I stroke her back whilst carrying her through to the utility room.

'Mum, could you get me a bucket, please?' I call.

'Where is it?'

'Cupboard in the hall next to the stairs.'

I strip down to my underwear and take Aria's pyjamas off. She's still crying. The carpet will have to wait. I need to get us both some clothes first. My head aches and I wonder absent-mindedly as I carry Aria upstairs to the en suite in my bedroom if there is any carpet shampoo left for the carpet cleaner.

In the en suite, I shower us both at a temperature that's marginally above arctic, but she still looks hot, and I don't want to make her any hotter. I'll take her temperature again in a second. It's a little hard to feel effective when you're covered in vomit. It's in my hair too – nice.

Aria continues to cling to me as I walk through to her wardrobe and fetch her clean pyjamas, then we go through to my room where I fling on the first thing I can find.

The bathroom is our next port of call where I take out the thermometer again: 39.4°C. That's significantly up on yesterday.

We go downstairs and Aria reluctantly detaches herself from me, whilst I arrange some cushions for her on the couch. I take advantage of this brief moment of respite to grab my phone and google 'What's a high temperature for a three-year-old?'

Various results appear and I scroll through. Essentially, the advice is to take your child to A & E if their temperature is as high as Aria's is.

'Mum, you got a sec?' I call.

Aria doesn't want me to leave the room. 'Let me put on the TV for you, sweetheart. I need to talk to Nana for a minute.'

I find an episode of *Paw Patrol* and, satisfied Aria is occupied, take Mum to one side in the kitchen. 'Her temp's 39.4, which is way too high. I'll give her some paracetamol again, then we're going to A & E. I'm not sure how long I'll be, but can you ask Dad to pick Hugo up again if need be?'

'Of course. You're doing the right thing. She doesn't look great. Do you want me to come with you?'

I consider saying for a second, 'No, it's fine,' then I realise that it will be better for Aria if someone is able to hold her hand and cuddle her, since I will be driving.

'That would be great. Can you sit with Aria in the back? I'll go grab a few things.'

Mum nods and goes to check on Aria in the living room, whilst I throw stuff into Aria's backpack: spare clothes, juice, snacks, a teddy, two books and my charger. The last thing I need is my phone dying on me.

Upstairs, I grab Aria's dressing gown, which I put in the backpack. Mum has carried Aria upstairs so I can swap her PJs for jeans and a long-sleeved top. I've put her coat on her and am unlocking the front door when I remember wipes and nappy pants. She doesn't usually wear them, even at night, but since she's under par, she may have an accident.

I'm putting our bags in the car when I remember I haven't given her the paracetamol so back I go, returning with the syringe and dispensing it into her mouth.

Aria's seat belt is fastened, then I take it off, deciding she will be too warm in her winter coat, so I divest her of that and put a hooded top on her instead.

'If you get cold, sweetheart, tell Nana and she will put your coat over you,' I say.

Although Aria's conscious, she's not terribly responsive, which worries me.

'Nana's going to sit beside you,' I say, 'so Mummy can drive. We're going to see the nice doctor at the hospital. The doctor will tell us why you were sick.'

A thousand scenarios hurtle through my mind in the fifteen-minute drive to the hospital. I can't help it. Meningitis is at the forefront. I know it shouldn't be, but I can't make it go away. Thousands of children have fevers

93

every day. But that doesn't make matters any better when it's your child and they're listless and limp. I'd rather she was bawling her eyes out, but ever since she threw up, she hasn't said a word.

I try not to drive too fast to the hospital. I know it's nothing life-threatening, but when your baby's sick, all you want to do is make them feel better and as quickly as possible. Mum sits in the back holding Aria's hand and talking to her. She asks her about Valentine's Day and who her boyfriend is, what activities they've been doing at nursery and if she has made Mummy or Daddy a card yet. I'm grateful for her attempts to distract Aria, but I don't hear my daughter reply.

By a stroke of luck, I find a space in the car park. The rain turns to sleet, and I feel like saying 'Really?' to the sky. I unbuckle Aria's seat belt and carry her into A & E, Mum following at my heels.

The waiting room isn't as busy as I thought it would be and I sigh with relief. The receptionist asks me for Aria's details and symptoms, then tells us to take a seat, someone will call us through shortly.

Ten minutes pass, then a nurse calls Aria's name. Mum and I both go through with her.

'Hi, Aria, I'm Maisie,' says the nurse. 'Not feeling too good today, pet?'

I detect a North-East accent, or perhaps it's the intonation she gave 'pet'.

Aria doesn't even shake her head, just lowers her eyes. Now I'm really worried. She sits against me, my hand in hers, until the nurse says, 'I'm going to check your oxygen levels, Aria,' at which point I have to separate from her. It's almost like a physical pain, and I see that mirrored in Aria's eyes. It's horrible being so powerless when your child is ill.

The nurse takes her temperature as she chats away to Aria as if they are new best friends. I crane my neck to see what she has written down as I can't make out what the thermometer says: 39.6. Oh no, it's getting higher. Mum catches my eye. She is sitting close enough to see the thermometer reading.

'Has she had any Calpol or ibuprofen?' the nurse asks.

'I gave her paracetamol half an hour ago.'

'Right, I'd usually have you sit back in the waiting room for a bit, but I'm concerned about her temperature. Let me get one of the doctors.'

She leaves the room and Mum and I look at each other. I don't want to say much in front of Aria, but I berate myself for not trusting my judgement and taking her to out-of-hours last night.

'Stop overanalysing it,' Mum says.

She knows me so well.

'I wish I'd brought her in sooner.'

'You weren't to know her temperature would keep climbing, and if you'd brought her in earlier, they might have dismissed it and sent her home. Think positive.'

I cradle Aria in my arms, and try to control my emotions. This is when it's hard that Ronnie works offshore. For all Mum is here, and she really is a godsend, in times like these, I'd like my husband not to be stuck hundreds of miles away in the middle of the North Sea.

'Do you think I should call Ronnie?' I ask.

'Not yet. Let's wait to hear what the doctor says.'

The nurse returns with a young female doctor. 'Hi, I'm Dr Yazawa, and this is Aria?'

I nod. Aria's eyes don't even raise to the doctor's.

'Is it OK if I lift her top up?'

I nod again.

'No rash,' says the doctor.

The nurse writes something down. I can't help it, I blurt out, 'Is it meningitis?'

My mother inhales sharply.

'Anything's possible until we've made a full examination of her, but I wouldn't jump to that conclusion yet,' the doctor tries to reassure me.

'OK.' It doesn't quite make me sigh with relief, but at least my overactive imagination calms down for a second.

The doctor carries out a thorough examination of Aria then says, 'As a precaution, I'd like to admit her because I'm not sure what's causing the high temperature. We need to run a few more tests.'

My stress levels spike.

'Nurse will get you checked in and then we can make her more comfortable and see if we can figure out what the issue is.' The doctor leaves the room and the nurse takes control again.

'If you wait here a second, I'll find out where we're taking her.'

Twenty minutes later we are in Ward 6B of the children's wing. Aria looks so tiny in the bed, but she is a little too big for the nursery. I worry that she'll fall out of the bed, so I barely move from her side.

'Go and get a drink,' Mum says. 'I saw a parents' room along the corridor.'

'No, I'd rather wait here.'

'I insist. And I think now's a good time to text Ronnie. And whilst you're at it, text Dad and tell him what's happening and let Gen know to get the bus home.'

'OK.' I turn to leave but Aria howls, 'Mummy, don't

go.' And then she bursts into tears. Huge, gulping sobs.

'It's OK, Mummy's here.' I soothe her with quiet words, stroking her back the whole time. I indicate to Mum that she should make the calls. My daughter needs me.

Aria's little body stills against mine, and her breathing returns to normal, except for the occasional jerky sob.

Mum is still out of the room when the consultant arrives. That was quick. He introduces himself as Dr Williamson and explains exactly why they are keeping Aria in for observation, how dangerous high temperatures can be and why there is a need for continual observation over the next twenty-four hours. He doesn't tell me not to worry, but then I am sure they are told not to make empty promises or give people false hope. I wish Ronnie were here. And where has Mum got to? That's not fair. She's taking care of the rest of my family, and the rest of my life.

I try to stay calm for Aria, who holds my hand limply as she lies on top of the starched sheets. This is wrong. This place is too clinical for my daughter, too devoid of colour. It should have rainbow walls. I know my thoughts are jumbled, but I just want to find out what's going on with Aria.

When Mum comes back, I'll change Aria into her PJs and see if we can let her have a little rest. Should we be keeping her awake? I had better ask the doctor or one of the nurses. Ah, here's one now.

'I'm here to check her obs,' the cheery nurse says.

'Is it OK if she falls asleep?'

'Yes, if her body needs rest, sleeping is fine.'

Although that sounded like something partway between a holistic therapist and a training manual, she might have a point.

'Aria, are you tired?' I ask her.

She tries to give a little nod, but it's so pathetic it makes me want to weep.

'Let's get you into your pyjamas then, and I can read you a story.'

I take her pyjamas from her backpack and only then do I notice the other people in the room. It's a four-bedded room, and there's a boy of about seven in the bed opposite reading a Diary of a Wimpy Kid book, a girl of perhaps ten lying on her front with headphones in, and the other bed is empty but made up as if expecting its next occupant any minute.

Mum returns. 'All sorted,' she says. She waits for me to settle Aria then continues. 'Ronnie has texted back *Tell Louisa not to panic. Aria will be fine. She is in the best place. Keep me posted. Tell her I love them both.*'

I digest this then say, 'Mum, why don't you go home? You can take my car. There's no point both of us being here.'

Mum nods. 'OK. What do you need me to do with the kids? And what about the show?'

'The show. I forgot about the damn show.' It's in two days' time. What am I going to do? I can't even think about that right now. I don't have the headspace. Aria is my priority. If I have to miss the damn show, so be it. Nothing is more important than my children.

'I don't know, Mum. I might have to cancel. Can you and Dad stay with the kids until I know what's happening?'

'Of course. We'll make them dinner then get some board games out.'

What do we tell them about Aria, though? I don't want them to worry, but we don't exactly have a lot of information yet. So I simply say, 'Good idea.'

'And there will be no talk of cancelling the show. I know how important it is to you and your business, and how hard you've worked. Plus, I'm rather looking forward to being involved. Give me your organiser's details and I'll get in touch with them, explain what's going on. That way we're covered for every eventuality. I can always rope in a few people I know to help.'

An image of Betty Fairfax, with her twinset and pearls, flits through my mind. I wave the uncharitable thought away. Mum is doing her best to help. The fact her friend's attire says more Women's Guild than luxury wedding is not her fault, and being present at the show in some capacity is far preferable to not being there at all, I think. I hope.

'Have you got everything you need for Aria?' she asks me.

'I think so,' I say, grateful I had the foresight to pack a bag – it must be a mother's radar.

Mum gives me a hug.

'Here's the organiser's details.' I pass her a piece of paper. 'Text me later?'

'I will.' Mum turns to Aria and kisses her forehead. 'Bye, sweetheart.' She clasps my hand and whispers to me, 'Don't worry. I know it's hard, but try. Why don't you read to her again? She looks exhausted. She'll probably be asleep in five minutes and then you can both get some rest.'

I smile faintly at Mum. Although I am shattered, I feel as if I will never sleep again. Taking her advice, I perch on the chair, and with one hand I hold the book to show Aria the pictures, and the other I place on Aria's arm for reassurance. Whether it's to reassure her or me, I'm not sure.

Mum's right. Ten minutes later, Aria's asleep. I pour

myself some water and sit down with my emails, answering the most urgent and planning for the eventuality of not attending the show. Mum has seen enough of my plans, and I have a printed itinerary, that she would be able to take care of the stand, but not without help. I hastily compose an email to the recruitment agency I use, marking it urgent and explaining the situation. I check my WhatsApp messages. There are some from my sisters and Ronnie, as well as a few from friends, who don't yet know Aria is in hospital.

I glance up and see my beautiful little daughter, her arms outstretched on the top of the sheets, her blonde curls mussed up, and I wish I could take away whatever pain or discomfort she's feeling. I don't practise religion but I pray to God that my daughter will be OK, that her fever will break soon and that the cause for it will become apparent.

Since there's nothing else I can do whilst I wait for the consultant, I reply to the messages I've received. They all say much the same.

Heard about Aria, hope she's OK. Let me know what's happening. Love you. Wendy x

Dad told me about Aria. How is she? How you holding up? Let me know if I can help with the kids or anything. Chin up. Jo x

Met your dad in town. How's Aria. Any news yet? Let me know – stay strong and try not to worry. Sam x

Sam told me. How is she? I can take care of the kids if you need me to, let your folks get home later. She'll be fine. The doctors know what they're doing. N x

I'm so emotionally spent I can't even deal with those right now, so I turn back to my emails. Great. Someone has misspelled their own surname and their mother-in-law's first name on their invitations. They didn't notice at proof stage. That's the whole point of the proof stage. And another client has been told her wedding venue is no longer available due to a fire and the invitations are at the printer. Normally, I'd call, but that's definitely not happening. To take my mind off things here, though, I bash out an email to James Simpson Printer & Co. advising that if the print job hasn't started yet, they should hold off until we hear from the bride and groom about an alternative venue, or indeed to find out if the wedding will go ahead on that date.

I work my way methodically through some of my emails, giving a rueful smile at the irony of my being able to get through my to-do list. I would rather have a list the size of a football pitch than my daughter being seriously ill.

I do as much as I can, I'm almost like a woman possessed, stopping only when I hear Aria move or sigh or breathe differently. Then I am suddenly aware of someone hovering over me. The consultant.

'Mrs Halliday,' he says. 'We've done some bloodwork and what we really need now is a urine sample to discount a UTI.'

I stare at him. He surely doesn't expect to be able to get a urine sample from Aria when she's asleep. As if reading my thoughts, he says, 'They can still urinate when they're asleep.'

'But how will I balance a sleeping child and that grey cardboard box thing? It's hard enough to hold that when they're awake and catch it,' I say.

'One of the nurses will help you,' he says.

I don't want to wake my sleeping daughter. As the nurse had said, her body obviously needs the rest, but I do as the doctor asks and wait for a few minutes to see if the nurse comes in. When she doesn't, I go out to the nurses' station and ask for help.

Five minutes later, we have the desired result, and Aria returns to sleep, which I'm thankful for. A nurse returns to carry out more observations on Aria. It's a different nurse to the one who took the urine sample away. I wonder what's happening with it and how long it will take for the results to come back, and what they may show.

What seems like hours later the dinner trolley comes round. I must not have noticed the lunch one.

'Would you like something?' the woman dispensing the meals asks.

My stomach rumbles, reminding me I haven't eaten since this morning. What time is it? I check my phone.

I finally realise I haven't answered. 'That would be great.'

When she sets the tray containing tomato and basil soup, beef casserole and fruit compote in front of me, I almost salivate. Who knew I'd be so delighted at seeing hospital food? It smells surprisingly good. Even more surprising, it tastes good too.

Later that night, I sit mindful of the fact I have other children to take care of. Aria has woken several times and hasn't rallied much. They've been giving her liquids through a drip in case she isn't getting enough.

The consultant comes to see me. 'Mrs Halliday, the urine test came back negative. It could be viral. It most likely is viral, but we will keep her here in hospital whilst her temperature is so high. It's a waiting game now.'

Message delivered, he leaves.

A nurse appears shortly after.

'Excuse me, could you keep an eye on Aria whilst I make a couple of calls?'

She smiles at me. 'Of course.'

I reflect on the fact it's only the fourth of February and already I've been at this hospital three times. I don't like the trend.

The first call is to Mum to discuss arrangements for overnight. I tell her Sam has offered to look after the kids, but she won't hear of it. She's already dispatched Dad to collect some things from theirs.

After we've discussed Aria, Mum says, 'The children are fine, and I also called the organiser. They said I can collect new passes on the day. I've packed up most of the stuff already, but realistically, I don't think you will be able to attend the show.'

She has voiced what I already know. There's no way I'm leaving Aria, even if the hospital does discharge her tomorrow. I won't let her go back to nursery for a few days after she gets out, whatever happens.

'I know. I've already contacted the agency to see if they can send someone to help you.'

'No need. The girls are willing to step up, but if you think it would be helpful, by all means.'

I thank Mum for her friends' offers of help, but Mum showcasing my business is one thing, the women who are in her book club are quite another. If she at least has someone who knows how a trade show works, it will help a lot. And they can keep her in lattes and muffins as well as hand out business cards.

We talk for a bit about the children and then our conversation turns to the details for the show. When we've finished I say, 'Can you put Genevieve on the phone, Mum?'

There's some crackling on the line as Mum passes the phone to Gen. 'Hello? Mum?'

'Hi, Gen, you OK?'

'Not really.' Her voice cracks. 'Will Aria be all right?'

'She'll be fine, sweetheart. She just has to stay here until the doctors bring her temperature down.'

'And how will they do that? Why haven't they done it already?'

She's asking the questions I mulled over earlier. How can they not know what it is?

'I'm not sure, but that's why she's staying in overnight, for observation. Has Dad FaceTimed you yet?'

'Yes, he called about an hour ago. He told us not to worry.'

'He's right. Listen, can you do me a favour?'

'What?'

'I won't be back tonight and Nana and Papa will stay with you whilst I'm at the hospital with Aria. Can you make sure Hugo is OK? He'll be missing Aria too. You know how he bottles everything up.'

'Yeah, he was saying how it would all be OK, and she was doing it for attention.'

'Uh-huh. That's his way of coping with it. We all deal with things differently. Can you be extra nice to him, please? Make life easy for Nana and Papa?'

'OK.' She pauses. 'Mum, give Aria a hug from me, please.'

'I will, sweetheart. Can you put Hugo on, please?'

'Sure.'

Hugo comes on the phone crying. 'Mum, I want you to come home, and Aria too. I don't like it without you. Is she going to be OK? What's wrong with her? I'll share better, please bring her home.'

My heart goes out to my lovely, sensitive boy. He shares beautifully with his sister. He'd give her the moon if he could reach it. I try to answer his questions as best I can and reassure him, but I'm not sure I'm quite managing it, perhaps because I don't feel reassured myself.

Later, I wake on the chair with cramp in my leg. A blanket has been draped over me. I must have finally fallen asleep. Nurses have been coming in every so often to do observations on Aria. I've lost count of the number of times. One nurse will come in to do temperature, then another comes in to check her oxygen level. She's attached to a monitor and it has dipped below ninety a few times.

I glance over at my sleeping girl and my heart almost snaps in two. She looks so peaceful lying there. I wonder if it's peace or delirium. Rousing myself, I go to ask the nurses for the latest update.

Chapter Twelve

Friday 5 February

No lists today – I couldn't care less. I just want my girl to be well.

In the morning, it's not the sun streaming through the window that wakes me fully but the overhead lights flickering to full power. It's never truly dark in a hospital room, as there are always lights on. Aria continues to sleep. She's woken a few times but she has mainly slept since we arrived in the hospital yesterday morning. Her little body must have needed it.

Breakfast is brought round and I attempt to eat some toast. My heart's not in it. I look at my still sleeping girl and will her to wake up. She wakes about half past eight and then falls straight back to sleep. I stroke her hand and wait for the next round of observations to be done. I message the family to give them an update, what little news I have, how she has passed the night. I'm not even sure if she is better or worse. The waiting is the worst thing. You would think the nurses or the doctor would keep you informed, but until the fever breaks they won't know anything more.

By the time the consultant comes round at eleven o'clock, Aria is awake and more alert than she has been in the past thirty-six hours. The nurse told me earlier that she still has a high temperature but it's not as high as it was.

During Aria's hours of sleep, I managed to catch up a bit with the most urgent work and place an online order to be delivered to mine so my parents at least have some food to feed the children.

I can't quite take Aria in my arms yet as she is still hooked up to machines, but the fact that she is more alert is heartening.

'She's not completely out of the woods yet,' the young consultant tells me, a different one to yesterday, 'but she's heading in the right direction. Let's keep her here until this evening, then if we're happy, she might get out in time for bedtime, but I can't make any promises.'

'No problem, Doctor. I understand.'

I hug Aria and read her a few Hugless Douglas stories, then when she is occupied doing a wooden puzzle, I text the family to give them the latest, even taking a photo of her to reassure them.

The day passes in a similar vein to yesterday, but this time with a notable difference – my girl is awake and talking to me and even takes some food, and keeps it down.

Mum comes in with Dad once the kids are at school and they quietly make a fuss of Aria. They sit with her whilst I go to call Ronnie.

'God am I glad to see you,' I say.

'You look shattered. How's Aria?' he asks. 'I'm sorry I'm not there. You must have gone through hell last night.'

'Ronnie, it was awful.' I will the tears back down. 'She's improving but they're keeping her in until tonight to see what happens. Her temperature has come down a little, but not enough to let her home yet.'

'How are the kids coping?' he asks.

'Not great. Gen's voice was wobbly and Hugo was really upset. I did my best to tell them it would be OK, but I don't think it helped that I wasn't there to tell them face to face.'

'I can imagine. Poor Hugo, and Gen always tries to be so strong. Listen, you take care of yourself too. Your parents have been great. If anyone else offers to help, take it. Once you get home, you'll need some rest too.'

'Mum's doing the wedding show for me tomorrow.'

'Oh, I had completely forgotten about that. How–? What–?'

I fill Ronnie in on how Mum and a temp that I arranged today with the agency will man the stand for me at the wedding show whilst Dad deals with the kids and I remain with Aria.

'Hell, this is when it's so difficult, for all of us, Lou, me being here. Sometimes, I really wish I'd made more of an effort to get a job on land.'

Him and me both, but I don't tell him that. I know that the only jobs available back then were low-paid and wouldn't have covered our needs, but I've always wished we'd been able to find a way back from it. It simply hasn't happened yet. Perhaps that's something we can readdress in the coming weeks and months. I sign off FaceTime after a bit more time chatting with my husband – it's funny, it's one of the few times in recent memory we've managed to talk to each other without being interrupted, but I'd have foregone that conversation if it had meant Aria not being ill.

I read a few more stories to Aria and she lies back afterwards to watch a children's TV show.

A few hours later Aria is given the all-clear. Her fever has broken and her temperature is lowering. Smiles all round and oodles of relief from me. I catch sight of myself in the mirror. Sunken eyes, pale grey skin and my hair is like a bird's nest. I don't care. Aria hugs me and I shower her with kisses. Once I've called Dad to come and pick us up, I dress her and pack her bags.

The list is back. *Buy chocolates for the nurses.*

I thought Dad would never let Aria go when he saw her. He dotes on her because she's my youngest. And she's a chatty wee poppet, endearing and affectionate. He doesn't have favourites, but I can tell that her having to be kept in overnight has brought out his protective streak. But that's nothing to the welcome she receives when we get home. It's all I can do to protect her from the stampeding hordes. Her brother hugs her round the neck and her big sister tries to pick her up.

'Careful, guys. Give Aria some space,' I say.

They ignore me of course. Their beaming smiles show their joy at seeing their little sister safe and well.

I hug the kids and we all slump onto the sofa. The three-seater is just big enough for all four of us. It used to be there was room to spare, and as I watch my children, I realise how much they've grown in the past few months.

'Mummy, can I watch Dora?' Aria asks, and with five words, everything is back to normal.

Chapter Thirteen

Tuesday 9 February

To-do list – lost track
Do I have all party bags?
Ensure kids wear correct party clothes for their sister's birthday
Remember to write a list of who buys Aria what for thank you cards
Order thank you cards – chase up what happened to the ones I ordered ages ago

My baby is four today. I can't believe it. How did that happen? We've put last week's scare behind us and are concentrating on giving her the best party ever. Sam, Nicky, Jo and Wendy all pitched in and helped me decorate the house. We wanted to make it amazing given Aria's had a terrible few days. I had some time on my hands, well, within reason, given that I didn't go to the wedding show. Mum didn't do too bad a job, as expected. If she's to be believed, though, the temp was worse than useless and spent her time chatting up the grooms-to-be. Apart from that, her presence allowed Mum to go to the toilet and also to grab a sandwich from a nearby stall for lunch. She apparently stood 'looking sullen and pouting' for the duration of the two-day event, and even Mum's none-too-subtle hints didn't make any difference. And not many people dare defy my mother. I should know.

The entire downstairs is festooned with unicorn paraphernalia. Pink and white unicorn banners billow from the archways in the kitchen and living room; there's a unicorn piñata currently leaning against the dining room door. Don't want her to spot it too early. Sam made the most gorgeous unicorn dreamcatchers and has brought some extra materials so the guests can make their own to take home with them. Nicky ordered some unicorn party boxes off Etsy and has been filling them with unicorn-themed treats and toys. If I were four years old, or even ten, I'd be dying to get my hands on one of them; they look amazing. I daresay Hugo will forego his unicorn ban for the party too. I know he secretly harbours an affection for them. The cake, ordered last-minute from a local bakery, who went above and beyond to pull it off, has six rainbow layers and a sparkly unicorn on top.

Mum and Genevieve were up late last night making unicorn party hat horns. A blue cone with silver swirls and a yellow hairband with a bow to hold it on. My girl so deserves this after everything she has been through. I hope she loves it as much as I think she will. She's so much better, but the virus, the doctors couldn't find anything else, really has taken it out of her. She's still sleeping a lot more than she was previously and she isn't back at nursery yet, but the doctors have reliably informed me that whatever it was will have passed its contagious stage, if it had one, so no need to worry about infecting any of the partygoers.

I glance round once more at all the décor and smile. For the first time in a week, I am relaxed, even though there is still much to do. Bear scampers down the steps when I open the front door, and I take him across to the grassed area and let him have a little pad about whilst I keep one eye on our house. It's a crisp morning and the ground crunches underfoot. My breath forms clouds in the air and I feel truly content.

Bear and I return home and I make a cup of tea and scroll through my work emails, stopping only to put on a load of washing. I want nothing to spoil Aria's day and as soon as she's up, I'm putting my out-of-office message on for the day.

The party is set to start at four o'clock. I want a good chunk of time with Aria and the family first. Ronnie will call her tonight. He's gutted to be missing her birthday, especially given how poorly she has been, and since it's only by one day, but I know he will make it up to her when he comes home tomorrow. Although I feel a bit drained by recent events, I also feel energised. Aria is four, and she's starting school this year. A new adventure is about to begin. And my life will change again. I just hope I'm ready for it.

'Mum,' I hear from the stairs. Hugo. I go out to the hall and beckon him down with one hand and place a finger over my lips with the other.

'Is Aria up yet?'

I shake my head. His face falls.

'C'mon into the living room and you and I can have some breakfast together before the girls get up.'

His face lights up at that. We spend little enough time together on our own. There's always either someone there or he has to go to school. And at the weekend and some evenings, he has swimming lessons and taekwondo. I feel as if sometimes we don't have enough time to simply *be*.

We settle down in the living room under a blanket.

Hugo snuggles in. He won't do that for much longer, he's already eight, so I want to make the most of it.

'So, what did you dream about?' I ask him as he lays his head on my shoulder.

'I dreamt about Transformers and how I was a famous inventor and I had created a new one. It was a new breed and I called them the Digiforms.'

I smile and marvel at his imagination.

'Want me to draw it for you?' he asks.

'Sure. There's some paper in the craft cupboard.'

Hugo returns with the paper and sets to his task, tongue sticking out one side of his mouth. I watch him draw. He's really talented. He certainly didn't inherit that skill from me. Maybe it's from Mum. She's pretty handy with a pencil and can paint too.

'Scrambled egg, Hugo?'

'Yes, please.'

He doesn't glance up, his focus on his drawing and the metallic pencils he has brought with him to colour his design.

I boil the kettle for tea and bustle about the kitchen making scrambled eggs. Quite glad I decided on that now, as I fancy some myself. I sing 'Baby Shark' to myself as I cook. Damn, I can never get that song out of my head. It's one of Aria's favourites. I turn around to put the milk back in the fridge and almost drop the carton. Aria is standing in front of me, a huge smile on her face and wearing five fancy dress costumes one on top of the other. I spot Cinderella and Jessie from *Toy Story* amongst them.

'Happy birthday, sweetheart.' I bend down and kiss her on the cheek.

'Mummy, there are unicorns all over the hall and in the playroom. I saw them.'

'Real unicorns? Do you think they're hungry? Shall we take them some breakfast?'

'No, Mummy, don't be silly. They're not real.' She rolls her eyes at me and just like that my Aria is back.

'Oh, well, why don't you tell me all about them?'

She winds her arms around my neck and allows me to lift her up.

'There are unicorns with lots of colours in their hair and balloons with unicorn bodies and big horns.'

I sit her on the counter and say, 'I wonder how they got there.' I change the subject. 'Hugo wanted to see you. Hugo?' I call.

Hugo doesn't stir. I guess he's caught up in his drawing.

'Never mind. Would you like some scrambled egg?'

'If I eat it, can I have Coco Pops afterwards?'

She's sharp is my girl. Coco Pops is a special treat. I don't want her subsisting on chocolate breakfast cereal.

'Hmm, you drive a hard bargain, but OK then, seeing as it's your birthday.'

'Thanks, Mummy. Can I come down now?'

I lift her down and tell her to sit at the table, then spoon the scrambled egg onto two plates. I take one over to Aria, then go to round Hugo up.

'Hugo, Aria's up. Wow, that's amazing,' I say, studying his picture. It really is. I am sure parents with Transformer-daft children have paid lots of money for pictures or posters for their rooms that don't look as good. Pride swells within me.

'Really?'

His lack of confidence melts my heart and I drop a kiss on his head. 'Really.'

'Can I give Aria her present?' he asks, bouncing into action.

'Soon. Let's have breakfast and then your present can be the first one she opens. Deal?'

'Deal!'

I hold my hand out for a high-five and he reciprocates. That boy packs some punch.

'Aria, it's present time!' Hugo yells after breakfast. 'Follow me.' Hugo leads Aria by the hand into the living room then bends down and extracts a lovingly wrapped present from beneath the coffee table. I said the boy was good at drawing. He made his own wrapping paper and drew a family of unicorns on it. The babies are lying at the foot of the parents and there are five unicorns in all, representing our family. Hugo told me this last night as I helped him wrap it. He wanted to ensure that when she opened it, if possible, the wrapping paper remained intact, so I used Blu Tack instead of Sellotape. Let's hope that worked.

'It's so pretty, thank you, Hugo!' She gives her brother a big hug round his middle. They hold each other like that for a bit longer than usual. I take it they missed each other when she was in hospital.

'Mummy, can you help me open it?' She looks at Hugo. 'I don't want to break it. Hugo made it specially for me.' She beams at him.

Hugo grins.

'Bring it here.' I carefully undo the wrapping paper in such a way that I am not revealing the gift inside.

I pass it to Hugo, who puts it in Aria's hands. She opens up the paper.

'A fairy garden! And it's got three unicorns. Thank you, Hugo.'

'Do you want me to help you sort out the pieces?' he asks.

'Yes, please.'

'Why don't you do it at the craft table?' I suggest.

'Good idea, Mummy,' Aria says.

She seems so grown up. I massage her curls briefly then take the box through to the playroom.

'Hugo, can you read Aria the instructions?'

He nods and I disappear upstairs to wake Gen. She won't want to miss her sister opening the rest of her presents, especially with recent events.

The fairy garden is ready and it's hard to tell who is more delighted, Aria or Hugo. They've sprinkled the grass seed, erected the arbour and placed the unicorns on the sparkly pebble path; they've even placed the wishing well at the end of it. The only thing they haven't done is sprinkled the fairy dust.

'We wanted to wait for you and Gen,' Aria says when I ask.

'Plus we couldn't get the lid off the bottle,' Hugo adds.

That's more likely. I smile as I remove the stopper, before handing the bottle to Aria. 'Sprinkle a tiny bit at a time or it will all come out in a rush.'

Aria's tongue is out in the same mode of concentration Hugo employed earlier. She sprinkles a section, then looks to me as if for approval. I nod and she hands the bottle to Hugo.

'Your turn.'

Hugo obliges, covering the arbour and some of the path. Before he can give it back to Aria, she says, 'Gen's turn.'

Gen is as keen as her siblings to decorate the fairy garden. I don't think I ever bought her one. Even I get to sprinkle magic fairy dust.

I go to hand Aria the bottle, but she shakes her head.

'Don't you want to finish it?' I ask her.

'No, I'm keeping some for Daddy. That way everyone in our family will have a part of the fairy garden.'

A lump rises in my throat and I fight back tears. She's a thoughtful wee soul and she's had such a terrible week and now her daddy isn't here on her birthday. Again. He wasn't here last year either. I make a mental note, again, to talk to Ronnie about changing jobs long-term.

'So,' I say, clapping my hands together, 'does anyone think Aria might have more presents?'

Aria squeals with excitement and her siblings laugh.

'Come this way, birthday girl,' I say.

Behind the living room sofa is a bundle of presents, which Aria, assisted by her brother and sister, soon make light work of opening. It's not all unicorn based, although it is heavily slanted towards the horned creature. And then there's the Hatchimals, Enchantimals, LOL dolls and a Belle costume to name a few. It's not even been that long since Christmas and I haven't had time to do another clear-out, so goodness knows where we will put all her presents.

Ding-dong. It's five to four. My sisters and their kids arrived not long after I returned from the school run. It has been a quick day. Sam, Nicky and their offspring arrived five minutes after that. This time, it's Natalya. She goes to the same nursery as Aria. Her father is from Kiev and is here doing his PhD. She's a sweet little thing and you'd never know she speaks Russian at home. She's so fluent in English and even has a Scottish accent.

She shrieks with delight when she sees the unicorn-covered house. She and Aria bounce up and down – who needs a bouncy castle?

Over the next ten minutes the other girls trickle in,

exclaiming enthusiastically at the décor. Finally the last girl appears, resplendent in a blue, white and pink rainbow unicorn costume. Not to be outdone, Sam, always one for a laugh, ordered herself an adult inflatable unicorn costume off the internet. She really wanted to get into the spirit of things. From the smiles on the girls' faces at the sight of her, she's pulled it off.

'She seems almost back to her old self.'

I turn to see Nicky smiling at me.

'Thank God. And thanks, all of you, for helping arrange this. She loves it.'

'Happy to help, you know that. Do you want a drink?' She gestures to my empty glass.

'Old-fashioned lemonade. Woo hoo!'

'Don't worry. We'll get a night out soon, once things have calmed down. And whilst I was doing all the research for the party, I came across lots of good stuff for us too.'

'Oh?' I say.

'Marshmallow unicorn gin. Unicorn tears raspberry gin. And you can buy sparkly unicorn dust to sprinkle over your Prosecco.'

'Good to know. Marshmallow gin? Really? Sounds awesome!'

'That's what I thought.' Nicky grins. 'So much so, I bought some. I'll keep it for when Ronnie's home.'

I return her grin. 'Sounds like a plan.'

Genevieve, who has declared herself party planner, says loudly, 'Who wants to play some party games?'

'Yay!' chorus the girls, and the few boys who have been badgered into being there because they're related to us or their mothers are my friends. Although, I'm sure some of them secretly love the whole unicorn thing.

Sam, Nicky and I hang out with Jo and Wendy as the

kids all try to pin the tail on the unicorn. Do you see what we did there? No point reinventing the wheel. It's fun watching them and it reminds me that the simplest things can give us the most pleasure. We howl when Gen tells them for the nth time that her bottom is not the donkey's – I mean unicorn's – tail.

Gen has created a Twilight Sparkle quiz – I had no idea what that meant. I thought that My Little Pony was, well, about ponies, but somehow they shoehorned some unicorns in there too.

Aria is in her element and her eyes twinkle as she stares enraptured by her sister. Gen appears to be quite enjoying herself and Hugo, well, Hugo is in the midst of things. He has a go at pinning the tail on the unicorn but has an epic fail and flounces off to eat some unicorn marshmallows instead with Mum.

I excuse myself temporarily from my chat with the girls and pad across to Mum, who is watching the kids, a smile creasing her face.

'Mum.' I slide in beside her.

'Hi, darling. How are you? They seem to be enjoying themselves.' She inclines her head towards the children.

'Yep. I'm glad we're keeping the piñata until the end of the games. They look crazed enough without filling them with sugar.'

Mum raises her eyebrows and nods in agreement.

'And talking of sugar,' says Hugo. 'I think it's time to refill these marshmallows.' He wanders off with the almost empty bowl.

'Listen, Mum. Thanks, for everything. I don't know what I would've done without you this past week.'

She goes to talk but I silence her by raising my hand. 'No, let me say this. You and Dad always do loads for me, all of us, anyway, but you should be away on your cruises enjoying yourselves and not having to worry about me and my lot, so thank you from the bottom of my heart.'

'Any time,' is all Mum says then puts her arm around my shoulder.

I refill the adults' drinks and sit back and allow my lovely girl, Genevieve, to compere the games. Aria's not the only one in her element.

Sam rustles up a plate of food for me and I begin to relax. Jo and Wendy took pole position in the kitchen and I was under orders to stay out and enjoy the party. They bought and prepared all the food and Nicky baked the muffins and cupcakes. I am blessed to have such good friends, and I certainly needed them, and my family, this week.

Happiness radiates from Aria and I turn away for a second as a tear threatens to broach my barriers. She's four. Time is speeding up. Soon it will be nursery graduation, uniform choosing, starting school, empty nest in many ways. As the children play pass the parcel, relief washes over me. She's fine, she's healthy, happy and surrounded by people who love her, and so am I.

Chapter Fourteen

Saturday 13 February

To-do list
Write cards for kids and Ronnie
Buy M&S Dine in 2 for £10
Chase up remainder of leads from wedding show
Call those clients who want to get married next Valentine's Day x 2
Blow up tyres – gauge said they were down at 25 yesterday – can't be good
Nutella
Wrap Valentine's gifts for the kids to Ronnie and vice versa
Make cards for Ronnie with Aria and Gen

'So, are we exchanging gifts this year?' Ronnie asks.

What I want to say is, 'No, I'm buying myself something from the White Company as you never remember to buy me anything, then turn up with garage forecourt flowers and a bar of Fruit and Nut,' but I desist.

'Yes.'

'Oh.'

Amazing how one word can say so much, isn't it? I remember I used to think Ronnie was romantic, back in the day, pre-children. He always seemed to remember what I liked and have it magically awaiting me before I was aware I even wanted it. He once bought me purple suede Doc Marten-type boots covered in silver butterflies. I mean, what kind of man would know his girlfriend would covet those had she known of their existence?

Now, we just exist. I'd say co-exist, but there's less 'co' as he's gone for half the month. And I get that he wants to spend time with the kids when he's home. I want him to. I need him to, for my sanity apart from anything else. And I completely understand that he needs some downtime as he works damned hard on the rig, but I honestly don't think any man, and I don't even care if he has been a house husband (hate that term), has the faintest clue about what really needing downtime is.

When I worked as a chief buyer I thought I was the busiest person on the planet. Copious meetings, deadlines, targets, budgets, hundreds of emails a day – it was nuts. It was a doddle compared to being a parent and having to be at the beck and call of a small person, or in my case one small, one middle-sized and one relatively large person, twenty-four seven.

I'd like to be able to carve out a tiny piece of time for me, for us, but the minute Ronnie gets some time to himself, he wants to watch *QI*, a zombie movie or a documentary about Ancient Egypt. I'm not saying he has to watch *Strictly* or *Big Brother*, I loathe those, but I wouldn't mind a bit of chat of an evening and not only on topics to do with the children. Our conversation ranges from 'Hugo needs money for that school trip to the Edinburgh Dungeon' to 'Aria is now a library monitor at nursery' to 'Gen placed first in her year for French' and 'the kids' taekwondo costumes need upgraded'.

Enough procrastinating. I have a lot to do today, Ronnie

here or not. I have a few client meetings; they tend to mainly take place when Ronnie is home or during Aria's nursery hours, if the time suits. Today I am back to my role of professional businesswoman, who sent her mum to a wedding show instead of her, albeit with very good reason. I'm meeting the bride and groom so I have a chance to listen to their requirements properly, see what I think is best for them and convey that to them in as simple a fashion as possible. Clear is best I always find.

I have two back-to-back meetings at a hotel I tend to meet clients at in the city. I am one of the hotel's trusted suppliers and they even include me on their suggested supplier list, which is nice, although I've probably earned it from the number of lattes and flat whites I've bought there over the years for myself and clients. One of today's clients is a couple who met at school when they were eight, then grew up together, separated at high school, married other people and twenty-five years later and now divorced, are marrying each other. Then I am meeting Finn and Alasdair. Finn's from the Cotswolds and Alasdair is from Ullapool. That's a fair trek. From what Mum can gather they can't quite decide on where to live never mind the wedding venue, although at least they have the date and have opted to retain their own surnames, Larson and Abernethy. A year tomorrow. Oh, how I love seeing the dynamic between a couple.

My first meeting is at twelve. Ronnie can sort the kids out. I have a few things to do this morning.

'Ronnie, Ronnie,' I whisper, my hand burrowing below the covers to stroke his stomach.

'Ugh-nuh,' he says, burying himself beneath the pillows.

'You're dealing with the kids today. Remember?'

Silence. I could bet money this is where he's wishing

he hadn't stayed up into the wee small hours watching vampire flicks.

'Ronnie. You need to get up.'

'Hmm?'

'I have a meeting, two meetings.'

No answer. I can feel my stress levels spiking. I put the overhead light on.

'What? Ugh!'

'Ronnie, get up. You're looking after the kids.'

Finally, an arm reaches out from under the covers. He's awake.

I'm going to treat myself to a working breakfast at Costa Coffee next to the hotel. I can marshal my thoughts, prepare for the meetings and work on my to-do list. That way, when I get back late afternoon, I can devote myself to the family again.

Ronnie sits up. I ensure he is compos mentis then run through everything he needs to know.

I count off the items on my fingers as I go. 'Remind Hugo to take his new taekwondo kit; Aria has a Valentine's card that she made last night for her teacher – remember to put it through her door. She lives a few streets away at 27 Laburnum Avenue; take the bins out before eight as the binmen come around quarter past. Oh, also, you need to take Aria to the library. The books are in a bag in the living room. Make sure there are six as she has a tendency to take them out of the bag at the last minute. Think that's it. Right, I need to go. See you around four.' I peck him on the cheek, ignoring his dropped jaw, and leave in a cloud of satisfaction that I've done everything humanly possible to enable my husband to look after our children for the next few hours.

Ah. Coffee. Decent coffee. I am now ensconced in a coffee shop, notes laid out in front of me, assessing my priorities. I ensure I have all the items I need for my meeting and then tackle my work to-do list. I sit happily, ordering different card types and envelopes in jade, midnight blue and rose. This part of my business has taken a back seat recently as I simply haven't had time, but it would make sense to be able to enhance this element of my product offering. A one-stop shop is what people want these days. Fewer suppliers. Less fuss. But to do that effectively, I really would have to hire someone to help out. And I need time to cost that and look at the tax and insurance implications of having staff. Even in the peace and quiet I have today, there's no chance of being able to do that, although now I think of it, I could contact Business Gateway and ask for a meeting. That would be a positive step. Before I can change my mind, I dash off an email and press Send. Excellent, something else done.

I scan my emails. I propose dates for two more meetings to discuss wedding invitation requirements, as well as confirm an initial Skype call with someone in Australia whose cousin used my services last year and who is getting married here later this year and would like me to create their stationery suite. I agree to send samples out to three couples and then I tackle the problem areas. I reassure the bride and groom who misspelled two names on their invitations that their invitations will be ready in time to go out on the fourth of March. The feedback from the printer, who had a huge lead time, has been that I will receive everything by the end of the month. I can Fedex over the parcel and they should have it next day. I look at my watch. It's almost time. I drain the last of my coffee, gather my things and head next door to meet my clients.

'And my vision for the wedding theme is swans. Swans everywhere, including on the invitations. I thought perhaps the swans' necks could be incorporated into one of the letters in the name,' Alicia says, pausing only to readjust the pink floaty scarf around her neck.

'OK,' I say, marvelling once more at where people's ideas come from, but enjoying the fact that no matter how random their ideas sound, it's up to me to make them become a reality. Her husband-to-be, Jay, sits there, giving the occasional nod or smile, holding his fiancée's hand, looking every inch the long-suffering husband. Already Alicia is giving me the impression she's high maintenance. Either that or she's one of the many girls who have had their wedding planned out in their head since they were eight. The groom is merely a necessary adornment.

We bounce ideas back and forth and I promise to send some artwork back to them by the end of the week. By the time our meeting has concluded, I have the impression that I will win the business as long as I can deliver the brief. We shake hands and I remain in the hotel after they leave, making some notes and waiting for my next appointment.

My second meeting is a breeze after the first one. The couple are so easy to deal with, so obviously in love and have the same vision for the wedding, which always helps. Although they too opt for a bespoke design, there isn't a swan in sight. They met in Hong Kong five years ago and want to have a silhouette of the skyline over the harbour on the front of the stationery. That's easy enough to incorporate. I land that gig, they pass me a cheque for the deposit and I promise to send them some initial designs within a few days.

I stay in the hotel for a little longer to make a few calls, including to the temp agency, and then I drive home via M&S and pick up some posh ready meals. One for tonight and another for tomorrow. And I nip into Aldi on the way back too for other essentials. All in all a productive day's work.

'Mummy!' Aria barrels into me the moment I push the door open.

'Hi, sweetheart. Have you had a good day?' I ask once she has given me a monster hug.

'Uh-huh, it was awesome.'

She's been watching too many American cartoons again.

'That's great. So what did you do?'

'Well, it's a surprise. You'll find out tomorrow. And, I forgot to show you yesterday, I brought Dal home.'

'Dal?' I quirk an eyebrow, wondering if I've missed something.

'Yes, Dal the duck-billed platypus, you know. Every week someone takes him home to live at their house. We have to look after him and everything.'

Ah, responsibility for a pet week. I suppose the upside is it's a plush and not an actual pet. I'm not sure there are many duck-billed platypuses in the Glasgow area, pets or otherwise, but who am I to question things?

'That's great news. Where is he?'

She races off to fetch him.

'Mum!' Hugo accosts me as I take off my jacket.

'How was taekwondo?' I drop a kiss on his head, and he puts his arms round me and hugs me tight. The heat from his little warm body is welcome after the cold outside.

'Good. Guess what? I met Mrs Ryan and she told me

my art project got picked for the headteacher's showcase.'

'That's brilliant news!' I hug him to me. 'Well done.'

He toiled over a jungle scene, checking on Google to ensure it was as authentic as possible. I'm really pleased for him. My wee trooper.

'That deserves a treat. I think after dinner, we might have some popcorn and a movie night.'

'Yes!' He punches the air. 'Can I choose?'

'Oh, I think so. Right, where's Dad?' Ronnie hasn't materialised since I came in, nor called a hello.

'I think he's in the attic,' Hugo says, not sounding terribly sure.

'The attic? Wonder what he's doing up there,' I say half to myself.

'Dunno. He disappeared about five minutes ago.'

I head upstairs and find Genevieve in her room listening to music. She waves a hello and takes her ear buds out long enough for me to tell her I'll be back to talk to her in a minute.

'Ronnie,' I call up the attic hatch. 'I'm back.'

'Oh, hi.' His voice sails down to me.

'What you doing up in the attic?'

'I'm looking for some…memorabilia.'

'OK…right, well, I'll see you in a minute.' I go back to Gen's room, wondering what memorabilia we can possibly have in the attic. Ronnie, to my knowledge, has never collected anything.

'So, Gen, good day?'

I don't hug her. She's reclined on her bed and I have done well to enter her room without being told to keep out. There are good days and bad days. Today is obviously a good day. And there is none of the tension that was between us last week because of her arriving home late.

We're back on track.

'Listen, I was thinking, I know you're a bit big for doing it–' I figured this was the best way to put it to her '–but do you think you could help Aria make a card for Dad?'

'Sure.'

She likes to help, Gen. And she loves the role of mentor.

'Great. And you know, if you wanted to do one too, Dad would love that.'

She rolls her eyes. Yep, I'm too transparent and my daughter is too clever. I'll leave it at that and see how it shapes up.

'I'll set up the art things in the kitchen after I unpack the shopping, OK? Maybe you could start that whilst I'm sorting dinner. Cottage pie OK?'

I hope so. I know there's one I made last week that's in the freezer and would require little effort. Gen's eyes light up. One thing I don't have to worry about with my children, is food. But with Gen being almost a teenager, she's at that stage where body consciousness starts becoming an issue, so I need to be aware and look out for any warning signs.

'Fine for me,' she says. 'I'll tell Aria we're going to make a card for Dad.'

Today's definitely a good day. I smile and head downstairs to put the shopping away.

When I finish I go up to ask Ronnie if he wants a cup of tea. I'm on the landing when I hear him talking on the phone. He's so quiet I can barely make out what he's saying. Usually he's animated and laughing. I frown as I wonder who he's talking to. *No she doesn't suspect anything*. What? *No, I've been really careful. She doesn't know. It's our secret.*

My breathing is coming in fits and starts. No, no, no! Not another panic attack. Surely not. Not Ronnie. Not us.

We're solid. Aren't we?

He ends the call and I tiptoe back downstairs.

'So, you were up there a long time. Find what you were looking for?' I say to Ronnie when he finally appears.

'Yes, thanks. What's for dinner?'

Is he deliberately changing the subject? I frown but open the fridge to show him the extent of the wares I bought in M&S. 'Either duck or sirloin tonight. We can have the other one tomorrow. I also bought Coquilles St Jacques starters, cheese for dessert for me and Millionaire's shortbread mousse or raspberry panna cotta for you for tomorrow too.'

'Hmm. Sounds delicious. Duck, if you have no preference. So, meetings go well? Can I retire yet?' he jokes.

Yes, Ronnie routinely says he would give up work if I made enough money from my business to keep us both – well, all – in the style we've become accustomed to. Sometimes I wonder if he's being serious.

To distract from my discovery, I fill him in on my meetings.

'So, the wedding fair did yield some good leads, despite your mum and the pouting temp being the face of the company instead of you?' He grins.

'Something like that. Actually, I wanted to talk to you about taking on staff. I made an appointment with Business Gateway this morning.'

He whistles. 'Check you.'

'I know. I'm quite pleased with myself. Anyway, Aria and Genevieve need the kitchen. They have some important Valentine's Day-related stuff to do, so if you could make yourself scarce, maybe play a board game with Hugo or something. We haven't played Connect 4 in a while.'

'OK, I can do that. It would be so much easier with a cup of tea, though.' He tries to do doe eyes but fails. He's too big for that, and quite frankly after what I overheard, he can go to hell. I still need some time to process it all.

'You're pushing your luck,' I say.

'One does try.' Ronnie grins again.

'Yeah, I noticed. I'll put the kettle on, you can sort the cups.' Last time I went to offer him a cup of tea, look where it got me.

His face falls, then he edges away towards the kitchen door. 'Sorry, can't, have to tell Hugo and set up the game. Remember to give me more milk than you usually do.'

I glower at him and return to my task of unpacking the shopping. I flick the kettle on, then retrieve the art materials and set them up in the family area of the kitchen.

Genevieve comes in, trailing an excited Aria.

'Gen says we're making Daddy a card.' Aria's eyes are shining.

'That's right, sweetie. Up you pop.'

She climbs up on her chair and starts chattering away to Gen about what colour card she wants; multiple love hearts and purple feature strongly on her wish list.

'How about a yellow card?' Gen asks.

Aria nods and then says, 'And I want to write "I love you, Daddy" with a giant love heart. Can you help me make the love heart? I don't know if I can do that by my own.'

I hide a smile. All my kids had phrases they mixed up. Aria's is 'on my own' and 'by myself'.

'Of course.' Gen squeezes Aria's arm in a sisterly gesture of affection and then draws a huge love heart. Whilst I potter around, tidying the kitchen, Aria adds some other decorations around that, then they use the glue stick together and add feathers and googly eyes to form the words (goodness knows what this creation will turn out like, but their father will love it), finishing with an excessive sprinkling of three colours of glitter.

Finally, I make a cup of tea for myself and one for Ronnie. I refrain from adding arsenic to his.

'Would you like a drink, girls?'

'Too busy,' says Aria, concentrating on her card, tongue sticking out of the side of her mouth.

Gen shakes her head, so I go check on the boys.

Ronnie is sitting on the floor with Hugo, Connect 4 between them.

'Four in a row again, Dad,' says Hugo, a smug smile on his face.

I ruffle his hair. 'Beating Dad again?'

'Yep, three–two. Can I have some juice, please?'

Sometimes I think that boy is telepathic. 'Blackcurrant?'

He nods.

'Well, when you ask so nicely how can I refuse?'

After dinner, Ronnie beckons Hugo into the kitchen.

'But I want to choose a movie, Mum said I could. And have popcorn,' he wails.

'I'm not asking you to do the dishes and we will still do movie night, I just need a little help with something,' Ronnie tells him.

I try not to eavesdrop but an excited 'yay!' from Hugo tells me he's more than happy to do whatever activity his father has planned.

Ronnie pops his head around the door. 'No girls allowed. For at least an hour. And no listening in.'

He knows me well. I retreat to the living room with

the girls. We're going to watch *Matilda* at Aria's request. Gen loves this movie too, so she's staying. I sit with them, promising them hot chocolate and marshmallows once the boys are done in the kitchen. Life can be tough sometimes, but it's moments like this, sitting with my girls, that I realise just how precious it is. But is my life really as secure as I thought it was? Is Ronnie cheating on me, and if he is, with whom?

Chapter Fifteen

Sunday 14 February

To-do list
Arrange presents and cards for Ronnie
Book cinema tickets
Text the girls – haven't spoken to them this week
Check with Wendy what time the clan is descending
Bake Valentine's biscuits with kids – ingredients? Recipe?
Note to self: Who mentioned the recipe?

Bear is lying at my feet and although I am not taking the day off, I am going to try to enjoy Valentine's Day. There's a special screening of *Aladdin* at the cinema today and it's about the only romantic film showing that's suitable for kids. So, with a nod to the day of love, I'm booking us tickets for it – all of us. There's enough in it to accommodate Hugo, so it's only Ronnie who will be rolling his eyes, but parenthood is all about compromises. I'll indulge him later, maybe not by watching a vampire movie but I might consent to a dystopian one, albeit he doesn't deserve it.

I left Ronnie's card and present on my pillow and tiptoed downstairs to get some peace. I'm reading now and it's bliss. I don't remember the last time I picked up a novel. I don't think it has been this year. How ridiculous

– it's mid-February, for goodness' sake. I decided that, for fifteen minutes, I wouldn't work, or order stuff online, or deal with my to-do list, I would just be, and I'm loving it. I'm losing myself in the latest chick-lit chart-topper in an attempt to harness my inner romantic. You'd think I'd be really romantic as I'm surrounded by brides-to-be and grooms-to-be, but it's not that simple. Even if you were romantic prior to having children, it becomes so much more difficult once you have them. You have to *remember* to be romantic; it doesn't come naturally as everything else takes priority. There's always something else to be done and someone wanting your attention. And, of course, there's the possibility that your husband might be a lying, cheating scumbag.

When Hugo gets up, unusually first, at eight o'clock, I realise I've had both a lie-in – until seven – and an hour with a book. Wow. Imagine if I could do this every day.

He hands me a card featuring lots of love hearts. Rainbow ones, purple ones, pink ones, and pretty much hearts in every colour of metallic pencil he has. I open the card and read: 'Thank you Mummy, for being you, for always helping me and giving me hugs and kisses. I love you Mummy xxx Hugo.'

A lump the size of a tennis ball lodges in my throat and my eyes mist over. I finally choke out, 'That's lovely, darling, thank you,' then give him a bear hug.

I go to the bookcase and take out a card I bought for him, one I think he'll love. It's covered in lambs and reads, 'I Love Ewe'. He laughs. 'Mummy, that's a terrible joke!'

'I know, that's what makes it so funny.'

I play board games with Hugo until Aria and Ronnie get up, and yet again we have to coax Genevieve out of bed. Ronnie plays with the children whilst I shower and then head to the shops, taking Aria with me to buy the missing ingredients for the Valentine's biscuits.

When we return there is much excitement.

'What's going on?' I ask Ronnie as I note the chirpy voices of Hugo and Genevieve coming from the living room.

'You'd better go and see for yourself,' he says, taking the shopping bags from me.

I walk into the living room to find the biggest balloon I have ever seen, in the shape of a heart, tomato red. A love heart weight anchors it to the floor. Next to it is a huge teddy bear which reads 'Please Be Mine'. I am transported back to the early nineties. Ronnie remembered after all. And here was me thinking he wasn't a romantic. Now I feel terrible.

I catch his eye and he smiles. Crossing the room to the gifts, I touch them, marvelling at the thoughtfulness. It's so unlike my husband. He doesn't do gushy. Maybe I got the wrong end of the stick last night.

'Thanks, Ronnie. You really are the best husband.'

Ronnie frowns then after a few seconds, he gives a nervous laugh. 'Oh, no, these aren't from me.'

I wrinkle my brow. 'They're not? Then who sent me them?'

'Eh, Mum, they're not for you; they're for Gen,' says Hugo, his eyes on the floor.

What? Genevieve's twelve. A card half the size of our coffee table takes pride of place beside the fireplace. It's covered in love hearts and has two grey teddy bears with huge smiles hugging each other.

'But where did all this come from? Who sent it?' I ask, gobsmacked.

'Secret admirer,' says Hugo. 'The doorbell rang, and

when I went to answer it, all that stuff was there.'

'Well, someone has certainly gone all out,' I say.

'Any ideas who it's from?' Ronnie asks me.

'None. Did you ask Gen?'

Ronnie nods. 'She doesn't have a clue, or if she does, she isn't telling.'

I take a second to overcome the embarrassment at thinking my twelve-year-old daughter's Valentine gifts were mine.

'I think it's sweet someone has made all that effort for her. And she deserves it. She's gorgeous and clever. Not that I'm biased or anything.'

'Impartial to a fault.' Ronnie grins.

'I wish someone would make that much of a fuss of me.' I realise too late I've spoken out loud.

Ronnie doesn't quite look as if I've slapped him, but the hurt shows on his face and for once I don't feel terrible at being the cause.

'Wendy and the gang are due any minute. She called earlier. Said they'd be half an hour tops. I might make myself scarce if that's OK.' He picks up his car keys from the table.

'As long as you make up for it later.' I know Ronnie won't want to listen to us sisters talking about men and work and housework and menial tasks, but I'm not giving him a free pass without anything in return. I already feel as if I have the term dogsbody tattooed on my forehead. Maybe cuckold, mug and 'the wife's always the last to know' are there too.

'I guarantee it,' he says with a little knowing smile. 'I might take a run up to B&Q. Perhaps we can get the Jack and Jill upgraded once the kitchen is done.'

Now he's talking. That's a productive use of his time

and earns him one brownie point, maybe two.

'See you later then. Remember we're going to the cinema. I'll see if I can get anything out of Gen.'

I get nothing out of Gen. There are clams that open up more than she did when I broached the topic, which makes me hope she isn't hiding something. Do I need to be worried about an older man? Well, I say man, but I mean boy, although really I'm thinking anyone above thirteen or fourteen as she's twelve. And I wouldn't even be happy with her going out with someone of thirteen or fourteen. Twelve max.

She uses the arrival of her cousins and aunt to her advantage and I don't have any other opportunity to quiz her. As soon as her cousins arrive, she directs the little ones into the playroom and offers to do their hair, but I see through her ploy. She's hiding something and I want to know what.

'So, Gen's got an admirer?' Wendy asks, indicating the array of gifts. They are of such gargantuan proportions and occupy such a vast part of the free space in my living room she almost doesn't manage to encompass them with one wave of her hand.

'It would appear so,' I say. 'How about you? No admirers ringing your doorbell and running away?'

'No, and to be honest, if they did, they'd be running away for the wrong reasons,' she says, her hands sweeping down her body.

'C'mon Wendy, you're not overweight. You just need to tone.'

'People have been telling me that my whole life. That's code for "you're fat".'

'Not from your sister it's not.'

'Hmm.' She doesn't appear convinced.

'So, does that mean Brandon didn't get you a present?' I ask.

'A present? He didn't even get me a card. And I bought him an ESPA gift set.'

'To be fair, you bought him that in the three-for-two Christmas event so you could get stuff for yourself,' I remind her.

'It's not the point, it's the thought that counts.'

It's best not to push it.

'And what about you? Did Ronnie get you anything?'

'If he has, he hasn't told me yet. Nor did he say anything about the Hotel Chocolat chocolates I bought him. A thank you wouldn't have gone amiss.' I debate whether to relay my suspicions to Wendy, but don't have the courage.

'These men need a kick up the backside. When are we going to bugger off to Italy for a week and leave them with the kids, see how they cope?'

'Don't tempt me. Nothing against my darlings, but I wouldn't say no to an all-expenses paid trip to Ischia.'

'I'd settle for an overnight in Dumfries at this point.'

I burst out laughing. Wendy can be so dry sometimes. When she's miffed, she is funnier than anyone I know. Her one-liners crack me up. She has a much more serious side and is definitely the more sensible of us three sisters but when she lets her reserve go, she does it in style.

'I think we can probably do better than Dumfries, but I know what you mean. Why don't we see if we can do something spectacular for whichever one of us has the next big birthday?' I suggest.

'That would be you. You're forty in two years' time.'

'Thanks for reminding me.' I raise my eyebrows at my sister. 'Well, the positive is we get to go somewhere. Where do you fancy?'

'Oh, where do I start? Jamaica, Barbados, Saint Lucia, Saint Kitts and Nevis, Bahamas. I could go on.'

I'm sure she could. She rhymed those off in about five seconds.

'Let's do it. I can always do something separately with the family, but why don't me, you and Jo do a girls' trip?'

'Yeah, I'll be allowed to do that,' Wendy says wryly, 'especially when we're already going away to the Lakes for your birthday this year.'

'I'm serious. Tell Brandon it's happening. He has two years to plan cover for the kids.'

'Can you imagine Brandon with four children to look after? In fact, don't, it's giving me palpitations already. But seriously, conjure up the image of Brandon looking after our children all on his own.'

To be honest, I can't. Brandon's a great dad, but he's a bit needy and a little self-absorbed – as far as he's concerned advertising is the centre of the universe. More than once I've wanted to kick him up the proverbial, albeit I love him, for not stepping up enough to help my sister with the kids. He has plenty of downtime but Wendy is frazzled and she works long hours too.

'We'll work something out, and we can train him. And Mum and Dad will help out.'

Wendy hesitates a fraction of a second too long. I know it's tempting her, so I pounce. 'Great, I'll talk to Ronnie and Jo, then I'll work it into conversation when Brandon's around. Easy-peasy. Cup of tea?'

Wendy nods. Cup of tea is code for 'change the subject'.

By the time Wendy and her brood leave, complete with copious amounts of Valentine's biscuits that the kids baked together, I barely manage to feed my lot and have them change their clothes before we need to leave for *Aladdin*.

'Stop pushing me, Hugo,' Genevieve shrieks in the cinema queue.

'Gen, calm down. Hugo, watch where you're going. Learn a little patience. The film will still be there when we get in. Now, who wants pick and mix, who wants a kids' box and who wants nachos?'

My children have very high metabolisms. They can eat whatever they like, then be hungry twenty minutes later. I have no idea where they put it. I'm sure I didn't eat as much as a child. So clearly they need snacks to go into the cinema with, despite having just eaten dinner, and apart from the fact I almost have to remortgage the house to pay for it. There should be a ceiling on how much cinemas can charge for food. It would save us all a fortune.

Finally, we take our seats, right in the middle of the row, after saying, 'Sorry, excuse me,' half a dozen times, clambering, and falling, over backpacks on the floor and narrowly missing upending someone's soft drink. We sit back, relax, well, as much as you can relax when someone is asking you every five minutes to open something for them, or telling you they've spilled their juice, asking if you have wipes or tissues, or saying they need to go to the toilet, or whining for you to take their jacket, they're hot and there's nowhere to put it.

I try to harness the Zen feeling I know will ensue once the film starts, so I concentrate on the many adverts and trailers. I am starting to wish I'd ordered some nachos for myself, and am tempted to steal some of Hugo's, but that's a no-no in our house. You want something, you order it; you don't presume to eat someone else's. Of course we should share, but we don't have to, and we can all get quite territorial about our food – me included. Try to separate me from the last chocolate digestive at your peril, or the last glass of red wine or the last wine gum. In fact, there's quite a list.

I wasn't aware I'd drifted off, but I must have as there's some unappealing drool coming out of the side of my mouth and we appear to be about halfway through the movie. How did that happen? Did my children simply shush the minute the trailers started?

Ronnie appears transfixed by the scene in front of him. I, meanwhile, am transfixed by this vision of peacefulness beside me. Three children, one husband, zero squawking. The only sound emanates from the huge screen in front of us. Now, this is obviously as it should be, but it's so rarely the case that it takes me aback for a second. Did they even notice I was asleep? How long was I asleep? Clearly my mind running amok has taken its toll on me. Aria is cuddled into me, eyes wide, staring at the screen. I take it the movie choice meets with their approval.

On the way home, Aria falls asleep in the car. Ronnie carries her in and takes her up to bed. I shepherd the other two in out of the intense cold. It must have started to snow whilst we were in the cinema and a thick blanket of the white stuff covers the streets. It's ever so pretty but not conducive to stress-free driving. I'm so glad Ronnie drove tonight.

Hugo is yawning his head off, so I convince him if he wants a bedtime story, now is a good time. 'Ronnie, why don't you read with Hugo and I'll put the steaks on?'

'OK, medium rare for me.'

'Seriously? You have to tell me that?' I say a tad sharply. He has the good grace to bow his head. 'Probably not.'

'Indeed. Now, teeth and story.'

'My teeth?' Ronnie asks.

'You're not funny,' is my parting shot before I open the fridge and take out the contents of our meal. Gen wanders in, mobile in hand.

'Did you like seeing *Aladdin* on the big screen?' I ask Gen to make conversation and try to wrench her attention from her phone. I'm aware that soon she will go to her room and do whatever almost-teenagers do of an evening. She has a TV, her iPod, a laptop, a games console and a mobile phone. She will never be lonely or lost for things to do. I'd like to add a bookcase full of books, but although she has that too, she isn't one for settling back with a good book unless prompted.

'Hmm? Yeah, it was OK.'

Don't enthuse too much. 'I remember when you wanted to be Princess Jasmine.' I smile, thinking back. It feels as if that was only a couple of months back not a good few years ago. Time is marching along at a crazy pace and I'm not sure I like it.

'I was only a baby back then,' she retorts.

'Hardly a baby, Gen, you were eight, but yes, you're four years older now.'

She stands straighter, the equivalent of a peacock puffing out its chest to show off its feathers.

'So, I love your teddy bear. Must have cost your admirer a fortune.'

She smiles, a secret smile, laden with intent. It kills me that someone has 'feelings' for my daughter and I don't know who it is. It pains me even more that Gen either doesn't feel she can, or doesn't want to, share their identity with me.

'Yes, I like it. I've named him Cuddles.'

Still a baby at heart. And I'd feel more relaxed about

Cuddles if I knew who had sent him and could be reassured he was twelve like her, but the fact I can't rule out it's someone older worries me.

'Good name,' I say, hoping she'll venture more information, but none is forthcoming. I decide to park my questions for tonight and keep my interrogation for another time.

'Can you tell Dad dinner's ready, please? And if Hugo's story isn't finished, would you mind taking over from Dad so we can eat?' It's already eight thirty and I'm super starving. I'm surprised I haven't keeled over as I've subsisted on very little today. A juicy medium-rare fillet steak in a peppercorn sauce with blue cheese crumbled over, mushrooms on the side and chunky fries will hit the spot.

'Gen's looking after Hugo,' Ronnie says when he comes downstairs. 'She was quite into the idea of doing his story.'

'She always did like Horrid Henry. But I think it's more to do with being able to get away from me.'

'Why, what have you done?' Ronnie's eyebrows knit together.

'I've been quizzing her to see if I can find out more about this admirer, but she has been evasive as hell.'

'Hmm. Look, let's put it to one side for now. You've made us a lovely meal, and we are about to sit and enjoy it on our own, for once, with a good Pinot Noir, so all is good with the world.' Ronnie takes a sip of his wine and tugs me towards him, then kisses me softly on the lips. 'Thanks for cooking dinner, although it's a pity we can't start with dessert.'

What? He's feeling fruity. Where did that come from? Does he think he's on to a promise? Fat chance.

'Hmm,' I say non-committally. Much as I would usually love a bit of action with my beloved husband, nothing, and I mean nothing, will stop me from eating my steak whilst it's warm. I've been salivating the whole time I've been cooking it. And then there's the small matter of his potential infidelity.

We settle down to dinner, an episode of *Masterchef* on in the background to allow us to eat and not need to make conversation. We are too busy enjoying the food. Interestingly, no children have strayed downstairs. Normally they would be down about ten times before settling, but not tonight. Part of me wonders if Ronnie has paid Genevieve to keep them out of the way and under control. Even if we were going to get 'acquainted' it wouldn't be for a while yet. The only way I'd chance that is if I had a lock on the living room and kitchen doors from the inside. With three children in the house the prospect of someone walking in on you at an inopportune moment is high. That's why, when I think about it, I realise we've only had sex once this year. Pity we won't be doing anything about that tonight. My original plan had been to redress that balance, but not after Phonegate. I may as well enjoy this meal and observe the contestants on *Masterchef*, people who actually know what they're doing in a kitchen.

For me, tonight *was* cooking: frying a steak. I did have to cook it; it wasn't as if it was one of those cook-in-the-oven thirty-minute dishes where you genuinely have to do nada, but it wasn't quite Michelin-starred cuisine either. I sip my wine. It really is very nice and it's slipping down easily, too easily. I need more food or I will end up wasted.

We scoff dessert pretty quickly and Ronnie makes coffee whilst I go to check on the kids. They're all asleep. I can't believe it.

A wave of sadness washes over me. I had been so excited at the prospect of a lovely evening, ending in a little romantic time for me and Ronnie, but recent revelations have put the kybosh on that.

I tiptoe downstairs and back into the living room and stop dead. Laid out on the floor are what I can only describe as floorbooks, like Aria has at nursery. A2 size, from the looks of it. They are arranged like clock faces. Each clock face has photos of our children; in fact they have a clock face each. Then I realise that the number of photos matches the age of the child. It's beautiful.

'What's this?' I ask, when I have recovered sufficiently.

'They're tableaux of our children and our life…'

Ronnie points behind him to a clock face that depicts eighteen years – the length of time we have been together.

Genevieve's clock has twelve points, Hugo's eight and Aria's four.

'I took a picture every February, not every Valentine's Day, as I wasn't always here, but the closest day to it, and I thought I'd give it to the kids when they were older, but when I was on the rig this time, I was thinking about how hard it is us being apart, and how sometimes we snipe at each other and barely have time for ourselves and each other. I wanted to remind you of all the good times we've had, and then show you that it can be wonderful too, with the kids, and that we don't need to lose "us" in the process.'

Wow, that was quite the speech from my husband. He usually stops after two sentences. I almost don't know what to say. The ground has been pulled out from under me. So, I do what I always do in difficult situations: I burst into tears.

Chapter Sixteen

Friday 19 February

To-do list
Have Ronnie confirm fitter is still OK to start Wed
Buy new school shoes for Gen and 2 new shirts (long-sleeved) for Hugo
Start clearing kitchen of clutter for work getting done
Get on top of work as won't be able to get much done next week

Ronnie is taking the kids to school. Bear and I are alone and it's bliss. This is when I revel in the solitude. Not even the rain lashing against the windows can dispirit me. I have a lot to get through, but it makes such a difference when you can focus.

I'm seeing Sam and Nicky tonight, yet another positive to Ronnie being around. Whilst he spends some time with the kids, I will have some much-needed adult time, not having to worry about little ears listening, and without being constantly interrupted.

I smile as I recall the beautiful tableau Ronnie prepared for me. I can't believe I thought he was cheating on me. I add another item to my list – *Take black suit to get dry cleaned*. I've adopted Ronnie's word for the present he gave me, and a wave of love for my husband overwhelms me. We have many things to be thankful for, not least our beautiful, clever, sweet children, I think, as I gaze at the photos of my cherubs from age one through until now.

My mobile rings. Back to reality. It's a number I don't recognise.

'Wedded Bliss, this is Louisa.' I listen to the caller, a Dervla Currie, who is looking for a meeting to arrange her wedding stationery. She has some very specific ideas, which is good. We agree to meet next week at a country club a few miles from Bridge of Weir, where she lives. Good. Some more business coming in, or potential business. I give a little fist pump when I come off the phone. It's always a boost when a former client gives your name out. I make a note to thank Mhairi Bramley, whose wedding invitations I designed last year. Word of mouth is key in my business and it costs nothing to be nice.

I trawl the John Lewis website looking for the exact shirts I bought Hugo at the beginning of the school year – slim fit. The regular ones were about twice the width of him. Pop in basket, checkout, done. Tick.

Time for the messages.

Ronnie: *Have nipped into Sainsbury's for breakfast. Will get what we need when I'm here. Did you say something earlier about me talking to the kitchen guys?*

I love my husband and he's a wonderful father, but sometimes he's as bad as the kids. How many times do you have to tell men something?

Yes, you were to phone the fitter to make sure they were definitely OK to start on Wednesday, you know, the day you abandon me to deal with it all x

I move on to the next. Nicky.

Is Khubla's booked for seven or half past? I'll be

dropping Xander at Sebastian's around five. Thx x

I tap out: *Seven – they need the table back by nine. Don't be late!*

Jo next. *Have you heard from Mum and Dad? I've dropped in on them twice in the past few days, but they've not been in and I can't get them on the phone. Did they say anything to you?*

I rack my brain for a reason my parents would be out of touch. Nope. I tell my sister as much then worry, so I try to ring them myself. Mum's phone goes to voicemail. Dad's is off. I call the landline. It rings out. Strange. I'll try again later.

'Only me!' Ronnie plonks four bags of shopping on the kitchen floor and envelops me in a bear hug, smooching me in a mock-Heathcliff way. I wonder what the bits and pieces are that he's bought, bearing in mind he's only here for another few days and also soon I won't have a kitchen to cook in for a week.

'I'm just on my way out. I thought you'd be back ages ago.'

'Aw, not even a little bit of canoodling time on the sofa?'

'Ronnie, it's quarter to eleven. And it's not that I wouldn't like a nice snog on the couch, but I do have a company to run and clients to meet.'

Ronnie sticks his lip out like a petulant three-year-old and I can't help but smile.

I sidle over to him and say, 'One snog. That's it.'

Half an hour later, more than a little dishevelled, I open the living room blinds. I love my husband.

My day flies by. Thank goodness Ronnie is around to pick up the kids and do the home front stuff as my phone does not stop ringing, I hold an impromptu meeting when a client doesn't turn up, only for the client to arrive over an hour late, with no apology. So when I reach home, I take my fill of cuddles and then go and have a bath before going out with the girls.

It has been far too long.

Whilst I'm casting about for something to wear and realising that I may have to go on a diet as everything is tight, my phone rings. Nicky.

'Hey, Nic. All set for our big night out?'

Silence.

She must have poor reception. 'Nic, can you hear me?' Then I hear her, a gulp, a sob, and then a string of expletives, all directed at her ex-fiancé.

'Nic, calm down. What's happened?' I hear cars go past on her end of the phone. She's outside.

'Sebastian…Sebastian cancelled. He's going to the theatre.'

'Cancelled? On Xander?'

'Yep. He's absolutely gutted. I hate that man, I hate him, I hate him.' She bursts into tears.

'Hey, hey, it's OK. Never mind him. We all know he's an ass.' I don't think I've ever uttered a truer sentence. 'Do you want to bring Xander round to mine, or do you want me to come round?'

I don't imagine she'd want to go out even if Ronnie would look after Xander. She sounds in a right state.

'Thanks, but no. Xander has locked himself in his room and won't come out. Says it's all my fault as his dad wouldn't have moved out if it wasn't for me arguing with him.' She sobs again.

Ouch. 'Nic, you know he doesn't mean it. He's just upset and hurting. You mean the world to Xander, and he

150

to you.'

'I know, I do. Sorry. Why is my life such a mess? I can't even go out for a night with my friends. I wonder if he did it intentionally because he knew I was going out. He doesn't want me, but he doesn't want me to be happy either.' Another sob.

I wouldn't put it past him. Sebastian really is that low, and he's all about control.

'Nic, you don't know that, but even if it was the case, don't give him the satisfaction. What I suggest is, you go and offer to play on the Xbox with Xander, or do something you know he'll really enjoy, then order in a takeaway. Spend some time together. Xander will be fine. Our kids are a lot more resilient than we give them credit for.'

Nicky sniffs. 'That's a good idea, Lou. I'm sorry about tonight.'

'Don't be silly. We'll rearrange for another time. You have other things to think about.'

'Would you mind telling Sam? I don't think I can go through explaining all that again tonight. Plus I really should go check on Xander again.'

'No problem. Text me later and chin up.'

'Thanks, Lou, you always know the right thing to say.'

'Love you. Give Xander a hug from me.'

'I will. Bye.'

When I hang up, the rage must show on my face as Ronnie walks into the room and stops dead. 'Are you OK?'

'I will be.' I fill him in on Nicky's feckless ex. Ronnie hugs me to him and I am so glad I married this man.

'C'mon. Let's get you a glass of wine.' He kisses my hand and I follow him downstairs.

Wine glass in hand, I try Mum's mobile again. It's ringing. I'm about to press the end call button when Mum answers.

'Hi, Louisa. How are you?' She sounds a bit breathless.

'Hi, Mum. What are you up to?'

'Oh, just keeping busy, you know.'

I do, but Mum sounds evasive. Should I be worried? 'Where are you, Mum?'

There's a pause before she says, 'We're actually out for dinner with friends.'

Friends? Mum and Dad don't really go out for dinner, except with us, and although this may seem strange to some people, never without telling us; that's how close-knit our family is. Everybody knows everyone else's business.

'Which friends?' I ask before I can stop myself.

Again Mum hesitates. 'Oh, Theo and Barbara. You don't know them.'

What is Mum hiding? 'OK. Well, have fun, and Mum?'

'Yes?' comes her strangled reply.

'Call Jo and Wendy. They've been trying to get in touch with you for days.'

'Oh-h-h, I will. Must dash. Love you.'

I'm about to say that I love her, too, but she has hung up.

I can safely say that was one of the strangest conversations I've ever had with my mother.

Shaking my head, I sit down at the table and tap out a message to my sisters. *Mum and Dad are fine. They're out for dinner with friends. They've just been busy x*

When I wander through to the living room, the kids are delighted to discover I am no longer going out, although I don't tell them why. Whilst they pile on top of me so we can all watch Luca, my thoughts return to Nicky. I exchange messages with Sam and tell her what's happened and that we will sort out a new date. How I wish I could sort out Sebastian.

Chapter Seventeen

Wednesday 24 February

To-do list
Download passport application form
Order laundry pen for us and electric blanket for Dad

'Bye, sweetheart.'

I am vaguely aware of Ronnie kissing my cheek. I roll over towards him. No matter that we have done this routine a thousand times, I still feel bereft at the knowledge he's leaving for the rig for his two-week stint.

I snake a hand around his neck, then the other one joins it. If I am losing my husband for two weeks again, I want a proper kiss, something to remind him of home whilst he's gone.

After a minute, Ronnie says, 'I really need to go. The flight's at half six.'

Sometimes I think it would be quicker for Ronnie to drive to Aberdeen, and he does sometimes, but usually he flies from Glasgow Airport. His bosses want him fresh when he arrives. The helicopter taking him out to the rig is scheduled for late morning.

'Hope it goes well with the kitchen. I'll text you when I get on-site.' His lips brush my cheek, and I am reluctant to let go of his hand.

'Yeah, thanks for that,' I joke.

'You're welcome.'

I am a tiny bit nervous about the kitchen work starting today, although I have prepared everything for the workmen and the house is full of boxes upon boxes of things I've packed away. It's now difficult to move in any of the rooms, as they're crammed full of kitchen stuff. Thank goodness we have a decent-sized house, otherwise it would be torture. At least it's only for five days.

We finally plumped for the company who had transformed a friend's kitchen. Always better to go off a recommendation, I find. We had to wait a good while for them to be able to fit us in, but now Owen and his merry men are due at nine fifteen, to give me time to return from the school run. Ronnie's friend had said they were clean, reliable, trustworthy and did a good job, all of which are important attributes for me. Plus, since they are honest, I can leave them a key and they can lock up if they finish for the day when I'm not home. And I am not planning to be home much, at least not with the kids. Too much mess.

Let them clean all the dust and stoor away whilst we're out. It will be challenging enough not having a kitchen for five days, although I have stocked up on takeaway menus – not that that covers all the bases as Aria will only eat boiled rice from the Chinese, nothing else, and the kids don't like Indian food, so pizza may well dominate our choices.

I turn the alarm clock towards me – five thirty. Ugh! I only have another half an hour to sleep. Should I get up? I have a lot to do. Sod it, I'm too tired.

The alarm shrills. Yes, I still have one of those old-fashioned ones with the jingly-jangly bells on top. Fortunately, my kids would sleep through a tornado. Six o'clock. I do not want to get up. I am always the same the day Ronnie leaves. I think it's part dread, part realisation, part my sleep being interrupted by his departure.

Right, no more procrastinating. A shower will sort me out.

I stand under the welcome jets of piping hot water, letting them wash away my sluggishness. With the fitters coming this morning and the school and nursery runs to do myself today, as well as a mountain of work to complete, I need to be on my game. Caffeine is required, and lots of it.

Downstairs, I ruffle Bear's silky coat and make a fuss of him. He's adorable and I love him, but I don't relish having to take him out for the toilet when I haven't even had a sip of coffee. He's giving me that intent, expectant look, then he jumps up at me, wagging his tail so hard I feel it will either fall off or he will take off from the momentum he's producing.

I sigh. Guess I am taking him out first.

When I finally sit down with my coffee, I can't even face the to-do list. I need ten minutes to myself. I plug in my headphones and listen to the latest Milly Johnson audiobook. She always makes me laugh. Light-hearted and upbeat, that's what I need.

Ten minutes later I am loth to break my stride but I know I must. The final items need to be tidied away for the kitchen fitters coming and I won't be able to use the kitchen sink, or possibly any water, I realise, whilst they are replacing the kitchen. I make a mental note to ask them about that. Kind of important since I am working from home.

Aria's backpack is ready, complete with dance shoes, as the nursery has started dance classes as an extracurricular activity. Hugo's bag has the right PE kit in it, although I haven't been able to find his rain jacket. I bet he left it at school last week. That's me just noticing. Bother. We'll never see that again.

Time to wake the cherubs. Thank goodness I had the foresight to bath the younger two last night. Gen, like me, prefers a daily morning shower, eschewing the bath at all costs. I'd love a bath, and could be doing with a pampering soak, but eight minutes does not a spa day make.

I lean forward to kiss Gen goodbye after pulling the car into the drop-off zone, having made it in time for the bell by a hair's breadth, but she already has her seat belt off and the car door open. A smile flickers on her lips.

'Bye, Mum!' And she's gone, bouncing along the pavement like a newborn lamb. Something makes me delay my departure. As she turns in at the school gate, a boy, almost a head taller than her, catches her up. His face lights up, breaking into a broad smile when she speaks to him. I wish I could hear what she's saying.

Is this who sent the Valentine's card, and the presents? The horn of the car behind startles me out of my reverie and I reluctantly move off from the drop-off zone.

On my way back from school, I listen to the radio and sing along, out of tune, but who cares? I stop at the red light and am tapping my fingers in time with the music when I hear a crunch and I'm thrown forward against my steering wheel. Ow, that hurt. What the…?

Horns blaze around me. I look in my rear-view mirror and a confused-looking elderly gentleman is peering through the windscreen of the car behind me. I open my door, ensuring I am not putting myself at risk from the traffic, and walk towards his car, glancing back at mine to see the bumper hanging down and one of the lights smashed. I could scream; I don't have time for this. I quell my annoyance as I approach the other car. The man looks about eighty, or ninety. He seems so distressed, I soften.

'Are you OK?'

'Yes, I think so, dear. I'm sorry about your car. I think I hit the accelerator instead of the brake. Never done that before.'

'Well, as long as you're OK and you feel fine to drive.'

He doesn't reply, so I continue. 'We'll need to exchange insurance details.'

'What's that you say, dear? I'm a bit deaf.' He points to the hearing aid in his left ear. I then see he also has one in his right.

Suppressing a sigh, I say, 'We need to exchange details.' When he looks at me blankly, I say, 'For the insurance companies.'

'Insurance?' He says it as if it's an alien concept to him.

'Yes, your car insurance. Who's your car insured with?'

'Oh, I wouldn't know a thing like that, dear. My wife dealt with all that sort of thing.'

I note his usage of the past tense and proceed cautiously. 'So who takes care of your insurance now?'

'I assume it's still going.'

My heart drops. Please tell me he's insured. Poor old soul. He's clearly lost without his wife.

'Would anyone else know? Do you have children?' His jaw is trembling. Hard to know if this is accident related or not. 'Is there someone I can call? I'm not happy you just driving away in case you *have* hurt yourself.'

The old man gives it some thought, then says, 'I suppose we could call Valentin.'

'And Valentin's your son, is he?'

'No, my grandson. My son's dead.'

'I'm sorry to hear that.'

He waves a hand at me. 'Long time ago. Gulf War.'

'Sorry, I haven't asked your name.'

'Kingston, Kingston Pendragon. Pleased to meet you...'

'Louisa,' I say as I think what a fabulous name he has.

Kingston rings his grandson, whilst I surreptitiously survey the damage to my car. If Ronnie were on the mainland, I would have let him know. As it stands, there's no point telling anyone at the moment. Oh wait, apart from the fitters. I look at my watch. Nine thirty. Conscious of the fact the fitters were due fifteen minutes ago, I fire off a quick text, explaining what has happened and that I will be there as soon as I can.

'Valentin, it's Grandfather.'

He sounds so posh. Who calls their grandad 'grandfather' any more? Who has done for the past few generations? I glance at the car that has hit me – it's a Jaguar. More than that I don't know, but I can see the emblem at the front of the bonnet.

Kingston mumbles a few more sentences to Valentin and then says, 'Louisa, my grandson wishes to speak with you.'

I'm surprised but take the phone he hands me.

'Hello?'

'Louisa, hi, this is Valentin.' His tone is sensuous, although the subject matter isn't. 'I'm sorry my grandfather ran into you, and I'll be there shortly with a friend to drive his car back as I don't want him driving. He gets confused sometimes. This may be the last time he's allowed to drive, to be honest. We've been trying to dissuade him for months, but no joy.'

My heart goes out to Kingston. He'll lose his independence. What a shame. I remember how my own grandfather felt when his licence was revoked. He was in a bad mood for months and became a nightmare of a back-seat driver with us instead, which riled us all no end.

I'm vaguely aware Valentin is still speaking.

'I'm sorry to ask this, but could you possibly stay with him until we get there? We'll be twenty minutes tops.'

I hesitate, but only for an instant. I know I have fitters coming but my conscience wouldn't let me leave Kingston here alone even if I wanted to.

'That's fine, Valentin. He seems unhurt,' I add to reassure him.

'That's good, but at his age, I'd rather have him checked out.'

He's probably right.

Kingston and I chat whilst we wait for Valentin to arrive. He's a very interesting old man. He tells me all about his grandchildren and great-grandchildren. Valentin's brother apparently has three boys, but it's clear Kingston has a stronger relationship with Valentin than with his brother Rufus.

The time passes quickly and soon a gunmetal grey Porsche parks up behind us. Two men get out; one is wearing designer sunglasses and is well over six feet tall with floppy black hair and a disarming smile, the other is considerably shorter with short blonde hair and piercing blue eyes. His black leather jacket hangs big on him as if he has lost weight.

Valentin, because it's clear designer boy is Valentin, shoots me an incredibly sexy smile, by default I'm sure, not choice.

'Louisa, thanks so much for looking after Grandfather for me.'

'My pleasure,' I say, smiling back, glancing at Kingston,

who winks at me.

Valentin pops his head inside the car. 'Grandfather, what scrapes have you been getting into this time?' His admonishment is good-natured but Valentin's disapproval is also clear, and his concern for his grandfather is palpable.

'I'll drive you back. Preston will take my car. Let me sort the insurance out with Louisa first and then we'll head back home.'

Kingston grasps Valentin's hand in his and kisses it. 'Thank you, my dear boy.'

'Right, Louisa, here's the insurance details and my address. I deal with all of Grandfather's correspondence now. He should have had a copy of the details in the car. That was remiss of me. I'll put that in today. If you give me your information, I'll put it into my phone.' He takes out his phone and taps my name, address, registration number, insurer and policy number into it.

When we're done, I turn to his grandfather again. 'Kingston, it was lovely to meet you, although it might have been better under different circumstances. You stay safe now. Thanks, Valentin.' I nod to Preston.

I arrive home, flustered, over an hour late, expecting to apologise to, if not irate, at the least, narked fitters. Our driveway is conspicuously empty. I know Ronnie told the fitters to park in the drive so we wouldn't get any gossip from the neighbours about vans blocking the road and limiting visibility going over the speed bumps. He also told them his car wouldn't be there, so they wouldn't be inconveniencing him, but there's no one here. Strange. I go indoors to see if they have popped a note through the door saying they had come at nine thirty, I hadn't been in and they'd nipped round the corner for a roll and sausage and would be back shortly. Nothing.

I take my phone out to see if they've texted me back. Nope. Oh well, I'll get on with some work whilst I wait for them.

I look at my lists.

Work

Order glossy, matte, metallic and cross-hatch card

Check with James Simpson's the status of the vellum invitations for the Jenner wedding

Chase up quotes did for McNally and Gladstone weddings

Banking

Home

Renew breakdown cover – compare prices as much higher than last year

Double-check next taekwondo grading and answer instructor's letter about the direct debit being rejected

Call credit card company about new card as mine no longer swipes

Wendy/Jo/Mum/Nicky re dinner (possibly)

As I dial the insurance company's number I realise it hadn't even occurred to me that I might not be able to drive the car, but fortunately it was driveable. I need to arrange a courtesy car, though, so I don't get pulled over by the police – my broken light will attract attention and the bumper is, well, bumping along. I can tie it up with a piece of string, I suppose, but it would be better if I could get a courtesy car before I do the school pickup. Not sure how likely that is.

Fortunately, my insurance company are very helpful and promise to have me a car by two thirty. I pay extra to have a car I don't need to shoehorn the kids into. I've never had a courtesy car. I had assumed the company would give me a car similar to my own, at least in size. I don't think a Fiat 500 is going to cut it. So I pay for a VW Golf. I feel a lot calmer now I've sorted the car situation.

Time to crack on again. An hour later, I've ticked off a few items on my list, hurrah, and am feeling a little pleased with myself, when I realise I still haven't heard from the fitters. I'll send them another text. That's not as pushy as a phone call, is it? But they are almost two and a half hours late, on the first day of the job. Surely they haven't forgotten? I'm not being unreasonable, I don't think, chasing them up.

Text sent, I call the credit card company, who promise to send me a new card forthwith. I then have another look at my work email and see with despair and not a little sadness that the Stevenson wedding is no longer going ahead. A parting of ways.

What a shame. I feel much sadder for the couple than at the loss of income. All the same, the wedding was in twelve weeks' time and their stationery is expected back any day from the specialist printer.

I reply to the Stevensons (well, they won't be now, will they?) telling them I'm sorry to hear that, and yes, I will cancel their order. They were very apologetic. I'm sure they have bigger things to think about now. All that money on the venue, the dress, the entertainment, all their friends to tell. I'm glad I only provide the invitations and wasn't their wedding planner.

I know I need to work out how much I have lost on the Stevenson job, but can't bear to do it now as I don't want it to ruin my positive vibe. However, I do still have to contact the printer – I know in my bones it's too late to stop the print job, but I have to try.

That wasn't a fun call. Lots of expletives used. My

printer is lovely but treats me like the sister he never had, so as a side effect, I get the full extent of his displeasure down the phone. The job was set up yesterday and is currently being boxed, every last part of it. What a waste.

James calmed down in the end and apologised. He told me he was only annoyed as they are under pressure and could have done with freeing up the time spent on this job if they'd only known. By the time I rang off, he had offered me a ten per cent discount, as I am such a good customer. So at least I am not completely out of pocket.

I tackle my WhatsApps next.

Wendy: *Hi, sis. Do you want to bring the cherubs here for dinner tonight since you don't have a kitchen? There's always plenty grub spare here as you know x*

That does sound like a plan, although my kitchen is still unexpectedly intact. What time is it? Five to twelve. Where on earth are the kitchen fitters? My hackles rise; I am a stickler for punctuality. I ring them.

'Hi, Owen?'

'Aye, that's me,' a voice replies.

'It's Louisa Halliday.'

'Oh, I meant to ring you.'

'Sorry?'

'Yeah, the units haven't come in yet.'

I clench my fist that isn't holding the phone. 'So didn't you think it might be helpful to tell me that before I emptied my entire kitchen?'

'Well, I was still hopeful we'd get them in on time.'

'So when are the units coming?' I hold my breath. Please say soon.

'Not sure yet. Maybe Friday.'

'Friday!'

'Latest, next week.'

'Please tell me you're joking. I've planned everything round this kitchen being put in this week. You're supposed to be finished by Tuesday.'

'Yeah, unfortunately some things are out of our hands.'

'But picking up the phone to let me know isn't.'

'Sorry, it was on my list to do.'

'Do you think in future you could let me know if there's a major change of plan?' I'm trying and failing to keep my cool. My voice is just the right side of high-pitched.

'Will do.'

'In fact, can you make sure you call me back tomorrow, with a further update?'

'Of course.'

I end the call, frustrated. Why would anyone think that was OK? How can he run a business like that? I was expecting him to start work here three hours ago. So much for relying on recommendations. Surely they must have known they couldn't begin work today? If the units weren't in yesterday, they were hardly going to be here for the start of business today when Owen and his crew were meant to begin my job.

My thoughts turn to Wendy's message. We do still have a kitchen but everything is packed away.

Hi, Wendy. Long story short, yes, can we come to you for food as I am scunnered x

The doorbell goes. I glance outside and see the familiar Europcar van with second driver to drive his colleague back. I walk around the Golf the man has brought for me, checking it for scrapes and scratches, but deem it OK. We're getting a bit close to pickup time, so I sign the agreement and thank them before dashing inside, picking up the treats and juices for Aria and the kids and hoofing it to the nursery. I say, hoof, it's more of a ten-miles-under-the-speed-limit dash. New cars make me nervous, particularly new cars that don't belong to me. I've never subscribed to this mindset of a car is a car. Yes, it is, but they are all different, and it takes me a little while to get used to one: the biting point, where the windscreen wipers are, which side the indicators are on, and God forbid if it's foggy. I'm not even sure I know where the fog lights are on my own car.

'Mummy!' Aria throws herself at me when I wave to her from the door of the nursery. I hug her to me, breathing in the lingering strawberry scent of her shampoo. The smell of young children, clean ones, should be bottled so their parents can hold onto it forever.

I hold her away from me so I can focus on her. 'Hi, sweetheart. Did you have a good day?'

'Yes, I made four cakes, and iced them all by myself, and I learned new words in Spanish and we went to the forest and toasted marshmallows and made a den.'

I'm tired just listening to her. Why was my nursery never as fun as that? Whilst Aria prattles on, I help her change her shoes and put her jacket on. Now I have my girl all to myself again. I sometimes feel Aria missed out, as when she came along, I already had two others who needed me, too, making demands on my time, so to have a little Mummy/girl time with her is always a bonus.

Aria and I arrive at Ferniehall Primary with minutes to spare. Thank goodness the traffic was light. There always seems to be some kind of roadworks to hold us up. At least Hugo is old enough to wait for me, which frees me from anxiety.

'Mummy!' Hugo spots me as I get out of the car and runs towards me. I envelop my lovely boy in an Olaf-type hug. He is in no hurry to let go and nor am I. I kiss his head before he jumps into the car and we set off for Hamwell to pick Gen up, Hugo chatting away about his day as we do so.

I beep the horn at Gen, but she doesn't see me. Then I remember I'm driving a different car, so get out and wave to her.

She crosses the road. 'Where's our car?'

'Someone hit me on the way back from school this morning. This is our courtesy car.'

Gen's face creases with concern. 'Are you OK? You weren't hurt, were you?'

'No, I'm fine,' I reassure her. 'But the car is a bit dented.'

'That's terrible, Mum, although at least you're OK.' Gen shakes her head. 'What happened?'

'An old man drove into the back of me. He was sweet actually. We had a good chat whilst we waited for his grandson to come and collect him.'

Gen looks at me as if I have horns. 'You waited with him, even though he hit you?'

'Yes, darling, he was very confused.'

'Should he have been driving then?'

'Not sure, to be honest. Anyway, how was your day?'

'Fine.' We are back to monosyllabic Gen then. Fabulous.

On the drive to Wendy's, the rain lashes the windscreen without letting up. Kind of apt given the day I've had. I also have a feeling of déjà vu as I retrace the road I took from the nursery to the schools. Pity Aria needed picked up first; I could have avoided driving to Lymeburn twice. I haven't told the children yet that the kitchen remains untouched, I've simply said we are going to Aunt Wendy's for dinner, which was met with a round of cheers. They love their aunt and their cousins. Fortunately, Wendy lives nearby, in Lymeburn. They see her and her brood more than they see Jo's lot as they live an hour away.

Even the dash from the car to Wendy's nineteenth-century sandstone villa has been enough to drench us, despite us putting up our hoods. We are all soaked through from the ends of our jackets to the tips of our toes. We ring the bell, once, twice, three times. Hurry up, Wendy, I plead.

My sister opens the door and gasps at the bedraggled bunch in front of her.

'In you come. I hadn't realised the weather was so bad. It was only spitting when I got back.'

We take off our jackets and Wendy hangs them on the airer in the laundry room. Once the kids have washed their hands, Wendy sends them through to the kitchen to see their cousins, where she has already prepared a lavish spread for them, like an indoor picnic. My sister excels at organising and entertaining.

She switches on her Nespresso machine and without even asking – she knows me too well – she makes me a cappuccino and brings out the Kit Kats.

'Is that a new car?' she asks.

'Courtesy car,' I manage whilst trying to swallow a piece of biscuit.

'Is your car getting a service? It was in for its MOT recently, was it not?' Wendy says.

'No, not a service. Someone hit me this morning on the way back from school.'

'You're joking!'

'Nope. 'Fraid not.'

'Are you OK? You could have whiplash.' Wendy places her hand on my arm.

'No, I'm fine. I was stationary at the time.'

'So what happened?'

I smile and say, 'I met Kingston.'

'Kingston?' Wendy raises an eyebrow.

'Yes, Kingston Pendragon, a lovely, sweet old man who was a bit befuddled. His wife died recently and he seemed so…lost.'

Wendy clucks. 'Are you sure he wasn't pulling a fast one?'

'No, for once it was legit. He called his grandson, who asked me if I could please wait with him until he and a friend came to collect his grandfather and pick up his car. I get the feeling his licence may be revoked.'

'Should be too, if he's a danger on the road.'

'There are far more dangerous drivers on the road than the elderly.'

'Good point. So what's happening now?' Wendy bites into a Kit Kat, her second, not that I am keeping tabs. I simply want to make sure there is another one for me.

'It will go through the insurance. I called earlier. His grandson Valentin gave me the details when he picked him up.'

'Valentin? What a fabulous, dreamy name.'

'Not half as dreamy as the man himself, if I were unmarried and ten years younger.'

'Ooh, pray tell.' Wendy rubs her hands together and leans forward.

'Mummy, I've done a soft poo,' comes a shout from the downstairs bathroom.

I'm glad it isn't Aria.

'Coming, Mols,' calls my sister. 'Sorry, sis, duty calls. If it's not one arse I'm wiping it's another,' she says, grimacing.

Whilst Wendy deals with Mollie, I check my messages

and emails, which are piling up.

Drat, I forgot to pick up Hugo's prescription. I'll need to add it on tomorrow's list.

Wendy interrupts my manic train of thought by re-entering the kitchen, glancing at my empty cup and fetching two wine glasses and a bottle of wine.

'I'm driving,' I remind her.

'It's posh juice, not wine. Do you honestly think I would give you wine?'

Actually, no. There's no one more sensible than my sister. And all mums are programmed to never even have one drink and drive.

Wendy sits down, breathes in deeply and exhales. 'That's better.' She picks up her 'posh juice', clinks her glass with mine and says, 'Cheers.' After taking a sip, she puts her glass down and stretches. 'So, tell me, what did you think of the fitters? Have they done much yet?'

Ah. 'Not much.'

'Oh, how so?'

'Well…'

When I've finished telling Wendy, her jaw is hanging open. 'You're kidding, right? That's ridiculous. If they haven't sorted it by tomorrow, you give me their number, and I'll get it done.'

I have no doubt that she would. My sister is indomitable when she wants to be.

'Let's see what tomorrow brings,' I say, in an attempt to calm her a little. I've had enough adventure for one day.

Chapter Eighteen

Thursday 25 February

To-do list
Ironing – it has spiralled out of control again
Feather duster
Athlete's foot cream (special request from Ronnie)
Packed lunch food
Arrange smear test – got letter in
Reply to wedding invitation – check with Ronnie if he
wants to go
Tyre check at petrol station – think may have slow puncture.
Can't get the warning light to go off and even though my
information panel tells me it's fine, I don't trust it. It's not
my car.

'I'm afraid the units won't be in until Tuesday,' Owen tells
me. At least this time his words are tinged with regret.

'Tuesday? You can't be serious. That will be almost a
week late!'

'My hands are tied. I'm at the mercy of the supplier too,
you know.'

He says it as if he's the one who is being hugely
inconvenienced. I understand that it may screw with his
schedule a little, and he will have to juggle a few things,

move jobs around to accommodate new commit dates, but is his kitchen packed in boxes, with nothing visible apart from the white, or in our case silver, goods? Somehow I don't think so.

I'm about to ask him what I am supposed to do, but stop myself in time. What's the point? He's right: if the units don't arrive, there's nothing he can do. The problem is, he should have made sure they would arrive in time, and he should have ensured the delivery was on track or told me in advance so I didn't pack up my damned kitchen a week early.

More upheaval. And then, when will they finish? That's if the units do arrive Tuesday. And where are they arriving? My house? The fitter's premises? The UK warehouse of the company that makes them? The docks? It's all a bit too vague for my liking. I dampen down my frustration and manage a relatively calm, 'Let me know as soon as there's any news.'

One thing's for sure, he won't be getting a tip. I always tip tradesmen, but the only one he will be getting from me is how to improve his customer service. Let's hope his workmanship is better than his logistics and organisational abilities.

I'm glad the kids are already at school and nursery as I come off the phone and let loose a stream of invective that would make a sailor blush.

Today's list starts with half of yesterday's, given the crash and the chasing of the kitchen fitters. I need to tackle these work emails and tasks first though. I swig from yesterday's bottle of sparkling water, shrink back at the taste of the flat, lukewarm water, and decide needs must for the moment. I've no time to go get another one as I must crack on.

I call James Simpson and ask for an update on the Ferris wedding invites. I received them three weeks ago, but I noticed that the foil hadn't printed through properly on one of the corners, and it didn't look very professional. James said he'd have a word with quality control and ensure it didn't happen again, but I had expected the job to be marked as urgent, to minimise the delay to the client, yet the invitation suite hasn't materialised so far. Turns out the job is next one up, tomorrow, and then it should only be two more days before the invites are with me. I really hope James isn't crossing his fingers behind his back, or fobbing me off, as I know the Ferrises really wanted to send their invites out last week. I am sick of apologising for other people's mistakes and delays. When I think about that now, I reflect on Owen and my kitchen units, shake my head and convince myself it's not the same thing.

My phone pings. Nicky. Oh, a little respite. I know I should keep working and going through this list, but I haven't spoken to her in a few days, and she was on my to-do list too.

When are we meeting up?

I type back. *Come round tonight and we can have a takeaway. My kitchen won't be started until Tuesday.*

That's terrible – about the kitchen. Sure to takeaway. Don't need to ask twice. The wee man will be thrilled too.

I smile at that. Our kids do get on well, which I am very grateful for.

Good. Something positive. Now back to work. The banking. I haven't done that for almost a week. Keeping on top of everything is becoming harder and harder. I then navigate to the site I use for laser-cut invitations and order, in cream organza, the eighty day invitations, sixty evening invitations, RSVPs and menus for the Hope wedding. I loved their choice. It's something that, had it been available when we were married, I might have opted for myself. I might have chosen the venue too, Thirlestane Castle, with its marquee in the Rose Garden.

A weight lifts from my shoulders each time I tick off a task. I open my email and refamiliarise myself with the details of the McNally quote I did – something I should be able to do at home. Not a high earner, but steady bread-and-butter work. Lovely couple, young, madly in love. Not everyone I see in my line of work is, you know. You'd think they would be, but sometimes it's people who by the time they have reached the ordering the invitations stage are rather more disillusioned with each other than they were when they first got engaged.

I fire off emails to both the McNallys and the Gladstones, asking if they would like to receive samples of any of the invitations we discussed or meet for a second chat. It's all I can do until they are ready to make a commitment. Some couples choose to wait until three or four months before they marry to order their invitations, whereas most do it between six to nine months in advance. The Gladstones are set to marry in September, so have seven months, whereas the McNallys have set a date of the twenty-second of June, so they really need to get a wriggle on.

My mobile rings. It's one of the clients whose email I haven't reached yet. Melissa Duggan. She wants to know if she can have some samples by the weekend. Lord knows how I will manage that, but since she has family over from Canada, who are leaving again on Monday, I promise to pop her something in the post. It will need to go first class later.

I scribble myself a note and carry on. Ah, the taekwondo. Do you know what, rather than phone about it, I will sort it out tomorrow when I take Hugo to his lesson.

Deciding I need a caffeine hit before I do anything else, and perhaps a sandwich, I rustle up a cheese toastie and sit back downstairs checking my list. I will do the work stuff once I've finished eating. Bear, of course, tries to muscle in on my lunch, and even though I gave him a dental stick before I started eating, he still sits in front of me, ears raised, tail wagging and bashing off the floor until it reaches a crescendo of hope. This dog's puppy eyes are too good. I tell Bear to follow me, then drop a piece of my toastie into his bowl.

I could really do with a nap, as I haven't been sleeping well, even a ten-minute power one would help, but right now, I have more pressing matters. Those samples. From the various boxes in my office, I put together a package for Melissa Duggan, slip in a compliments card and wrap it in a bow, before sealing it in a box, ready to be taken to the post office on the way to do the school pickup. I need to leave in the next five minutes or I'll be late.

Fortunately, the school pickups go without a hitch; however, we've only been home from school fifteen minutes when the doorbell goes.

'Nicky!' I throw my arms around my friend and kiss her cheek. She is equally exuberant. It has been ages since we saw each other, but it feels even longer. Xander gives me a brief hello and then disappears into the playroom to find Hugo, who is playing on his Xbox.

I put the kettle on and Nicky slumps down on the sofa.

'Hard day?' I ask as I spoon coffee and sweetener into cups for us.

'Something like that. Cancelled wedding.'

'What is it with everyone at the minute? Has there been

175

a full moon recently? I had a cancellation the other day.'

'Well, this one was unavoidable. The groom was killed in a hit-and-run.'

'Oh my God!' My hand flies to my mouth. 'That's terrible.'

'Yeah, the bride told me by email. She apologised but said she was still too in shock to speak on the phone, which I completely understood.'

I nod, then shake my head at the senseless death of a young man, due to someone's dangerous and cowardly actions. I shiver and then try to turn the conversation to something more positive.

'Quite a few more quotes have come in this week, plus three requests today for meetings.'

Nicky accepts the coffee I hand her, takes a sip then says, 'I've had to turn work away this week. Same day as another wedding I already have arranged. Pity, as it's a big one, three hundred guests. I think I would have been in action all day, from the sounds of it, and it would certainly have been more lucrative, but I'm looking forward to the wedding I'm doing the photos for that day – it's at Alnwick Castle.'

'Where Harry Potter was filmed?'

'Yep. We always talked about taking the kids there, but we never have.'

'I know. Hugo mentioned it again a few weeks ago, and even Gen, albeit she wouldn't be caught dead saying so, would love to visit it.'

'Well, here's a crazy idea…'

'What?' I look at Nicky, seeing the glint in her eye. I know that sign. She's scheming something.

'Well, if you aren't doing anything the weekend of the eleventh of November why don't you come down with me and we can all stay over? I'd only be working one day. We could all go the next.'

I don't know off the top of my head if we're free that weekend. With a family like ours, there's always something going on or being planned, but I mull the idea over in my head. It would mean I could look after Xander for Nicky – he's never any problem. He and Gen could help with Hugo and Aria. It's definitely doable, if I'm free. Even if Ronnie's home, I'm sure he'd be happy to have the weekend to himself. And Mum would take Bear. Bear has no shortage of willing volunteers to care for him. He is such a softie, he melts the heart of anyone he meets.

'It could work,' I say tentatively. 'Let me look at the dates to make sure I'm not double-booking myself.'

'No problem. Anyway, tell me about this kitchen.'

I fill Nicky in on the non-existent progress.

'That's ridiculous. Couldn't they have told you about the delay before you packed your life in boxes?'

Her indignation on my behalf makes me smile. Nicky doesn't suffer fools, and she always fights her friends' corners. A better sounding board I couldn't have.

We chit-chat for a bit, catching up on the minutiae of daily life, dealing with and fending off various requests and demands from our offspring.

'Lucky Star or Musharatt's or Domino's?' I wave the menus in front of Nicky.

Xander strolls in. 'Domino's! Domino's. Please, Mum.' He tugs on Nicky's sleeve.

'That OK with you?' Nicky asks.

'Sure, mine would prefer pizza anyway. Do you want pizza or shall you and I have Indian or Chinese? It's no problem to get both.'

'Whatever you fancy. I'm easy – quite partial to a

vegetarian hot one, or whatever Domino's call it.'

'Lucky I have a jar of jalapeños in the fridge.' I pat the Smeg for emphasis. 'At least I didn't have to empty that.'

'Just as well. I still can't believe they're leaving you in the lurch like this.'

I sigh. 'I know. I hope they get a move on. I don't want workmen in whilst I'm packing for the Lakes. You know it takes me days.'

'Same, and there's only two of us.'

'Oh, before I forget, I have something to tell you.' I close the door so the children don't overhear.

'What is it? You've gone all secretive,' Nicky says.

'I think I saw Gen's admirer.'

'What? Where? When?' Her eyes are almost popping out of her head.

I smile at Nicky's barrage of questions.

'Yesterday, at the school gates. She couldn't get out of the car fast enough, didn't even kiss me goodbye.' Nicky's eyebrows raise at this. 'And as she was going through the gates this boy caught her up and smiled at her then they started talking.'

'Well, that's innocuous enough. Could have been anyone,' Nicky says.

'Not the way they were looking at each other. You mark my words, that was the boy.'

Nicky frowns. 'So do you think they're boyfriend and girlfriend then?'

'I hope not. She's a bit young for all that.'

Nicky makes a non-committal noise. 'What was he like?'

'Of the glimpse I had of him, tall, lovely smile. Can't really say more at the minute.'

'Eye colour?'

'I was too far away, but I shall report back once there are developments.'

'Please do. Very exciting.' With no further information forthcoming from me, Nicky says, 'Right, shall we phone this order in?'

'Yeah, let me see what everyone wants.' I am en route to the playroom when the doorbell rings.

Who's that? I'm not expecting anyone. Probably someone wanting to clean my gutters or my monoblock.

I open the door and my face breaks into a smile. 'Valentin. What are you doing here?'

Valentin smiles and produces a hand-tied bouquet of the most gorgeous flowers. I recognise some of them – calla lilies, green carnations, pink lisianthus, but a couple are new to me.

'I wanted to thank you properly for looking after my grandfather, and for being so kind,' he says.

'No need to thank me. Anyone would have done the same thing.'

'No, they wouldn't have, and this is just a little gesture of appreciation from me and Grandfather.'

'Well, thank you. Sorry, would you like to come in for a cup of tea?'

Again with the killer smile. 'A cup of tea would be great, thanks.'

How middle-aged must I sound? Cup of tea? But then, he is driving, so I couldn't exactly offer him anything else, unless he wants a Pepsi Max.

I usher him into the living room, where Nicky, whom I had momentarily forgotten, is tapping away on her phone. She looks up at my return. 'Who was it? Oh! Hi.'

Valentin's eyes alight on Nicky, his smile widens and he holds out his hand. 'Valentin Pendragon, nice to meet you.'

Nicky blushes. She has always been terrible at hiding her feelings. Interesting. There is a definite frisson between this pair. Nicky can't take her eyes off him, although, to be fair he is the epitome of gorgeousness.

'Please, sit down,' I say as I take a cup out of the cupboard for him. 'How do you take your tea?'

'Milk, one sugar,' he replies, his eyes never leaving Nicky's face.

I'm beginning to feel surplus to requirements in my own living room, and am torn between introducing Valentin properly and interrupting them, because the chemistry between them is unmistakable.

Once I've made the tea, I fumble for biscuits, leaving Nicky and Valentin to chat.

'Mummy!' Aria hollers. 'I'm hungry.'

Damn. I forgot I haven't placed the pizza order yet. Valentin's arrival threw me off kilter.

'Sorry, I need to take the kids' pizza order and then I'll be back. Help yourself to a chocolate biscuit.'

'Don't mind if I do,' says Valentin, with that oh-so-beguiling smile of his.

I take my time dealing with the kids. It's been a long time since I've seen Nicky react like that to a man, and I see potential straight away given how Valentin responded to her too.

'Mummy, I want cheese and pineapple,' says Aria.

'Can I please have pepperoni, Mum?' Hugo asks.

'I'll share a medium one with you, if you like,' Gen offers.

I have no idea where my daughter puts it. I know it's her age, but I don't recall ever being as slim as she is now, even though I did plenty of sport as a child. Xander bizarrely wants an anchovy pizza. Must be a new thing. I thought children loathed anchovies; they're not often welcomed by adults either.

When I return to the living room, Valentin and Nicky are deep in conversation. I watch them for a second without their observing me. Valentin roars with laughter and Nicky giggles. It's too long since I saw this side of her – she's so girlish. Her relationship with Sebastian ripped her heart out. Could this be a stepping stone on the way to mending it?

Finally, I have to make my presence known. 'Right, I have the kids' orders. Valentin, we're calling out for pizza. Hungry?'

'Oh, I don't want to impose,' he says, whilst his eyes flick to Nicky.

'You wouldn't be. The more the merrier. And it's the least I can do after you've brought me such beautiful flowers. Man cannot survive on chocolate Hobnobs alone.'

What am I saying? I am spouting a lot of nonsense. I need an excuse to leave the room.

'Well, that would be great, thanks. I'm starving. Skipped lunch because of a meeting that ran over.'

'Perfect. What would you like?'

'A Vegi Supreme Italian crust, please.'

'Give me five minutes to place this order, and I'll be back.' I seize the opportunity to make myself scarce and do a little happy dance once the door has closed behind me.

But not before I see Valentin mouth 'thank you' at me. Nor before I see Nicky's smile ratchet up a notch.

'The pizza van is here,' shrieks Hugo about twenty minutes later.

Shouts of 'hurrah' come from the playroom. I had purposely found some tasks I needed to do so as to leave

Nicky and Valentin alone together. I am crossing my fingers here. He's lovely, concerned for his grandfather, so clearly a good person, and particularly easy on the eye. Nicky needs a Valentin in her life. If I didn't already have a Ronnie, I'd need a Valentin in my life.

For once, I let the children eat in the main dining room. I don't want to break the spell between Valentin and Nicky, and I fear that if I make them move to the other room, that may well happen.

During dinner, Valentin tells us more about his grandfather, some of his scrapes and japes. He once was stuck in a lift in Jenners with a famous screenwriter, and by the time they were rescued, the screenwriter was taking notes of his anecdotes. We laugh, as it's so easy to do; Kingston's quite the character and so full of charm. Valentin speaks with fondness of his grandmother. It's clear that although he is close to his grandfather, he was equally so with his grandmother and feels her loss keenly.

Xander wanders in. 'Mum, can I have more juice, please?'

Valentin's eyes raise, as if it has only now occurred to him that Nicky may have children, or indeed a partner or husband. His brow creases for a second, but then when Xander slips his arm round his mum in a half-hearted hug, Valentin's smile returns.

Valentin glances at Nicky's left hand, which is ringless, and he visibly relaxes.

Nicky is oblivious as her attention is on Xander, whom she then introduces to Valentin.

'And what year are you in, Xander?' Valentin asks.

'Primary six.'

'Ah, so you'll be around ten or eleven then?'

'Ten and three months,' Xander says, which makes

us laugh. Additional months are important when you're young. When you're older, you'd wish them away if you could.

Xander soon wanders off with his juice to the playroom. A Disney movie is playing for the younger ones and Xander and Hugo are busy on Skylanders. I often feel I speak a language known only to parents of children of a certain age. I used to play video games myself when I was a kid, but technology moves at such a rate of knots that I can't keep up with the games, terminology and capabilities. I just buy the kit.

When I return, Valentin is on the phone. 'No problem, Grandfather, I'll be there soon.' He disconnects the call and shoots us both an apologetic glance.

'I'm afraid I have to go. Grandfather's had a fall.'

'Oh, that's terrible,' Nicky says.

I nod in agreement. 'Hope he's OK. Send him my love.'

'Unfortunately it happens more often than I would like, but he won't let me stay over with him. He has carers but they're not live-in. That may have to change. Anyway, thanks for the pizza…and the company.' He smiles at me then his eyes meet Nicky's and linger there a little longer than would be usual if there was no chemistry between them.

I show Valentin out, thank him for the flowers again and return to the living room. I wonder if it took all of Nicky's restraint not to accompany me to the door. She is sitting on her hands. It looks like I gauged that right.

I quirk an eyebrow at her. 'So, what's going on with the delectable Valentin then?'

Nicky grins. 'He asked for my number, then whilst you were away doing whatever you were doing, he asked me out. If I can get a babysitter for Xander, we're going out tomorrow.'

'Wow! He moves fast.'

Nicky's grin widens. 'I know! I couldn't be bothered with the whole playing hard to get thing. Where's the fun in that at our age, and in my situation?'

'So, how are you feeling?' I ask as I sit back down.

'Honestly? Euphoric. I didn't think I would ever feel this way about a man again, but to quote Drac in Hotel Transylvania – the third one, I think – I zinged!'

Another thing about parents is they have a universal knowledge of animated films. I know exactly what she's talking about.

'Well, looks like things are on the up and up, Nic. How about a virgin mojito?'

'Sounds fab.'

I'm so pleased for her. Nicky deserves someone truly lovely like Valentin. Perhaps fate intervened yesterday with Kingston. If he hadn't hit me, Valentin and Nicky wouldn't have met. Every cloud really does have a silver lining.

Chapter Nineteen

Friday 26 February

To-do list
Laundry/ironing
Washing machine repair man
Check kids bags for forms from school
Vet re Bear's paw
Collect parcels from post office – they couldn't be delivered as we were out

Three Amigas WhatsApp chat
    Nicky: *I think I'm going to be sick.*
    Me: *You'll be fine. Your hair looked lovely earlier and your make-up. And you showed me your outfit. Send us a selfie.*
    Sam: *Yeah, I never saw you made up. Take a few.*
    Nicky: *How's Xander?*
    Me: *Stop procrastinating. Send us a pic. Xander is fine. He and Hugo haven't left the playroom. I think the Xbox is about to go on fire.*

A few minutes pass with no one making any comment. I wait until I see Nicky typing again, then three photos ping in. One close-up of her face and hair, one full-length and one top half. She hates doing selfies, so her eyes are looking anywhere but at the spot she should have been focusing on. Despite this, she looks amazing. It gives me a warm feeling and I realise I am excited for her. She deserves this, deserves Valentin. And if he doesn't turn out to be as nice as I've pegged him, he'll have me to deal with.

Sam beats me to it. *If his jaw doesn't drop when he sees you, he's blind.*

Me: *I couldn't agree more.*

Me: *And he wouldn't be worthy of you. Stop fretting, he's lovely, you had great chemistry and you're going on a date. Have fun. With a man. Remember that? It's allowed, you know!*

Nicky: *Gotta go. Think that's him at the door.*

Me: *Knock him dead!*

Sam: *You got this! Don't do anything I wouldn't.*

Nicky sends back a stream of emojis which are so random it's hard to know if she has leant on her phone by accident.

Silence descends and I assume she is now with Valentin. I pray it goes well. As I leave the living room, Aria barrels into me. She needs to go to bed. I allowed her up later than usual as she loves Xander and he is good with her, and she was manic when she found out he was having an impromptu sleepover. However, if I don't get her down soon, she will be overtired for her friend's party tomorrow.

I peek round the playroom door and see the boys have moved from the Xbox to the sofa, where they are now watching a movie. Gen has joined them, unusually. Ah, *Inside Out*. She loves that film, as does Aria. The opening credits are rolling, so I resolve to bath Aria then do her stories and get her to bed before she realises she's missing out. I'm guessing they haven't told her what they're watching, or I would have had a tantrum to deal with.

Once I've settled Aria, I enter the playroom, ask the kids if they want popcorn, and when it's ready, I ensconce myself on the sofa beside them. My Friday night may not be rock and roll, but I'm content and I'm surrounded by those I love, and anyway, I do love a good Pixar movie. It's just a pity Ronnie isn't here to enjoy it with us.

Chapter Twenty

Saturday 27 February

To-do list
Hugo's friend's mum re pick Hugo up for taekwondo
Clothes shopping with Gen
Mum re meet for lunch
Wrap present for party Aria 11.30
Nicky!

I don't want to get out of bed today. I can tell it's freezing. My central heating is making such a noise that it can only mean it has had to crank itself up to the max to stave off the worst of the cold.

I am itching to message Nicky, but it's too early for her. She'd kill me. I have my fingers crossed her date went well as Nicky has so much to offer, and she could do with the boost to her confidence after Sebastian decimated it. And what better way to lift your self-esteem than having someone like Valentin showing an interest in you. I think about how sweet he was and how well mannered. Oh my goodness, I'll be joining the knitting circle next. I should be thinking more of how hot he was, for my friend, of course.

When did suitability become more important than

chemistry? Or maybe they should go hand in hand. I never had that problem – Ronnie was always the full package. I know I'm lucky, but as with everything, there's a catch. He's only mine half the month. The rest of the time he belongs to his rig and his colleagues.

I'm looking forward to seeing Mum for lunch today. We haven't seen each other for a while. She and Dad appear to be busy, but with what is anyone's guess. Whenever I call the house, there is never any answer. It has taken some getting used to, my parents having lives. I suppose that's what happens when people retire. I wonder if they've booked another cruise or holiday yet. I'm sure Mum won't pass up the opportunity to pick up some brochures today when we're in town.

So, I need to drop Aria at her friend's party at half past eleven. It's at her house and, at three hours, is a little longer than most kids' parties. I know the mum quite well, so I have no qualms about leaving Aria with her. She said there would be no room for them to play if all the parents were there too, so she wanted only those parents whose kids were particularly clingy to wait. Aria doesn't fall into that category. Much as my daughter loves me, she can equally walk into a room without a backwards glance to me. I love her confidence and wish she could sprinkle me with some of it.

Hugo's friend's mum is picking him up at nine thirty and they are away most of the day at a taekwondo tournament. Normally, I would go with him, but the logistics with Ronnie being away means it's not feasible today. Fortunately, I took Hugo and Jonah to the last tournament, so Jonah's mum is returning the favour.

The plan is to hit the shops with Genevieve and buy her some casual clothes that we both agree on. Not too much black, nothing too short or skimpy. She's twelve not sixteen nor auditioning for a cheerleader squad. Then at one o'clock we'll meet Mum for lunch at Princes Square.

The clock chimes eight o'clock. Crikey, how did it get so late? Hugo needs a shower and so do I. I run upstairs to start cajoling my lovely cherubs to get out of bed. I stand in the doorway of Hugo's room, smiling at my beautiful boy. He suits his glasses, has the air of a mini professor, but when he's asleep like this, no glasses on, I love taking in the length of his lashes, the peaceful expression on his face, the way his hair sticks up in all directions. He lies with his arms above his head as he has always done since he was a baby, oblivious to the world around him.

I leave him a moment and cross to Aria's room. Her blonde curls peep out from under her duvet as she lies diagonally across the bed. It never ceases to amaze me the positions children find comfortable. How she isn't freezing, I don't know, yet when I touch her skin and press my lips to her cheek, she is toasty.

To complete the perfect image I have of my children, I enter Gen's room. It's immaculate. The teenager she is soon to become has thankfully not emerged yet. Gen lies with her duvet wrapped around her, her face the only visible part. She's mumbling. I can't tell if she's sleepy and talking to me, or talking in her sleep. I wait, then she gives a gentle snort and turns over. I smile to myself and return to Hugo's room. I needed that – my perfect children – of course they're not, but they are to me.

'Hugo,' I whisper in his ear as I stroke his damp hair off his forehead. It curls more in his sleep, aided, I guess, by the copious amount of sweating, young children tend to do. He grunts and snuffles into his pillow. 'Hugo, c'mon, sleepyhead, time to get up.'

I sit down on his bed and hug him to me. 'Today's the taekwondo tournament.' That does it. Hugo leaps out of bed as if I've told him there's a fire, grabs his glasses and whirls towards me.

'I'm going to get my new belt today, Mum.'

'I know.' I smile at him and ruffle his hair as he hugs me. 'In the shower and I'll get you some breakfast,' I tell him, handing him his clothes, which I set out last night.

He salutes me and heads for the Jack and Jill bathroom he and Genevieve share.

Xander stirs from the other bed. 'Hmm, what time is it?'

'A little after eight. Good morning. Are you having a shower here or at home? Mum will be round for you about nine.'

'If I say home, do I get more sleep?' he asks with a yawn.

I grin. 'Fifteen minutes.'

I give Gen and Aria a lie-in as they don't need to be anywhere quite so early. Whilst Hugo gets ready, I make a start on ironing their school clothes for the week ahead, and when I hear him humming 'Can't Stop the Feeling', I smile to myself, pack the iron away and shake some cereal into a bowl for him.

'Mum, I will get my belt, won't I?' Hugo says between mouthfuls of Shreddies.

'Of course you will. You'll ace it.'

'Thanks, Mum.' He gives me his trademark goofy grin.

Soon after, the doorbell rings and Hugo plants a kiss on my cheek, before running to the door and high-fiving his friend. Jonah's head pops round the door, 'Hi, Mrs Halliday.'

'Hi, Jonah.' I raise my hand in greeting. Jonah's a lovely boy. He looks like he should be in a boy band in a few years: perfect white teeth, floppy dirty blonde hair falling into his eyes, but he is the sweetest boy and may he never change. He is also Hugo's best friend, so he clearly has good taste.

'Good luck,' I say to them both.

Xander tumbles downstairs half asleep and grunts a yes to some toast and milk. He doesn't say much in the time between surfacing and Nicky coming to collect him at nine. His eyes are fixed on YouTube as he takes bites of toast, crumbs falling around him, missing the plate entirely.

When the doorbell goes, I rush to answer it, hoping to get Nicky alone to see how her date went. But no sooner have I opened the door than Xander pushes past me to hug his mum, and the opportunity is lost. She's smiling, though, so surely that's a good thing. As Xander walks to the car, I motion for her to call or text me.

'Mummy, can we go to the party yet?' Aria asks.

'It's not time yet, honey.'

Aria sighs in exasperation. 'How many more minutes?'

I glance at the clock. 'We'll leave in half an hour. That's thirty minutes.'

'I know half an hour is thirty minutes,' my daughter tells me. 'I learned that at nursery.'

So my teaching her the time didn't sink in, but the nursery teacher managed it?

'Gen's painting her nails,' she informs me.

'Ah, is that what she's up to?' I ask, distracted momentarily.

'Yes. She has a boyfriend now.'

I almost choke then recover enough to see if I can wangle any information out of my youngest. Devious, I know, but needs must. 'What was his name again?'

'Mummy, how could you forget? It's such a funny name.' Aria rolls her eyes at me. 'And I like it. In fact, I might call my boy that when I grow up.'

I wait, patiently, for her to reveal the mystery boy's name. I have a face, perhaps, from the school gates. Is Aria about to enlighten me? 'Hmm,' I say, non-committally.

'Rain is such a cool name. And maybe if I had more than one baby, I could call them Snow and Wind. Ooh, or Storm. I like that.'

I don't think Aria's children will thank her for that, but I feel pretty certain she'll have changed her mind by the time motherhood strikes; however, I now have a name: Rain. What kind of name is Rain? Is his father a Native American, or his mother a hippy? Before I can wheedle anything else out of Aria, she says, 'Can I go watch Gen paint her nails?'

If it stops you asking me how many more minutes until the party, then yes. 'Sure.'

I tidy up the breakfast things – three breakfasts I made in total – cereal for Hugo, granted that doesn't take much effort – a roll with bacon and egg for Gen, and toast with jam for Aria. It's at that point I realise I haven't eaten, so I pop a slice of bread in the toaster as my stomach rumbles.

The clock says ten thirty. I fire off a quick message to Nicky. *How did it go?*

I stand still for a minute to see if she replies. Nada. Nicky either replies immediately she sees the message, or if she is caught up in doing something, it can be hours. I'm guessing it's the second one.

I've just finished my toast when my daughters bounce downstairs, Gen sporting pastel-coloured nail varnishes with sparkles on them, each finger a different colour. Aria's hair has been plaited, in all honesty far better than I can do it. My heart swells with pride at the closeness of my two girls. They dote on each other.

After wrapping the Melissa and Doug toy we've bought for the birthday girl, I motion to the girls that it's time to go, and we set off for the party.

Once we've dropped Aria off, Gen and I chat like best friends in the car on the way to meet Mum. We discuss what clothes we're looking for, and I remind Gen of the rules of what she can and cannot get, and I turn it into a joke so it doesn't ruin the mood. I'll buy her a wee gift since we're having Mummy/girl time, but she doesn't need to know that in advance.

I'm so glad to have my own car back, I think as I reverse into the almost impossible to find parking space in the centre of town.

We've traipsed through Dorothy Perkins, John Lewis, Tommy Hilfiger, and my eyelids are starting to droop and my feet beginning to ache. Now we're in shop number four.

'Mum, I like this one,' Gen tells me, bringing out a rainbow-coloured chunky knit dress. It's very Boden-esque, albeit we're in Next. We can just about agree on Next. My inability to throw good money away doesn't allow me to shop at some of the cheaper stores, as I know the clothes won't last. I'm sure there are bargains to be had, but I don't have the patience to separate the wheat from the chaff.

I try to think of an appropriate response. If I say, 'That's sweet,' I feel she may glare at me and put it back. Struggling to find a word that won't make her scowl, I settle for, 'You'd look good in that.'

'Can I try it on?'

'Of course. Aren't you trying anything else on?' I ask, as that's the only thing she has in her hands.

She glances round, scanning the racks and rails. 'No, I'm good.' She hesitates. 'Maybe some boots.' She cocks an eyebrow in the direction of footwear.

'We can look in a minute,' I concede. 'Let's see the dress on.'

Gen disappears into the changing room and I check my phone for messages and emails whilst I wait.

Nothing from Nicky. A message from Mum saying she's already in town and can come shopping with us if we wish. I'm enjoying it being the two of us. Do I pretend I haven't seen it? I hate lying, even by omission. Would my mother give Gen more freedom than me with what she wears? Possibly, although I don't recall her and Dad being overly strict with me. Would Mum be offended if I said I'd prefer if it was just me and Gen until lunch? Probably, plus Mum speaks first and thinks later, so no doubt Gen would find out her nana had been free to see her earlier and I had decided for whatever reason not to meet her until our lunch date. Why is life so complicated? Even with your own family.

My heart stops when Gen comes out of the changing room. She looks so much older, more sophisticated. She looks fifteen, not twelve, her glossy hair swishing like that of a catwalk model. I am both proud and nervous. My cells contributed to this fabulous, stunning girl. And clearly she has my brains too. The woollen dress hugs her slim frame and I can see a soupçon of the woman she will become.

She gives me a twirl and smooths the dress down as she studies herself in the full-length mirror. 'Can I have it, Mum? I love it.'

'Me too,' I say, before I've even looked at the price. We

don't do clothes shopping in person often. It's mostly done online, so unless it's a hundred pounds, she can have it. Gen wanders over to the footwear section, and I decide to text Mum back once we've chosen some boots.

Mum, we're leaving Next. Off to Monsoon. Will we meet you there?

In Monsoon, Gen looks like Christmas has come ten months early. She fingers the material of a few dresses, picks up a floaty scarf and wraps it around my neck.

I smile. 'We're not here to shop for me. What do you like?'

'This dress.' She gestures to a pale pink prom dress. It's lovely. She would look amazing in it, but it's not prom, it's February and she'd be freezing. In fact, I have no idea why these kinds of clothes are on sale at this time of year.

'What about something more for this season?' I say meaningfully, indicating the long-sleeved tops and jackets. Gen starts browsing the rails as my phone beeps. It's a message from Nicky, but as I'm about to open it, Mum enters the shop, waving at me.

'Hi, Nana,' Gen calls. 'I didn't know you were coming shopping too.' She looks delighted. I don't know whether to be happy or insulted. Is my opinion not good enough? Apparently not, because as soon as my mother has enveloped me in a cloud of Versace, my daughter whisks her away to ask what she thinks of a couple of tops she has singled out. I like the one with cap sleeves.

Since they're otherwise engaged, I sneak a peek at Nicky's message.

I'm dancing on air. Is it too soon to be in love? He's incredible. I want him.

I laugh at this last. I'm tempted to ask her if they got to first base, but figure she'll tell me what she wants me to know, and we're not eighteen any more. Unfortunately.

Happy for you, hon. Are you seeing each other again? I type back, safe in the knowledge that Gen is caught up with my mother, and I am not neglecting her on our Mummy/ girl day out.

No reply. I hope that means she's busy with Xander and not that she and Valentin haven't arranged to meet up again.

I turn round to Mum and Gen but they're gone. I'll wait here until they come back. I glance at my emails until Gen returns and says, 'Mum, Nana and I like these.'

I survey the tops and skirt she has chosen and say, 'That's fine. Do you need to try them on?'

'Already did.' Gen smiles. 'And Nana says they look wonderful.'

I'm glad Gen isn't yet at that age where she believes that if her nana thinks something's wonderful she's not meant to like it.

'Great, let's pay for this lot, then we can go get some lunch. Unless you have any shopping to do?' I turn to Mum.

'Not here, Louisa. John Lewis will do just fine for me, and I'll go there after lunch, give me more time. I know you have to be back for Aria.'

'Thanks, Mum,' I say to her as I put my arm through hers, whilst Gen links her arm through my other one.

We stroll into Princes Square and take the escalator up to Zizzi's. It's Gen's favourite restaurant, and one Mum approves of, and I also like, so win-win. As we wait for the waitress to seat us, my phone pings. Nicky.

We're going for lunch tomorrow afternoon in Edinburgh. Sebastian has Xander. I'm very excited but nervous too. I can't rush off easily if it all goes pear-shaped.

The waitress seats us and since Gen and Mum excuse

themselves to go to the loo, I take the opportunity to reply to Nicky.

Why would it go pear-shaped? Think positive. You are a clever, funny, sexy woman, the equal in every way to Valentin Pendragon. Have fun. I want details!

I can't resist. The need to know if they at least kissed is killing me.

No answer. I am going to kill her!

Lunch is a pleasant but slightly too rushed affair. I hate having to run from one thing to the other, but I am aware of constantly clock-watching to ensure I am not late back for picking up Aria. You'd think I'd be used to it, but I'm not sure parents – or at least mothers – ever get used to it, the inability to completely relax. Even when the kids are on an overnight, which happens about once a year, I can't relax, wondering if they have managed to fall asleep OK, if they're being problematic for whoever is looking after them, playing up, or staying up way past bedtime.

One surprise that came out of lunch was Mum confided that she and Dad are stopping cruising for the time being. They want to explore other options, whatever that means. As long as it doesn't mean they're getting divorced, I'm happy. My parents are the benchmark by which every marriage is measured. If they can't make it work, there's no hope for the rest of us. They make it look easy.

It was lovely to catch up. We don't do this often enough, especially just the three of us, and Gen is getting to that age where she appreciates being in adult company and being treated more like a grown-up. It was funny to hear her giving opinions on current affairs. She seemed better versed in some of those topics than me. I wonder if there's a debating team at school. Gen would shine at debating.

She certainly gives me a hard time when arguing a point. That's the thing with having clever children: sometimes they outsmart you.

We've been home about an hour before Jonah's mum drops Hugo off. I'm surprised to see her come up to the door and equally surprised that Hugo storms past me and runs upstairs.

I frown. 'Hi,' I say to Jonah's mum, 'is everything OK?'

She sighs. 'Yeah, he's just really upset.'

When she doesn't elaborate, I say, 'About what?'

'Oh, sorry, I should have said. He didn't earn his green belt.'

'What? Oh no. I thought he was ready.' Now I feel terrible for suggesting he went for it, but his instructor also thought he was ready. Would it have made a difference if I had been there to watch him compete? I guess I'll never know, but I share his disappointment.

'Thanks for letting me know and for taking him. I better go and see how he is. See you next week?'

We say goodbye and I seek out Hugo. I find him in bed under the covers.

'Hugo.' Silence.

'Honey, it's not the end of the world. You'll be able to do it again soon.' And next time I will be there to watch you, and help you beforehand too.

Sniffles come from under the covers and I can see his little body heaving as he tries to hide his sobs from me. My poor boy. Doesn't he know he never needs to hide his emotions from me? He'll be feeling humiliated, but Ronnie and I, and his sisters, are here to help him overcome that. That's what families do. We lean on each other. I pat the covers until I find his head. 'I'm sorry you're sad, sweetheart. And I know it hurts, but it will make you stronger, I guarantee you. You are brilliant at taekwondo. In fact, I pity your next opponent.'

He sniff-cry-giggles then says, 'Can I get a tissue, Mummy?'

'Of course you can. Give me a sec.'

Whilst I go to the bathroom for tissues, I can't help but think that no matter how awful Hugo feels now and no matter how much I empathise with him, he will never want for love from us, his parents, his siblings, and my heart goes out to Xander. Once again, I damn Sebastian.

Chapter Twenty-one

Sunday 28 February

To-do list
Dig out salopettes and snow boots
Get sledges out of attic
Find thick gloves and my cashmere scarf
Recycling
Clean out cutlery drawer and pot cupboard

Last day of the month. A day closer to spring. Thank goodness. It's snowing heavily. I hope it doesn't stop Nicky from meeting Valentin. Sebastian is picking Xander up at ten as he usually does. That gives Nicky plenty of time to get through to Edinburgh. Maybe Valentin is collecting her. Surely he would be, if they are going all the way to Edinburgh, unless they're going together on the train. I try not to worry on her behalf. Worst-case scenario, they don't go to Edinburgh, but meet closer to home. Perhaps that would be better; they could go to Nicky's, since Xander won't be home. Oh la la, I must stop getting carried away.

My phone beeps. Ronnie. His messages have been short and to the point the past few days, asking about the kitchen progress and the kids. I love that he wants to know all this stuff, but sometimes I'd like him to ask about me. I don't mean that to sound needy or pathetic, but I miss being able to talk to him about what programmes I'm watching on TV, or something funny I saw in the street, or whose nose is out of joint because their neighbour has a new summer house. Gossip, I suppose, I mean, but not in a bad way, in a natural, bouncing off each other kind of way.

Ronnie: *How's my girl?*

Me: *Which one? You have two.*

Ronnie: *The third one.*

Me: *Ah, me? I'm good, thanks. Juggling some work and household admin whilst Gen is at gymnastics. Mum took her for me. Saved me a bit of time. They've been getting really close. You ought to have seen them clothes shopping yesterday.*

Now it's me who's talking about the kids.

Ronnie: *That's good. How about Aria and Hugo?*

Me: *Aria's building a Lego set in the playroom and Hugo is boinging on the trampoline.*

Ronnie: *In February?*

Me: *Yes, you know he doesn't care.*

Ronnie: *Don't you have any snow? Aberdeen is having blizzards.*

Me: *Yes, we've had a foot overnight. He's got a parka on and hat, scarf and gloves, and he cleared the trampoline of snow. He's enjoying himself, so I've left him to it, particularly as he isn't on the Xbox.*

Ronnie: *Fair point. Can I call you tomorrow? About nine? I miss you.*

Me: *Nine's fine. I miss you too. Seems ages since you left and it's only been a few days.*

I think of all that has happened since I last saw my husband: Kingston crashing into me, Valentin bringing me flowers, the chemistry between Nicky and Valentin and their dates. That's months' worth of events.

Ronnie: *Love you.*

Me: *I love you too.*

Sometimes communicating with my husband makes me lonelier and lonelier. I ache at the fact he hasn't even been gone half the time he will be. This half-life doesn't get any easier.

I was so busy fretting over whether Nicky's date would be cancelled because of the weather, that I temporarily forgot it's my turn to host the Three Amigas Sunday lunch, or in this case the Two Amigas. Normally, Nicky would have come, but I don't hold it against her that she has taken Valentin up on his offer. To be honest, even without Valentin in the mix, she would have had a kid-free day, with Xander being with her ex, so it is my lot and Sam's.

Time runs away from me and when I next look up, it's because the doorbell has ding-donged. One o'clock. How did it get to be one o'clock?

'Come in, guys!' I hug my friend and cuddle the two cherubs. They look adorable in matching cream faux-fur gilets and chunky Aran jumpers. Ava's blonde locks tumble around her shoulders and Emily's curls bounce as she runs into the playroom to seek out Aria, no doubt. I love how my friends' kids feel so at home in my house, and vice versa. I wouldn't have it any other way.

'Hi, Mum.' Gen appears, her face flushed and healthy. Continuing with the gymnastics class was definitely a good idea. She tried to get out of it a few months ago, but I know what it's like when girls go to high school, they don't exercise as much, so I cajoled her to stick at it a bit longer and it has paid off. She now has a few close friends there and one of her classmates, who moved into the area recently, has joined the club, too. Her next competition is in a few weeks. It amazes me how flexible she is. I certainly am not, not any more, but gymnastics was never my bag; I wasn't graceful enough. I just about managed to play wing defence in netball.

'Hi, honey. How was practice?'

'Good.'

'Did you shower at the club?'

She nods.

'Fine. Lunch will be in about an hour.'

'Cool. I might go listen to some music.'

She has already bounced back out of the room before I can reply. I bite my lip to prevent myself from parroting 'not too loud'. Much as I love my mother, I have never aspired to be her, but I often find myself trotting out her stock responses and I cringe every time.

Forty-five minutes later, we're all sitting in the dining room, and for once silence reigns. Having takeaway every day is a time saver, but I am beginning to get sick of it and can't wait until my kitchen is complete so I can cook in it. I sip my one small glass of Pinot Gris, safe in the knowledge I don't have to go anywhere today.

The restlessness soon kicks in once the plates are cleared.

'Mummy, can Ava and I leave the table, please?'

'OK, we'll have a half-hour break before dessert. Banoffee pie.'

'Yay!' Ava shouts and sprints out of the room, Hugo on her heels. Aria and Gen follow suit with Emily close behind.

Sam and I smile at each other. Peace at last.

'I wonder how Nicky's getting on,' I say.

'I know! I can't believe I've not seen what this Valentin

looks like yet.'

I blow out a breath. 'He's bloomin' gorgeous. And lovely personality. The full package. Oh, I forgot to tell you, Nic's not the only one who has a new boyfriend.'

'Oh?' Sam scrunches her forehead, intrigued.

'You remember I told you Gen got a huge card and presents on Valentine's Day?'

'Yeah.'

'Well, I saw this boy with her at the school gate recently, and the way they looked at each other…let's just say I remember being that age and looking at a boy like that.'

'Ooh, how exciting. Your baby's first love.' Sam is almost jumping up and down with glee. 'So, has she told you anything about him?'

'God no. I had to tease the detail out of Aria.'

Sam splutters. 'What?'

'Yes. Aria is the person in the know in this house, apparently. She told me his name's Rain, and from what I glimpsed of him at the school, he's very tall, almost a head taller than Gen, and has short blonde hair, slightly longer on top.'

'Sounds lovely.' Sam sighs.

'Yep, dreamy, but Rain?'

'Maybe his mum was a hippy,' Sam says, taking a sip of her no-alcohol Prosecco.

'That's what I thought. Great minds,' I say.

Sam grins then sighs again, but this time it's not with happiness. 'I hope Nic has half Gen's luck. Surely it must work out for her this time.'

'Hey, we could google him,' I say. 'I mean, it's a long shot, but there might be an image of him somewhere.'

'Good idea. Why didn't I think of that?' Sam rolls her eyes as if to say she's a dimwit.

I type Valentin Pendragon into my phone, not really expecting anything to come up, but there are loads of results, and when I click on images, all of the top results are him. I suppose the name is a little unusual, classy, foreign.

Valentin does it again. Pendragon heir raises six hundred thousand pounds for cancer charity

Valentin Pendragon's skydive for Alzheimer's UK

Valentin Pendragon expansion plans

Pendragon hires new CFO – and a picture of Valentin shaking a fifty-something's hand.

Pendragon to open twelve new restaurants in Scotland and North-East by end of next year

Valentin Pendragon scoops first place in the restaurant awards for the second year running, this time for his French bistro, La Bohème

The news articles go on and on.

'Lou…Lou…Louisa,' Sam says, her eyebrows scrunched up in concern.

'Yeah, I'm fine.'

'He's not married, is he?' Sam whispers.

'No, well, not that I saw.'

'So, what is it?'

'He's one of *the* Pendragons.'

'The Pendragons?'

'Yes, as in the restaurateurs. The son of Luka Pendragon, the one who died in the Gulf War. That must be why he stays with his grandfather. Poor guy.'

'But surely he's absolutely minted!' Sam says.

'That's putting it politely. His grandfather, Kingston, is one of the top hundred wealthiest people in the country. There's barely a town without a Pendragon restaurant in it, and they're still expanding.'

'I take it Nic doesn't know.'

'I don't imagine so. You know Nic, she would never think to google someone, and she's so far out of touch with dating, she wouldn't realise you can do that, or if she did, she wouldn't. She'd think it would spoil the magic or something.'

Sam nods in agreement. 'So, you're telling me that Nicky, the sweetest, most caring person on the planet, is out for lunch with a millionaire who is really into her?'

My brow furrows. 'Yep. Things could get very interesting. But the big question is, do we tell her or not?'

Chapter Twenty-two

Tuesday 2 March

To-do list
Doctor's appointment
Leotard – Gen gymnastics
Pick up dry cleaning
Check if Hugo and Gen's walking boots fit them
Buy Aria walking boots – must do today – express delivery

'Don't worry about a thing, Mrs Halliday,' says Owen as he walks past me into the kitchen with a toolbox and a kitbag. 'It will be mostly done by the weekend. Possibly need Monday to set the finishing touches.'

I breathe a sigh of relief. Finally the work on the kitchen is starting. I have a couple of meetings with clients today, so I'm going to remain at the hotel afterwards and avail myself of their Wi-Fi so I will at least get some headspace to work. Plus it doesn't do any harm to charm the hoteliers a little.

I need to schedule my time carefully this week, doing only the bare minimum. The kitchen was originally supposed to be finished tomorrow, and I hadn't factored in the inconvenience of having builders here all week. Not ideal when I have to pack and buy in groceries for our trip.

They'll have to put the fridge in the garage for me. I can't possibly lug it in myself.

As I'm leaving, I see to my great relief that Owen's men are unloading the kitchen units from the lorry. They ask me if they can store them in the garage until they are ready, in case the weather changes. I don't really want them sitting them on the melting slush anyway. I'd cleared a part of the garage for them yesterday. That wasn't fun. I managed it whilst Hugo, for once, without complaint, sat and did his homework, Gen was at her friend's and Aria was playing with her Little Live Pets. Who knew we had so much stuff? I wish I'd had more time to sort it all out. Half of it could probably be thrown out. Why are we keeping a cafetière from fifteen years ago? In case the other breaks? We have a De Longhi pod coffee machine now.

And why do we have eight old mobile phones, and planks of wood, and bikes nobody will ever use again, and a trike for Aria? Much of this will need to go to the recycling centre once I have time and volition again. I'm so glad we bought a house with a designated second living room, which then became the playroom. I couldn't have coped if we'd had to convert the garage. Where would we put everything? We'd need to install a row of sheds out the back to cope with the sheer quantity of 'stuff' we have.

Seat belt finally on, I am about to pull out of the driveway when Owen waves to me.

I lower the window. 'Yes?' I try not to be snippy, but I have only thirty-five minutes to get to the West End, and traffic along Byres Road can be a killer.

'Sorry, but where do you keep your biscuits?' When I don't immediately answer, he goes on. 'For when the lads have their break.'

They arrived fifteen minutes ago and they're almost a

week late in starting the job. I grit my teeth and say, 'I've left coffee and tea, sugar and biscuits in the utility room, where the kettle is, as I imagine you'll pull my kitchen apart first.'

'Thanks.' He gives me a thumbs up.

'Owen,' I say, 'the work will definitely be finished by Monday, right?'

'Sure as death and taxes, Mrs Halliday.' He winks.

His response doesn't provide me with the comfort I'd hoped for. I really must ration the biscuits tomorrow, or not buy any more.

I raise the window again. I've released the handbrake when my phone trills. I glance at it and see it's a WhatsApp from Sam. *Hi. Any further thoughts on what we should do about V?*

I haven't exactly lost sleep over this, but when I have a moment to myself, it has been occupying the little space left in my brain. On the one hand, Nicky's our friend, we should be truthful with her, but on the other hand, I don't want her to feel overwhelmed or out of her depth when she and Valentin are getting on so well and starting to get better acquainted.

She called me on Sunday night and said they'd had a lovely afternoon padding about Rose Street, strolling along to Charlotte Square where the book festival is usually held. They'd had lunch in a little Greek taverna and talked non-stop. Time had passed too quickly, but they were arranging another date. She's a little concerned about getting too involved too quickly – she doesn't know the half of it – and she has to ensure she doesn't spend too much time away from Xander. Plus, appropriate babysitters are an issue, despite Xander saying he doesn't need babysitting. Her parents aren't very hands-on, so really it will have to be when Xander can stay here, or with Sam, or when he's at his dad's. I'm sure Nicky doesn't want Xander at Sebastian's any more than he already is. Xander has already passed on some less than savoury details of what his father has said about his mum – to me, not to her, fortunately.

As I drive to One Devonshire Gardens, I mull over the dilemma of what to do about Nicky and Valentin. Should we simply let things take their course? Would I want her to tell me if roles were reversed? Yes. But then I'm nosy, and probably a lot more confident than Nicky. Aargh, this isn't getting any easier. I arrive at the hotel with five minutes to spare and discover my client already seated. I hate being wrong-footed like that. I prefer to be the one who looks calm and professional when they arrive. At least it's a client I've met once before. Her friend used my services two years ago and she accompanied her to the appointment as the groom-to-be 'wasn't good at that sort of thing'.

I'm pleased to see her fiancé is with her. They look great together, like an advert in a country living magazine. They already have coffees, so I introduce myself to Clive and say hi to Olive again then signal for the waitress to bring me a latte. She knows me well and knows my order.

It turns out that the wedding will be here at One Devonshire. It's funny. I'm usually good at marrying people with their venues, pardon the pun, but I didn't have this pair down as choosing this type of hotel. It's all very decadent, understated, olde worlde but with a familiar feel to it, as if you've dropped in to your great-aunt's drawing room. OK, my great aunt didn't have a drawing room either, but I'm sure you get the idea.

I finish my first meeting with a signed contract and a commitment date for six weeks' time. They oohed and aahed over all the offerings. I didn't think they would ever make a decision and I was beginning to worry that this meeting wouldn't be over by the time the next one was due to start.

Once the Duncans have left, I scribble some notes, check my emails and rattle off a few responses. I am grateful that the next client is a little late. I even managed to nip to the loo. By the time they arrive, I am composed again, despite part of my brain whirling away at the thought of the new emails I have to deal with by close of business today. The Farnsworth wedding invitation suite goes like a dream though. Yasmin and Zane are a sweet twenty-something couple, who would have been happy if I'd penned their invitation on the back of a Sainsbury's receipt. However, I managed to convince them, given the boutique nature of their wedding, that it would look really luxurious to have the invitations in either cream or purple silk with a contrasting ribbon or font to finish it off, since the two bridesmaids are wearing purple silk sheath dresses. That idea wowed them, so that was then a done deal. And it won't be too expensive per se, as they only have fifty guests. I leave with a contract for that, too. Today is shaping up to be a good day.

I am walking down the steps towards the street when I hear the concierge call me.

'Madam, is this your phone?'

What? How did I leave that behind? I'd be lost without my phone. My whole life is on there: my family, my friends, my business.

'Yes, thanks, you're a lifesaver.' I accept the phone graciously and see I have a missed call from Owen. I dial his number and it rings eight times before he finally answers.

'Mrs Halliday. I'm afraid we have a problem.'

Chapter Twenty-three

Wednesday 3 March

The snow has completely disappeared now, but I still shiver as I cross to the grassy patch opposite the house with Bear for him to go to the toilet. It's quarter past six and the looming rain clouds do nothing to dispel my bad mood. I hate starting the day in this way, but how am I supposed to not be stressed out? Talk about bursting my bubble, as well as busting my ass. Owen certainly did that yesterday. Euphoric after landing those two contracts, I would have liked a little more time to enjoy that feeling before Owen broke it to me that two of the units the manufacturer had sent were the wrong size. Aargh. First the delay, then this. Of course, Owen only noticed after they'd taken my units out, some of which they'd hacked to bits to get out, so now I'm left with, literally, a building site in my kitchen. Everything is covered in dust, too. Nice. I'd say surfaces, but I don't have any as he and his crew removed the worktops. What a mess. I've basically had to close the door on the kitchen – at least they hadn't taken that off – to avoid seeing it all the time, but I did lie awake for hours last night thinking about it all.

Owen promised me the correct units would be here today as the manufacturer is sending them Express. I should hope so. I wish people took as much pride in their work as I do with mine. It never ceases to amaze me what shoddy customer service organisations can get away with. Small businesses definitely don't have that liberty. Nor would I want to have. It's a matter of personal pride and integrity.

I boil the kettle and make myself a coffee. The coffee machine is packed away for now. So Nescafé it is. I take my coffee through to the living room and sit down with today's list.

To-do list
Post office with Abercrombie and Ferris invitations
PayPal re business account
Call Joanna and Wendy about holiday arrangements
Pay factor
Up personal pension contributions
Read school newsletter
Return permission slips

It's twenty to seven. I grab my laptop and tap away at the keys, putting together some quotes for the new requests that have come in. As I've done many times before, I count my blessings, focusing on something positive. I have plenty of work and we don't need to worry about money. Others are not so fortunate. I do wonder why, though, whenever we are preparing to go on holiday, nothing goes according to plan. OK, perhaps having the kitchen replaced ten days prior to our trip wasn't the best plan, but it was meant to be finished by now. And I would still have had a few days' grace before our trip to organise and pack everything.

Next the banking, PayPal and invoices. I could do these in my sleep and probably have fallen asleep doing them before. By the time I've finished, it's time to wake the kids for school.

Gen mumbles OK to me, when I wake her; Aria snuggles into me and I lift her up. She's getting too heavy to do that with now, but she won't be babyish enough to want it for much longer, so I make the most of it. However, when I go to wake Hugo, I find him sweaty; no surprise there, but when he tries to sit up in bed, he says, 'My tummy hurts, Mummy. I don't feel very well.' Before I even have time to be concerned, he throws up all over my slippers. Fortunately, I had put Aria down on the bottom of the bed before I tried to wake him, so she has remained unscathed. I kick my sick-covered mules off, pick Hugo up and carry him to the bathroom. I'll have to go back and check his bedding shortly, but for now, I need to ensure he's OK and that he won't be sick again. I wonder what has set him off, though. We all had the same for dinner, and he hasn't been eating many sweets, nor is he allowed fizzy drinks.

If Aria is getting heavy and almost too difficult to carry, Hugo is virtually impossible, but I manage to deposit him on the side of the bath whilst I ferret in the bathroom cabinet for the thermometer. There's no way he can go to school. It has a strict policy on vomiting – keep kids off for forty-eight hours. I can't even ask Mum to sit with Hugo whilst I do my work tasks as I know she is booked in at a health spa today with Dad. I'll juggle it somehow. All of this is running through my brain as I take his temperature, 38.3 °C, then press a cold facecloth to his forehead.

'How are you feeling now, honey?' I wipe his mouth with some toilet paper and through his tears he tells me he still doesn't feel well, then promptly vomits all over the floor.

Aria, who has followed us to the bathroom, stands there

watching, aghast.

'Aria, go wake Gen again. Tell her Mummy needs her, Hugo's sick.'

My youngest scampers off and I turn my attention back to Hugo, who is looking sicker by the minute. He starts to cry again and I gather him to me. Sometimes a hug from your mum is all you need, but I'm not sure it'll suffice this time.

'Hugo, lean over the bath whilst I get you fresh pyjamas. These ones are soaked through.'

He doesn't answer me. I bring some clean clothes for him from his room. Some vomit made it onto the carpet after all. Great. However, it looks like his bedding was spared. A positive. I think he needs to go back to bed.

Gen strolls in, her bed hair sticking up and her eyes heavy with sleep. 'Hugo OK?' She yawns.

'No, hon, he's been throwing up. Can you do me a favour and get Aria ready for me, and sort breakfast?'

'Sure. Hugo, hope you feel better soon, buddy.' I refrain from smiling at this touching comment from my daughter. She and Hugo may be at loggerheads much of the time, but she loves her brother really and will be sorry he is unwell.

Hugo remains ashen and unresponsive. I'm starting to get worried. Often when the kids are physically sick, five minutes later they bounce back, literally sometimes, on the trampoline. Not today.

'Aria, c'mon, I'll make you some Frosted Shreddies, your favourite.'

'Yay!' says Aria. 'What's Hugo having?'

As Gen escorts her downstairs, she replies, 'I don't think Hugo's hungry at the minute.'

I put Hugo in the shower cubicle and help him wash. He starts to cry again.

'It's OK, honey. I'm here.' I hate it when the kids are ill.

I dry Hugo and put him back to bed, wondering if I should administer Calpol now or wait to be sure he won't be sick again.

The doorbell rings. Nicky. Thank goodness. Once I'd settled Hugo and checked on Gen and Aria, I'd asked Nicky if she could do me the huge favour of dropping Aria at nursery if she didn't have work on this morning. Since she had set aside the day to organise albums from a couple of weddings, she was fortunately free to do so. I'd called the nursery to explain Aria would be late in and who would be bringing her. Hopefully, Hugo will be well enough later for me to collect her, otherwise I'll need to come up with a Plan B, which I pray won't involve taking a sick kid in the car. That never ends well. And Gen, she was amazing, taking care of Aria whilst I calmed Hugo down, then seeing herself off to school.

I usher Nicky in.

'How's he doing?' Her face creases with concern and sympathy.

'I don't think he has much left in him. He's asleep now. I gave him some Calpol and stroked his back until he fell asleep.'

'Funny, that always works with Xander too. Whoever discovered that worked was a very wise woman indeed.' Nicky sets her bag on the sideboard.

'Aria, come and see Auntie Nicky. She's taking you to nursery.'

Aria steamrolls into the room and almost knocks Nicky flying.

'Hey, munchkin, you coming on an adventure with me today?'

Aria's face splits into a wide grin. 'Yes, Mummy said I'm going in your car today.'

'That's right.' She musses Aria's curls. 'Where's your backpack? We don't want to be too late for nursery. You'll miss circle time.'

Aria loves circle time. She is such a chatterbox, she is always joining in. Confidence is not something she lacks, despite her young age.

'I'm taking my Doc McStuffins backpack today,' Aria announces.

'Good choice,' Nicky says, giving her a high-five.

As Aria shrugs her jacket on, with my assistance, Nicky mouths to me, *I'll tell you everything later*. No guesses what, or rather who, she's referring to there.

With the house to myself, except for a poorly, sleeping cherub, I try to recalibrate my schedule. I wonder if Gen could take the invitations to the post office for me after school, but I might miss the last post. Would they still get there in time if I waited until tomorrow? But then there's no guarantee Hugo will be all right tomorrow. And, I've just remembered, he can't go to school tomorrow either because of the forty-eight-hour rule. Drat. Gen is my best bet. I'll prepare everything and send her to the post office a few streets away if Hugo isn't feeling better.

The breakfast things tidied away, I check on Hugo again. Still asleep. Good. Rest is what he needs. Owen and his team will be here any minute. Worst possible time to have a child unwell, when you have workmen in the house, but it can't be helped. I wonder if I could slip some noise-cancelling headphones on Hugo without him noticing. Those Bose ones are really quite effective: a birthday present last year from Ronnie. Pity I rarely get a chance to use them.

I am about to get back to my to-do list when my phone rings. Mum.

'Hi, Mum, how are you?' I am aiming for chirpy instead of despondent, but I obviously don't achieve that as Mum says, 'What's happened? Is everyone OK?'

'Yes, Mum. We're fine, although Hugo's off sick today.'

'Is he all right?' My mother's voice is laced with concern.

Why do people always ask that, me included? Clearly if someone's off sick, they're not all right, they're sick. 'He'll be fine after some rest, I'm sure.' I glance at the clock, wondering how long Mum's call will last, what she wants and how both will affect me getting on with everything that needs done whilst Hugo is asleep. I admonish myself for feeling less than interested in talking to Mum right now, but I am a little overwhelmed.

'Do you want me to come over?' she continues.

Honestly, yes, as I could then get so much done, knowing that she could help with Hugo, but first of all, he's my son and I should be looking after him, and secondly, I don't want my parents becoming ill if what he has is contagious. And I know they have their spa day planned.

'No, Mum, it's OK. Thanks for the offer though.' I wait for her to tell me the reason for her call, then before she can tell me, I add, 'Although if you or Dad are back from your spa day before school pickup and could collect the kids, if Hugo's still out of sorts, I'd really appreciate it.

'That's why I was phoning. The hotel called us to tell us there has been an "incident" in their spa, so they've had to cancel our booking. They've given us the option to cancel completely or postpone and have a free lunch as compensation too.'

'Oh no. You were looking forward to it so much.'

'Not to worry, it'll keep. And yes, we can pick Aria and Gen up. Give my boy a kiss for me. I'd best let you get on. I imagine you'll be snowed under with Hugo ill and a house full of workmen.'

I smile at Mum's intuitiveness. 'Thanks, Mum, bye. Love you.'

Mum responds in kind, then as I hang up, I cotton on to what she said. Workmen. Where are they? It's quarter to ten. They were supposed to be here at nine. It has kind of worked in my favour, I suppose, what with Hugo being ill, but even so their non-appearance concerns me.

I will call Owen in half an hour if they still haven't shown up. In the meantime, I'm about to crack on with my to-do list when the doorbell goes. Must be the postman, although I'm not expecting any packages today, I don't think.

'Good morning. Are you the homeowner? I'll tell you what it is, we're in your area to discuss home insulation–'

'I'm sorry, this really isn't a good time, but thanks.' I smile and close the door.

Right, where was I? My eyes dart around the room. Ah, to-do list. I nip into the kitchen, grab a pad and pen and go through each cupboard adding items to my shopping list. I open the fridge to scan its contents then hear a noise upstairs, then retching. Oh no, my poor boy. I sprint upstairs and find Hugo half in, half out the bed. There's vomit all over the floor.

'Sorry, Mummy,' Hugo says as I put my arm around him. 'I couldn't get to the bathroom in time.' Then he bursts into tears.

Poor love. 'Don't worry, sweetheart. I'll clean it up. We just need to concentrate on getting you better.' His pyjamas appear to have caught half of it. I divest my son of his vomit-stained Toy Story pair and grab a facecloth from the bathroom to wipe his mouth. When he's cleaned up, I rummage in his drawers for some fresh pyjamas.

'Mummy, what's wrong with me?'

'I think you have a bug. Hopefully, it will pass soon.'

'A bug, like an insect. Do you think something bit me?' His eyes go wide.

'No, nothing like that. A sickness bug.'

'But how did I get it?' His face crumples.

I refrain from telling him he probably picked it up at school. I don't want to put him off going back.

'These things are usually a mystery. Let's get you back to bed.' I check his sheets weren't affected and then help him put his clean pyjamas on.

Hugo slips meekly into the bed. He's hot to touch, but is he hotter than earlier?

My son lies still as I make up a story for him. Soon he is asleep again. Poor little mite. I edge out of his room and head downstairs to put his pyjamas in the wash.

I'm closing the washing machine door when my mobile rings in the other room. Desperate for the sound of 'Firework' not to wake Hugo – we all love that song – I rush into the living room where I left it and swipe to answer.

'Hello?' I say, out of breath, casting an eye skyward, listening for any hint of movement from Hugo's room. I'll put the phone on silent after this call.

'Mrs Halliday, hi, it's Owen here.'

'Hi, Owen. I was about to give you a call. I thought you were coming at nine.'

'Yes, well, the thing is, one of our clients, whose garage conversion we were unable to finish because the owner was ill, has called to remind us we promised to do it as soon as he was better.'

Horrified, I clutch my phone tighter. 'Owen, are you telling me you're not coming today?'

'Erm, actually, we won't be able to come for the rest of the week…' I go to intercede but he rushes on, 'but I promise you we will be there first thing Monday morning.'

'You'd better be, Owen, and I'll be interested to hear details of the discount you're giving me for the huge inconvenience you're causing me. See you Monday,' I say before hanging up. It's times like these I wish I had the kind of phone I could slam down. It would be far more satisfying.

With my head in my hands, I sit on the sofa. When will this damned kitchen be finished? Started? The place looks like it has been hit by a meteor. I take deep breaths and try to concentrate on the positive – at least they won't disturb Hugo today.

A cup of tea. Isn't that the cure for all ills? That will rally me. Then I can start packing for our trip. I suppress the little voice that says, *If it goes ahead.*

I sip my tea, reading a book, a luxury, something to put me back in the frame of mind to cope with everything that's going on. As I boiled the kettle, it hit me that the workmen are returning on my birthday. Thanks for that. Instead of the nice quiet 'me' time I had envisaged, I will be surrounded by workmen banging and clanging. Just the way I wanted to celebrate my birthday.

Hugo doesn't wake right through lunchtime and I make the most of the time I have to power through as many of my tasks as I can. At one, I prepare myself a ham sandwich and sit down to go through my messages, starting with making arrangements for my birthday weekend away.

I love us all spending time together: my sisters, their children, and my children, as they, and we, all get along so well. It's a miracle really. Most families have some sort of tension, but not ours, unless you count the strife between Gen and Hugo, and that's simply a little sibling rivalry.

Jo, are you picking up the food from M&S? I text to Sisters Like These group chat on WhatsApp. I think for a minute then type, *Wendy, do you still have that rattan picnic hamper? The handle has broken on mine. I'm doing an Asda order now for the non-M&S food. Anything you want me to include?*

Wendy is the first to reply. *Yeah, it's in the loft. Will look it out. I'm doing the M&S run after work today. Jo has a meeting. How's the kitchen coming along?*

Me: *Don't ask. Suffice to say I'm still living in Beirut.*

Wendy: *Oh no! How come? Weren't they coming back today?*

Me: *They had to return to another job. Only silver lining is Hugo is off ill so at least his rest isn't interrupted.*

Wendy: *What's up with Hugo?*

Me: *Vomiting.*

I try not to think what my sister will be thinking, which is, will he be OK for the weekend and will he pass it on to them?

A message pops up, but not from Wendy, from Sam.

Have you had any thoughts about what we should do about Nicky? x

Crikey, I had completely forgotten about Nicky and Valentin. Must be the poorly boy upstairs addling my brain, or perhaps the cowboy kitchen fitters.

I compose a brief reply explaining about Hugo, and Sam comes back soon after.

Poor wee man. Give him a hug from me. Hope he feels

better soon x

My phone beeps a message alert. Wendy. *Tell him we're looking forward to seeing him at the weekend. Sending healing vibes to him and strength for you.* My sister then sends me lots of uplifting emojis: bottles of wine, love hearts, smiling faces, teddy bears – I guess that's for hugs. It makes me smile. Wendy is fierce when at work, but she's a hugger and the sweetest person ever to those close to her. She has no idea what a lift she has given me on what has been a nightmare of a day.

Chapter Twenty-four

Friday 5 March

To-do list
Call school
Finish packing
Tie up work loose ends
Remember to get kids McDonald's for dinner (pre-hol treat)

It's still dark when I get up. Five thirty. It won't be light for another hour at least. I hate getting up in the dark. The sun at least buoys your spirits. I've lost track of my tasks the past few days. I know some things have slipped through the cracks, but I'm powerless to do anything about it. Once again, I remind myself why I hate going on holiday, until I get there, when it is marginally better. It's like moving house all over again. And I have so many messages and emails I haven't replied to. Nor have I decided what to do about Nicky. I really need to get back to Sam on that. I won't have time over the weekend. My family is so intense and being with them is all-consuming. I love it, of course, but it leaves little time for anything else. So I will need to address the Nicky issue today.

Bear has a quick pee at the tree across the road, whilst I

stand hopping from foot to foot, freezing. I wish I'd put on a jumper rather than throwing my raincoat over my pyjama top. The stars twinkle above me in the remarkably clear sky, and I am thankful for the opportunity to witness this moment, where everything is calm and still, and the stars sparkle like diamonds in the cloudless sky.

Nicky. What to do? What if this thing with Valentin doesn't go anywhere? I mean, hopefully it will, but I know Nicky will retreat into her shell if she finds out Valentin is loaded. Money-grabber she isn't. I know she wouldn't feel worthy, as if she wasn't in the same class, in the original sense of the word, as him, not just out of her league.

I sip my coffee that I left in the utility room before I took Bear out. It's lukewarm. I pop it in the microwave for twenty seconds, enough for it to be warm, but not enough that it pings, in case this is the one time the kids decide to be light sleepers. I smile at the things we mothers have to think of to get a moment's peace. And we're generally not doing it so we can carve out a little 'me' time, but rather simply to have some sanity in an overloaded day and when we have a to-do list that never ends.

Hugo, fortunately, is well enough now to go on holiday. That could have been problematic, not to mention he would have cried the place down if he had been unable to spend time with his cousins and go to the villa. He has been so looking forward to it. My kids love a change of scene. Who doesn't? His vomiting lasted all of Wednesday and he was a bit peaky yesterday too, but he ate a few bites of lunch and a little more at dinner last night, so he is definitely on the mend.

It's too early to reply to any messages, so I attack the emails, and dig out my pension details from the sideboard. I have been trying to up my contributions for, well, three months, but there's always something more pressing. I swore to myself I would do it before my next birthday, and since we're away at the weekend, today's the day.

I log in and it says – *The username is not recognised.* For the love of… I try again. Same result. I haven't used the account in ages. The money just comes out of my account. Bollocks, I'll need to call them.

The clock shows it's seven fifteen. Time to wake the cherubs.

'Mum, I don't have enough room in my suitcase.'

I enter Hugo's room. His backpack is filled with cuddly toys and I suppress a smile. His overstuffed suitcase contains books, comics, two board games and Xbox games. I'm not sure how he is going to play them as we aren't taking the Xbox and the villa doesn't have one – the general idea being to detach from our busy lives and embrace nature for the weekend. Noticeable by their omission are his clothes.

'Hugo, what are you going to wear when we are at the Lakes?'

He scrunches up his forehead as if I have asked him something too taxing, then ventures, 'Clothes?'

'That's right. So where are yours? In a hidden compartment? Under a cloak of invisibility?'

He's halfway to admitting his error, but my reply pulls him up short. He scowls then folds his arms in front of his chest. 'Mum, it's not kind to be sarcastic.'

How I hate when my own words are used against me. I sigh. 'You're right, sweetie, but you're eight, and you should know you need clothes for going on holiday. Why don't we just put it down to you being unwell the past few days?'

His face brightens but then falls again.

'What is it?'

'Well, if I couldn't fit everything in before, if I add clothes, I definitely won't be able to close the case.'

I glance at the case, grab a few items of clothing from his wardrobe and chest of drawers, move things around in the case, and say, 'Voilà.'

Hugo stares at me as if I'm a miracle worker. 'How did you do that?'

'It's a mum thing.' I give him a hug. 'Now, are you done? We don't have long before we have to pick up Aria and Gen.'

He nods and follows me downstairs.

'Yay, we're going on holiday tomorrow!' Aria shouts. She fist-bumps Hugo, who grins. 'High-five, Gen!'

Gen submits to her sister's enthusiasm and smiles.

'I'm taking my Polly Pocket toys and Suzi Sloth,' says Aria. 'Mummy, can I take my Trunki?'

'Sure, sweetie,' I call over my shoulder as I negotiate a roundabout.

It never ceases to amaze me how mothers can multitask to the extent they can hold full conversations with their children, and make sense of them, whilst they're driving. Whether it's listening to their rendition of 'Silent Night' at Christmas, being bored to death about their latest YouTube fixation, or the constant demands to have their own channel (Hugo), we absorb it. Ronnie tells me he zones out and resorts to grunts when the kids ask him questions in the car, and my sisters and Sam tell me their husbands are the same, so it's definitely a male thing.

Aria loves her Trunki. We bought it when she was two, and she has taken it on every holiday, weekend break and sleepover. Fortunately, she can now wheel herself as she rides it, and I don't have to push her.

'How was school, Gen?' I make the same feeble attempt as always, although I know I will be met with a monosyllabic response.

'Fine.'

As expected.

'There's a new girl. Freya.'

Information. I can barely believe it. It's possibly the most exciting thing Gen has communicated to me about school in the past year.

'Oh?' I refrain from saying, 'that's a lovely name' as that's what my mother would say, and I guess it's probably not very cool to do so.

'Yeah. She moved here from Aberdeen. She talks really fast and has a funny accent. Some words we can't make out, but she seems nice.'

'And is she in your class?'

'She was in my French class and maths, but I didn't see her in English or art.'

'And have you spoken to her?' I probe, wondering how the girl must be feeling having to start over at a new school.

'Mr Montford asked her to sit beside me in maths, so I kind of brought her up to speed on what we've been doing.'

'And did you see her at break or lunch?' I ask, keeping my tone nonchalant.

Gen has a very small circle of friends. She could do with adding to them.

'No, maths was in the afternoon. But I said I'd see her at break on Monday.'

'That's good.' I smile inwardly, thinking of my lovely girl taking the newbie under her wing. It's nice to know you have kind kids. Makes you feel you've done a decent job.

After dinner, it's bath time for Aria and Hugo. Gen will shower in the morning like me. I see her point: she's too old for playing with ducks and sticking foam letters on the tiles. Hugo pretends he is, too, but I still find his foam cars and other vehicles across the tiles, on days where I know Aria hasn't had a bath. So unless it's Ronnie using them, it means Hugo still plays in the bath, which I think is sweet. Like most mothers, I fear my kids growing up too quickly. In the fast-paced immediate world we now live in, it's all too easy for them to become mini-adults by the age of ten. I don't want that for my troop.

Soon the kids are in bed, except for Genevieve. She sits in comfortable silence with me on the sofa, stroking Bear's ears. He does have the softest ears ever. It's almost therapeutic running my hand over his silky coat, but the ears are like velvet. It calms me, so I know how Gen feels. As I try to reduce the items on my to-do list and unfortunately add more to it as things occur to me, I sneak a glance at Gen. Her honey-coloured hair is pulled back in a ponytail and she's wearing a unicorn onesie, a joke present from Nicky last Christmas. Joke or not, she loves it. She pretends she wears it as it would be rude not to, since it was a gift, but I don't buy it. I know how much unicorns were a part of this girl's formative years. She looks about nine, not twelve. Her dewy skin is blemish-free. My girl is gorgeous, not that I'm biased. She has her Totes on – also unicorns – and her feet are up on the coffee table.

Gen heads to bed at ten and it's a good few hours before I manage to do the same. I need to be able to channel my inner bright-eyed and bushy-tailed holiday persona tomorrow morning, but I'm so knackered I can't even make myself get back out of bed when I realise I haven't brushed my teeth. There's nobody beside me to breathe on anyway.

Crying. Am I still dreaming? Nope. Definite sobbing. Must be Aria. It's two thirty. I've been in bed less than two hours. I jolt out of bed and go through to Aria's room where she is sleepily wandering about, sobbing her heart out. Night terrors. She can't even see me or hear me. The first few times this happened, it freaked me out, but after a call to NHS 24, who assured me it was quite common, I felt reassured. I pick her up and take her to the toilet. If she's coming into my bed, I don't want her having any accidents. I don't have the rubber-backed sheets on mine.

I rock her on my lap, brushing her soaked hair away from her face. Once I've settled her in my bed, I grab the thermometer, this is becoming a habit, from the bathroom and check her temperature. She's fine. Sweaty. Thank heavens. And I'm not only thinking about perhaps having to cancel the break or the fact Hugo is only now well enough to go. It's often the case that one of your children is sick, as if they're on rotation. School has a lot to answer for. Hotbed for germs.

Aria turns over in her sleep and snuggles into me. Relieved, I throw the duvet off, bring the sheet up to our chins and fold my arms around my beautiful daughter.

Chapter Twenty-five

Saturday 6 March

To-do list – it's done, well, just about and as much as I'm doing before this break.

Darkness envelops me when I wake, except for the tiny glow of Aria's night light, which I brought in once I settled her last night. Yes, it involved getting back out of bed, and yes it was an effort to unwrap myself from Aria's warm embrace, but I had no choice. The dark freaks her out, and if she'd awakened in complete darkness, the ensuing shrieks would have meant no one got any sleep for the rest of the night.

Bear hurtles up the stairs to meet me. I shush him and manoeuvre his not inconsiderable bulk back downstairs. It's a chore as he's forty kilos and is so excited. He knows something's going on. I swear that dog knows that my bringing out the suitcases means he is being farmed out to someone. Although he always has great fun with whichever family member takes him, when we return from holiday, we have to ensure an adult greets Bear first as he would bowl the kids over, like a Pro-Bowler landing a strike.

The only way to calm Bear down is to feed him. I delve his measuring cup into his sack of dog food and then sprinkle his food into his slow feeder. That's a laugh; Bear doesn't know how to eat slowly. I stroke his ears affectionately, yawn, then gather my wits about me and put the kettle on.

Mum and Dad are coming for Bear at nine. That gives me a couple of hours to finish packing, feed the children, shower and hopefully do as many last-minute things as I can. I do not, I repeat not, want to be constantly on my phone whilst I am on holiday. I have a golden rule: phone gets checked first thing in the morning for emails and last thing at night. Nothing in between. Family time is too important, and I already feel the pressure of having to be, in effect, two parents in one, the weeks Ronnie is away.

I know we're only away for two days, but the Lakes is only two and a half hours away and, I don't know, somehow when you do something with your weekend, which doesn't involve cleaning, groceries, washing, ordering stuff off the internet, paying bills, with the occasional fun time thrown in for good measure, time lasts longer.

Unbelievably, when Mum and Dad drive up at ten to nine, the house is in some sort of order and we're almost ready.

Mum gives me a hug that almost squeezes the life out of me. Of course, I wouldn't have it any other way. I'm big on affection myself. 'Do you want us to come in to settle him before we take him in the car, or do you need to get off?' she says.

'I'll make some tea. We're not meeting at the villa until twelve, so as long as we leave by half past, we should be there in time.' I plant a kiss on my dad's cheek. 'Hi, Dad, your favourite bundle of fun awaits,' I say, indicating the living room.

'Which one? Aria or Bear?' He grins.

'Take your pick. Although the hairier version is with you for two whole days.'

'Good point. Aria, sweetheart, come and give Papa a cuddle.'

Aria launches herself at her papa and I smile at the loving family tableau they present.

Mum grabs my arm as I head to the kitchen. 'I'll do it, love. You finish packing the car.'

I glance to the open doorway and see I've left my boot open. Mum knows me well. Even for only two days, there's no way that's all the luggage we're taking. That, and the giveaway signs of the holdall, Trunki and backpack still in the hall.

'Did you remember to check your tyres?' Dad asks when I finally return from packing the car. I should have drawn the line at Aria's sixth giant teddy bear. We're only away for two days, one night.

'Yes, Dad,' I fib. It's only a little white lie. I did check them, but it was in January. Dad forgets that new cars have gauges to tell you if your tyres need pumped up, or if your screenwash is low. Ah, that's something I haven't done. Where is the screenwash? In the shed? In the garage? Do we have any? Right, stop panicking. Even if we don't have any, I can stop at a petrol station and get some.

'So, what are your plans for the weekend?' I ask as I run a brush through Aria's curls. 'Hugo, put your shoes on, it's almost time to go.'

'We thought we'd take Bear for a walk along the canal. It's meant to be decent today and tomorrow, if chilly. You will take care on the roads, won't you, Louisa?' Mum peers at me, anxiety written all over her face.

I do wonder if anyone has ever said no to that question.

'Of course, Mum. That sounds great. Bear will have a

ball.'

'I'm looking forward to it, too. We have a lot on next week, so a few days of walking this chap will do us the world of good.' Dad runs his hand through Bear's soft coat.

'Great. Well, Bear's things are ready. If you give me your car keys, I'll pop it all in the back.'

Dad riffles through his pockets, then tosses me his key. 'Don't put it on the sheet or cushions, those are for Bear.'

'Nothing but the best for your boy,' I say, smirking.

Dad winks and says, 'You know it.' He's obviously been watching too many American films, or should I say, movies.

Soon after, we drive off, waving at my folks, with Hugo 'barking' at Bear, and Aria doing her best to imitate him. It's good to know I'm not the only one in this family who's barking. Genevieve tuts at their immaturity. She was so helpful when Hugo was sick the other day, I only hope this run of sweet behaviour can last the duration of our break. It should do as she loves spending time with her cousins, but she is that little bit older now. I pray the novelty doesn't wear off before the weekend is over.

The kids sing along to Abba in the car for a bit, chair dancing to 'Mamma Mia' then start making requests. I draw the line at Justin Bieber. I know Hugo likes him, but I also want my ears not to bleed. We settle on 'Can't Stop the Feeling!'– another Justin, but at least I like this, too. Who couldn't after watching *Trolls*?

Half an hour passes, and a fly on the wall would think we were the perfect family, but my cherubs soon tire of being in such a confined space together.

'Mum, can I play my Switch?' Hugo asks.

'Do you have it there with you?'

'Er, no,' Hugo admits.

'Well, you'll have to wait until we get there, and I guess you won't want to play on the Switch as soon as you see all your cousins, will you?'

The question's rhetorical. Of course he will, despite loving his cousins. They can sometimes be as bad as him, if not worse.

'But I don't want to wait,' he moans. 'I'm bored.'

Crikey, I wish I had time to be bored. I'm sure if he wasn't in a car seat, Hugo would stamp his foot right about now. My boy is usually sweetness itself, but when he goes in a strop, he really lets rip. I look heavenward in an attempt to communicate to the Almighty that I would like that not to be the case today.

'That's because you're boring,' Genevieve replies, rolling her eyes at her brother.

Oh no, not both of them. I need them to keep things on an even keel whilst I'm driving. Thankfully, the conditions are OK, but I still have to concentrate on the road.

Genevieve and Hugo have a sibling spat, and for once I zone out, instead focusing on the road ahead and trying to bring to mind the idyllic villa I booked after an eye-watering amount of consultation with my sisters.

I've never been to Grange-over-Sands, even though I've been to the Lake District many times. It's hard not to, when we only live a few hours away, although there are so many great places in Scotland to visit, too. So I am really looking forward to it. And I really feel as if we will be living a life of luxury. Holstead House is a Victorian villa overlooking the bay, with seven bedrooms and a huge, lush garden filled with flowers I can't name. Flowers aren't my forte. I'm better with animals. It also has three bathrooms, a games room, a dining room, two lounges and even a cinema room. I am so excited about the cinema room.

I envisage me and the girls sitting back with a glass of wine watching a romcom once the kids are in bed, chilling finally.

My reverie is disturbed by a small voice, growing somewhat insistent. 'Mum. Mum!'

Hmm? 'Aria, sorry, sweetie, I was dreaming.'

'I need the toilet,' my delightful offspring informs me as I pass the slip road for the services. 'Won't be long till we get to the services,' I tell her, smiling. 'Hold it for now.'

I catch Genevieve's eye; I know she was about to point out we just passed the services, but a warning look from me and she sits back and pops her earbuds in. Not sure why she didn't do that earlier when she and her brother nearly came to blows.

A few miles pass, my anxiety levels spiking after glancing every so often in the rear-view mirror. Aria is doing the equivalent of hopping from foot to foot, but in a car seat. She is wriggling around, and I can tell she is crossing her legs, which means she is bursting.

'Mummy, I don't think I can hold it in much longer.'

I hope it's only a wee she needs. That would be bad enough.

'Gen, can you put Aria's extra hoodie from the parcel shelf under her bottom, please? I can't stop as we're on the motorway.' Just in case Aria can't hold it in, I don't want her soaking her car seat.

Gen nods and twists around to grab Aria's hoodie.

'Stop it,' Aria squeals. 'You're making me need the toilet more.'

Gen tries to calm Aria as I focus on driving at the maximum speed without going over the limit, for both safety and not being caught by a speed camera on the motorway reasons.

'Aria.' I try distraction techniques again. 'If you can hold it in, I have a Freddo in my bag you can have once we get to the services.'

'What are services, Gen?'

'It's like a petrol station with restaurants and toilets, for people when they go on holiday,' Gen tells her.

'So, like us? We're going on holiday.' She beams, as if pleased with this discovery.

'That's right, petal,' I tell her. Six miles to go. Come on, service station, hurry up.

Between distraction from Gen and cajoling from me, we finally make it to the next services. I yank the handbrake on, tell Gen to keep an eye on Hugo, jump out, run round to the other side of the car to undo Aria's seat belt and help her down.

'Come on, sweetie. Let's get you to the toilet.'

'Oh, I don't need the toilet any more, Mummy.' She smiles.

I move her to my side and stare down at the car seat. Her spare hoodie is soaked through. Now I'm standing there, I can smell pee, and when I lift the hoodie up, a very damp car seat greets my eyes. I groan.

'Gen, I'll open the windows. I need to go get something to clean that seat with, at least until we can get to the accommodation and shove it in the washing machine. You stay here with Hugo.'

Gen is quite restrained in her response, probably because she thinks the world of her little sister. Aria's party dress is the first thing I lay hands on in the boot, so it looks like it's her lucky day. She plagued me this morning about wearing it and I told her it wouldn't be very comfortable for travelling in. She's having the last laugh now.

'Yay,' says Aria as she notices the dress.

I suppress a growl and head to the toilets so I can clean her up and change her leggings and pants, and socks, I see too. Yep, this is how all holidays should start… Relaxing? I think not.

Holstead House is even more spectacular than I had envisaged. The photographs don't do it justice. It's stunning. It does help that the sun comes out as we arrive at the iron gates. I key in the code the owner gave me, and they sweep open. I stare in awe at our home for the next two days. I can't believe we can afford this. It looks like somewhere the aristocracy would stay, back in the good old days.

As I drive the car into one of eight parking spaces, the main door opens and Wendy dashes out, assorted children following her.

'You're here. I was beginning to get worried.'

I step out of the car and she looks into my face as if trying to ascertain if anything is wrong.

'We had a little incident.' My eyes move towards Aria, who, having clearly undone her seat belt herself, bounces out of the car and into the throng of cousins.

'Jo's sorting lunch,' Wendy advises me. Maybe it's a warning; Jo isn't known for her cooking.

I raise an eyebrow.

'You'll see.' Wendy smiles and envelops me in a hug. 'This will be the best birthday weekend ever. Isn't this place amazing?' She gestures to the frontage of the villa.

I nod. 'It's even better than I expected.'

Wendy grins. 'Wait until you see inside. We haven't allocated any bedrooms yet, although as you can imagine the kids have explored every room, well, those that they could find. I'm sure they still have a few left to investigate.'

Unpacking the car can wait until later, and I'll retrieve the car seat cover and hoodie once I've said hi to Jo. Don't suppose she'd be too impressed if I greeted her with a hug and a peed car seat cover.

My four nieces and two nephews permit me to hug them and kiss their heads or cheeks, depending on which is easier for me to reach, then they abandon me and Wendy, and zoom into the house, chattering like a troop of monkeys. I haven't seen as much of them recently and I can see the differences in them more than usual; Jackson has taken a stretch, the twins are definitely faster than before and Aurora is coming out of her shell. We really need this weekend to reconnect and have some downtime together, not just the adults with each other but also the kids.

We follow the children inside and Wendy regales me with certain features she likes in the hallways: the original cornicing; the gorgeous stained-glass windows in the hall which portray various scenes of the sea, although I have the impression the owner may have a predilection for mermaids. Not a choice I'd usually associate with stained glass, but we are near the sea. A lighthouse and the stormy sea are depicted in another, with yet another displaying a quiet cove with children sailing boats in the sea.

The hall is so long and wide there's even room for a chaise longue. I will be having a sit on that later; I love chaise longues. I would really like one at home, but it's simply not practical.

The house has a relaxing feel to it, despite its grandeur. The enormous mahogany spiral staircase is like something the rich and famous descend to make a grand entrance, in a movie. My mum brain kicks in and has a momentary panic about the possibilities for trips to A & E caused by our cherubs sliding down the banisters. Hopefully, the three of us have brought them up well enough for them to know that's out of bounds, but there's always a renegade.

'In here,' Wendy says, opening the door to a room at the end of the long hallway.

'Sis!' Jo leaps at me. We are an affectionate family. 'Great to see you. So what do you think of the place, in the flesh?' She throws her hands out, indicating the high-ceilinged lounge, with an ornate chandelier hanging down from a stuccoed rose centrepiece. At the far end of the room stands a baby grand. How did I miss that in the description? Pity I don't know how to play…but Wendy does: the only one of us to persist with the piano lessons Mum made us take. I wanted to continue with my lessons, but seeing people cover their ears every time I tried to play a tune was kind of off-putting.

The chesterfield and chairs are as elegant as I hoped. I wasn't sure they'd be comfortable, but I'd always wanted a sofa like this and never had the chance to try it out. It's not the same bouncing on a sofa in a furniture store for all of two minutes; I need more time. This weekend should give me that. I run my hand reverently over the sides then the buttons. This must be very old, although it's in great condition.

'Sorry?' I blink myself out of my reverie and concentrate on Jo.

'Look at the view,' she says, standing back from the bay window to give me the opportunity to get in closer, not that she really needed to as the windows are huge and there are three of them. Wow! What a view. Fortunate to see the sea from here on a clear, sunny day, I drink it in. I'm sure the water's freezing, but it looks so inviting. What a difference from the torrential rain when we left home. March sure is a strange month.

'It's incredible.' Aware my jaw has dropped, I close my mouth again.

'And it's ours for two full days. Squee!' Jo grabs me by the waist and does a little jig, propelling me along with her. She does tend to go a bit tonto when her kids aren't in the room, as if we're all still teenagers, but that's the whole point of this weekend, to have fun, so I decide to embrace it fully and actively dance with my sister, despite the lack of any music.

Jo spins me around and I come to a stop facing the hallway. 'Aargh!' I scream at the top of my voice. A man in a white coat is facing me, his eyes wide, his mouth agape as if in terror. It's me who's terrified. 'Who are you? What do you want? How did you get in here?' The questions tumble from my mouth, but he doesn't get an opportunity to answer me.

Wendy lays a hand on my arm and gives it a calming rub. It's not working. 'Surprise, Lou!'

My panic subsiding, I stare at my sister in horror. 'No, you haven't. Please tell me you haven't got me a stripper.'

'A stripper?' Jo's brow furrows. 'Why would we get you a stripper?'

Now she's said it, the idea is beyond cringeworthy. I'm almost too embarrassed to turn back to the guy who is the source of this conversation.

Wendy smiles at me, and I see the man stifle a smirk. 'He's the chef, Lou. We hired caterers for some of the meals this weekend. We didn't really go to Marks. We wanted to surprise you.'

Well, you've certainly managed that. Oh my God, I am absolutely mortified. Ground, please, no, I mean, really, please, open up and swallow me. My face burns like molten lava. I am terrible at hiding my feelings. I glance back at the 'chef' and mutter, 'Sorry for the misunderstanding.'

His blue eyes twinkle. 'No problem. I'm flattered. And I've been called many things, but didn't realise I was stripper material.'

Seriously, he has to leave the room now, or I will have to. I'm about to combust.

He turns to Jo. 'When would you like me to bring in the starter?'

Jo glances at me. 'Eh, perhaps in fifteen minutes, Caden. Could you prepare us some aperitifs first? Your recommendation, but can you make one a virgin.'

She did that on purpose. It's not possible for me to feel any more humiliated than I currently do.

'Certainly.' He bows and leaves the room, but not before I noticed the hint of colour that crept up his cheeks. He bowed?

He has been gone about half a minute, during which I have been rooted to the spot, unable to speak. Jo and Wendy fix that by bursting out laughing.

'Stop it, Wendy. You'll make me wet myself.' Jo holds on to a chair for support.

Tears are streaming down Wendy's face, and her mascara starts to run. 'I cannot believe you thought the chef was a stripper. That is the best laugh I've had in ages.' She comes and hugs me, then says, 'If that's any indication of what's in store for the rest of the weekend, I'm so glad we're here.' Then she dissolves into another fit of the giggles.

Jo snorts, then hiccups. She's terrible. When Jo starts a fit of laughing, she can't stop and often has to sit down and try to calm herself, but that can take a good ten minutes.

'Well, if you're quite finished getting your kicks at my expense…'

I'm joking, and my sisters take it as such.

'Where's that drink when you need one?' I mutter just as the chef returns. I flush red again. I know I do, as I can feel it rising from the tips of my toes to the roots of my hair. Now it looks like I'm an impatient mare, when nothing could be further from the truth.

'Sorry, ladies. Does anyone have any allergies? For the drinks.'

'No, we're good, thanks. Good of you to check though.' Jo gives him a dazzling smile. My sister seems quite taken with the chef. I may have to remind her later she's a married woman, although I suppose she would only be window-shopping, and you know the saying, 'What happens in Grange-over-Sands stays…' Yeah, it doesn't work quite as well as with Vegas.

I lower myself onto the chesterfield and sigh with contentment, although a cup of tea would go down better, or a latte, right now. I'm not sure I know how to drink during the day any more, even if it is with a meal. On that note, I wonder what's for lunch.

As I am about to ask my sisters about the menu, a scuffling sound in the hall alerts me to our offspring.

'Mum, can I share a room with Jackson?' Hugo asks.

'Of course,' I say, assuming this would have been the case anyway.

'The thing is, he told Aurora last week he'd share with her.'

Jackson slopes in behind him, a tad sheepish. Quite right too; he's getting Hugo to do his dirty work for him. My beloved nephew doesn't like confrontation but neither does Hugo.

'Boys, I'm sure you can share with Aurora too. Have you been to see the bedrooms?'

They shake their heads.

'Well, if I recall correctly, there were two rooms that had enough space for three people in them.'

'Really?' Jackson says, relief written all over his face.

'Really,' I reply. 'Why don't you go and find out which rooms they are?'

The boys bolt for the door and I call after them, 'Take Aurora with you.'

Keeping the pace is what family holidays are about. Oops, Freudian slip; I meant keeping the peace, although keeping the pace is valid too. Not sure I can always hack it.

Our chef-waiter enters carrying three glasses on a round tray.

'My take on Cosmopolitans.' He beams as he hands us a glass each, and this time he does make eye contact. Hopefully, my two faux pas have been forgotten. Anyway, it's my birthday celebration, so if anyone is allowed to make a tit of herself, it's me.

'Tell me if you can work out my secret ingredient.'

My sisters raise their glasses to me, 'Happy birthday, Lou.' We chink glasses and then Jo says, 'In advance.'

Wendy rolls her eyes and we all take a sip of our cocktails. It's divine. I haven't had a Cosmopolitan since I was in New York before Gen was born. Mmm. Delicious. But there's something different; a sweetness, but not sugar.

'Caramel?' I guess.

The chef, Caden, shakes his head then smiles, his eyes twinkling. 'Good guess, though.'

'Almond?' asks Jo.

Caden's forehead creases. I'm guessing he wasn't expecting that flavour to come across.

'Nope.'

'Honey?' Wendy is last to have a go.

'Nope. Looks like it will have to remain secret,' he says, catching my eye. His lips twitch in amusement.

'We'll get it before the meal is over,' Jo says with confidence.

'One way or another,' Wendy says with a wicked grin.

I raise my glass to take another sip but a voice interrupts me. 'Mummy, I need my Trunki. My teddies are in it.'

I sigh and go to heave myself out of the chesterfield.

Wendy stays me with a hand. 'Chill. I've got it. Keys, please. C'mon, Aria, let's get your Trunki.'

I relax back on the sofa, but then sit bolt upright. 'Wendy, I'll take her. I need to get the car seat cover and hoodie and shove them in the machine anyway.'

My sister gives me a pitying look. 'Do you think I can't handle a wee bit of, well, wee? I told you, I've got this. R & R time for you this weekend. You need it, especially after…'

'After what?' I ask, alarm clearly etched on my face as she waves a hand at me to dispel any manic thoughts I might be having.

'I was about to say "after the fiasco with the fitters", but we're here to forget about all that. Enjoy your drink and then Jo can give you the tour.'

I give Wendy a grateful smile. I'd say she doesn't know how much these simple gestures mean to me, but she does. That's what sisters are for.

'But what about the kids?' I ask to her retreating back.

'Taken care of. Now, relax, that's an order.' She really can be quite bossy sometimes.

'What did she mean?' I ask Jo, who has already finished her Cosmo.

'Hmm? Do you think it's some sort of syrup?'

'What?' I ask.

'The secret ingredient.' She rolls her eyes at me. Frankly, I think I should be rolling mine at her. She's the one who wasn't listening to me.

'Possibly. What did Wendy mean, the kids are "taken care of"?'

'Oh, that. She means Michael, the entertainer we arranged for the afternoon so we can have lunch in peace. And their food's sorted too.'

'Entertainer?' My mouth drops open. My sisters really have thought of everything. I feel humbled, and I have a lump in my throat at their thoughtfulness.

'Yes, they have a magician who will also cater a silent disco for the older ones and a Tumble Tots-type experience for the little ones.'

That sounds amazing, I think. Not sure if I'm more pleased that my kids will have the opportunity to enjoy that – Hugo will love the silent disco, so will Gen – or the fact that I may manage to eat a meal without anyone asking me for something, or interrupting me to tell me the Wi-Fi has stopped working. This is like a dream. I had better make the most of it.

Wendy heads off, and Jo heaves herself out of her wing-backed chair and plonks herself down next to me on the chesterfield. 'Cheers, sis. Hope you have a wonderful birthday on Monday, and don't worry, we'll make sure you have a fantastic weekend here.' She chinks glasses with me then adds, 'Even without a stripper.'

I'm about to retort but she beats me to it. 'Although, wouldn't it be nice if Caden was a stripper? I mean, he has a look of Tom Ellis about him.'

She knows Tom Ellis is my favourite. Ever since I started watching *Lucifer* a few years ago, I've had a thing for him. 'Yeah, yeah, you're funny,' I tell her, trying to ensure the heat doesn't rise to my cheeks again. The thing is, Caden, who wasn't officially introduced to me, is hot. I mean, hello? Not sure what age he is. Early thirties? As I mainly kept my head down in embarrassment, I didn't get a good look at him, but I saw enough to see he was…divine is the only word that fits. How apt. Just like Lucifer. Those dark curls, the height – he must be six feet two at least – and lean. Right, must stop self getting all hot and bothered. Am married. But one can fantasise, right? Especially on one's birthday weekend.

'Right, let me take you on the tour, madam,' Jo says, holding out her arm for me to link mine with hers. I love it when we're like this, me and my two sisters together. It reminds me of how things were growing up, the three of us sharing a room. Dad offered to give up his study as a bedroom for Jo, but she chose to stay with us younger ones. We were inseparable. Sure, we had our own friends, but we were the closest sisters could be. I smile at Jo and kiss her cheek. 'Lead the way.'

We ascend the gorgeous staircase with its hand-carved motifs – more detail I gleaned from the website. The upper hall is just as breathtaking with its original oil paintings and seascapes.

'We haven't divvied up the rooms yet, but I recommend this one for you.' Jo opens the door into an enormous bedroom, with its own dressing room. Standing pride of place is a mahogany four-poster super king-size bed. I sit on it and discover it's a waterbed. Wow! It feels so weird.

Jo laughs. 'Lie down. It's amazing. I promise you, you won't be disappointed.'

I do as she tells me and have to agree. This must be the next best thing to being cushioned in the womb – the bed moves with me and embraces my aching muscles.

Must I really go back downstairs? Can't I chat with my sisters tomorrow? Surely one of them will watch the kids when the entertainer goes. Oh, this is heaven. I want one. I wonder how much they cost. Can you put one upstairs? Well, clearly you can here. Wonder what limitations there are. My brain races. It doesn't know how to stop.

'I don't want to leave,' I confess.

Jo sits down beside me, and I almost slide off with her additional weight.

'Oi, I was enjoying that.'

'Heaven, isn't it? I wonder how much they cost,' she says wistfully.

'I was just thinking the same thing. If only.'

'I know.' Jo moves round to the other side of the bed and lies down, almost catapulting me to the ceiling.

'Ha, ha, ha. Sorry, didn't realise that would happen.'

'I'll bet,' I say, pretending to be miffed at her. 'I think it might take some getting used to, though, if there were two of you in it.'

'Would make us roll closer to our hubbies, though. Perfect for those romantic moments,' Jo says, winking at me.

'Yeah, right. Like we have many of those, with three children and a husband who lives away two weeks of the month.'

Jo's mouth drops open. 'But you and Ronnie surely–'

'Don't!' I raise my hand out at chest height to stop her. 'I'm not discussing my sex life with you. Some things should remain unsaid between siblings.'

'Fair enough. As long as you're getting some.'

'Jo!' I glare at my sister.

'All right, all right, keep your knickers on. Or not.'

I give her my most scathing look, which seems to work.

'On with the tour.' She jumps off the bed and I follow,

loth to leave it.

The rest of the villa is as grandiose as my bedroom. Hand-carved headboards, marble fireplaces, underfloor heating, and there is even a sauna at the end of the hall. Decadent. I shall be using that. I mentally work out which of the rooms to allocate to the children. I spot the room Hugo has bagsied with his cousins. His hoodie is partly on the bed, partly on the floor. There's tons of room for them all. I wonder if the games room is upstairs or down. I haven't even seen the remainder of the downstairs yet.

'How about this room for Aria, Mollie and Logan?'

'Yeah, I'm sure Wendy will go for that.'

'Where do you want to sleep?' I ask.

'Well, I thought perhaps this room for Wendy, so that she can have the twins in with her as it has a connecting door via the Jack and Jill bathroom.'

'That's a great idea,' I agree. 'So you would be where?'

'There's still a few other rooms, so maybe this one?' She opens another door to a tastefully decorated room in Cath-Kidston-style print. 'Then I could keep an eye on the boys and Aurora.'

'Sounds like a plan. Let's see what Wendy thinks.'

We descend the staircase. It's tempting to slide down the banister, even for me. Lord knows how the children will hold out. I feel like a queen arriving to meet her subjects. The cacophony of noise from the room to our left indicates that's where the children are holed up. I pity the entertainer. It's quite an age group to cover. He seems to be keeping them engaged, though, so I will concentrate on enjoying a meal with my sisters.

'Let's not open that door.' Jo inclines her head to the room where all the noise is coming from. 'They sound like they're happily distracted.'

I couldn't agree more, on both counts. She shows me where the toilet is, the study, the boot room and then says, 'And last but not least, the kitchen.'

She waits whilst I walk in ahead of her. I'm in love. The midnight blue units and island are so me. And someone who knew how to design a kitchen with love clearly put them in; in dire contrast to the bog-standard kitchen found in a new-build house like ours. Ours is a big house, but sometimes I'd like to be able to tweak its layout. OK, more than sometimes, often. I try not to caress the black granite worktops. I would die for a kitchen like this. Oh my God, how middle-aged am I? I should be having orgasms over the food, not the furniture. Or possibly the ultra-hot chef standing looking at us with an air of amusement.

'We were keeping the best for last,' Joanna says breezily. 'Lou would love a kitchen like this, right, Lou?'

Caden's ice-blue eyes find mine.

'Yes,' I mumble.

'We were killing time until lunch by doing the grand tour. Lou can't wait to sleep on the four-poster waterbed tonight, can you?'

'Looks comfortable,' I croak as my face flushes. I need to get out of this room before I turn bright tomato.

Caden's eyes hold a question, as well as a soupçon of mirth.

'Well, I'll have to make extra sure the food exceeds expectations too then.' He smiles.

I back out of the room; I have no idea why. All that's missing is a curtsey. What am I doing?

Once in the hall, Jo takes me by the shoulders and pivots me round. 'This way.'

We retrace our steps to the lounge, where I have never been so glad to see a glass of wine waiting for me, although a litre of water might be better for quelling both my embarrassment and my desire. I'm married, for goodness' sake. Then a little voice says, *You can still appreciate great beauty*. To no avail, I try to get the voice to shut up; instead it says, *And nice eyes, gorgeous smile…* Shut up! Jo looks at me in alarm and I wonder if I said that out loud. After a minute, Jo says, 'You OK? You look like you've seen a ghost.'

I give myself a shake and say, 'Yes, I'm fine. Do you want some wine? Looks like Caden brought it through for us whilst we were doing our tour.'

Wendy waltzes in, smiling. 'They're having a ball. Could we book the entertainer for the duration of the trip, do you think?'

We laugh. 'You don't mean that,' I say.

'Don't I? I could happily while away the time chatting and chilling, even without alcohol.' She holds her mocktail aloft. 'Chin chin! To Lou, happy birthday.'

We chink glasses again. I guess Jo and Wendy drew lots for who was the designated sober person this trip. I take a sip of my wine, sit back and exhale. It's amazing how the strain and stress floats away when you have two minutes to yourself, where you don't have to be constantly at someone else's beck and call and can formulate coherent thoughts.

Jo raises her glass again. 'To peace and quiet!'

'To peace and quiet,' we all agree.

We take another sip and I fully relax back into the chesterfield. I wish I could do this once a month. I think once a week would be pushing it. I love my own company, albeit I don't have much time where I'm not actively doing something for my family, but if I had to share my downtime with anyone, it would be these two here. They are always there for me, and I know how lucky I am. Many siblings aren't close, so I appreciate what I have, and when things are tough, I know I can depend on these two.

'So, Jo, what's new with you? I feel as if we haven't talked properly for ages.' I put my glass on the marble coaster and sit back.

'Certainly not without interruptions,' agrees Wendy. 'I know you love it there, but we miss you since you moved to the Trossachs.'

'You make it sound as if it's across the Irish Sea or something. It's not even an hour's drive.'

'I know that, but we were so used to popping round to see you, and you us, and it's considerably more difficult now with all the activities the kids have,' I say ruefully.

'I'm thinking of taking the kids out of their activities for a year.'

'What?' Wendy and I say in unison.

'Well, since we've moved up there, Travis is working even more hours because it's his restaurant now. So, that leaves me with the kids more and more. It's almost as bad as it is for you when Ronnie is away, sis.'

Privately I think it can't be, but I humour her and continue to listen. 'Hmm,' I say non-committally.

'And now we live in one of the most beautiful parts of Scotland, with all the walking, cycling, mountain biking, open-water swimming and fishing you could ask for, and it seems silly to take them to dance lessons and taekwondo, rushing from one place to another and putting ourselves under so much stress.'

'Open-water swimming?' I almost spit out my wine. 'You do know the Trossachs is still in Scotland, not the Bahamas?'

'Yes, yes, I know, but I think it could be character-building for the children.'

'Are you nuts?' Wendy says. 'They'd freeze to death. Even putting them in a full wetsuit, they'd be freezing. It's March. It was snowing last week. Don't you remember when the twins were born, I nearly gave birth in the car as we couldn't get through the snow? Brandon had to dig the car out of a snowdrift after they were born so he could get home. And you want the cherubs, who are four and seven, by the way, not fourteen and seventeen, to plunge into the freezing water?'

Jo rolls her eyes. 'I will be with them,' she says, as if that makes it all right.

'I should hope so!' I pipe up. 'But Wendy's right, Jackson can't even swim, and he's only four. He hasn't even started school yet.'

My sister doesn't half have some outlandish ideas and sometimes it requires me, the voice of reason, to temper them. But this time we have to adopt a two-pronged approach. I love my niece and nephew, and I'd like them to stay alive. So Wendy weighs in again. Where I am the voice of reason, Wendy is the master of calling a spade a spade. She has no qualms at being direct, even if it means her hurting someone's feelings, if it's something they need to hear. This is something Jo needs to hear.

'Jo, I understand that you want to embrace this whole new life you have in Balquhidder and take advantage of the natural amenities the countryside has to offer, but don't you think you're being a little extreme?' Wendy asks.

'No.' Jo isn't defensive, but matter-of-fact. 'I think it will be good for us.'

'Maybe when they're a little bigger,' I say, whilst thinking 'a lot bigger'. 'Why don't you concentrate for now on getting to know all the footpaths, walks and cycle routes? There are so many up there. We could come up too, later in the spring.' Once the snow melts.

'Lunch is served,' a voice I'm coming to know all too well says. 'Please, follow me.'

I stumble on Bambi legs behind him, unsure if it's the wine or the sound of his voice that has put me off balance. Jo is asking Caden something, I can tell from the intonation of her voice, but my brain won't let me catch up.

Caden ushers us into the dining room, where little silver nameplates sit at our places for lunch. It's a nice touch, and I wonder if Caden or Wendy took care of that.

We sit, then all gaze up at Caden, whose chef whites are still pristine despite having concocted the wonderful dishes which lie in the centre of the table.

'The idea is that you share each dish, try a little of everything. Like tapas, but English.'

He smiles and my insides go into spin-cycle mode.

'First up, we have scallops with chorizo and hazelnut picada, then charred spring onions and romesco, baked feta with sumac and grapes, and finally grilled lobster tails with lemon and herb butter. Any questions?'

I'm dying to ask him what picada is, although from my limited knowledge of Spanish, A-level, I wonder if it's spicy. I also have no idea what romesco or sumac are and debate googling them on my phone. At least I know what lobster tails are, not that I've eaten them often, if ever. I've had lobster once or twice before, but frankly I can't remember which part.

The three of us shake our heads. Jo is already eyeing up the scallops, as am I, when I am not eyeing up the other tasty morsel in the room. Get a grip, woman. I stay mute, whilst Wendy asks what sumac is. If Wendy doesn't know, no wonder I didn't. She has dined in far more restaurants than me and considers herself a foodie. It will be interesting to see if she's miffed at not knowing what it was. That said, the good thing about my sister is she is so direct, she doesn't care if it makes her look gauche.

'It's a spice, often used in Middle-Eastern and Mediterranean cooking,' Caden explains. 'I use it in a lot of rubs.'

Once again, my mind goes off on a tangent, thinking of him rubbing me down, although not with sumac. I'm thinking more massage oil. Jesus wept! I cover my hand with my mouth as if to prevent myself from voicing my thoughts.

'Anything else?' Caden asks when Wendy has thanked him. 'No? In that case, bon appétit!'

To avert attention from me blushing again, at my less than pure thoughts, I spear a scallop and transfer it to my plate. Oh my God, it is amazing. I'm having a food orgasm. I don't remember the last time I had one, but it was before the kids were born, I'm sure. That and any other kind, my subconscious tells me. Shut up, I say, not wanting it to spoil the moment. The scallop is so soft, it melts in my mouth. Wow! So he's not only gorgeous, but talented too.

No one says a word, we're all too busy enjoying the food. I'm sure my sisters are having food orgasms too. How can they not? It's incredible. Although, perhaps my experience has been somewhat heightened by the bonus of Caden's presence today.

I opt for the baked feta next, allowing the salty taste to flood my mouth, appreciating every bite. This food is heaven on a plate. I'm either simply not used to eating such fine cuisine any more or this is the best food I've ever tasted, and I don't mean that because I'm biased towards the chef.

I sigh with contentment and my sisters both look up.

Wendy speaks first. 'I don't have the words to describe it,' she says. 'Everything seems an injustice, unworthy.'

Trust Wendy to be poetic and to find exactly the right way to describe it, even though she thinks she hasn't. If this is the starter, what will the main course and dessert be like? I pray I get to eat them without being interrupted. Much as I love my children, right now I almost love this food more.

'These lobster tails are to die for,' Jo chips in. 'Do you think it would be crass if I asked for more?'

'He might not have any more,' I say. 'And remember we have our main course and dessert to have.'

'True. In that case, do you think if he has any more, he could leave us a doggy bag for later, for when we're watching a movie once the kids are in bed? How decadent would that be? A midnight feast of lobster tails!'

'Yeah, tell him to add a few oysters, some foie gras and some caviar. That'll keep us going and in the style we'd like to become accustomed to,' jokes Wendy. At least I think she's joking.

'Well, I'm asking him after we've finished our food,' Jo says. 'You don't get if you don't ask.'

True, but I thought Wendy was the direct one out of the three of us.

'Good idea,' says Wendy, wiping her mouth with the crisply starched napkin. Honestly, the service, the food and the surroundings as well as the accoutrements are better than most restaurants I've been in, possibly every restaurant I've been in.

I thought we'd chit-chat over our starters, but we're so busy savouring the food, the flavours, commenting on the dishes, that we don't get a chance.

We sit back, contented, after we've finished everything.

'That was what the word "amazeballs" was invented for,' says Jo with a sigh.

I nod and breathe in and out, replete. I'm so blissed out, I don't even notice Caden until he is almost upon me.

'Did you enjoy that?' he asks, smiling, but with a quiver to his voice that suggests he is really hoping we did.

'Caden, that was incredible,' I breathe.

'Thank you,' he says humbly. 'I'm so glad you enjoyed it.' His eyes twinkle and my imagination runs wild, wondering what it would be like to say those four words to him with a different meaning, after a certain activity had taken place. For the love of God! Has he spiked the food with some love drug? Are scallops an aphrodisiac as well as oysters? I make a mental note to check Wendy was kidding about asking for those for a midnight feast. That's the last thing I need right now. I need my libido to take it down a notch, not go into overdrive.

'Yes, Caden, that was incredible,' Wendy parrots, then shoots me a look when he turns to Jo.

'And I third that,' says Jo, smiling sweetly at him.

'Excellent. Are you ready for your main courses then, or would you like a break first?' he asks, bestowing his smile first on Jo, then Wendy until finally it rests on me.

I'm grateful when Jo causes us to break eye contact. 'Depends how long the magician keeps the kids entertained,' she says matter-of-factly.

'Good point,' I say, then exhale in relief.

'Two and a half hours,' Wendy says. She'd know, she booked him. 'So–' she looks at her watch '–we have another hour and fifty-five minutes.'

My sisters appear to be waiting to take their cue from me, so I glance up and say, 'Maybe give us a ten-minute break?'

'Of course. That'll give me time to clear this lot away.' He gathers the plates together and asks if we need any refills – yes – before he sweeps from the room.

I exhale again. Wendy and Jo turn to me the minute Caden has closed the dining room door.

Wendy squints at me and asks, 'What is going on?'

'Yeah, I can see it too,' Jo agrees.

'See what?' I ask, frowning at them both.

'You like the chef,' Wendy says.

'What she said,' Jo says, draining her glass and putting it back on the table.

'I do not!' I reply hotly. Clearly I have protested too much as my sisters immediately say, as if they're stars in a panto, 'Oh yes you do.'

'Guys, I'm married, remember?'

'Doesn't mean you can't find someone attractive, and he cooks well too. Bonus,' says Jo.

'Are you two actively wanting me to be unfaithful to Ronnie?' I almost screech.

'God no!' Wendy assures me. 'But the very fact that's your reaction shows you do fancy him.'

I stop resisting for a second. What's not to fancy?

'Lou, it's your birthday. We can all fantasise. There's nothing wrong with that. And heaven knows, with you and Ronnie being apart so often for so long, a fantasy to keep you warm at night isn't a bad idea. It's not as if you're doing anything. But we can all dream.' Jo smiles at me.

She's right there. I've never once thought of cheating on Ronnie. I wouldn't. But who says I can't have a far-fetched daydream about a hunky young chef being interested in me, or that I can't lace with meaning each of my words to him, or his to me? Nobody. It's not hurting anyone. And Jo's right, it's my birthday, well, almost. It would be nice to think that a gorgeous guy might consider me attractive. Self-consciously I glance down at myself. The cobalt blue jumper dress I put on this morning is still clean, which is surprising since Aria was crawling over me earlier, and the accessories I chose – watch, silver necklace and matching chunky bangle – make me somehow look hip and young, well, younger than my thirty-eight years. I'm so used to being in jeans or work suits, I'm no longer sure what's trendy. Wendy picked out this dress in Whistles last year and bought me it for Christmas. It's flattering and I love it. Most of my wardrobe is utilitarian.

Wendy brings me out of my reverie. 'Earth to Lou.'

'Sorry, I was miles away.'

'I bet you were,' says Jo, her lips curling upward.

'Just try not to do the melty voice thing when he comes back,' Wendy advises.

'What melty voice thing?' I say, full of indignation.

'The breathy voice, the Scarlett O'Hara one,' clarifies Jo.

'I don't…I didn't,' I protest, but my sisters simply look at each other, then me, and smile.

'She's got it bad,' says Jo.

'Oh yes,' agrees Wendy.

The door opens and we all freeze.

'Your drinks, ladies.' Caden places our drinks in front of us, then announces, 'Lunch will be five minutes,' before breezing out of the room.

Wendy and Jo fall about laughing.

'Oh my God, do you think he heard us?' asks Jo, stifling a giggle.

I groan. 'I hope not. How embarrassing.' As if I wasn't mortified enough already. I'm beginning to miss the safety of being Gen, Hugo and Aria's mummy. Why did I think that was hard sometimes? This is a minefield. My phone beeps in my bag, providing a welcome distraction. I raise my eyebrows hopefully at Wendy. She is very strict about no phones at the table, and that extends to adults too. I am too, but I am dying to know if it's from Nicky.

'Oh, go on then, it is your birthday, after all.'

I take my phone out. It is Nicky, updating me on her and Valentin. I really hope this works out for her. Once again I think of how she needs a Valentin in her life. *Like you need a Caden in yours*, says that mischievous subconscious again. I ignore it.

'Nicky.'

'As I was saying–' Wendy stops when the door opens and Caden wheels in a hostess trolley.

'Ladies, your main course – roast duck breast with figs, rosemary and garlic-fried potatoes.'

Caden gently places the plates in front of us. 'Careful, the plates are hot.' He beams at us all as we inhale the aroma – I love rosemary, and figs. Did Wendy tell him what to cook, or is this all his own invention? If so, he seems to have telepathically known my favourite foods.

'Can I get you anything else?' he asks, his cheeks dimpling as he smiles.

Jo mumbles something unintelligible and Caden turns to her. 'Sorry?'

'No, nothing, I have a frog in my throat, that's all.' She glances at us and then says, 'I think we're good.'

'Well, I'll leave you ladies to enjoy your mains. Please let me know if you need anything else.'

His shoulders are broad and his arms well-defined. I'm not sure I've ever noticed anyone's arms before, not even Ronnie's. It's this place, this house, this village, this food, this company, this alcohol – it all has me under its spell. I'd like to say the sooner we get out of here and back home, the better it will be, as I won't have all these feelings racing round my mind, desperate to escape. But I can't, as the truth is, apart from really enjoying myself with my sisters, I'm also enjoying the smiles Caden is throwing my way, the way his voice sounds like honey, his smell. Hello, how did I notice how he smelled? And if I'm honest, the way he has been looking at me. Yes, I am attracted to him, and no, it won't go anywhere, but I'm pretty sure the attraction is mutual. Also, my sisters are both very good at reading people and their chemistry – they're rarely wrong, and they both sense it.

I return to the present to find my sisters silently eating their duck, and I realise I haven't started, so I dig in.

'How was the duck?' Caden asks when he returns to take our plates. Since every plate is empty, I think he has his answer, but either he wants an opportunity to talk to us, or me, or he wants to ensure we didn't scarf it down as we felt obligated.

'It was wonderful,' says Wendy. 'Absolutely delicious.'

'Mouth-watering,' Jo agrees. 'Best piece of duck I've ever had.'

I have no idea if Jo is intentionally laying it on thick or if it is the best she's ever had; it's hard to tell with her.

Finally, Caden turns to me, and I say, 'So succulent and fragrant. Really lovely dish, thank you.'

'You're welcome.' His eyes linger on me for longer than is necessary, unless my imagination has run away with me. I will my face not to flush, not now.

Caden stows the plates on the hostess trolley and leaves again.

'You're almost purple,' whispers Wendy.

'Oh no, at most I thought I might go tomato. I thought I could feel my ears redden.'

'Redden? They look like they're on fire!' says Jo.

My ears going red are my tell-tale sign that I'm mortified. They're always giving me away. I hope Caden didn't notice.

'If it's possible, I think they're getting redder.' Jo frowns.

'That will be because I just thought of him noticing,' I say.

Wendy chips in, 'Don't beat yourself up, he is seriously hot. You're only human.' She pauses. 'But if I'm not mistaken, it's not only you who fancies him.' She sits back with her napkin in her lap and quirks an eyebrow at me.

'Don't be ridiculous,' I say dismissively. 'He does not fancy me.'

'Yes, he does,' agrees Jo, her head nodding as vehemently as a dog wagging its tail.

'How do you know that? What makes you think that? He can't do,' I bluster.

'Er, we have eyes,' says Jo.

'And ears.' Wendy grins. 'I don't think he used the same seductive tone to us that he did to you.'

'Bollocks!' I say. 'He spoke exactly the same way to all of us.'

'Did he? Are you sure about that? Care to wager?' Wendy asks.

My sister can be very annoying sometimes, especially when she's adamant she is right about something; now is one of those times.

'I won't wager he fa–' The words choke in my throat. Caden enters the room again, this time bringing the most opulent-looking desserts.

He assumes his usual position. 'Ladies, I have a trio of desserts for you this afternoon.'

I notice a smudge of what looks like strawberry jam on his otherwise immaculate whites.

We all sit expectantly waiting to see what delights Caden will place in front of us.

Quite frankly he could say 'bin liner, salt shaker and toilet roll' and I would still be enthralled as I could listen to his voice all day. I love his accent. Definitely Yorkshire, although my geography isn't good enough to pinpoint where.

Caden lays the desserts on the table as he introduces them. 'First up, molten *dulce de leche*.' A lazy smile crosses his face as he sets that in the centre. 'Next, we have pistachio soufflé with pistachio ice cream, and finally lavender poached pear with Poire Williams pudding.' He looks at each of us questioningly, so I smile and incline my head slightly, not trusting myself to speak. I'm guessing he wants to know if it meets with our approval. It most certainly does, and even if it didn't, I wouldn't be telling him so.

Caden once again tells us if we need anything, to holler, and leaves the room.

'Are you getting a sense of déjà vu?' Jo asks.

'What do you mean?' I say, furrowing my brow as I raise a mouthful of the *dulce de leche* to my mouth.

'Well, gorgeous man delivers food, leaves us, we eat, he brings food, leaves us, we eat–'

'Yes, yes, I get the picture. Now, will you shut up so we can eat?' I dig my spoon back into the *dulce de leche*. I cannot believe I still have space. Thank goodness we didn't have a big breakfast this morning. It's blissful eating this meal far from the land of endless list-making that is my norm.

'This lavender thing, forgot what he called it, is delicious,' says Jo. 'Why can't I cook like that?'

'It's called baking,' Wendy says. 'The fact you can't get the terminology right is probably a giveaway.'

'Yeah, yeah, we can't all be Bake-Off finalists, you know.'

Wendy watches *The Great British Bake-Off* religiously. I have no inclination to watch programmes about baking or indeed any reality TV programmes. I can bake a few things, but when I have free time I prefer to do other things: listen to music, read a book, chill in the garden, although if I did that in March, it would be chilling of a different kind.

I don't do resolutions as such at New Year, but each year on my birthday, I do have a think about what I'd like to achieve over the coming twelve months. I've always wanted to learn another language. Perhaps this year will be the year. Either I'll upgrade my Spanish or choose a new one. I should aim high. Maybe Mandarin or Japanese. It's probably a pipe dream, but dreams are there to be aspired to, aren't they?

We eat the rest of our desserts in relative silence, communicating mainly through gestures or facial expressions, anything to avoid us having to stop eating; the desserts are sublime.

I look at my watch. It hits me that soon we will have the children back and we can prepare for our evening together. The kids so look forward to their movie and games nights with the adults, and it's not just for the popcorn. Between us we must have about fifteen board games. We're only here for two days, but when you have children of all different age groups, it's easier to bring a variety. There's nothing worse than someone saying they don't like anything you've brought for them to do. It spoils it for everyone else.

My sisters have their heads bent together and are giggling about something. I look at them fondly and think about how they have excelled themselves this time in arranging everything, and I applaud Wendy in particular for giving me a stress-free, child-free afternoon. It has been so nice to feel like an adult again, thinking adult thoughts – actually, maybe that part wasn't such a good idea, but I mean, having adult conversation that didn't revolve around brands of nappies, taekwondo outfits or the latest K-pop band.

'Well, was it everything you had hoped for?' Caden stands in front of us, his hands behind his back, his eyes glinting with mischief. Was that a double entendre, or am I detecting nuances that don't exist? I need a cold shower. He filled our drinks up when we finished our main courses, too, so I must be on my third glass by now, and it's beginning to show. At this rate, I'll need to have a sleep before games night.

'It was,' Jo says, just about keeping her face straight.

'Most definitely,' Wendy adds.

'I-I really enjoyed it,' I say. Does he look a little hurt? 'It was fabulous,' I gush. 'All of it.' I can't stop myself. Now I've started I can't stop. His food has been wonderful. Credit where credit's due. The fact I fancy the pants off him and am having wildly lustful thoughts about him is just a bonus, or not, I think dryly. 'I haven't eaten this well in years,' I say.

'You've been going to all the wrong places then,' he says. And this time there is definitely a twinkle in his eye. My sisters notice, too, and they sit back as if they're watching a table tennis match. Entertainment on the cheap. Who needs a cinema room when your own drama is playing out for all to see?

'Well, thank you, all of you. It has been my pleasure to cook for you today. I am so glad you enjoyed everything.'

'Caden? About those lobster tails…'

Wendy and I roll our eyes. Sometimes our sister can be a total embarrassment. And believe me, today, I've had more than my fair share of mortification.

We manage to get through the coffees and petit fours without any further incident, and surprisingly without any of the kids appearing. Secretly, I think Wendy or Jo, or both, have paid off Gen to keep the kids in line, with the help of the entertainer. There's no way he's that good or that the kids have been so well-behaved without help.

'Returning to our earlier conversation, Lou's right,' Wendy says. 'Steer clear of the open-water swimming. And when have you ever shown an interest in fishing?'

'Well, I thought it would be good for Jackson, and Aurora's a tomboy, as you're well aware.'

'Do you have any idea how boring fishing is?' Wendy asks, shaking her head. 'You would lose it with the kids after five minutes. Jackson's too little. He'd be too excited and scare away the fish. Aurora too, even though she's seven. She's not known for staying still.'

'That's true,' Jo admits. 'But I want us to have a different life to what we had in the city.'

'And you can still have that,' I say. 'You already have that.' But without endangering my niece and nephew, I don't add.

'You don't need to do everything all at once, Jo.' Wendy pats our sister's arm. 'Otherwise, you're trading one busy life for another. If you really do want to embrace the country life, then by all means ditch the kids' activities, and take them on some walks, go look for flowers, print them off lists of spring, summer, autumn, winter items to find in the forest. Don't get ahead of yourself.'

Jo nods and says, 'When you put it like that, it makes sense.'

Relief is the order of the day. Not sure I'll ask Jo again what she's up to. It's too exhausting. But seriously, crisis averted.

And talking of crisis. 'Mummy!' Aria runs into the room, big fat tears rolling down her little face, chocolate all over the little white fur shrug I bought her to go over her party dress. Is that snot on her chin? As if on autopilot, I reach for my bag. I rummage in it but come up short.

'Here.' Jo hands me a packet of wet wipes and I use one for Aria's chin, then another for her eyes. 'What's the matter, sweetie?'

Between sobs, then hiccups she says, 'I haven't won a prize. I'm the only one.'

Wendy shoots me a look then hightails it out of the room, presumably to the kids' lounge.

'Everyone else has got a colouring book,' Aria wails. Then she bursts into noisy sobs again.

'But maybe it's your turn to win a prize now,' I say, cuddling her to me, all thought of the state of her and her grubby dress almost forgotten.

'Do you think so?' She looks at me, a smile forming on her lips.

'I do.' I clean her up and give her another hug. 'Why don't you go back to the party games and win the next one?'

I'm glad to have dodged a bullet. I thought she was about to go into full-on meltdown mode there, but fortunately not.

'But I want to stay with you, Mummy. I miss you.' She

snuggles in against me. No matter how creased or crumpled your child makes you when they paw your clothes, when they *need* you and tear at your heartstrings, you'd have to be an ice queen not to melt.

Jo is about to intervene, I guess with some reason why she'd enjoy being back with the other children, so that I can enjoy my 'me time', but I shake my head and sit back with my daughter on my lap, feeling thankful. These are the moments to remember. All too soon she will be grown up, or like Genevieve, whom I have to coax these moments out of. The warmth of her little body snuggled into the crook of my arm makes my heart sing.

Wendy returns just then with a colouring book. She is so adept at reacting to situations. 'Here we go, poppet. Why don't we open those pencils and we can colour Peter Rabbit in together?'

'In a minute, Auntie Wendy, if that's OK. I want to snuggle Mummy for a bit longer.' My daughter and I share a smile, and when she turns away, I do the same with Wendy.

'Aria, why don't we go and sit on the sofa? There's a table there you can sit your colouring book on. That will be easier, won't it?'

She nods solemnly and then together we move her things to the coffee table. Once we're settled my sisters join us.

'That was ace,' says Hugo, bouncing into the room and plonking himself beside me on the sofa. 'The magician taught me three new tricks.'

I smile at my son's enthusiasm, glad he enjoyed the afternoon's entertainment.

'Do we have any cards, Mum? I want to show you the trick too.'

'Er…' I rack my brain, trying to recall if I did pack any cards. It feels like I packed everything we own, but did I put cards in with the Trivial Pursuit, Monopoly, travel chess and Connect 4 set? Not to forget the huge Snakes and Ladders set Hugo begged me for five minutes before my parents arrived. 'I'm not sure. Why don't you have a look in the games bag? It's the one with the green and white stripes.'

'Thanks, Mum.'

Aria finishes colouring her picture of Peter Rabbit and Mrs Tiggy-Winkle and proudly shows it to the twins, who have entered the room, along with all the other children.

Wendy is missing again, but I think she has possibly gone to thank the entertainer. I'd like to thank him myself, given the spring in my boy's step. Aria is happily chatting, so I ask Genevieve how she managed with the show, expecting her to be disparaging as she's the oldest and quite probably beyond these things, but she surprises me.

'It was really cool. Hugo loved the magician, but he was fantastic. He even showed us a couple of tricks.'

'So Hugo said. He really enjoyed it,' I say. Who would have thought Gen and Hugo would find common ground in magic?

'Yeah, I really liked the walking through paper one, as well as the one where you made your cup look like it had gone through the table.' Gen's face radiates happiness. Who knew magic could have this effect on my children? So, I tell Gen I look forward to her showing me how to do it later, and confirm that yes, we do have paper cups somewhere and I head off to find Wendy and the entertainer.

I'm walking along the black-and-white chequered floor of the hallway and am about to enter the other lounge, when Caden opens the door and steps backwards right into me.

'Jesus!' he yelps. 'Sorry, I didn't see you there. I was busy saying bye to Michael.'

'You know the magician?' I ask, surprised, trying to think of something mundane to say so I don't stand there mute. Caden's even more gorgeous up close, and we're pretty close at the minute.

'Entertainer,' he corrects me, smiling.

My pulse quickens. He could entertain me anytime, Caden that is. What is wrong with me? Am I going through the change? Surely it's too early, but why am I flushing? Why am I daydreaming about having wild, passionate sex with a stranger, even if he is drop-dead gorgeous, when I have a perfectly good husband at home? Or not – he's on an oil rig. But similar concept. I'm taken, yet my hormones have gone into overdrive.

'I-I was looking for my sister Wendy,' I stutter out.

'Been and gone. Think she went upstairs.' He fixes me with a look that I can't decide if it's going to make me swoon or throw up.

'R-right. I best go look for her then.' I turn to go but stop when Caden says, 'Lou, wait. Can you give her this when you see her?'

My heart almost stops. Lou. He called me Lou. It's so intimate somehow. I pivot round and he hands me a hairbrush, a smile playing on his lips. Wow. His hand grazed mine, and I feel as if I've had an electric shock.

'I think it fell out of her bag.'

I take a few seconds to compose myself then say, 'OK, thanks.' Then I turn and flee, my heart pounding. I have got to stay away from this guy. He's trouble, not through his own fault, but he's dangerous for me.

'Lou,' I hear, although the timbre of the voice is quite

different this time. I glance up. Wendy is waving at me from the top of the staircase. 'Can you come and help me with these games? I've no idea why they were put upstairs.'

Relief envelops me. Safe. I can do safe. I climb the stairs, taking deep breaths as I go, and not because I'm out of puff. It would be fair to say that a certain someone has upset my equilibrium.

'You can't swap until all the properties are bought,' Hugo says. He's very strict about rules in games and proper gamesmanship. Gen is more relaxed and Jo, well, Jo would bend every rule if she could, and that's in life too. We're playing in teams, and the little ones keep trying to put houses all over the board even when they don't have a full set. They just like the houses and are now fighting over who is going to get the last hotel.

'Perhaps we should get Frustration out for the twins, Aria and Jackson,' I say.

'But Mum said we'd play Hedbanz after,' says Aurora, pouting.

'We've got all night. We can play both.' I try to smooth things over.

'So what time's the movie then?' Gen pipes up just as her phone pings. She grabs it and a smile breaks over her face. Rain?

'Yeah, and what movie is it?' Hugo asks. 'I want to watch the latest Spider-Man.'

'No way,' says Gen, glancing up from her phone. 'We can watch an animated one so the little ones will like it too. Spider-Man is too grown up for them.'

My children are close to blows, and unfortunately I'll have to intervene to stop a war erupting.

'Let's toss a coin,' I suggest.

Groans all around, then Gen shouts, 'Heads.'

'I want to be heads,' wails Hugo.

Give me strength. My kids are fabulous, but sometimes, I wish they wouldn't fight over the least little thing. Sometimes it feels like they actively seek out reasons to argue with each other.

'Fine, since you can't agree,' I say, trying to keep my tone neutral, instead of the high-pitched one fighting to leave my mouth, 'we'll let Aunt Wendy decide.'

The scowls my children give each other would be worthy of two teenage girls. They open their mouths to protest, but I quirk an eyebrow and they know the matter is closed.

I defer to Wendy, who, after much consultation with the twins, chooses *Incredibles 2*. I sigh with relief: problem solved – for now. The clock shows five thirty. The cherubs will start getting hungry again soon.

'What are we doing about the kids' dinners?' I ask Wendy and Jo.

'Oh, Caden's taking care of it. He did their lunch too,' Wendy says.

Although it's outside his area of expertise, he served up pizza, sausages, pasta and hot dogs buffet-style. We'll eat later, although how I'll manage to eat after the lunch we had, I don't know. As if reading my mind, Wendy says, 'We're having a light supper.'

'Ah, great, I'm so full from lunch still.'

'Me too.' Jo pats her stomach. 'I only have room for liquids,' she says, refilling our glasses then her own. The handily positioned ice bucket has made it all too easy to drink more than I'd intended.

I love *Incredibles 2,* although I would also have been

happy with Spider-Man. I'm a big kid at heart, so I have no problem watching animated movie after animated movie. Looks like Hugo will get his choice tomorrow morning. We all squashed in to the cinema room, younger children and popcorn balanced on our laps. By the time the movie was finished, the twins and Aria were fast asleep, and I relished in the feel of Aria's warm, trusting little body against my neck, and the smell of her strawberry shampoo. I've had a fantastic day; the food was amazing; we've had lots of downtime with the kids; there's been no housework to do, just being, living in the moment for once. It has been wonderful. And catching up with my sisters and relaxing with them has been fantastic too. This is my favourite type of holiday. I'm very lucky the girls organised this for my birthday. It will help me get through yet another birthday alone since Ronnie isn't back until Wednesday.

Once the kids are all in bed, most asleep – except Genevieve, who is on Instagram with her friends, showing them how gorgeous the villa is, and possibly texting Rain – Jo, Wendy and I retreat to the conservatory. The night is cold, but we open the doors for some air and take in the stars in the cloudless sky. A crescent moon hangs overhead. It's almost like a scene from *Peter Pan*, it's so perfect.

I slowed down on the drinking front. I'd forgotten how quickly wine goes to my head. If I hadn't I would have been asleep during the movie. We decided not to have our grown-up movie tonight; instead we're going to chat and play Trivial Pursuit. Jo is so competitive. I love Trivial Pursuit, but Wendy always wins. Tonight, I'm determined to beat her.

We spend a blissful couple of hours trying to gain pieces of pie, and unfortunately, Wendy wins, again. At least I was second.

The wine flows as we chat, and I feel bereft at the fact Caden isn't serving it to us. Look at me, not only am I missing the hot chef, I'm missing being waited on. I was disappointed earlier when Wendy told Jo she'd 'dealt with' Caden after he left our light supper in the fridge for us. He'd gone without saying goodbye. What an idiot I am. Of course he did. He's the hired caterer and I'm the birthday girl, with a husband and three children.

We're all struggling to stay awake. It's half past twelve. Wendy's eyelids are drooping and I wonder if it's because she's the sober one. She gives a huge yawn and gives in. 'I'm going to bed, or I'll be useless in the morning.'

'I'll be up in a minute too,' Jo says. 'Once I've finished this glass.'

We say goodnight to Wendy and she heads upstairs.

'So, did you have a good early birthday, sis?' She slurs her words slightly. I'm hoping she's had more to drink than me, as I don't want to be at the slurring words stage.

'It has been brilliant, all of it.'

'Good.' She nods, then nods again, then looks like she has fallen asleep.

'Jo,' I say. No answer. 'Jo,' I try again. I stand up and shake her awake, which takes considerable effort. 'Time for bed.' I help her stand, unsure if her inability to do so independently is caused by tiredness or alcohol. I'm so glad her room is nearer the beginning of the hallway. With much huffing, I get her upstairs, take her shoes off and then lay her on the bed. I don't bother with her clothes. It won't be the first time she has woken up in them. I fold the duvet over her then tiptoe out of the room, although why I'm bothering I don't know, as I don't think she would hear if an asteroid hit right now.

Remarkably, I'm more awake now, although breathless after assisting my sister upstairs. I pause. I could go straight to bed, or I could go back downstairs and make myself a cup of tea. Woo hoo! Party girl, drinking cups of tea on a Saturday night. But then again, I've had rather a lot of wine during the day, so I've hardly been restrained.

Kettle on, I check my messages. Drat. I have loads of new emails. I make a note on my phone of actions I need to take – I'm compos mentis enough to know not to reply to emails at this time of night or when I'm tipsy. When the kettle is ready, I pour myself some chamomile tea, hoping it will help me sleep, then I have the genius idea of sitting on the chaise longue in the hall. This is the most peace I'm likely to get here to use it, so why not? Who cares that it's one o'clock in the morning?

I pull over a side table and pop my cup and saucer on it then go back to my messages. A few have come in from Nicky and Sam, as well as from Mum and one of Hugo's friends' mums about an upcoming birthday party. It has been so weird, but nice, to detach from all things social media and any kind of communication today, apart from my one message from Nicky earlier. Maybe I should try to disengage more often. It has worked wonders for my stress levels, unless that was the wine.

I'm almost at my last email when a noise behind me startles me. I jump, wondering if one of the kids has wandered down, but I don't see anyone. Then the noise comes again. I realise I haven't locked the outer door, although the inner one is already locked. It was probably down to me to lock the outer one as I am last up, but it hadn't occurred to me until now. It's probably the wind banging a branch against something. Hoisting myself out of the chaise longue with more reluctance than I can describe, I go to the door, intent on locking the outer door. I almost have a heart attack when I see a shadow through the stained glass. That's no branch. That's a person. It hits me that we are three women with nine children in the house and I panic. 'Go away,' I shout-whisper, eager not to wake the others. 'I'm calling the police.'

The letter box slams open and a voice calls, 'Don't call the police. It's me, Caden.'

Caden? What's he doing here? At one in the morning? 'Caden?'

'Yes, I've lost my phone. I've looked everywhere for it, but I've only now worked out where I last had it. It was in the kitchen when I was preparing the desserts.'

'OK.' I try to calm my pounding heart. I hesitate.

'Can we stop talking through the letter box? I feel enough of a prat as it is,' he says.

'Of course,' I say to the letter box, then realise what I've done and open the door.

He smiles at me, his cheeks dimpling again. 'Thanks. I'm so sorry to disturb you, and it's ridiculously late, but I know you are all going out tomorrow, Wendy told me earlier, and I didn't want to wait and ask the next family to come here as I can't afford to lose it…'

'Breathe,' I tell him. He inhales deeply, and I say, 'Right, you were saying?'

'All my business contacts are in it and I have a job tomorrow that I need it for, or there won't be any food at the wedding I'm catering.'

'No problem. On you go.'

I wave him in and close the door, then follow him, although I'm not sure why, into the kitchen.

'It must be here somewhere,' he says, in frustration.

Deciding that it would probably be best if an extra pair

of eyes helped out, I scan the surfaces, then the nooks and crannies, and am about to check the bin when he says, 'Would you mind calling it? Unless it's dead it should ring.'

'Sure. What's the number?'

I tap in the number he gives me and a few seconds later, it starts to ring. I hear something in the far end of the kitchen, but it's not a ringtone; he must have it on vibrate. We're both searching for it, when I spot it. 'There. It's in behind that cookery book.' We reach for it at the same time and his fingers brush the back of my hand. I jump back as if burned and he looks at me, an unfathomable look in his eyes.

He picks up his phone and stares at it. 'Great, I have fifteen new messages.' He sighs. 'No rest for the wicked.'

His comment lies in the air between us and I don't immediately respond.

'I better get going. Thanks again for this.' He waves his phone at me, then puts it in his back pocket. He hesitates when I don't move.

'I wanted to say thank you so much for making my birthday special. The food was truly incredible.'

He scans my face. 'It was my pleasure.' A silence falls and now it's him who seems reluctant to leave. 'Would you mind if I had a glass of water before I go? I meant to pick a bottle up on the way, but I was trying to get here as quickly as possible, given the hour.'

'Sure, or you could join me in a glass of wine, if you like?'

He eyes me, uncertainty flickering in his eyes. Did he see my china tea cup when he came in?

'Just the one then.' He meets my eyes and I wonder if I've made a huge mistake.

We sit in the conservatory as the girls and I did earlier.

The lamps are down low and the view of the stars is excellent despite the doors now being closed.

'So, how did you get into catering?' I ask.

'My dad was a chef, had his own restaurant. I'd like that too someday.'

'But you wanted to branch out on your own first?' I ask.

'Not exactly, my dad died a few years ago, leaving loads of debt, so Mum had to sell the restaurant.'

I mentally kick myself for putting my foot in it. 'Sorry to hear that.'

'All water under the bridge now. I'm happy doing what I'm doing, so maybe not inheriting the restaurant was the best thing for me.'

We talk about food, restaurants, his home town of Sheffield, and how he ended up living in Grange-over-Sands. He likes water sports and that was a big pull for him in making his decision to relocate here.

He listens as I regale him with tales of life in Ferniehall. He has never been to Glasgow, but has always wanted to visit. He has been to the Edinburgh Fringe Festival twice, but it was too quick a visit for him to fit Glasgow in too.

Eventually, Caden says, 'I really need to go.'

I look at my watch. It's five to three. Holy moo. How did it get to be that time? I will never get up tomorrow.

I carry our glasses through to the kitchen and put them on the worktop. I turn to find Caden looking down at me, his eyes dark.

I go to thank him again, but he stops me by putting his finger to my lips. He must have read my mind. He's clearly decided I've thanked him enough. He removes his finger from my lips, then leans forward and kisses me on the cheek. 'Happy birthday, Lou.'

I glance up at him, but he moves his head at the same

time and our mouths collide. Oh my God. That was an accident. I try to move, but I'm frozen. He places a feathery kiss on my lips and I almost pass out from desire. Gee whizz, thank goodness he's going. I can't cope with this. This heat must be what the menopause is like. Then he kisses me again, more firmly, and before I know it, I'm kissing him back, my hands snaking up into his hair, then down to his shoulders, his back, his bum, his chest. Oh my God, I'd forgotten what this felt like. I feel so alive, every cell in my body responding to his touch. We haven't broken apart yet and I'm scared to breathe. I don't want this moment to end.

'Oh God, you taste so good,' Caden moans. Just like that my ardour disappears. I'm married. What the hell am I doing?

'Stop. Stop! I can't.' I push him gently away from me.

'Sorry,' he says. 'I misread the signals. I'm so sorry.' He runs his hands through his hair.

'No, you didn't,' I say. 'You're an incredibly attractive man, with an amazing talent, and you seem a genuinely nice person. But I'm married. Oh my goodness, I've never done this before, and I don't intend to again. This isn't me,' I wail.

'Me neither,' he says. 'I've never kissed a married woman in my life. I just, I-I don't know, I felt a connection to you. I can't describe it.'

He doesn't need to; I know what he means. I felt it too.

'I think I'd better go,' he says, his eyes downcast.

'I think that would be best,' I say.

'Bye then.' He eyes me with what I think is regret and leaves the kitchen.

I slump down to the floor and cradle my head in my hands. What have I done?

Chapter Twenty-six

Sunday 7 March

To-do list – who cares?

Today passed in a blur. I don't recollect much of what happened. I gave perfunctory responses to everything, I managed to deal with the kids, smile in all the right places and show enthusiasm for the gifts everyone had bought me. But I felt like I was living outside of my body. I've spent most of the day tormenting myself. I keep asking myself if I led Caden on, and the truth is, yes. I didn't mean for anything to come of it, but I was enjoying his attention.

Jo had arranged for us to go on the Lakeside and Haverthwaite Railway, but it was all I could do not to throw up. Naturally, I was sitting opposite the direction of travel, which made me feel so much worse. I've hardly eaten a thing, blaming my lack of appetite on having gorged myself on the magnificent food yesterday, but my sisters know me. They know something is up. I know they're just waiting until they can get me alone again. I want to go home, to where it's safe, and there are no sexy men to waylay me. I know it was only a kiss, but if he hadn't spoken, the spell may not have been broken, and who knows if I would have let it go further? I feel sick at the thought.

It's a relief when it's time to head back to Scotland. I'm glad everyone enjoyed themselves, it has certainly been a memorable trip, but there are certain parts I'd rather forget, although they won't leave me alone.

All the kids are asleep when I pull into our driveway. At least the timed lights have come on, making the house look inviting.

I turn round and look at my children: Aria's head has flopped to the side and she has drool all over her chin; Hugo is lying back against his car seat, his mouth wide open, catching flies; Gen, headphones in, is a picture of perfection. They always are when they're asleep. I can't ruin their lives. I can't tell Ronnie. He would be so hurt. I try to put thoughts of Caden and what happened out of my mind, and instead start unpacking the car.

As I step into the house, my feet crunch on several letters, and I pick them up and put them on the hall table. I miss Bear. He always bounds towards me when I open the door, my faithful friend. Mum and Dad are bringing him back tomorrow. Maybe. Sometimes he ends up staying there for longer, when we go on holiday, as they consider Bear being on his holidays too, and if he's having a ball, they beg to keep him for an extra day or two. How I could do with him now, although perhaps it's best he's at my parents', what with the fitters coming back tomorrow.

I stand, hands on hips, looking at the kitchen, the state of it. Somehow it no longer touches me. I have bigger issues now. How am I going to live with this guilt?

Whilst I'm organising the last load of bags, Gen stirs and then wakes. I give her a hug, which startles her. 'Are you off to bed now, hon, or are you staying up a while?'

'What time is it?' she asks me.

'Quarter to ten.'

'Oh, I'll just go to bed then.' She hauls herself out of the car. 'Night, Mum.' She kisses me on the cheek and I feel worse than ever for my traitorous behaviour.

I bring the other two in from the car, and after making them go to the toilet, I change them into their pyjamas and put them to bed.

I stay up way after midnight, going through my work emails and trying to get ahead, since I plan to take my birthday off tomorrow. Although now I don't think I want to be alone with my thoughts.

The spa appointment is booked though and I've arranged to have lunch at One Devonshire, on my own. The kids wouldn't like this kind of food and my sisters and friends are working. I'm always there with clients and I've always wanted to go for lunch or dinner, not just coffee.

Midnight. The clock strikes and I stare at it. Happy birthday to me. What's happy about it? As per tradition I make my resolutions for the year. They're different from how I envisaged them. Be a better person. Stay faithful to Ronnie.

With a sigh, I heave myself off to bed, not feeling one bit celebratory. My last thought before I drift off is 'Should I come clean to Ronnie?'

Chapter Twenty-seven

Monday 8 March

Happy birthday to me! Well, you know what they say: fake it till you make it. But at least there are no lists, only lovely appointments to look forward to.

For once Owen and his boys turn up on time, which is just as well as I have places to be. I'm not in the mood to make small talk. All I want is for him to finish this job. He assures me it will all be taken care of and be finished by Wednesday latest. I wish I could believe him.

The rain is horizontal and the wind unrelenting as I dash from the car to the salon.

As the masseuse at Optima Spa unkinks all the knots in my back, I do my best to focus on the soothing music. I deserve this massage. I deserve to relax. I am owed this. Yes, I kissed someone else the night before last, but surely one simple kiss doesn't outweigh an entire year's worth of good deeds? I need this massage, now more than ever.

It's no use; the Native American pan flute music isn't working. 'Relax your body,' says the ridiculously pretty masseuse. It's all right for her, I think grumpily. She hasn't just cheated on her husband. She's probably too young, or sensible, to be married anyway. And I didn't exactly cheat on Ronnie, I participated. It's not like I slept with Caden.

A tiny voice whispers, *But you might have done. Not that there would have been any actual sleeping done.* Aargh! Get out of my head.

Fortunately, after my massage I had a relaxing facial, which was exquisite, and did wonders for relieving the tension headache that had started to come on. Later, I lie in the relaxation room and drink some tea I've never heard of. I could sit here forever. Here I feel as if I am in a bubble, where no trouble can follow me. Once I leave this room, however, that will change. Back to normality, or what passes for it now. How can anything ever be the way it was before? The rational part of me knows I'm belabouring the point, but the irrational part of me keeps saying, how could you?

My phone rings as I'm getting dressed. It's Wendy. Wendy? She must be having an early lunch.

'Wendy? I'm getting ready at the spa. Did you get back in good time last night? Kids OK?'

'Lou. Happy birthday first of all.'

'Thanks. Early lunch?'

'Lou, what's going on?'

The abruptness of her tone startles me. 'Sorry?'

'Something happened whilst we were away. Want to tell me?'

'I-I don't know what you mean,' I say, unconvincingly, even to my own ears.

'Right, I'll meet you at One Devonshire. I'll call ahead so they can change the table to two. Bye.'

She hung up. No, no, no! The last thing I need is Wendy quizzing me, and she never takes time off work. She must strongly suspect something is up. What am I going to do?

In the car, I'm about to drive off when my phone rings

again. What does Wendy want now? But it isn't Wendy.

'Sorry to bother you, Mrs Halliday. It's Owen.'

'What is it now?' I snap uncharitably.

'Nothing to worry about, but in case you come back and we're not here, one of my guys has had a bit of an accident.'

'An accident?' My heart sinks.

'Yes, he fell off a ladder. It's nothing serious, but I do need to take him to A & E.'

I feel faint. My kitchen will never be finished. Then my charitable side kicks back in and I think of the poor guy who is hurt. The lads all seemed very nice. I wonder which one it is. It's not their fault their boss has zero organisational skills.

'OK. Thanks for letting me know.' I'm about to press End when Owen says, 'I may have to stay with him until the doctor sees him.'

I suppress a sigh. Of course he will. 'Yes, that's fine. I'll see you later.' Not how I had envisaged my birthday, at all.

Wendy is already seated when I arrive at One Devonshire. Is it wrong that I'm miffed that my sister is joining me? Not only because I know she is suspicious about my behaviour, but because I had been so looking forward to this, just me, sitting in the window table, which I asked for specially. I wanted to soak up the atmosphere, enjoy the luxurious surroundings and the food – although to be fair, I have had so much wonderful food the past few days.

Wendy rises to greet me. 'Hi, sis.' She kisses me on the cheek and hugs me. 'Happy birthday.' Her smile doesn't reach her eyes, and she seems…apprehensive.

I forego pleasantries, sit and say, 'So, how come you managed to get away today?'

Realising I'm not in the mood for small talk, she dispenses with it too.

'Some things are too important not to deal with straight away.'

I quirk an eyebrow at her.

'Lou, don't do that.'

'What?' I say. 'Raise an eyebrow at you?'

'Don't be facetious. You know what I mean. Don't deflect.' She turns to the waiter who has approached our table. 'Just a bottle of sparkling mineral water for now. Can you give us ten minutes or so before we order, please?'

Wendy is a no-nonsense sort of person. Nobody ever initiates an argument with her. The waiter has clearly understood she doesn't want him interrupting our conversation for at least the next ten minutes, and he scuttles away.

Once he has gone, Wendy turns to me. 'Lou, birthday or no birthday, you're going to tell me what's going on. Have you had some bad news? Is one of the kids sick? Are you sick? Tell me!'

Oh God. I've managed to panic my sister into assuming the worst, all because I kissed another man and don't know how to deal with it. Now she has taken time off work to prise it out of me. What a mess.

'It's not what you think,' I say, then realise how ridiculous that sounds. It really isn't what she thinks, but isn't that always what cheaters say when they are found out? Ironic that it genuinely fits this situation.

'Right,' she says, drawing out the word, then folds her arms and sits back, evidently waiting for me to elaborate.

I feel sick again. Wendy loves Ronnie. She'll be appalled. She would never do anything like this to Brandon. I take several deep breaths and then blurt out, 'Caden kissed me.'

'What?' Wendy looks flabbergasted. 'How? When? Where?'

I can see the cogs turning in her head.

I sigh. 'He forgot his phone. Left it in the kitchen.'

'But he never came back for it. We would have seen you. You never left us apart from to go to the loo.' She scrunches her forehead.

'You're right, I didn't, but he came back after you guys went to bed. I'd made myself some chamomile tea and was sitting on the chaise longue.'

'As you do,' said Wendy, unable to resist a smile.

'Indeed. And I let him in and helped him search for his phone.'

'And then he kissed you?'

'No, not then. It was when he was leaving. We'd had a glass of wine…'

'You had a glass of wine with him?'

'Well, yes, seemed churlish not to.'

'Weren't you on chamomile tea by then?'

Wendy doesn't miss a trick. 'Yes, I was, but, well, I was hardly going to offer him chamomile tea.'

'No, just yourself,' Wendy mumbles.

I glare at her. 'That's not fair.'

'Isn't it? I'm not being judgmental here, just playing devil's advocate. You invite a man you barely know to have a drink with you in the small hours of the morning, when you know how gorgeous he is and that you're both attracted to each other.'

'I didn't know he was attracted to me,' I blurt out. 'I thought you pair were just messing.'

'I don't see you protesting you didn't find him attractive,' Wendy says.

'Of course I found him attractive. I have eyes. You and

Jo thought he was hot too.'

'Yes, we could appreciate he was a good-looking man, but we didn't feel a frisson when we looked at him, and it was pretty obvious that you did, and he did too.'

'It wasn't obvious to me,' I mutter darkly.

'Well, you never were one to notice what's in front of your nose,' Wendy says, playing with the bangle on her wrist.

I say nothing. She's right about that.

'So, what happened?' she goes on. 'How did the kiss come about?'

'You sure you're not judging me?'

Wendy rolls her eyes. 'I guarantee I am not judging you.'

So I bring her up to speed.

'Wow. That is pretty definitive. But it was only a kiss. Rap yourself over the knuckles and don't do it again. You've learned your lesson. What's the problem?'

How do I tell her that if Caden hadn't spoken when we broke apart, I would have undone the belt on his trousers, had my fingers poised ready to slip into the loops?

'I feel as if a temporary madness overcame me.'

Wendy sighs. 'Did anything else happen?'

I hesitate. 'Not exactly.'

Wendy rests her elbows on the table and lowers her voice. 'So what exactly did happen?'

'Nothing like that,' I say quickly. 'It's just…it was so good…and if he hadn't spoken and made me realise what I was doing, I'm not sure I would have stopped at kissing.'

Wendy looks at me, her eyes full of sympathy, not judgement, thank goodness. Why I'm surprised at that I don't know, as she always has my back. But I don't usually have major transgressions she needs to consider.

'Don't think about what you didn't do, focus on what you did, and why,' she says. She sounds like a younger, female version of Gandalf, dispensing advice. It's either that or a fortune cookie.

'But I feel so guilty,' I wail. 'Even though I didn't do… much, I feel terrible.'

Wendy sits back and steeples her fingers. 'Lou, stop beating yourself up. It was a kiss, that's all. A mistake. And it's done now. It's not like he lives round the corner or anything. He lives more than a hundred miles away. Put it in a box and let's not talk about it again.'

'I thought you'd be angry at me.'

Her eyes widen. 'Angry? Why would I be angry with you?'

'Because you love Ronnie. You two get on great.'

'I do love Ronnie, you're right, but I love you more, and nobody's perfect. You've been married thirteen years, and this is the first time you've even kissed another man. That's some feat, believe me, especially in this day and age.'

'But you would never do anything like this. I can't believe I have.' I flop my head in my hands.

Wendy leans closer to me and says, 'Wouldn't I?'

'What?' I say, my blood running cold.

'Lou, like I said, nobody's perfect. We all make mistakes. Mine was called Christopher. Two years ago. Sales conference in Birmingham. And I didn't just kiss him.'

'Whaat?' I yell, then lower my voice when I realise people are staring at us. 'Sorry,' I mutter, smiling shyly at the other diners.

'It went a good bit further than kissing, although we didn't sleep together. It took me a while to come to terms with it, and it was only that one night, but Brandon and I had been having some problems, and I felt invisible. Christopher saw me.'

I refrain from making a joke about how much he saw of her, albeit that would usually be part of our arsenal of witty repartee.

'I can't believe it. You guys are rock solid.' I shake my head as if doing so will somehow make it untrue.

'We are.' Wendy nods. 'And so are you and Ronnie. So, now you need to think about why it happened and what you need for it not to happen again with someone else in the future. That's what I did.'

'You did?' I lean forward, my chin resting on my hand.

'Yep.' Wendy sits back as if that's the matter settled. 'Shall we eat?' she says, picking up the menu.

'Ye-yes, I guess so.' I too pick up my menu, with slightly more of an appetite than I had fifteen minutes ago.

Despite still reeling from Wendy's words and admission, and them whirling around and around in my head, somehow I manage to enjoy my meal. My sister is good company and it's rare, almost unheard of, for the two of us to be out on our own. It's almost like there's no show without Punch; Punch being Jo in this scenario.

When we leave ninety minutes later, I'm still a little lost, but feel marginally better than I did before Wendy offered her sage advice.

School pickup goes without a hitch, the kids jabbering about the second birthday cake we're having for me. The first one we had at the villa the other night, but it didn't last long. Our children are vultures. It's takeaway again tonight, so I don't have to cook on my birthday. Pizza Hut. We've agreed to have a movie night. We never did get to see Spider-Man, the new one, so we aim to snuggle under the throws after dinner and have a movie night. I'm growing to like this life of leisure where I don't work. Pity it's back to the grind tomorrow.

The children spill out onto the drive and I fish in my pocket for my key. Only then do I remember Owen's call, having had too much else on my mind. Once the children are ensconced in the playroom, I steel myself to investigate the kitchen, but the mess greets me before I reach it. Half of my living room has plaster and dust everywhere. The TV, all forty-two inches of it, has slipped off one of its wall brackets and is dangling precariously from the other. Owen failed to mention that he had wrecked my living room too. Did the young boy fall off the ladder from the kitchen into the living room, somehow grabbing my flat screen on the way? You couldn't make this stuff up. I pick my way through the mess in the living room until I reach the kitchen; it's a disaster zone. I half expect Miley Cyrus and her wrecking ball to jump out. The units that have been put in are damaged, possibly from when the lad fell off the ladder.

I groan and return to my chaotic living room. I can't put this right just now. I have to feed the kids and I've promised them a movie night. Surveying the scene around me, I come to a decision: takeaway in the playroom then everyone upstairs in my bedroom for movie night.

When they're asleep, I'll take photos of the damage then tackle the mess of my living room. I hope Owen's insured. I've had just about enough of his company, accident or no accident.

Half eleven. That's what time it is when I sit down, having done my best to tidy up and clean the living room. With half an hour left of my birthday, I allow myself a glass of wine. My phone beeps. A text. I haven't even looked at my messages today. I've barely answered phone calls, but I had been hoping for a call from Ronnie. I know it's often difficult on the rig, but I did think he would make the effort today.

I scan through my messages. One from Sam wishing me happy birthday, same from Nicky, also saying she had a great time on her date with Valentin, and she hopes we enjoyed the Lakes. Mum and Dad have messaged me, saying they've left messages on my voicemail and that they'd like to keep Bear a bit longer, must have been either when I was in the spa or at lunch with Wendy, but nothing from Ronnie. Although I have no right to, I feel despondent. I miss him. Perhaps if I didn't, this wouldn't have happened. My earlier doubts crowd my mind, and I begin to feel maudlin. Best if I stick to the one glass of wine. I boil the kettle and prepare a chamomile tea. Another message. Maybe this will be Ronnie. But it's a number I don't recognise.

Hope you've had a lovely birthday, Lou. I enjoyed meeting you. Some things are simply not meant to be. I hope your husband realises how lucky he is, C x

I cradle my head in my hands and burst into noisy tears, muffling them with a cushion.

Chapter Twenty-eight

Wednesday 10 March

Ronnie's coming home today. I don't know what to do. Do I tell him or not? Wendy made me feel I was making a mountain out of a molehill, but why do I find it so terrible then? I suppose because if the roles were reversed, I would be devastated. Then I think about the fact Ronnie has had plenty of opportunity over the years, with his overnights in Aberdeen before they fly out to the rig, and I torture myself over and over that he might have had a fling, might have slept with more than one woman, many women, in fact. This isn't helping.

The house is still a tip. Owen and his remaining lad are trying their best, but it's not enough. His other apprentice has broken his leg. The kitchen is nowhere near ready and my life is falling apart. Thank goodness I can design cards from anywhere. And I am grateful I left some space in my diary this week as I'm in no fit state to put on a bright smile and ask engaged couples what their ideal wedding stationery is.

It's not easy holding it all together right now. And the text from Caden didn't help. I didn't respond, of course, and I blocked his number, but between that and my house looking like a demolition zone and my shredded nerves,

I've had better days. It also worries me how I will react when I see Ronnie. Will he be able to tell? Will I be able to keep it from him? Am I making too big a deal of it? God. One kiss. Well, a little bit more than that, and I can't deny it was good, but am I so starved for affection that the first time I meet a sexy chef, I let him put his tongue down my throat? The answer, unfortunately, would appear to be yes.

'Er, Mrs Halliday.' Owen breaks into my thoughts. I've taken refuge in the playroom as it is the only place in the house I can get any peace.

'Yes?' I say, taking my headphones off.

'I wanted to give you an update on the damaged units.' He clasps his hands in front of him almost as if he's praying. Maybe he is.

I wait. And wait. Eventually, I say, 'So?'

'Well, the factory doesn't have any more of that batch in stock, so we may have to send the good ones back and get a whole new batch.' At least he has the good grace to look shamefaced.

This is not good. This drama is unravelling me. That's the last time I take a recommendation from a friend. 'OK,' I say, drawing the word out, hoping he will take that as a sign to elaborate.

He hesitates then says, 'The thing is, it will be about a week before they can get them from another factory and send them up to us.'

Words fail me. I don't want to cry in front of him, but it's becoming very difficult, which he must notice as he says, 'Don't upset yourself, love, we'll get it done.' He gives me a small smile.

I don't doubt he will get it done, actually I do, but when will he get it done?

'It's fine,' I say. 'My husband will be taking over dealing

with you for the next two weeks. He's due home shortly.'

The momentary look of horror on his face before he can mask it is almost worth my having undone years of what the suffragettes fought for. But I do genuinely feel that sometimes workmen try to pull a fast one with women, even strong women. So let me introduce Owen to the man of the house. Ronnie's a pussycat, so let's see how he likes having to be tough on the tradesman.

I don't imagine Ronnie will be too impressed to come home and find the house in such a state. He wants to relax when he gets back after two weeks on the rig, and the work should have been completed long ago.

My phone rings and I use it as an opportunity to get rid of Owen. 'I need to take this,' I say.

He walks to the door and closes it behind him. With a sigh, I sit on the sofa and press Answer.

'Lou! Thank goodness. It's Sam.' She garbles all her words, so it sounds like one word.

'I know it's you. What's up? Where's the fire?'

'It's Nicky. Go on to the *Daily Record* website.'

'OK.' I stand up from the sofa and cross to my laptop, then sit down on the swivel chair in front of it. 'Give me a minute.' I bring up the site and gasp at the first article. *Pendragon heir beds beautiful mystery brunette* reads the headline. A photo, indisputably of Valentin and Nicky, sits below the text.

'I've found it. Let me read it a sec,' I say to Sam, who, if her breathing is anything to go by, is very agitated; either that or she's auditioning for a job on an X-rated phone line.

Playboy Valentin Pendragon does it again. His usual type, dark-haired, long-legged, dark-eyed, the mystery woman made no comment when asked how long she had been having a fling with one of Scotland's most eligible bachelors. Recently returned from his home in Perugia, Italy, the father-of-one was spotted in Michelin-starred bistro, Clariers, on Tuesday night. The couple looked rather cosy, but declined to talk with us, or pose for the cameras. But will Arabella Aschiero, his Italian wife, or rather ex-wife be impressed? Despite the couple's split at the end of last year, Arabella was recently quoted as saying 'The marriage is far from over. We are working at it. All couples have rough times.' And is this true love for Valentin, this time? Or is it yet another gold-digger?

Oh my God, Nicky has been papped. Although my first instinct is to feel terrible for the developments the article has revealed, part of me is proud that my friend is cool enough to be papped. But those terrible things they've said about her; Nicky doesn't even know who his family is, and she's the last person to be interested in material things.

'Are you still there, Lou?'

Coming back to the present, I nod, then remember Sam can't see me. 'Yeah, I'm here. Bloody hell.' I exhale noisily.

'I know. I haven't been able to get hold of Nicky yet. Poor Nic. I'm going to drive round. Lucky I was off for a doctor's appointment this morning.'

'I'll come too.'

'No, we don't want to overwhelm her, and Ronnie's due back today, isn't he?'

'In an hour, but he'll understand. I'll text him.'

'Seriously, Lou, I've got this. You wait for Ronnie. I'll update you once I talk to her.'

'OK,' I say numbly.

I read the rest of the article, then google Valentin Pendragon and numerous articles relating to his more recent exploits come up. A photo of a stunning woman, who is clearly Arabella, as she is as Italian-looking as a Ferrari and sleek like one too, appears, her arm draped possessively over her *husband.*

How could we have missed this? We already googled him, for goodness' sake. I guess we should have gone past the first page of search results. How could we have all got this so wrong? He seemed so perfect, and perfect for Nicky. Was he too perfect? He was so nice, but I suppose all charmers are; that's their MO. Thank goodness Nicky hasn't slept with him yet. Has she? Oh Lord, I hope not.

My fingers itch to text her, but I trust Sam to assess the situation and report back. In the meantime, I try to keep busy, which isn't hard as I have a lot of work to catch up on, but I find it difficult to concentrate.

My phone beeps with a text. Mum. *Is that Nicky in the* Daily Record *with Valentin Pendragon?* She has attached a photo of her holding the physical copy of the newspaper. Holy moo, it's on the front page.

The front doorbell rings, and for a moment I think it's Nicky come seeking refuge, although hopefully they don't know where she lives. Images of the press staking out Hugh Grant's home in *Notting Hill* flit through my mind. God, Nicky would hate that. I pray to the man upstairs that the worst news is past.

I fling open the door and my husband opens his arms to me. My face falls momentarily and he must notice as he says, 'That's not quite the welcome home I was hoping for.'

'Sorry, come in. Give us a hug. There's a lot going on.'

'Or not,' Ronnie says, his face falling when his eyes take in the devastation that is the living room and dining room. 'What the hell?'

'Never mind that. We'll deal with it later.'

'But they're already behind schedule, by miles,' Ronnie protests as he drops his holdall in the hall and wraps his arms around me. For a moment I lose myself in his embrace, then reality returns as my phone starts to ring.

'Give me a minute, hon. Bit of an emergency.'

Ronnie gives me the long-suffering husband look and pads off to inspect the kitchen, which he will note is absent of kitchen units and indeed kitchen fitters.

'Lou, it's me,' Sam gasps out. 'I've been to Nicky's house, but there's no answer. I can't tell for sure if she's there or not. What are we going to do? I've texted her and phoned her, but it goes straight to voicemail.'

I marshal my thoughts. 'Worst-case scenario, she'll have to pick Xander up from school later. We could intercept her there.'

'We're not on a sting, Lou!' Sam says. 'And what if she didn't send Xander to school? What if she couldn't face that?'

Drumming my fingers against the table, I debate what the next step should be. 'I'll phone her and text her, then I'll contact her mum, and if that fails, I'll contact Valentin. I still have his number.'

'Do you think that's wise? I'm sure he's the last person she wants to speak to right now.'

Sam makes a fair point, but what else can we do, and what do we have to lose?

'Let me see what I can find out, and try to keep calm.'

'OK,' Sam says, 'but I'm so worried about her. You don't think she'd do anything stupid, do you?'

The thought hadn't even entered my mind, but now that Sam has voiced it, it has me concerned too. 'No. She wouldn't do that. She has Xander to think about, and anyway, nothing's that bad.'

'Right. Good luck, Lou. I need to get to school.'

I hang up the phone and go to find Ronnie. I'll need to fill him in and explain why I may have to head out the moment he arrived; otherwise he may get a complex.

'Ronnie, there's a bit of a situation,' I say as he turns to me, his face pale. He has clearly taken in the state of the kitchen.

Quickly I bring him up to speed, then peck him on the cheek, grab my things and promise to be back as soon as I can.

Nicky's mum hasn't heard from her and is also frantic with worry. I reassure her that I'll find her and make another couple of calls, including to Valentin, with no success.

I ring Nicky again, but the phone doesn't even ring, going straight to voicemail. So I google the phone number of Pendragon Enterprises.

'Good morning, I'm looking to speak with Valentin Pendragon, please.' I keep my tone professional.

'Mr Pendragon is in a meeting at the moment. Can I take a message?'

'Is he in the office today?'

'Yes, but he has appointments all day.'

'No problem. I'll try him later. Thank you.' A plan begins to form in my mind.

My clothes won't convince them I'm a client, so I need to think outside the box. The address is in the West End of Glasgow, off Argyle Street. I have about half an hour to streamline my plan. Either that or I'll have to wing it.

The sleek glass building is fitting for the wealth I now know the Pendragons have. I'm not sure if I'd been expecting camera crews and reporters to be flocking outside, but the exterior of the building is eerily quiet. All I can hear is the hum of the passing traffic.

My hands are clammy and my heart is pounding, but I steel my resolve and approach the Pendragon building. They probably have CCTV covering every nook and cranny, so I try to act as normal as possible and not like someone faking their confidence.

As I reach the door, an opportunity presents itself. A girl is juggling rather a lot of items and keeps dropping something.

'Let me help you with that.' I smile.

'Thanks. I'm already late for this presentation. My car wouldn't start and I was tasked with bringing these materials in. My boss' PA has phoned me ten times.'

'Oh no. That's stressful. Here, I'll get the door.'

'Thanks.' She shoots me a grateful glance. 'I'm Judy. I haven't seen you here before. Are you new?'

'I'm Louisa.' I almost tell her the truth about Valentin's grandfather hitting my car, but then realise they may not want that to be common knowledge. 'I'm a friend of Valentin's.'

'Oh, yes, he's a great guy, great boss,' she says, almost as if she's worried she's given me the wrong impression.

'He is, but he works too hard.'

'He does.' She nods.

'Which is why I'm here to take him to lunch, and I'm not taking no for an answer.'

'Good for you. Quite right. All he does is hold meeting after meeting, and there are only so many deli sandwiches you can eat.'

'Right. Well, there's a new steakhouse opened on Byres Road, and I made a reservation so he can't fob me off with excuses.' I lean forward conspiratorially. 'Although I have to get past the gatekeeper first.'

Her eyes twinkle. 'Bernadette. Don't you worry, leave her to me. You can just come to the meeting room with me. I'll tell her you're a consultant. You'll just need to sign in.'

'That's great. Thank you.'

Judy is as good as her word. 'Morning, Bernadette. How's your grandson? Isn't it his birthday this week?'

Bernadette, who until then was surveying me like a predator ready for its next meal, softens and says, 'Yes, he'll be three. Do you want to see some photos of him?'

'I would love to,' Judy says, 'but can it wait until after the meeting? I'm already so late.' Her eyes lower to all the paraphernalia she is carrying.

'Of course.'

'Louisa, can you sign in?' Judy says, inclining her head towards the book on the desk.

'Sure.' I scrawl my name and turn to go, but Bernadette says, 'We need your company details too.'

I feel as if her hawkish eyes see right through me. I do have a business card with me, but I'm not sure that a card bearing the words Wedded Bliss will get me into that meeting. Brazening it out, I hand Bernadette my card and about-turn. I wish I had eyes in the back of my head to see her expression. I can almost hear the cogs turning and see her forehead scrunching in puzzlement.

'Ready?' Judy asks.

'Absolutely.'

'Sorry I'm late, everyone.'

From the corner where I'm waiting by the door, I can just see into the room. Valentin is sitting at the head of the table, whilst, I presume, an associate gives a presentation. Judy approaches him and whispers in his ear. Lip-reading comes in handy sometimes. I see him mouth *'What?'*

'Excuse me, everyone. Let's take a ten-minute break here to gather our thoughts.' He strides out of the conference room towards my hiding place.

'Louisa!'

'Hi, Valentin.' I give a wry smile.

'What are you doing here?'

His incredulity bugs me, so I say, 'Trying to look after my friend. Or rather, trying to find my friend.'

'What do you mean? Is Nicky all right?'

'That's what I'd like to find out. When did you last hear from her?' I feel like the Gestapo, but this is no time to mess around.

'This morning, about seven. Why?'

'And she was fine?'

'Of course she was fine. Why wouldn't she be?' Valentin's face creases as if he's confused.

'I'm taking a wild guess here, but I don't imagine she was very happy about you being photographed last night.'

'Oh, that. No, she was fine. It was an inconvenience, sure, and a little embarrassing for her, but I drove her home, we had coffee at hers and then I went home. She was fine then too.'

I huff out a breath. 'Well, Valentin, she hasn't been seen or heard from today. There's no answer from her house and her mum is worried, as are Sam and I.'

'I don't understand.' He runs a hand through his hair, as if that will somehow give him the answer.

'Valentin, seriously, you don't know? You can't hazard a guess?'

'Guess what? Know what?'

He honestly doesn't know. 'Have you seen the headlines today?'

He shakes his head. 'I've been in a meeting since eight

o'clock. We've been thrashing out a contract with Tokyo. What headlines?'

I groan and bring up the article on my phone, then pass the phone to Valentin.

'Oh no! Oh God, poor Nicky. It's not what it looks like. This is nonsense. Oh shit.' He hesitates, then says, 'Excuse me a minute. I need to fix this. It's all my fault, or rather all my ex-wife's fault.'

He re-enters the conference room and pulls Judy to one side, and although I don't hear what he says, I get the gist: he's coming with me.

When he returns, he says, 'Look, let's grab a coffee in my office so we can work out how best to track her down.'

I nod and follow him to a huge corner office with an amazing view over Kelvingrove Park and the art galleries.

'Please, take a seat.' He busies himself with the coffee machine to the left of his walnut desk, or is it mahogany? Hard to tell. Some expensive wood.

'What would you like?' he asks me.

'Latte,' I say.

Two minutes later we're sitting with our coffees, as Valentin tells me his version of events: how he returned from Perugia recently after finalising his divorce, how he had been living in Italy full time until now to be able to maintain contact with his son.

'Arabella and I have been over for a long time. She cheated on me, more than once. I could never trust her again. I'm not the playboy the press makes me out to be, far from it. Yes, I was photographed with lots of women in the past, some friends, some more than friends, but only when I was single.'

I remain silent so he will continue. 'Arabella won't accept that we're over, even though we have been for many years. She's always coming up with ways for me to have to return to Italy. Now, with the conclusion of the divorce, she's clearly out to stir up trouble. I don't want to hurt her, but I haven't loved her for years. My priority is some normality for our son. So I won't bad-mouth her in public, or expose her lies. But we are over. I would never have started anything with Nicky otherwise. I'm not only separated, but divorced, and was divorced and a free man before I met Nicky.'

'But have you told Nicky you have a son? She hasn't mentioned it to me.'

Valentin sighs. 'No. When you're wealthy and have children, it becomes complicated. Protecting Mario is my number one priority. With a famous mother and a famous family generally, it's hard to do so, but I don't bring the subject of him up until I know someone really well. I would have told Nicky in a few weeks, but I had to be sure that what I think we have is real before I risk my son getting hurt.'

'I understand, but equally Xander could get hurt if you were to become involved in his mum's life and then it all ended.'

'True.' Valentin dips his head. 'But Xander's life wouldn't be played out in the media.'

'Like Nicky's hasn't been.' I can't help the barb from spilling out.

'Touché. Well, it wasn't supposed to. And if Arabella hadn't been so vindictive and determined, it wouldn't have been. Anyway, now you know the story, what do we do to find Nicky?'

'I don't know. We've tried contacting her in every way we can think of. No joy. I suppose we could try messaging her and saying it's not true. I should do that as she would expect you to say that. But, Valentin, you need to understand, Nicky is fragile. She finds it hard to trust. I really hoped you'd be the guy to change that, but she clearly hadn't realised who you were. I didn't.'

'And I didn't explain. It's hard when you meet someone new. I wanted her to like me for me. It's the only way I can be sure it's authentic, if I don't give the background detail on my family.'

'It's not exactly truthful, though, is it?'

He closes his eyes momentarily. When he opens them, he says, 'I suppose not. Right, why don't you fire off that message, and I can rack my brain for anywhere she might have gone.'

I do, but no reply comes. I ask Valentin to send a message, stating that we're together and are worried about her. Still no answer. I tell her Sam and her mum are beside themselves. Still no answer. I don't know what else we can do. Did she take Xander to school? We could go there and wait, although stalking someone at a school doesn't seem like a great idea.

My phone rings. I grab it up, then realise it's Sam. My relief dissipates, then I wonder if she has any news.

'Sam, have you heard from her?' The hope in my voice is almost tangible.

'No, afraid not. However, I have heard from Sebastian.'

'Sebastian?' Now I'm confused.

Valentin's brow furrows.

'Nicky called him this morning, said she had an emergency and could she drop Xander off for a few days. She said she'd explain more later. He took Xander, obviously, but didn't think too much more of it until the newspaper dropped onto his mat.'

I groan. 'So we know she's not expecting to be home

for a couple of days.' I drum my fingers on the desk as if it will help me think better. 'No, I reckon she's away licking her wounds somewhere. I'll check her house again, see if I can be certain she isn't hiding out inside the house with bottles of wine and tubs of ice cream, but if that doesn't turn up the goods, we'll have to wait until she's ready to talk to us.'

Valentin nods as if thinking over what I've said. 'I think you're right. We need to let her know she has our support and that we're here for her when she's ready to come back and talk.' He turns to me. 'I'm so sorry about all this, Louisa, what a mess. Poor Nicky. She's too nice a person to have to deal with all my baggage.'

'Valentin.' I put my hand on his arm. 'Hopefully, Nicky simply needs some time and then you and I can both explain to her the way things really are. You're great together. Nicky needs someone like you.'

He raises an eyebrow and smiles ruefully.

'OK, someone like you, but without the drama and the vengeful ex-wife.'

'I can't believe all this has happened. I feel as if I'm in a nightmare.' He drags his hands through his hair again.

'Don't worry. She'll be in touch soon. She has to be.' I smile. 'I'll let you know if I find her at the house, or if I hear from her.'

'Please, let me come with you. It's the least I can do.'

'Thanks, Valentin, but you have a meeting with Tokyo to get back to, and I honestly think it would be best if you're not the first person Nicky sees.'

He sighs. 'You're right. Please find her, Louisa.'

'I intend to.'

'Any joy?' Ronnie asks me when I finally return home.

'Afraid not.' I collapse into his arms. 'Thanks for picking the kids up.'

'They are my kids too, remember.'

'Indeed. How is everyone?'

He beams. 'Delighted to see me, of course, although Aria hadn't realised today was Wednesday and thought I was coming home tomorrow.'

'I reminded her this morning,' I say. 'That girl has selective hearing.'

'She certainly does. Anyway, do you think we could sit down for five minutes and talk about Nicky, and this–' he sweeps his hand in the air to encompass the wrecked living room and non-existent kitchen '–nightmare that Owen has left us with?'

I honestly want to say no. 'Can it wait until tomorrow? The kitchen part? I'm wrung out and still worried about Nicky, and let's face it, the kitchen has been a state for two weeks now, what's one more day? Plus, talking about it won't change matters.'

'OK, deal.' Ronnie smiles at me. 'So, would someone like a relaxing shoulder massage?'

'I thought you'd never ask,' I say. 'But first let me say hi to the kids.' I kiss him on the cheek as I pass him to seek out my cherubs.

The younger two are watching a Disney movie, looks like *The Hunchback of Notre Dame*.

'Hey, guys.'

Aria is entranced by the movie, but Hugo launches himself at me, wrapping his arms around my waist and burying his head into my stomach. I hug him back; after the day I've had, my son's affection helps soothe away the stress.

'Mummy!' Aria has finally noticed me and jumps up in

her Paw Patrol onesie and forms a group hug with me and Hugo.

'Mummy, Daddy's home and he let us have pancakes from Tim Horton's for dinner, and he said we could play a game when you got home, before we go to bed. And he gave me strawberry milk.'

Aria's verbalised stream of consciousness makes me smile, despite the gruelling day, and I enfold her in my arms and thank heaven for my children. Whenever I am feeling blue, they always put a smile on my face and make things brighter again. If only I could track down Nicky, everything would be well with the world.

Gen is in her room, listening to her iPod.

'Hi, Mum, is Nicky OK? I saw what the paper said.'

The difficulty with social media, the internet and having children who are almost teenagers is, they often know things before you do, and also there's no hiding anything from them.

'She'll be fine, thanks for asking.' I omit that I haven't spoken to Nicky yet.

'Good. I like Nicky.'

'Me too. Have you had dinner?'

She nods. 'I don't want to see another pancake ever again.' She pats her totally flat stomach. Ah, memories, I remember when mine was like that.

'Do you want some hot chocolate? I can still use the microwave.'

'No, thanks, I'm so full.' She smiles at me then raises her eyebrows. 'Mum, when will the kitchen be finished?'

I sigh. 'That's a good question.' I kiss her on the forehead and she hugs me. With my emotions all over the place at the moment, I'm more grateful for that hug than she will ever know.

'Oh, that's so good. You really know what you're doing. I'm so glad I married you.'

Ronnie grins. 'Right, that's you done. Pass me the Hobnobs.'

I sit up from where I've been leaning against the couch whilst Ronnie massaged my shoulders and revel in the bliss I feel at having the tension eased from my body. The Hobnobs are out of reach at the other end of the table, and I groan at having to move already, but I can hardly refuse when my lovely husband has massaged me for twenty minutes.

We watch a few episodes of a box set we are both happy to sit through. It's easy to forget how chilled it is when we are both home; it definitely alleviates the pressure, but I sometimes still find it hard to relax as I feel I should get all the stuff done I don't manage when he is away. But this is our time, albeit we're in a partially damaged living room, next to a kitchen with no door, which unfortunately means we have full view of the chaos and detritus within.

'Do you want some wine?' Ronnie asks.

'Only if you're not drinking.'

'I don't fancy it tonight, but I imagine after what has been happening with Nicky, you might need one.'

'Pity I don't drink brandy. I could be doing with some for the shock.'

'I'm sure she's fine, Lou.' Ronnie puts his arms around me and I snuggle into his chest. 'She probably feels humiliated and betrayed and needs a few days to get her head straight.'

'I know. It's just she has never not contacted us before. She must know we'd be worried.'

'She'll be in touch soon. I know she will,' Ronnie says.

'Especially with everyone leaving her messages.'

I hope he's right.

'Lou, Lou, wake up.'

'Hmm?' I struggle to open my eyes. When I do, Ronnie is standing over me.

'Lou, it's one o'clock, you need to go to bed.'

I don't even remember being sleepy. I must have conked out. Poor Ronnie. First day home and I don't spend any time with him, then I pass out on him, perhaps mid-conversation. He really is one in a million.

Ronnie offers me his hand, and I grab it and let him pull me up. I feel as if I'm in a fog right now and can't wait to be in bed with my husband, snuggled up. Warm. Safe. A known quantity, no complications – not like poor Nicky. Although a little voice, more distant than before, reminds me I have had my own complications recently. Not even my guilt over what happened with Caden gives me a sleepless night, however, as I don't even remember my head hitting the pillow. My last thought was, *Please let Nicky be OK.*

Chapter Twenty-nine

Thursday 11 March

Nicky is my first thought when I wake. I pick up the phone from the bedside table to see if she has called or messaged. Nothing. Then I notice the time. Ten o'clock? I've overslept. How? The kids have school. I jump out of bed and then realise there's no Ronnie-shaped lump beside me. He must have taken the kids to school. I breathe a sigh of relief.

After doing the maths, I discover I slept nine hours after I went to bed, as I vaguely remember Ronnie telling me it was one o'clock, and who knows how long I had been sleeping on the couch beside him before then?

I pad downstairs, but Ronnie is noticeable by his absence. It feels like half the day is gone. Normally, I'm reaching for the crackers and cheese at this time, staving off hunger pangs until lunch as I've been up for a good four hours at least. Today everything is out of sync.

I go about my day on autopilot, checking my phone every five minutes in case I've somehow missed Nicky's call or message. I do the housework, answer the emails, engage with the kids when they return from school, but I don't really feel present. All I want is to know Nicky is OK.

And as for my list – it can sod off today. There are more important things in life.

Chapter Thirty

Friday 12 March

Now I know what Groundhog Day feels like. I've been here before. No news. No progress. I'm starting to get scared. Nicky is so responsible, especially with regards to Xander, and her not calling me, Sam or her mum to let us know she is all right is killing us. I'm honestly thinking about calling the police, but what would I say? 'My friend was papped with Scotland's most eligible bachelor, his jealous bitch of an ex-wife made up some rumours about her and she's devastated and now she's missing?' It sounds preposterous, like something out of an upmarket version of *The Jerry Springer Show.*

The day passes in a kind of daze, again. All I can say is thank God Ronnie is home this week, as I am worse than useless. I can't focus, I keep getting distracted and I have achieved literally zero.

Even overhearing Gen talking to Rain on the phone as I folded sheets in the next room only made me smile a little.

It frightens me that my friend is out there, distraught and alone, and doesn't feel she can turn to anyone, not me, not Sam, not her own mum. Nicky's lack of confidence and low self-esteem run even deeper than I ever suspected. I grit my teeth. Sebastian has a lot to answer for. If it wasn't for his treatment of her, she'd be as strong in her personal life as she is in her professional life, but he just seems to deal her blow after blow after blow. I suppose at least he is taking care of Xander. But wait, Xander's his son, too. Why wouldn't he look after him? God, he's such a terrible person I've almost completely blanked the fact he was instrumental in Xander's creation. Thank goodness Xander is like Nicky in nature.

It's late when I finally go to bed. I wake on the couch to find a blanket draped over me, the living room tidy. I feel very thankful for my husband tonight, particularly as I climb the stairs then snuggle into him in bed, even though his mouth is half open and he is emitting not so gentle snores. I take comfort from his warmth and broad back and hope that Nicky decides to come home soon.

Chapter Thirty-one

Saturday 13 March

To-do list
Contact Valentin and Nicky's mum
Grocery shopping
Pay bills
Book restaurant for us all for tomorrow (problem – last-min cos of kitchen)
Pick Hugo's new glasses up from optician – phone first

The kids have eaten and are squashed up on the couch beside Ronnie, Gen too, when I finally get out of bed. Another restless night, worrying about Nicky. The touching family scene brings a much-needed smile to my lips, and I sense that familiar lurch in my stomach when I think of how much I miss Ronnie and having him as part of our family on a daily basis. Why can't he get a job on the mainland? Maybe it's time he tried again. I tell myself to stop it and to concentrate on what's important at the moment: Nicky.

No messages on my phone. I check as I boil the kettle. Valentin is frantic, Nicky's mum is too, and Sam and I are next in line; however, I've got to believe Nicky knows what she's doing. She told Sebastian she'd be a few days, and she won't want to be away from Xander for long.

Hopefully, she'll be back any day.

'Budge up,' I say to Gen. She rolls her eyes, but in a good-natured way, and makes room for me. The best thing about a corner sofa is we can all fit on it. Despite my concern over Nicky, I can still bask in the glow of this touching family tableau. The five of us all together. 'Woof,' Bear says. OK, boy, I meant five humans. Six if we count you. He must be telepathic as he seems mollified and lies down at Ronnie's feet. Funny how he casts me aside when Ronnie returns, a bit like the kids do too.

'So, what we doing today?' Ronnie asks.

'Well, I need to get the shopping, and book a restaurant, last-minute, for our families for tomorrow. That'll be fun.' I pull a face.

'Yeah, it's a pity someone else couldn't do that for you.'

The irony isn't lost on me. Ronnie could do it, especially as it's Mother's Day and I'm supposed to be the recipient of the pampering, along with my two sisters, my mother and Ronnie's. But that would never occur to him.

Everyone was supposed to be coming here. We had lunch at Wendy's last year on Mother's Day, but of course, with no kitchen, and a living room that needs repairing, that's not an option. I drink my coffee faster, realising what an uphill struggle I have ahead: finding a restaurant will be no mean feat. And, of course, we want somewhere nice, which also has decent food and caters for everyone's preferences and allergies and isn't too far for everyone to travel to.

I make my calls first. Valentin's phone goes to voicemail and I leave him a message telling him there's no further news, but as soon as I hear anything, I'll be in touch.

'Louisa? How are you? Have you heard from Nicky?' her mum asks.

'No. You?'

'Not yet.' Her voice cracks.

'How's Xander doing, do you know?'

'I spoke to Sebastian last night and Xander is a bit withdrawn but generally OK. I'm a little worried he might think she's not coming back.'

'Oh, he wouldn't think that. Don't concern yourself about that. He knows his mum adores him. Does he have any idea what made her go away? Has anyone explained the situation to him?'

'I don't think so. How do you explain that to a ten-year-old?'

Good point. There's not much difference between an eight- and a ten-year-old maturity-wise, and Hugo wouldn't understand, despite being an empathetic little boy.

'If you hear from her, can you let her know we love her and miss her, and we're here for her?' I say.

'Will do, Louisa. Thanks, love.'

I could do without this right now; in fact I could do with cancelling Mother's Day altogether, quite frankly. It's the last thing I want to be doing, but unable to do anything on the Nicky front until she decides she's ready to come back, I acknowledge it's time to phone these restaurants. I try six without any joy. Then I have a brainwave. Perhaps Travis could help.

Five minutes later, I'm back to square one. Travis' phone just keeps going to voicemail and the restaurant phone is ringing out. I must remind him when I see him that that's bad for business. I'd ask Jo if she knows if Travis might be able to help, but Jo is so hands-off with regards to the restaurant, that I probably know more about it.

Forty minutes later I'm ready to scream. I've called sixteen restaurants and not one can give us any time of day tomorrow for lunch or dinner. My phone rings in my hand as I'm about to call the seventeenth, The Hungry Horseman, a country pub about twenty miles away. We've never even eaten there, and I haven't had time to check the reviews, but I'm becoming desperate.

'Valentin, have you heard anything?'

'No, not yet.' He sighs. 'It's taking too long, Louisa. She obviously doesn't believe me. I don't know what to do, I lo–'

Was he about to say he loved Nicky? Oh God, in different circumstances that would be so romantic.

'I like Nicky so much, and I'm furious at Arabella for all the trouble she has caused with her lies. Maybe I should leave Nicky alone. Then she wouldn't have to deal with all the drama that follows me everywhere.'

I sense his desolation over the phone line. 'Valentin, don't be too hasty. Nicky is taking some time to get her head together. Let her decide if the chaos that surrounds you is too much for her.'

After a few seconds, Valentin says, 'You're right. Thanks, Louisa. I'm so glad you're Nicky's friend. If I can ever do anything to help you, please let me know.'

An idea forms in my head. 'Valentin, since you're in the industry, you don't happen to have any idea where I'll be able to get a lunch reservation for tomorrow for eighteen people?'

'Eighteen? Wow, you guys really like to celebrate.'

'Yeah, we're a big family. It was meant to be at mine, but the kitchen isn't finished, or anywhere near finished yet. In fact, it's barely started.'

'Hmm. Let me get on the case. We have a few restaurants with tables on retainer, but not usually for quite so many people. I'll see what I can do.'

'Thanks so much.'

Hope surges through me as I hang up. If anyone can find me a restaurant, Valentin can, with all his connections. And maybe it will keep my mind, and his, off Nicky for a little while.

'Ronnie, you OK with the kids whilst I sort out some admin and catch up with a bit of work?'

'Sure. We're watching *Cinderella*, aren't we, guys?' He smiles at each of our brood and they gaze up at him adoringly. I'm a tad resentful that he is getting to hang out with them, whilst I have to do all the boring stuff. Plus, he's home, and I'm still running around like a headless chicken taking care of everything. Oh well, tomorrow will hopefully be different. One of the two days per year where I should be getting looked after. I laugh. Yeah, and pigs might fly. I've already had my birthday, alone. At least the weekend was really good, and we were all together, except the husbands. Pity my two 'special' days are in the same week. Then I have to wait another three hundred and sixty days for another one.

'Are you picking your folks up from the hotel later, or are they coming straight here?'

'Hotel?' Ronnie's brow furrows.

Dear God, please tell me he has remembered I told him to book a room for them? 'Ronnie, have you booked a room for your parents like I told you to on Thursday, given they can't stay here as the place is a mess and we don't have a functioning kitchen?'

'Er...' He makes that hangdog expression I hate.

'I don't believe it! You haven't. Ronnie, I asked you to do one thing.'

'A lot has been going on,' he says, his chin jutting out in defiance.

Honestly, sometimes he's worse than a child.

'Ronnie, they're your folks, you sort it out.' I slam the door, my teeth clenched so tight, I'm sure they'll go through the gums soon.

The door rocks on its hinges, and satisfied, I storm upstairs. I don't usually lose my temper, but sometimes the lack of awareness my husband shows and the expectations he has of what falls under my remit gnaws away at me until finally I explode.

In my office, I sit down and open my laptop. First, the bills. Then I go through today's mail. I open a letter from my pension provider. That's a laugh. I've hardly paid anything into it for the past decade, but it does remind me that I still need to phone them to reset my password. I tackle the work emails and messages, place some orders, and then see one that says *Urgent – reminder*, from someone called Gayle Richards.

Gayle Richards? I don't recall the name. I open the email. Oh God. I've dropped the ball. I remember now, but it's because I spoke more to her sister than her, as she was really shy. I was supposed to send her some samples, and if they were happy with them, they would place the order. They want the invitations ASAP as they are having a last-minute wedding in Inverness. And I haven't done anything with her email. This is so unlike me. Suddenly, exhaustion overwhelms me. I take great pride in my work and to make a mistake like this really rankles.

'Hello, is that Gayle? This is Louisa Halliday of Wedded Bliss. I've just seen your reminder email. I am so sorry, somehow it slipped through the net. Let me sort those samples out, and I'll hand-deliver them today.'

Gayle protests that I don't have to do that, but I do. I need her to understand my service level is usually good and that I always do my utmost to ensure the client is happy.

Her address is on file. She lives in the Southside, in Giffnock. It's not too far, but it's a journey I could have done without today, especially given I still have the Mother's Day lunch to finalise.

I spend the next half an hour creating Gayle's samples. I'm about to move on to the next batch of emails when my phone rings. Valentin.

'Valentin!' I say almost breathlessly. Even though I've been sitting most of the time, the adrenalin that surged through my veins at my messing up the samples has tired me out.

'Good news, Louisa. My brother's girlfriend's father owns a restaurant and he has had a cancellation for a large party. He could take the eighteen of you tomorrow. It might be a little cramped, but I can vouch for the food, and it's a really quaint place, a seventeenth-century inn.'

He gives me more details, including the address and the owner's name so I can ask for him when we arrive, and I jot it all down.

'Valentin, you're a lifesaver. Thanks so much. You have no idea how much you've saved my bacon.'

'Anytime, Louisa. Anyway, I had better go, but I'll be in touch if I hear from Nicky.'

'Me too. Chin up, Valentin. She'll be back.'

'I hope so.' His voice cracks and he struggles to cover it up.

It's only when I venture back downstairs that I realise Ronnie didn't come after me when I had my meltdown. Does that mean he's indifferent? Surely shouting at me to defend himself or coming to see if I was OK would be normal reactions in that situation?

Ronnie looks up. 'Hi.'

I can't tell if he is annoyed at me or not. 'Hi,' I say back.

'The folks are booked into the Travelodge.'

I raise my eyebrows so much they must surely disappear into my hairline. 'Travelodge?'

'Yeah, eh, it appears there's a medical conference this weekend and all the big hotels are full.'

'You could have put them a little further afield, even up towards the West End.'

'Actually, the nearest decent-sized hotel with amenities I could get them was Linlithgow, and I didn't think they would want to be so far from us.'

'Linlithgow? Must be some conference.'

'I think there's a Star Trek convention too, in the SEC.'

I try not to smile at that. 'Well, at least you have them booked in.' I'd love to be there when he tells his parents. A Travelodge is not their idea of a hotel, I'm sure. They're more used to four- and five-star hotels in country settings. It's tempting to suggest he get them tickets for the convention, but I know when I've taken it too far.

'OK, so that's settled. Right, I need to drop some samples over in the Southside. I'm supposed to be taking Gen "shopping", but that will have to wait. I'm sure she won't mind.'

'I'm sure she won't.' Ronnie knows Gen isn't happy about having to go bra shopping. Whereas many girls would be excited about it, she doesn't want to acknowledge that she's growing up in that way. I can't blame her. I didn't want to when I was her age, and I don't want her to now; it seems like only yesterday she was crawling around the floor and we were doing tummy time.

'I'm sorry I lost it earlier, I just have so much to do–' I don't add 'all the time', but I'm thinking it.

'Don't worry about it,' Ronnie says.

No apology from him then. 'Right, I won't be long. What time are your parents coming over?'

'They said about six.'

'Fine. That'll give us–' emphasis on the 'us' '–time to give the kids their dinner and get everything organised.'

'Uh-huh,' Ronnie grunts, turning back to the film. 'See you when you get back.'

I'm pretty sure he hasn't been listening to a word I've said. Obviously the Ugly Sisters are more interesting.

'You really didn't need to do this,' Gayle says when I ring her doorbell. 'It would have been fine posting them over.'

'Not at all. I'm so annoyed with myself for missing the email. I can't apologise enough.'

'Well, I'm very grateful, not sure the other half will be, though, as that changes our plans for tonight. I'll be practising with my calligraphy pens before making a start on these, and he'll be assisting me.' She grins. 'Thanks again.' She hesitates then says, 'Do you want to come in for a coffee? You've come all this way.'

'That's really kind, and usually I'd say yes, but I have a jam-packed day today and the in-laws descending on us at six.'

'Ah, understood. I don't have any yet, mine are still in training, but I can imagine.'

I laugh. 'Mine are OK, in small doses.' I consider telling her about the kitchen saga, but realise that will only delay me further, and let's face it, she probably doesn't want to know, and she definitely doesn't need to. 'Well, enjoy your evening of calligraphy. If the invites are OK for you, let me know and I'll courier some over on Monday.'

'Will do. Thanks again.'

I drive home, relaxing a bit more now that I have

smoothed things over with the client and all is well with the business side of my life. Don't get me wrong, of course I still have a lot to do, and I haven't had a chance to investigate taking on a temp yet, or even had time to look at the financials properly to see if the business can afford it, but I hate incompetence, particularly when it's mine. So I'm glad I've resolved my latest bout of it.

When I arrive home, I drop my key and bend down to pick it up as the front door opens. I wonder which exuberant child is about to pounce on me, but when I stand up, my eyes lock on Nicky's.

'Nic!' I yell and fling my arms around her. 'You're back. Thank God. You had me so worried.' My eyes are wet, and I have to release her to wipe away my tears, and to avoid leaving a damp patch on her top.

Nicky gives a rueful smile. 'I'm so sorry. I really didn't mean to worry you, or Sam, or Mum, or anyone really, including Valentin.' It's then I notice Valentin is behind her. He slips his arms around her waist from behind and she leans into him. 'I just lost it, lost myself, had a meltdown. I couldn't cope. I've no excuse though.'

'Never mind, you're back now, safe and well. Right, can we take this indoors? I'm freezing.'

Apparently Nicky, Valentin and Xander turned up soon after I left for Giffnock, so she has had time to introduce him to Ronnie, and the two appear to be getting on well. We leave them talking in the living room and Nicky and I go through to the playroom. Aria, Xander and Hugo are outside on the trampoline, but Ronnie has promised to keep an eye out. Gen is in her room – surprise – listening to music.

'So you and Valentin are OK?' I ask once we are

ensconced on the sofa with a cup of tea.

'Yes, I just saw red. First of all the embarrassment of being in the newspapers, but remember I don't know him that well, and when I saw his wife's horrible comments, well, I flipped.'

'It must have been awful.' I pat her arm.

'It was, and it brought back all my insecurities, what with Sebastian doing the dirty on me with Brittany. I couldn't see past that, and I had to get away. I thought history was repeating itself. I thought Valentin had either gone back to his wife, or lied about having split up from her in the first place.'

'I understand why you might think that,' I say, pushing a plate of chocolate biscuits towards her. 'But Valentin isn't Sebastian.'

Nicky sighs. 'I know. He's pretty great.' Her face breaks into a broad smile.

'He is. Apart from being wonderful towards you, for which I am his biggest supporter, he got me out of a tight spot earlier.'

Nicky quirks an eyebrow and I fill her in on Valentin's mercy mission to find me a new venue for tomorrow's lunch.

She gives a lazy smile. 'I like him, Lou, I really do.'

'Well, that's good, because he seems pretty into you,' I say as I snap a Kit Kat in half.

'Yeah, I might hang on to him, if I can see past all the wealth. You know none of that matters to me, right?'

'I know.' A thought occurs to me. 'You have let your mum know you're all right, haven't you? She was going out of her mind.'

'First place I went then we collected Xander together.'

'Thank goodness for that. Right, Nic, excuse me,

but talk to me whilst I tidy and order the kids' dinner as Annabelle and Phillip will be here shortly.'

'Oh, we should go,' Nicky says.

'Only if you have something better to do.' I grin.

'There's plenty of time for that. Anyway, Valentin and Ronnie appear to be bonding.'

I crack the playroom door open, so I can see through to the living room. 'Yep, they're still chatting away. Sounds like they're talking about films.'

'Valentin's a real film buff. He especially likes Italian films, a side effect, I guess, of having lived there.'

'Does he speak the language?'

'Yes, I think he speaks Italian, French and Spanish. His family is dotted around the place.'

'Makes sense. Anyway, let me call a takeaway.'

No sooner have I arranged for the kids' food to be delivered than the doorbell goes. I frown, wondering who it can be at this time. Five o'clock. Funny time for Jehovah's Witnesses or salesmen. And it's Saturday.

I peer through the spyhole. Annabelle and Phillip? They're not due for another hour. Great. I look like a bag of rags, again. With my best fake smile plastered on, I swing the door open. 'Annabelle, Phillip, how lovely to see you. Come in.'

Phillip gives me a hug, but Annabelle restricts herself to a tight smile.

'And where are my grandchildren?' she says in a manner befitting Queen Victoria.

'In the garden, I believe. Why don't you go through and see Ronnie, and I'll round them up?' I'm making my children sound like sheep. Anything to get away from Annabelle's critical glare. Every time she's here, it's as if she's scrutinising everything, from the skirting boards to the light shades, checking for motes of dust. She is adept at insinuating she has found me and my efforts wanting. Well, this time she has plenty to complain about, the state the kitchen's in.

I beat a hasty retreat, ducking my head into the playroom on the way. 'Back in a minute. Got to deal with the in-laws.'

She chuckles. I can't help thinking if she married Valentin, at least she would inherit his grandfather, and he's lovely.

'Hugo, Aria, Grandma and Grandpa are here.'

'Yay!' Hugo jumps off the slide and Aria off the swing. They love their grandparents. The affection Annabelle withholds from me, she lavishes on my children.

Nicky has joined the circus in the living room when I return with the kids. I'm guessing she was summoned by Valentin or Ronnie, as Annabelle will have given Ronnie the third degree about Valentin, or perhaps she quizzed the man himself. She doesn't understand boundaries, and despite being an out-and-out snob, her behaviour often isn't very polite, and can in fact be downright invasive. There are no taboo areas with her.

Gen slopes in just as Hugo sits on the edge of Phillip's chair and they launch into a discussion about the solar system. Meanwhile, Aria has plonked herself in Annabelle's lap. To me, it would be like putting my head inside a lion's mouth, but Aria has a different effect on Annabelle. She becomes softer somehow, not as brittle. Maybe I'm being unfair; she does adore the kids, after all.

I turn to see Gen and Nicky, heads close. Try as I might, I can't hear what they're saying.

'That's a great idea,' I hear Ronnie say.

Wondering what I've missed, I spin round to see Annabelle looking self-satisfied, as she often does when she gets her own way.

'What's a great idea?'

'Mum and Dad are babysitting tonight so we can go for a drink with Valentin and Nicky.'

Whilst I'm sure Nicky and Valentin would like some alone time, they're both nodding at me, smiling, so Annabelle hasn't put the kybosh on things.

'Well, that was a gift,' Ronnie says as he puts his arm round me in the pub. The Golden Goose is less than a mile's walk from our house, but it's too cold to do so in this weather, so the four of us jumped in a cab.

'Yes, I wasn't expecting them to offer to do that. Really kind.' Somehow around Ronnie, I can't tell him how I really feel about his mother. I did at the very beginning, but soon realised I was fighting a losing battle and it wasn't worth the aggro.

'Good job they'd already eaten at that bistro round the corner from the Travelodge.'

'Yes, what a godsend,' I say, thinking back to Annabelle's exact words. 'We found a charming little bistro a stone's throw from that "lodge" you put us in, Louisa.' Clearly the reason she's not in a five-star hotel is my fault, never her beloved son's.

She has never called me Lou, which I'm glad about, as we don't have that type of relationship. I think I am pretty easy-going, barring the occasional meltdown at my husband when he tries my patience, but she has never been warm towards me.

Valentin and Nicky return with the drinks and I breathe a sigh of relief. Discussing Ronnie's parents isn't on my list of top ten favourite subjects.

We pass the evening pleasantly. I haven't laughed so much in ages, and it's lovely to be out with another couple. I can't remember the last time we were, not even with my siblings and their husbands. That's what happens when you have kids; you always need to think of the babysitting situation first.

Valentin and Nicky are so sweet together and he gets my vote. He is funny, attentive, without being overbearing, and when he smiles at Nicky, it lights up his whole face. As for Nicky, she is transformed in his presence. I didn't think I'd ever see her like this again. She's like a love-struck teenager, all girly and giggly, and I know it's not an act. Oh to feel like that again. *You did feel like that*, a voice reminds me. *Last weekend*. I quiet the voice and concentrate on another of the tales about Italy and his family Valentin is sharing. It's a place I've never been and I would love to go. If only I could find the time, and have the opportunity.

Nicky has gone to put some music on the jukebox, so I nip to the loo. When I return, Nicky is still mulling over her choices, and I think about joining her, but I'm too thirsty. As I approach the table, I hear Ronnie saying, 'Yeah, the kitchen's a nightmare. I think if I'd been here, it would have been a different scenario. I wouldn't have taken things lying down. Lou's a lot less forthright than me. Workmen like that will walk right over her. It's not right, but she doesn't have the wherewithal to stand up to them. She's too nice.'

Valentin listens but doesn't say anything. As if miffed that his new friend hasn't agreed with him, Ronnie changes the subject. I detour to the jukebox after all, to make the final choices before returning to the table.

We walk home, as tipsy people often do; it always seems a good idea at the time.

'Ronnie, I heard you telling Valentin earlier that I didn't stand up to Owen. You don't really think that, do you? I've told you often enough how many times I've had to push him on it.'

'Hmm?' says Ronnie, his eyes a little glazed. Now clearly isn't the time to discuss this, but we will. I'm not having him portray me as the meek little woman who needs a man to stand up for her to get things done. I've never been that person and I never will be.

It's quite late when we return, and by that time I'm mellowing slightly towards Ronnie. That's what being exposed to almost sub-zero temperatures when you've had a few will do to you. He has still been an insensitive git though and has some serious making up to do.

We're all giggly and shushing each other. I'm looking forward to having drunken sex with my husband and he me, if his roving paws are anything to go by. It's not only Nicky and Valentin who can act like teenagers. We'll get rid of, I mean say goodnight to, Phillip and Annabelle, and then it's all systems go. The kids will be asleep by now.

'Hi, Dad,' Ronnie says. 'How was everything?'

'No problems. Kids great as ever. In fact, Gen only went to bed twenty minutes ago. We've been watching Batman, not sure which one, there are so many now. It was good, though.'

'She does love her superheroes.' I smile. Phillip is OK, it's his wife who tests my patience.

'I can't believe how late she stayed up,' he says, impressed. 'Outlasted her grandmother.'

Outlasted? Does that mean Annabelle is asleep? I glance round the room, half expecting Annabelle to be hidden under a sleeping bag or a bundle of coats.

Phillip clocks what I'm doing and says, 'She made herself up a bed in the spare room. Anyway, when I think about it, it makes more sense us staying here than at the Travelodge. You two will have had a few drinks, I bet, and I know you always like someone to be sober in case anything happens to the kids. So, we may as well stay, if that's OK with you, especially as Annabelle is already dead to the world.' He smiles fondly. I wonder if he loves Annabelle so much he simply doesn't see how prickly she can be to others.

'Right, cup of tea, Dad?' Ronnie says over-brightly. He doesn't meet my eyes. Am I unreasonable to be unamused that my spawn of Satan mother-in-law has taken it upon herself to stay in our house even when we specifically asked them to go to a hotel this time? If I didn't know better, I'd almost think she'd engineered our trip to the pub with that exact aim in mind. That's the problem with Annabelle, she makes me see conspiracies everywhere. What bugs me is, in addition to turning up nearly an hour early tonight, she has seen fit to sleep in our spare room, which is a total dump at the minute as our kitchen is out of action and we've redistributed items into the garage and the spare room. I didn't know to change the bedding, so she will be sleeping in potentially musty sheets. No one has stayed over since the family at New Year. Knowing Annabelle, she's probably raked through the drawers to find sheets and clean pillow cases, moaning all the while. I bet poor Phillip has had an earful about the state of our house.

Tomorrow could be a real test. Then I become annoyed at Ronnie. If he had remembered to book his parents into a decent hotel when I asked him to, Annabelle wouldn't have the hump about being in a Travelodge and I wouldn't be lumped with her overnight and tomorrow morning. I could just about get through lunch, as there are a lot of us, so I can sit at one end and coordinate it so she sits at the other end, but now I have to endure almost an entire day of her.

Finally, after watching a bit of TV with Phillip, a political programme, of course, which I find mind-numbingly boring, not least because we don't share the same views and I have to listen to him expound on why his view is the right one, Ronnie and I go to bed.

'I thought Dad would never shut up,' Ronnie whispers as he slides into bed beside me.

That makes two of us. God, that's so bitchy, but is it too much to want a little privacy and peace and quiet? It's bad enough the kitchen is a bomb site and no-go area, but for Annabelle to start poking her nose into the upstairs rooms, then pulling a Goldilocks manoeuvre, it's not on.

'Come here, you.' Ronnie lunges towards me, but somehow I find it distasteful rather than sexy. All of a sudden I am sober.

'I've missed you, Lou. The thought of making love to you again is what keeps me going when I'm on the rig.'

Normally, I would think that was quite a sweet and open comment to make, but tonight I bristle. He wants to make love when his parents are in the next room? The parents I didn't agree could stay. Sorry, but my ardour has totally dissipated.

'I can't with your folks here,' I say.

'They're fast asleep.' He kisses my neck.

'Ronnie, not tonight.' I turn away and hear him huff then turn his back on me.

Too bad. If anyone should be taking the hump tonight,

it should be me. I drift off thinking about Annabelle and voodoo dolls.

Chapter Thirty-two

Sunday 14 March

To-do list
Get everyone to the restaurant without coming to blows
Write cards and presents
Find something decent to wear
Order light jackets for kids
Order new backpack for Hugo – he has ripped one of the bottle pouches – Nike

Happy Mother's Day reads the banner across the living room door. I smile and push the door open. Good. No one up. It's surprising though, as it's eight o'clock. I've had a decent amount of sleep, and although I'm a little hungover, I need coffee more than extra time in bed. Bear bounces up to me. 'Hello, boy. You hungry?' He jumps up as I bend down to put my trainers on. Slobber covers my face. 'Bear, down!' Yuck.

As it's Mother's Day, I'm not working today. The end of the world could come, and it might with Annabelle around, and I wouldn't bat an eyelid. I deserve this day off.

Bear doesn't want to go out after breakfast, so I leave him be, instead making myself coffee and grabbing a romantic novel to read – Sophie Kinsella. I haven't read one of hers in ages. I love her books.

Are the kids in the playroom? I wonder. It's not like them to sleep this late. I peek round the door. No one. Come to think of it, where's Annabelle? Not that I'm looking for her, but she's always up with the larks.

It's then I see the note on the playroom table. 'We decided not to wait for you to get up. The children, Phillip and I have gone for a walk to the duck pond. We will treat them to breakfast on the way back. Annabelle.'

Whilst I'm certain Annabelle wasn't simply leaving me and Ronnie to have some alone time, I'm not complaining about having some extra time to myself. I intend to have a bath after this coffee.

'Mummy, Mummy, where are you, Mummy?'

I jolt awake. I've fallen asleep in the bath. My hands are like prunes. How long have I been in here? I lever my body out of the bath and wrap a towel round me as Aria knocks on the door. Just as well I locked it. The last thing I need is Phillip or Annabelle surprising me naked.

'I'll be out in a minute, sweetie. I'm getting out of the bath.' Once I'm decent and have a towel wrapped around me, I open the door to find my enthusiastic daughter waiting on me. She hugs me so hard she almost dislodges my towel, but I grip it tight. She looks fit to burst.

'Come into my room and tell me all about your walk.'

She trots along obediently beside me, then as soon as I sit on the bed, she is off like a racehorse. 'Mummy, I saw fifteen ducks. Hugo thought it was fourteen, but I told him he was wrong, so he counted them all again to be sure, and I was right.'

'Well done,' I tell her, hugging her to me as I pull my T-shirt over my head.

'Thanks, Mummy. And we saw two boys flying kites, a red and yellow one that looked like a dragon and a blue and green one that was like a sea monster. One of them got stuck in a tree and their daddy had to go up the tree and rescue it.'

'That's exciting,' I say, as I guess that's the level of response she's hoping for.

Hugo wanders in then – thankfully I'm dressed – and picks up the story.

'Hi, Mummy. It was so cool. We saw Canadian geese and two hedgehogs, which Grandpa said was unusual because they're usually only seen at night, and a red squirrel – those are almost as rare nowadays as seeing hedgehogs during the day, I think.'

Sounds like the kids enjoyed themselves, and that's all that matters. I hug them both to me.

'Mummy, you smell nice,' says Aria.

'Thanks, poppet.' You've got to take compliments when you can get them when you're sliding down the slope towards forty.

'Are you sure this is the place?' Annabelle asks once we've parked the cars and are standing outside the inn. It's gorgeous, steeped in character, with ivy trailing down over the trellises, and writing in elaborate cursive above the doorway. A colourful shield hangs above the script, depicting a scene which reflects the inn's name, Lochview Inn. And it's not just a clever name. The view across Loch Tay is spectacular.

'Quite sure.' I point to the name. Then I can't resist. My inner devil gets the better of me. 'My friend Valentin Pendragon recommended it. Remember, you met him at ours last night.'

Annabelle scrunches up her forehead. 'You don't mean he was Valentin Pendragon of those Pendragons?'

'Which Pendragons?' I ask, keeping my face the picture of innocence.

'The millionaire restaurateurs.'

'That's right,' I reply cheerfully. My guess was right. Annabelle doesn't read the tabloids, only *The Independent*. She wouldn't have come across the shot of Nicky and Valentin.

For once, Annabelle looks impressed. Ha ha, one point to me. Game on.

Jo and Travis walk towards us. Jo is holding Jackson by one hand and Aurora is swinging one of Travis'.

'Afternoon. Happy Mother's Day.' Jo kisses me on the cheek. My sister has lost weight. I'm not sure how; she eats even more chocolate than me. Maybe it's the country air now she is living the idyllic bucolic life.

'Annabelle, how lovely to see you.' Jo is so effusive even Annabelle can't dampen her spirits. She simply has to go with the flow, and I inwardly applaud my sister.

Phillip envelops her in a hug and tells her she's looking well. Jo compliments him and he blushes, at which Annabelle frowns.

'Your parents not here yet?' Annabelle says, scanning the car park.

'No, we asked them to arrive a little later, since I'm the one who made the booking and have the contact with the owner,' I say.

Annabelle gives me an odd look. If I didn't know better, I'd say I'd managed to impress her twice in one day. Her face looks weird, though, as if it pains her to look impressed.

'Inside, everyone. We can't stand out here in the cold.'

She marches off, the children following her as if she's the Pied Piper. Traitors.

The foyer is warm and inviting. I immediately relax. I can put up with Annabelle for a couple more hours if these are to be my surroundings.

'Good afternoon,' I say to the maître d'. 'We have a booking for Halliday.'

'Let me check.' He runs his finger down his list, but frowns.

Oh no, nothing can go wrong now, please. We've had such a fight to get here.

'I don't–'

'Valentin reserved it yesterday for us,' I whisper. 'As a surprise.' This way Annabelle won't know I didn't book it myself.

'Ah yes, I recall, I spoke with Mr Pendragon myself. Come this way.'

He leads us to a table next to huge bay windows overlooking the rolling hills and the peaceful scene. Soon spring lambs will abound here, but for now there are only a couple of ponies and a few cows dotted here and there.

Sneakily, I wait until Annabelle sits down then position myself as far away from her as possible, Aria on one side, Gen on the other. Hugo stays with Ronnie. Opposite me is Jo, who has a child either side. My parents can sit next to Aria.

'Mum,' I say, standing up when I hear her voice, 'Happy Mother's Day.'

'And to you, Lou.' She hugs me, then turns to Jo and does the same.

'Can I sit next to you, petal?' she asks Aria, who beams at her and nods.

'Dad, would you mind sitting the other side of Mum?

That way Wendy can sit opposite you when she arrives.'

'You know me, easy to please.' Dad winks. He clearly knows my game plan of avoiding Annabelle. He's seen the way she treats me, as if I'm not good enough for her son, although I was apparently good enough to bear her grandchildren, but naturally they all inherited their father's traits, never mine.

Wendy sweeps in soon after, in a flurry of hugs and kisses. 'You OK?' she asks me.

I nod, knowing what she's referring to. Caden.

'Ronnie, how are you?' She pats my arm and moves off to speak to my husband.

Brandon is his usual disinterested self. I don't even merit a hello. He just manages to raise his attention from his phone to say, 'Annabelle, Phillip, such a long time.'

Not long enough for me.

Valentin was right. The food is exquisite, and I love the feel of the place, so welcoming. The staff are lovely, and although the inn is busy, given the occasion, we're not sitting on top of each other even though Valentin had warned me that might be the case.

The afternoon passes in a flurry of anecdotes. We can't really hear each other from one end of the table to the other, so we have kind of split into two groups – Ronnie, his parents, Travis and Brandon in one, and the rest of us in the other. Our group is considerably bigger. The children swap seats with the adults so they can be closer to their cousins between courses. Wendy brought colouring books for them all, so they're all entranced by those, which allows us to eat in peace. The kids pick at their food, apart from Hugo, who wolfs his down, and even Genevieve makes a good attempt, but the others are too interested in playing and being together.

Dessert comes and goes, and whilst I am sitting with my coffee, Aria swaps places with Mum. Good, I've been wanting to catch up with her properly. It also seems a good time to give her our gift. It's a collection of all the best moments of our childhood – me, Jo and Wendy – as well as some photos of all the grandkids, some on their own, some with us, but most with my mum and dad. I had suggested doing a similar thing for Annabelle, but Ronnie said she would rather have a voucher. Typical.

'Mum, this is for you, from the three of us. We hope you like it.'

My sisters nod.

As Mum is unwrapping her present, we hear from the other end of the table, 'A trip to Venice, oh thank you, Ronnie, what a wonderful present. You're too kind.'

And I can't help but think, yes, he is too kind. That's not quite what I thought he meant when he said she'd prefer a voucher. How much did that cost? He has never taken me to Venice. I haven't even got a birthday present yet. He said he'd like me to pick something myself. Maybe I'll go into the travel agency and book myself a holiday, tell him that's what I chose. God, I wish I dared.

Mum looks at me, then my sisters, as if asking permission to carry on unwrapping. We nod in unison. She removes the tissue paper surrounding the box, then takes out the photo frame featuring fifty photos of her nearest and dearest. She studies each picture in turn and then her eyes well up, and before we know it, she has burst into tears.

'Mum, Mum, are you OK?' I ask, as my sisters come round the table and, like me, pat her arm and try to calm her. Dad is trying to see what's going on, but I nod to him that we have it under control. Finally, she stops sobbing, touches my cheek, then hugs the three of us to her chest. 'It's the most wonderful gift I've ever received. Thank you. I couldn't ask for better daughters. I'm so proud of the women you've become and the things you have all achieved.'

We hug for the longest time, then sit down and finish our coffee and tablet.

Afterwards, Jo and Wendy take the kids outside. Aria is still attached to me; Gen is talking to Ronnie, and Hugo has gone with his aunts.

'So, how are things?' Mum asks me. 'Did you enjoy your birthday trip away?'

'I did. Getting away somehow makes the time last longer. I didn't have to do housework, or constantly be on my phone checking client emails. I was able to detach from the drudgery of everyday life. It was bliss. I had time to chat, properly, with Jo and Wendy, and the kids had a ball, all of them being together.' I neglect to mention my kiss with Caden, obviously.

'And what about you? When are you next off on your travels? Have you and Dad picked up any more brochures?'

'Actually, I've been meaning to talk to you.'

'Oh? That sounds ominous.' I frown, worried what is coming next.

'Not at all. It's a good thing, at least we think so.'

'OK.' I wait for Mum to elaborate. When she doesn't, I say, 'Don't keep me in suspense. What is it?'

'Well, Dad and I have decided that although we like cruising, it would mean missing too much time with those who are important to us. You. The kids. Wendy, Jo and their kids. So, we want to be around to help out more. Mainly you, but also Wendy.'

'That's so magnanimous of you, Mum, you and Dad, but these are your twilight years. You're meant to be cruising, travelling the world, playing carpet bowls, doing macramé and playing bridge.'

'I don't belong in an Agatha Christie novel just yet, you know,' Mum says, feigning indignation. At least, I think she's feigning it. 'And we will still have plenty of retirement time, don't you worry. But–'

'But what?' I press her.

'But, well, nobody tells you how boring retirement is. It seems like this great thing, as you have all this time on your hands, but then you realise that what you enjoy is actually what you were already doing. Sure, it's good to try new things, and we've found new hobbies and interests since we retired, but the novelty is wearing off. So–' she pauses '–I, we, want to help you and your sisters, with childcare, giving you some time back to yourself, watching the kids so you can have weekends away, that sort of thing.'

'Mum, that's incredible. Thank you.' I fling my arms around her and nuzzle into her shoulder. Now my eyes are wet. 'This is turning out to be one tearful day.'

Mum laughs. 'That wasn't the plan. Anyway, I have a couple of other things to add.' She turns to Dad. 'Martin, can you come in on this for a sec?'

Out of the corner of my eye, I spy Annabelle earwigging as best she can from the other end of the table. Ha ha, not a chance she will overhear us, not from there, especially as my parents are softly spoken.

'I was telling Lou about our plans to help the three of them out.'

'Oh yes. Great idea of your mother's, I thought.'

'Thanks, Dad, I know you'll be a big part of it and a great help too.' I give him an awkward hug over Mum's back.

'Anyway,' Mum says, 'I have two more things I wanted to let you know. One of the ways I personally want to help you is with the business. I know you're struggling to cope with the demand, as well as run the house, deal with the kids when Ronnie's away and Bear too. So, since I have a little experience–' she emphasises the word 'little' and holds her thumb and forefinger together to show just how little '–I wondered if you'd be happy for me to come on board. You've been worried about taking on someone new, in case you can't afford to pay them, or the business can't support them. Why not take me on? I really enjoyed doing the trade show for you, even though it was all new to me. But I'm not too old to embrace a new challenge.'

I study Mum. She's deadly serious. The fact that she has put this level of thought into this touches me more than she will ever know. Do we ever truly stop helping our children? It doesn't look like it, although I consider myself extremely lucky. My mum is the kind of mum I hope I am, the mum I aspire to be.

'Mum, if you really want to work with me, I'd love to have you on my team. I'll pay you going rate, too.'

'Nonsense. You can pay me once I start proving my worth. I don't need the money, you know that. Knowing I'm helping you have an easier life is my reward.'

'Mum, am I dreaming?'

'Ha ha, very funny.' She swipes me with her menu.

'Seriously, you are the best mum in the world. Happy Mother's Day.'

'And to you, my darling.'

Chapter Thirty-three

Wednesday 24 March

'You all packed?' I ask Ronnie.

'Yep.' He looks at me ruefully.

'I can't believe it's time for you to go already. These past two weeks have gone by too quickly.'

'Well, you know what they say, time flies when you're having fun.'

'Hmm,' I say. I want to tell Ronnie that he needs to start looking for a job on the mainland again, that this two weeks without a husband and father lark has gone on for long enough, but the timing is wrong, plus he'd only tell me I have Mum and Dad on tap to help now, which solves one problem, but not the other: we can't work on our relationship when he is away.

'At least the kitchen is operational again,' he says, doing jazz hands, as if that heals all ills, although to be fair, it does help a lot. The kitchen being finished has restored my sanity. And interestingly enough, it wasn't Ronnie's intervention that got the work done double-speed once the new units arrived, it was me standing over them constantly until it was finished, mobile in hand, checking emails. I barely left the living room. Owen quickly got the message that I wasn't to be trifled with.

Plus, I negotiated a fifteen per cent discount, much as Owen blustered about it. I put my foot down, citing the great inconvenience we'd endured over an extended period, and giving examples, whilst remaining empathetic about the young boy breaking his leg. Grudgingly, Owen gave in and conceded the discount, but I think I may need a different kitchen fitter in ten to fifteen years' time.

The kitchen is gorgeous. I almost want to cook in it. In fact, scratch that, I do want to cook in it. I saw the design in Vogue magazine last year when I was in the doctor's waiting room. I immediately fell in love with the forest green units and the Spanish-style archway that split the family area from the cooking part of the kitchen. Plus, the island is huge. I would be happy to work there, with all the light spilling in from the garden. I am going to become a bona fide culinary whizz. Maybe Mum can help with that too.

Talking of Mum, she said she'd drop by later. I turn to Ronnie, stretch up to kiss him on the lips, and then he's kissing me, as if he doesn't have a helicopter to catch in a few hours' time.

'You know you can't be late.'

'I'll drive faster.' He moans, his breath coming in quick, sharp gasps.

Ding-dong.

Who can that be? Mum isn't due for another two hours. And unlike Annabelle she would never arrive unannounced, two hours early.

'Leave it,' urges Ronnie.

So I do, until the doorbell rings again. Frustrated, Ronnie pulls away from me and goes to answer the door.

'Hi there, can you take a parcel in for next door?'

'Yeah, no problem.' Ronnie's tone is gruff. To have his

intimate moment interrupted by the postman when the parcel's not even for us. That will please him.

Sure enough when he returns, his face is like thunder

'Someone up there doesn't like us, or me at least,' he says.

I laugh. 'It'll keep.'

'Yeah, but it's two more weeks. This is killing me, Lou.'

That's quite the admission from Ronnie. Usually he brushes it off when I talk to him about working away. Maybe he is ready for a gentle reminder, but not right this minute. Timing is everything.

'I know.' I wrap my arms around him and hug him to me. It's hard to tell who is hugging who the hardest. Finally, we release each other.

'I better go.' Ronnie leans over and kisses me chastely on the cheek, then picks up his bags and opens the living room door.

I follow him to the car for our ritual goodbye, well, our second one. I know farewells are hard, but I still treasure every moment with my husband.

'By the way, there'll be a delivery next week. I'll text you the time and day,' he says.

'Delivery?' Ronnie rarely orders anything; I take care of that side of things.

'A gift.'

'Now I'm intrigued.' Could he be getting me a birthday present after all? Not letting me choose my own?

'I like to keep you guessing.' He smiles and rolls the window up.

On the doorstep, I stand and watch my husband drive away, waving for what feels like the longest time. Will this hollowness I have inside ever go away? Every time he drives off to go back to the rig, I experience the same pain, as if his absence is somehow gouging out my insides.

I go back inside, send messages to Sam and Nicky to see if they want to meet up at the weekend and then burst into noisy tears. I've never felt so lonely, or so alone.

'Hi, Mum.' I open the door wide to let her through and she hugs me then shrugs off her coat.

'Brr, it's freezing out there.'

'I know. I saw Ronnie off earlier. I had to come in and go under a blanket for a bit afterwards. I was chilled to the bone. Tea? Coffee?'

'Latte, please, if you're making proper coffee,' Mum says, rubbing her hands together to get warm. 'How is Ronnie?'

'A bit forlorn, to be honest. I had the impression he didn't want to go back this time.'

Mum remains silent for a few seconds then says, 'Maybe it's time for him to look for something more local again.'

'Hmm,' is all I say.

'And the kids?'

'The usual, good, although they've already managed to damage one of the kickboards of the new units.'

Mum frowns. 'How did that happen?'

'Oh, they were playing with Bear and somehow the board under the oven got bashed.'

Mum shakes her head in disbelief. I know the feeling. 'The kitchen is gorgeous though, despite it being the longest makeover in history.'

'Yeah, it was a while coming, a long while, but it's in now, and I love it.' It's true, I feel as if it has my stamp on it now. Everything is where I want it to be, I have more units and room for both a tumble dryer and a dishwasher, instead of having to choose. I came in here this morning when I got up and simply stared around me. Owen and his team completed it last night about seven. I asked Ronnie to take the kids to Pizza Express so the men could work on to finish it off. I'm so glad I did. It's like a totally different room.

'Anyway–' she cuts into my reverie '–I never did get to talk to you about the second thing.'

I quirk an eyebrow at her, not sure what she's talking about.

'When we went for lunch on Mother's Day, I said I had two things to tell you.'

'I thought it was that you had stopped cruising and you were going to help the three of us.'

'OK, so that was point 1A and 1B,' she explains.

'Right?' I say cautiously.

'Well, you know how you called me that time I was out for dinner with Barbara and Theo?'

'Yes,' I say, wondering where this is going.

'I wasn't out for dinner with Barbara and Theo. The second thing I wanted to tell you was Dad and I have bought a house in Arran for the family. Barbara and Theo are the current owners. We're selling our house and moving into something more manageable, and that means the family can enjoy breaks to Arran whenever it's available.'

'A house in Arran? Wow! That's fabulous, Mum.' I hug her.

'Yes, we've always wanted a place in Arran, but it wasn't feasible when you were growing up. Although there would have been benefits: the beach, the countryside, the community feel, I don't think you would have appreciated missing out on the cinema, the theatre, things like that. So we didn't move then, but now we'll have the best of both worlds. We can come and go to the cottage as and when our schedules allow, and we can spend a bit less time there in winter, when the ferries are unpredictable and the weather is quite frankly, what is it you say, pants?'

I laugh. Hearing my sixty-eight-year-old mum say something is pants is too funny.

'Mum, that is brilliant news. You and Dad will have such a fantastic time.'

'And so will you. I say cottage, but it has four double bedrooms, so it's very spacious. And there's a second living room and a games room. So if we all wanted to go over together, we could get camp beds for the kids. I can't think of anything I'd rather do than spend more time with all of you.'

A tear slides down my face. Its twin soon slides down Mum's. Then we take turns at crying.

'We're a right pair, aren't we?' she says, choking back a sob.

'We are indeed. I love you, Mum. You're so selfless and the best role model a girl could have.'

'That's all I ever wanted. Now, this coffee's gone cold, can I have another?'

Some things are changing, but not everything. I smile. Just as it should be.

Chapter Thirty-four

Tuesday 30 March

The kids are at school, Mum has gone to the post office with some samples and I've just bought a new foil transfer tool and foil quill for Wedded Bliss. Mum is on her fourth official day with me, and so far she has been a godsend.

I'm still euphoric from Mum telling me about the cottage on Arran, which we will now have use of. We're going to see it this weekend and I can't wait. I love Arran. It has always been special to me, ever since I went as an eleven-year-old. Plus, I had been splitting my lists into two groups: work stuff Mum could help me with, and things that I had to do myself for work and for our family. It's amazing how much more I feel in control now that I can attack 'the list' with renewed vigour. I'm starting to control the to-do list, not the other way around.

My phone beeps. I finish composing the email to a potential new client and then glance at my phone. It's from Ronnie.

Hi Lou, forgot to message earlier in the week, busy. The gift is coming today, around 12. Travis is bringing it. Hope you like it. Ronnie x

Travis? I frown. Travis? Why is my brother-in-law bringing my birthday gift? And how big is it if Ronnie couldn't have it delivered by post? I stare at the screen as if I can deduce from the message what the gift might be. Nope, I have no clue. I'm stumped.

Mum returns from the post office, bearing two fudge doughnuts. I've noticed one drawback to Mum working with me: she's always bringing me treats. I swear I've put on a few pounds already in four days.

'Here you go.' She hands me a doughnut and a napkin. 'What's wrong?'

I look up from my phone. 'Sorry?'

'You're away in a wee world. Penny for them.'

Mum's quaint expressions always make me smile.

'It's nothing. Ronnie texted me saying Travis is delivering a gift here today.'

'A gift. Why not use a courier? What's Travis got to do with it? And isn't he working?'

'Your guess is as good as mine. Jo hasn't said anything to me. I'll text her.'

'She'll be in meetings,' Mum reminds me. 'Did he give you a time?'

'Yeah, about twelve. Right, let's forget about it for now, we may as well crack on with work. Can you take this next batch and sort the suites out – day invitations first, evening invitations next, gift list, RSVPs, menu, children's menu?'

'Got it. I'm on it.'

Mum cracks me up. One minute she's talking as if she just walked out of a Victorian novel, the next she's like a judge off *The X Factor*.

The morning passes quickly as we work through the to-do list. The doorbell rings. I glance at my watch. It's ten to twelve. I look through the peephole. Travis.

I open the door and Travis saunters in, empty-handed,

hugging me and Mum. 'Get the kettle on, then, sis. What kind of house is this?'

Bewildered, I do as bid, all the while trying to listen to what Travis and Mum are whispering about next door. Bear starts to bark. 'It's only Travis, boy. Calm down.'

I'm about to go into the living room with the tray of tea things when Mum comes into the kitchen and prevents Bear from leaving.

'What is it? He's fine with Travis. In fact, he's fine with everyone. He'll want to see him.'

'That's fine, but in a minute. Travis wants to give you your gift in peace.' I go to protest but she silences me with a 'Bear will only be overexcited to see Travis and jump all over him.'

I dip my head, acknowledging she's right, then walk through to the living room. I almost drop the tray. There, in front of me, is the most adorable puppy I've ever seen. It's a Beagle, black and brown and white, with the most hangdog, no pun intended, expression ever. Its eyes are huge, and its ears so floppy and silky.

'Oh, Travis, he's gorgeous. I can't believe you guys got a puppy. Jo didn't tell me. The kids must be so excited.'

'Er, Lou–' he raises his eyes to meet Mum's '–the puppy's not ours, it's yours.'

'Mine? But–' I glance at the adorable bundle leaping around in front of me. He doesn't even seem scared, and it is a he, I ascertain, patting his coat and checking underneath '–we have a dog already.'

'I know,' Travis says, 'but Gen told Ronnie she wanted a puppy for Christmas, and she was really upset when she didn't get one. It has been preying on Ronnie's conscience for a while, so he decided to get her one. He's lovely, isn't he? You couldn't not love him, look at those eyes.' He sounds almost desperate to hear me say I'm happy about the pup, but all I can think of is my husband making such a huge decision without me, especially when it's me who will have to look after it. Puppies take a lot of work, and it will need trained. I wonder how old it is. Questions flit through my mind, but the main one is 'Why did Ronnie think this was a good idea?' We have Bear. What if Bear's nose is put out of joint? I voice this last sentence and Travis says, 'Ronnie thought it would be good for Bear, having a playmate around the house.'

'Did he now? I take it he didn't think of the widdling and the cleaning and the chaos a puppy can cause, never mind a dog who feels its territory is being encroached upon.'

I come to the end of my tirade, and Travis' shoulders drop and his face flushes.

'Sorry, Travis, I'm not taking it out on you, I'm just shocked. And Gen will love it, of course she will. It's a big undertaking though.'

I put my hand under the puppy's chin and let him come to me. He is a lovely little thing, and that would be great, if we didn't already have a dog. What the hell is Ronnie thinking? I honestly can't believe it. It's like a cruel prank. I've finally got some help in the shape of Mum, and now I'll have to find and pay for a dog walker for two dogs. So much for my stress-free life.

I lift the puppy up and cradle him to my chest. It's not his fault. 'Has he got a name?'

Travis shakes his head. 'No, Ronnie wanted Gen to have the final say on the name, although Hugo and Aria can make suggestions too, as can you,' he adds hurriedly.

'Glad to see I'm allowed some say in the pup,' I mumble.

'He's been as good as gold on the way down, haven't

you, buddy?'

The pup leaps out of my arms and runs over to Travis, who pets his ears.

'How did you get roped into this anyway?' I ask Travis. He and Ronnie don't spend much time together, so entrusting him with something as momentous as this seems odd.

'Simple, really. The puppy is from a litter born in the next village to us. I did all the paperwork with the owners this morning and here he is. Plus, I was coming into Glasgow for an interview, so it all really fell into place.'

'You went for an interview? I thought you loved the new job?'

Travis laughed. 'Not for me. I was hiring. Looks like I was successful too. In fact, I can't stay long as he's in the car. I've already offered him the job of sous chef, and since he had the time, I offered to drive him up to see the restaurant, get the lay of the land.'

I can see Travis is excited over his new hire. 'Let me just secure this little fella. I'll have to bring out the stair gates again. I thought I was done with all that.'

'Well, you're only thirty-eight, Lou, you never know, not too late to hear the patter of tiny feet.'

I glare at Travis.

'OK, got it, not funny. Anyway, let me introduce you both to my new chef. C'mon.'

'Wouldn't it be easier to bring him in here?' I say. 'I can't believe you left him in the car. You didn't even do that with the dog,' I joke.

'Fair enough. Be right back.'

'I'll get another cup,' Mum says. I nod and wait for Travis to return with his new recruit.

I have my back to the door when Travis comes in, as

I'm pouring another cup of tea.

'This is Liv, my mother-in-law, and this–' he waits until I straighten up and turn '–is my sister-in-law, Lou.'

I can't breathe. My vision blurs and I pray my family don't notice.

'Caden. Nice to meet you, Lou.'

My lips are dry and my words stick in my throat, but somehow I manage a hello.

One thing's for sure, the puppy is no longer the greatest complication in my life.

THE END

Did you get your free short stories yet?

TWO UNPUBLISHED EXCLUSIVE SHORT STORIES.

Interacting with my readers is one of the most fun parts of being a writer. I'll be sending out a monthly newsletter with new release information, competitions, special offers and basically a bit about what I've been up to, writing and otherwise.

You can get the previously unseen short stories, *Mixed Messages* and *Time Is of the Essence*, FREE when you sign up to my mailing list at
www.susanbuchananauthor.com

Did you enjoy *Just One Day – Winter?*

I'd really appreciate if you could leave a review on Amazon or Goodreads. It doesn't need to be much, just a couple of lines. I love reading customer reviews. Seeing what readers think of my books spurs me on to write more. Sometimes I've even written more about characters or created a series because of reader comments. Plus, reviews are SO important to authors. They help raise the profile of the author and make it more likely that the book will be visible to more readers. Every author wants their book to be read by more people, and I am no exception!

Have you read them all?

The Dating Game

Work, work, work. That's all recruitment consultant Gill does. Her friends fix her up with numerous blind dates, none suitable, until one day Gill decides enough is enough.

Seeing an ad on a bus billboard for Happy Ever After dating agency 'for the busy professional', on impulse she signs up. Soon she has problems juggling her social life as well as her work diary.

Before long she's experiencing laughs, lust and … could it be love? But just when things are looking up for Gill, an unexpected reunion forces her to make an impossible choice.

Will she get her happy ever after, or is she destined to be married to her job forever?

The Christmas Spirit

Susan Buchanan

Natalie Hope takes over the reins of the Sugar and Spice bakery and café with the intention of injecting some Christmas spirit. Something her regulars badly need.

Newly dumped Rebecca is stuck in a job with no prospects, has lost her home and is struggling to see a way forward.

Pensioner Stanley is dreading his first Christmas alone without his beloved wife, who passed away earlier this year. How will he ever feel whole again?

Graduate Jacob is still out of work despite making hundreds of applications. Will he be forced to go against his instincts and ask his unsympathetic parents for help?

Spiky workaholic Meredith hates the jollity of family gatherings and would rather stay home with a box set and a posh ready meal. Will she finally realise what's important in life?

Natalie sprinkles a little magic to try to spread some festive cheer and restore Christmas spirit, but will she succeed?

Return of the Christmas Spirit

Susan Buchanan

Christmas is just around the corner when the enigmatic Star begins working at Butterburn library, but not everyone is embracing the spirit of the season.

Arianna is anxious about her mock exams. With her father living abroad and her mother working three jobs to keep them afloat, she doesn't have much support at home.

The bank is threatening to repossess Evan's house, and he has no idea how he will get through Christmas with two children who are used to getting everything they want.

After 23 years of marriage, Patricia's husband announces he's moving out of the family home, and moving in with his secretary. Patricia puts a brave face on things, but inside she's devastated and lost.

Stressed-out Daniel is doing the work of three people in his sales job, plus looking after his kids and his sick wife. Pulled in too many different directions, he hasn't even had a chance to think about Christmas.

Can Star, the library's Good Samaritan, help set them on the path to happiness this Christmas?

Printed in Great Britain
by Amazon

83689457R00212